TINY
DARK
DEEDS

TINY DARK DEEDS

COURT LEGACY: BOOK THREE

EDEN O'NEILL

Court High

They The Pretty Stars

Illusions That May

Court Kept

We The Pretty Stars

Court University

Brutal Heir

Kingpin

Beautiful Brute

Lover

Court Legacy

Dirty Wicked Prince

Savage Little Lies

Tiny Dark Deeds

Eat You Alive (forthcoming)

CHAPTER
ONE

Sloane

Fox News.

MSNBC…

CNN.

There wasn't a station my brother or I could turn to that wasn't stating the same thing.

This can't be happening.

I literally didn't believe what I was seeing. This had to be a lie, a mistake.

"You're everywhere," Bru whispered beside me. He eased in at my side, flipping to another news station.

The same thing.

Bru appeared in awe himself, and I swiped the remote from him, clicking through stations at a rapid pace. There had to be some kind of mistake here. I wasn't this… girl they kept talking about on TV.

I wasn't a Mallick.

This had to be bullshit because I *wasn't* one and definitely not *a twin*.

Ares's twin.

My swallow shifted my throat, each and every news station reporting the same thing. An anonymous tip had been apparently given to the authorities about who I was. From there, they claimed I'd been kidnapped by the very person who'd done it. My father, Godfrey Sloane, was being accused of taking me and not just once but twice. I'd been stolen initially from a hospital shortly after birth and again today. My parents… Godfrey *and Marilyn* were kidnappers…

And I was the kid.

My brother adjusted a blanket around my shoulders. When it'd gotten there I didn't know. I did recall flinching when he'd put it on me, and only partially because my shoulder still fucking hurt from that fall in the warehouse.

My stomach coiled, twisting, and clamped up. I gripped the remote in an iron hold, each pant of breath meeting my brother's hand when he rubbed my back.

"Sloane, this is insane," my brother gasped out. He rubbed his mouth a beat, his expression haunted, and it had to match mine. He raised a hand. "But this tip they keep talking about. The anonymous one?" His hand lowered. "How did they even know *this baby* is… you? And how did they know you were even kidnapped today? One better, how did they know you were coming here after it happened—"

"I don't know, and this is a lie." I wasn't this girl, and whoever had made this tip had to have made a mistake. I shut off the television. "Where's Callum?"

"I think still downstairs." Bru's knees hit mine when he turned. He was still in his jean jacket and sweats from when we had pizza the night prior.

At Ares's…

I hadn't even had the thoughts to go over all that, *kidnapped* and held against my will after and then all this?

My brother cuffed my arm before my thoughts could run

away with themselves. "You heard Lucas, and it's a good thing he was proactive about securing the floor from the press. When you hadn't arrived yet, I didn't know what the families would do before you got up here. They really think you're this girl."

By families he meant all the families, *Legacy* families, and the only reason they weren't here now was because they'd left to come back with an army. An army to get *me* according to the press.

Dorian and his family had been amongst them.

I'd seen them on the news too, his beautiful parents and the dark prince in the middle of them. All the Legacy parents had been visually striking, Bow and Thatcher with their parents. Wells with his.

I'd gone to my knees on the floor when I'd seen the Mallicks, Brielle I'd met. She'd been there on the TV with her husband, Ares's dad Ramses.

I searched his face, hers too, and even Ares's. He'd been with his parents, of course, and they all had dark eyes, a glow to their skin like mine…

I didn't care what I saw on that screen, or what *the world* was telling me. These people all had to be making a mistake. I'd wanted to go downstairs after seeing them all, but security told my brother and me we needed to stay put until we were heard from either Lucas or Callum. Neither one of us had our phones either. Mine had been destroyed, and apparently after the press had been blowing up my brother's phone, he'd given it to Callum's PR people to man.

My brother's hands came to my shoulders. "We'll figure this out."

We would figure this out.

That was if I didn't faint first.

We waited for a little bit longer and by then, I'd been given some hospital scrubs. I still smelled like gas, hair thick and matted with sweat. I tried not to cry when I saw myself in the mirror, face bruised and with so much weight to my limbs. I was physically holding the weight of all the thoughts circulating in my mind. Who was I?

And who were those people downstairs who thought they knew who I was?

A doctor came in to look at me too at one point. No serious injuries besides my bruised hip, shoulder, and face. I was holding a can of Coke that'd gone warm by the time Lucas returned to the hospital room. Staff had given it to me, but I hadn't drunk it.

I got up with the assistance of my brother, my hip still warm from my fall on hard concrete. I'd been surrounded by fire then, gas...

The click of a cane came behind Lucas, an older man and my brother's guardian. Callum always sported a suit, but his tie was absent today, the top buttons undone and his jacket gone. He appeared exhausted, a tension around his eyes, and I wondered how long he'd been awake.

"Sloane." A large breath escaped him, one that rose his large shoulders. His cane tapped the floor as he ventured over to me. "You're okay?"

As okay as I could be considering the situation. My throat constricted again. "What's going on?" No one was giving us answers, not security or even the news at this point. Eventually, my brother and I had turned it back on, but they just kept repeating the same stuff we'd seen. "Why is the news saying what it's saying about me?"

"And who told them all that?" My brother had his jacket off, his Adam's apple flicking. "They got the world down there thinking that Sloane is some face on a milk carton. She has parents. *We* have parents. Well, we had..."

His speech croaked, and I couldn't help myself when I placed my arm around him. All this was fucked up, our parents and that situation.

"They're calling them kidnappers." Bru's expression pinched, mouth tight, words squeezed tighter. "Now, I know what Dad did was fucked when he took you, but he's had mental issues."

"It goes beyond that, Bruno." Callum gestured to Lucas, and in the next second, his head of security was leaving the room. Bru and I found out he was in charge of the fleet outside the room.

Lucas shut the door, and with his absence, things got so quiet. Callum advised my brother and me to take a seat, and though I took one, Bru chose to stand.

Bru's hand locked on my shoulder, tight, and I reached back for it. It was as if I was bracing myself as much as comforting him.

"I'm afraid what the news is saying is true." Callum had taken his own seat, an easy chair in this luxurious hospital room. The place looked more like a hotel than an actual room to tend to patients. Callum's hand rubbed the top of his cane. "I know because I'm the one who told them."

Bru shifted behind me. His hands catching my scrubs in a way that made me think he was attempting to keep himself on two legs.

"What are you talking about?" he started, and I blinked.

"I'm saying I'm the one who leaked the information to the press." He tucked the cane against his chair. "At the time, we didn't know exactly where Sloane was. We were able to track her via GPS since Godfrey had taken Bru's vehicle, but he abandoned the car a fair distance out from where we ended up finding her. Lucas combed the area visually for long enough where it made us all nervous. For all we knew, Godfrey could have hopped a train with her or changed out cars even. I hoped by telling the press what was going on would help toward the quick capture of Godfrey."

"But why all that other stuff?" Bru came around the

couch. "That stuff about Sloane being a missing kid and all that—"

I clung to Bruno's arm.

Mostly because of Callum's expression.

Tension thinned his lips, the skin at his eyes taut and rigid. His mouth parted. "Because it's true."

Bruno tucked in beside me.

And I wasn't breathing. I gripped his leg. "What do you mean it's true?"

Callum's hands came together. "I mean you are a missing person," he stated, then glanced at my brother. "And she's not your sister. At least, not biologically."

Bru started to speak but I got up. "What are you talking about, Callum?" I asked. "Why are you saying this?"

"I'm saying it because it's true, Sloane." Callum rubbed his hands. "And though it pains me to say, though I wish that *wasn't* the case, it is, and now that I know the truth, I'm giving it to you. It's something I suspected for quite some time, but until I had solid proof, I couldn't present this information to you. I have it now, and Godfrey trying to destroy the evidence of such, of what he'd done, only corroborates just what my team and I have discovered. Him taking you and trying to *get rid of you* only validates that he and his wife did indeed take you. They took you from here, Maywood Heights, and raised you as their own."

My lips moved, twitching. "How do you know?"

"It started after I gained custody of you both. My suspicions." Callum's head tilted. "Your records weren't panning out, Sloane. In fact, they appeared fabricated. *All of it* from your birth records. Social security…"

I shook.

"None of it appeared right, and that didn't sit well with me."

Bru put his hand over mine. "What made you think she was Pilar?"

Him *saying that name* made me twitch.

That's not my name. That's not my name.

"My team found out all that for me. They have their ways, but it took some time." Callum panned in my direction. "They presented to me the strong possibility that you were this missing girl, Pilar Mallick, and as soon as they did, I started the process of undoing all Godfrey and his wife had done. That meant you coming home and back to your family."

My breaths labored again, thoughts the same. "My family."

"The Mallicks, dear." Callum nodded. "Ramses and Brielle Mallick. You are their biological child. A twin."

A twin.

"One who was taken from a hospital not far from here," he continued. "You were very sick the week of your birth and your kidnappers..."

I cringed.

"Godfrey and Marilyn," he corrected, knowing to do that for some reason. I knew what he was saying. I knew what was claiming *they were*, but still. Callum's expression hardened. "They took you. He and his wife lived in a town not far from Maywood Heights. Godfrey actually worked for me during that time. He left the company abruptly. It was unusual considering his more senior position, but in business there's often movement."

"But why would they do that?" Bru rocked and when I returned beside him, but then his eyes twitched. "Am I taken too? Kidnapped?"

"No, Bru," Callum said, and both my brother and I sighed. Callum lifted a hand. "You are biologically Godfrey and Marilyn's, but according to the file and the information my people were able to gather about your parents, the two had quite a bit of difficulty having children. We believe that was why Sloane was initially taken—"

"But how was he alive?" I stood. "Godfrey? Also, you said he tried to destroy the evidence? You mean me?"

The words chilled, the thought making me completely ill. Me in that fire...

That I was evidence to destroy.

Bru took my hand while I stood, but I wouldn't sit down.

I honestly didn't know if I'd be able to get back up.

"We found the details surrounding all that about an hour ago, the faking of his death and his motives surrounding it." Callum paused, his lips pressed together. "Godfrey had been staying at a motel, and the establishment contacted the authorities after seeing Sloane's story on the news about a kidnapping and who'd done it." Callum shifted in my direction. "You see, they found a journal. The ravings of a madman, they said. It gave details about a plan to wash himself of sin. Cleanse from wrongdoing."

I wavered, and Bru stood up beside me.

"I believe we saw the result of that." Callum exchanged a glance between my brother and me. "The plan was to fake his death, eliminate Sloane, and eventually come back for Bru and start a new life with him. The motel ID'd Godfrey from the footage on the news and contacted the hospital where Sloane was staying."

Oh, God.

"Of course, I'm sure Godfrey's plan didn't involve me finding out the truth." Callum's eyebrows narrowed, his eyes scanning the floor. "He must have found out some way that I was asking questions. Gathering evidence to make things right." He sighed. "This feels like my fault what happened. I should have been more careful about the investigation, as well as spoken up sooner. My people and I weren't being quiet about what we were looking into, and I suppose we didn't think we had a reason to considering your father's passing."

"Why didn't you? Speak up sooner?" Bru rubbed my arm, and I was at a loss for words. How was all this true?

How was this my life?

I leaned into my brother, and using his cane, Callum stood. He faced my brother. "There's a lot of parties involved here, Bru. A lot of people who could be hurt if evidence was unfounded or not factual. I had you kids moved here when we were mostly certain. Once we were, I planned to reveal the information delicately. First to you kids, then well, the Mallicks of course. The family."

But Dad got in the way of all that, Godfrey…

"It's unfortunate how it all ended up happening. And I do take responsibility." Callum frowned. "I've known for a few weeks now, and I was trying to find the right time. It's difficult. There are other factors."

I glanced up, eyes itchy, face hot. My tongue felt thick in my mouth, and with as dry as my throat was, I didn't know whether speaking would result in speech or tears. I blinked down one. "Factors?"

Maybe it'd been more than one tear. Maybe it'd been a river. Because next thing I knew, my brother was helping me to sit, and Callum was giving me his handkerchief.

God…

I sobbed against my brother, my body shaking, and I was sure I was fucking ugly-crying. I couldn't stop.

"It's okay," Bru kept saying, his hand covering my head. He moved my hair out of my face, his big arms wrapped around me as if shielding me from the fucking world. Maybe he was.

"What factors, Callum?" Bru continued, but our guardian didn't say anything. He appeared pained when I looked at him, Callum. He was always such a serious man, albeit kind. He'd always been so good to us.

I could always rely on him.

I had always been able to, a rock for my brother and me.

He took care of us, did that and in more ways than either of us could have ever believed. Godfrey had been his friend, and he stood up. He *did something* when others... well, others could have remained quiet.

The fact that he took care of us financially only drove the point in more, the man coming forward. He lifted a hand, and when he waved it, Lucas came back into the room.

I pulled apart from my brother when he did, and Callum's expression turned grave.

"I have to tell you kids something, and once I do, I'm going to be handing you off to Lucas here," Callum said, his security standing by the door. "He'll oversee anything you need and aid with the reunification process regarding Sloane and the Mallicks."

I didn't understand, letting go of Bru.

"I haven't been completely honest with you children. Honest about myself and who I am to this town." Callum's hand rubbed his cane. "I haven't, and because of that, I don't expect you to want any further contact with me. Especially you, Sloane, and you'll understand when I tell you. That's why Lucas is here. He'll be taking over for me after what I have to tell you both."

Bru's mouth opened, and my brow lifted.

"I hoped to shield you children from who I was. I didn't want my history to be any part of the horrible ordeal you kids have already had..."

"Callum?" My voice rocked, wavering on the end.

"But I know now that was weak of me. Selfish." He shook his head, his hair a graying blond. He was a lot older than he appeared. I would have said late fifties, but I knew him to be older. His head tilted. "I was protecting myself as much as I was trying to protect you kids, and that wasn't right. In any case, it's moot because I'll be making a statement to the press regarding my role in your lives. It's time I stop hiding and let everyone know the truth. I'm not who you kids think I am."

My fingers bit into my arms, my hands gripping them. "Who are you?"

I heard myself speak the words, ask the question. I thought I'd be prepared for the answer. I mean, I'd asked it...

I'd asked *for* it.

CHAPTER
TWO

24 hours before the news broke…

Dorian

"What do you mean you found her?" Ramses's voice drifted into the air, and I think it gave us all pause.

And froze the shit out of Wolf.

He'd been the one to call him. Well, *I'd* been the one to call my god dad *for him.*

Wolf was on my phone.

I'd connected my buddy to the person he needed to speak to, and right now, he wasn't speaking. He started to and actually had done pretty well.

Wells, Thatcher, and I coached him on. Thatcher had his hand braced on Wolf's shoulder, his expression grim, serious. He kept squeezing Wolf's shoulder, his elbow hooked across the top of Wells's beside him. Wells stood tall in front of Wolf, hands buried deep in his coveralls. He pulled one out and touched Wolf's other shoulder.

I held the last position, the one where I was taking Wolf's hand and making him physically bring that phone speaker to his mouth.

He'd lowered it.

I stepped back after that, but not far. My own shoulder didn't leave Wolf's. They touched, and I wasn't going anywhere.

None of us were.

"I'm going to repeat myself, son." Ramses's deep tone edged differently now. It encompassed an unease when it was normally lax and easygoing. Out of all my god dads, Ramses was without a doubt the one most relaxed. He was the peace-maker, the one all of us went to (adults included) for a level head and reason. Ramses didn't have his own problems. Even when he had them, he didn't *have* them. He brushed that shit off like nothing. "Ares, what do you mean when you said you found her?"

Wolf had given him that. My friend had gotten at least that out.

Wolf's lips moved, but no speech passed them. Face red, eyes haunted, he looked like he'd be sick right in front of us. He dampened his mouth. "I said I found her, Dad. I did. I swear to God I did. I found *her*, Pilar."

The name gave me pause, my swallow hard. I closed my eyes but only gave myself a moment.

Get your shit together.

Now wasn't the time for me to break down, but I noticed more than one eye on me in that moment. Wolf was completely distracted, but both Wells *and* Thatcher were looking at me.

"You okay?" Wells mouthed, and I barely kept eye contact before I was squeezing Wolf's arm.

I covered the phone. "You can do this."

He *had* to do this, had to for her.

Wolf waited patiently for his father's response, his face aglow, and the brick fireplace did that. We were still at his house, pizza boxes open. The pies had grown cold when none of us had the stomach to fucking eat them.

Ramses sighed into the line. "We've talked about this, son," he stated, another breath in his voice. He'd regained his calm, my godfather so collected. "You can't find Pilar. She is gone, and we will not be getting her back."

He probably thought he had to say such things. Wolf had a history. Ares thought for a while he could find her and actually to the point where he'd become obsessed.

He'd even ran away.

It'd been a dark time, a real dark fucking time, and put the fear of God in all of us. We thought, for a time, we might lose our best friend, Thatcher, Wells, and me. Ares had gone into a deep depression, and even his parents couldn't pull him out of it, *his parents* who had so much love and support just like the rest of ours.

Thatcher, Wells, and I had a lot of regrets back then. Regrets that we let Wolf go as deep as he had into that dark cloud. His depression had started during the countless days in which he'd searched for his long-lost sister, the days which turned up empty each and every time. Why the guys and I felt responsibility for that was because we'd covered for Wolf. He'd run away quite a few times dating back to as young as elementary school.

He'd been searching leads.

That last time he'd left, left *to find her* had been so fucking bad. Ramses and Brielle ended up finding him in California of all places. At twelve years old, our buddy had hopped on a bus and traveled thousands of miles because some chick over there simply had the same *name* as her. He'd done things like this… rash and crazy things to chase the memory of a person he'd never gotten to meet. It never was Pilar in the end.

His searches always came up empty.

Wolf's anger signaled the end of his searches. He'd never been Mary Sunshine, but without his searches… without *hope*, his depression unfurled into something else. He got real mean, nasty and self destructive, and I think a part of him hoped that he'd been the one taken from the hospital that day instead of Pilar.

If only so his parents didn't have to deal with him.

Of course, he'd never say that, but all of us knew him. We knew *his heart.* He was shit at hiding it just like the rest of us.

That was why I was especially being so rigid now, refusing to feel anything. I couldn't. I couldn't break fucking down when my best friend was trying to tell his dad something way bigger than me. It was bigger than what I was feeling.

Stop being a bitch.

I realized I wasn't breathing. It wasn't until Wells cuffed my arm, the other hand still on Wolf. I wanted to shove Wells away. I wasn't a bitch. I was *fine.*

So why the fuck did I let him stay?

I said nothing, letting him do that shit, but I didn't look at him. I refused, squeezing Wolf's arm.

"This isn't like before," Wolf's voice cracked into the line. His eyes pinched tight. "Dad, it's different."

"Different how?"

Wolf shut down in that moment, his mouth moving again with no words. He scrubbed a heavy hand into his hair, and I thought he'd rip that shit out when he gripped it. That was when I took the phone, giving him a moment. Wolf backed up; his long wingspan locked above his head.

"Ares? Son—"

"It's me, Ramses. Dorian." When I took over, the guys all looked at me, and Wolf whirled around. I lifted a hand, letting him and the others know I had this. "Um, he's not lying. Wolf. He's telling the truth. She's back. Pilar's back." It felt weird calling her that. She wasn't Pilar. She was my *little fighter*. She was… "You've got to listen to him. He's telling the truth. She's back."

Nothing but silence hit after what I said, and at this point, Wolf had gone sheet white. He edged in closer, and Thatcher rubbed his shoulders.

"Put my son on the line, Dorian," Ramses said, but Wolf had that look about his eyes again. The look where I didn't know whether he'd be sick or spiral out.

I lifted a hand to him, again letting him know I had this. I *had this.*

Be strong.

Be like Charlie.

I channeled someone else in that moment, someone who had been that person for me. If Charlie was here, this shit wouldn't have been a thing. He'd be the one talking, *being strong* for everyone else and getting shit done.

Stop bitching out.

I started to be that person, move my fucking mouth, but then I heard a voice.

"Ramses?" My dad's smooth voice drifted into the line. It made me stop full stop. Gave me pause. "What's going on? You look like you've seen a ghost."

I was at a loss now. My dad was wherever Ramses was, and I felt suddenly like a kid then. Like I'd gone from eighteen to four and couldn't make my lips move. Like I'd destroyed the house and blamed it on Chestnut.

Like I needed my dad like a little kid.

It was a weird place to be, as much comfort as unease knowing my dad was there. I wanted to talk to him as much as I wanted to hang up the phone.

"My dad's there?" I asked, and Ramses said yes.

"He drove out for poker night," Ramses continued, but his voice sounded so far away. "And I don't know, Royal. It's our kids, but they're not making sense. They're saying things and…"

Though Ramses clearly didn't have the phone close, it wasn't hard to make out the struggle in his voice.

"Talk to him," I heard Ramses say, but then I heard my name. I heard my father speaking my name.

"What's going on?" he asked after and this time, I noticed my friends around me. I took inventory of each and every one of them. I noticed the pain in Wolf's eyes and the plea in Wells's and Thatcher's. They all wanted me to do something.

Even if they hadn't asked.

When this night began, I'd planned to call *my parents*. I was going to call my dad, but Wolf's family took priority. This was their family, this was *them*, and when it came to me, I should have only been there for support. I needed to just be supportive.

But how could I when I felt like I was dying?

"Dad," I croaked, my throat fucking working, tight. "Dad…"

My chest tightened, my limbs heavy, and I felt cold while at the same time being hot. Like I was frozen but drowning in lava. Like I couldn't *breathe*.

"Dorian Riley," Dad whispered and unusual in the sense. My father was never one to handle me with kid gloves. That was Mom. Never dad. "What is it, son? What's wrong?"

I turned away from my friends. Why couldn't I stop feeling so fucking cold and hot? "Dad, you're going to hate me." He would. How couldn't he after what I had to tell him? I went behind his back. *I lied* to him. "I lied, Dad."

"Lied about what?" The room was so quiet, on both our ends. "What did you lie about? Tell me."

It was the ultimate lie, the ultimate betrayal. How could I tell my dad that I'd reached out to someone who hurt him so badly? How could I tell him that same person may or may not have Wolf's twin sister? She might go to him. She trusted him, and why shouldn't she?

She didn't trust you.

My chest caved again, ripped raw from the inside out. I felt like I was cut in two, bleeding.

"Whatever it is, we'll handle it," Dad said, his words thick but steady. "We'll fix it, and I won't hate you. Just tell me what it is. Tell me the truth."

The truth was madness, painful, but it had to be done. All this was bigger than me.

My love for her was secondary.

CHAPTER THREE

Present

Dorian

Ares's house was chaos…

And we were at the center of it. Us kids got the kiddie table while the parents worked around us, and what used to be Ares's house became a hub. The parents brought in their resources of cops, lawyers, and anyone else they believed could be of any use. Adults were moving in and out of rooms, opening and shutting doors, and us kids couldn't do anything about it.

They wouldn't let us.

We'd done our part, mucked shit royally the fuck up, and now, *our parents* were attempting to undo all the shit we'd gotten into. We hadn't seen any of them in what felt like hours, and Thatcher, Wells, and I hadn't seen Ares or Bow in at least an hour. Ares left with his parents to go back to the hospital barely after leaving it, and Bow was on the cusp of a panic attack after everything in the last twenty-four hours. She'd ended up going with her mom and Cleo, Wells's mom, to drive the block and calm down. The Mallicks hadn't been able to sit still either, hence why they were back at the hospital now. From what I understood, they still couldn't get in, but I didn't blame them for being there.

I should be there.

My mom hadn't let me when I'd suggested it, neither of my parents listening to me at this point. I'd talked enough I think for both of their likings, and though my mom had said I couldn't go back out, she'd ended up joining the Mallicks. She'd gone along with them and my god dad Knight. He had ties to the military, and from how it had sounded as they all left, he was trying to get in contact with old friends. He was trying to get in that hospital, and I wondered if that meant completely stepping over the law and anything else. The law wasn't on our side here. My parents, *our families*, had the cops in their pockets, but even they couldn't get into the place where the news was saying Sloane was being held.

My grandfather had locked it all down, and though the news was saying otherwise, I knew the truth. According to the media, the general public was being kept out of the hospital by their security and for the safety of Sloane herself. They were trying to protect her, the reports stressing the need for it.

She'd been kidnapped.

I didn't know the details from there. None of us did, and at this point, the news knew more than fucking we did about Noa. We knew she'd been taken, taken by who was supposed to have been her dad. He took her again and...

Well, now she was back at that hospital. We'd all seen her on the news being rushed in. That'd been hours ago, though, and Thatcher and Wells watched that shit the press was going on about now. My friends gauged their time between studying me pacing and that gossip shit on the tube. They'd stopped telling me to sit down a long time ago.

I suppose they'd gotten tired of me telling them to fuck off.

I was spiraling at this point and well aware of it. I didn't know what my grandfather was doing. I didn't know his plans, but I did know he *had to be* in that hospital with my girl. *Mine*, and that fact alone had me with a bandaged hand. I'd punched a mirror in the bathroom about an hour ago.

I'd be answering to that eventually, my hands working, fingers flexing. Wells had pulled all the little pieces of glass out while Thatcher had swept up the mess, and not one word was exchanged between the three of us. They hadn't dared, and I hadn't either.

I might scream if I did.

"I can't do this shit," I huffed, heading toward the door. I passed the couch that held my buddies along the way, their heads angling back. Thatcher was up off the couch in seconds, and Wells bounded over it.

"Parents told us to stay put." Wells raised a hand to me, bold enough to do it. Out of all of us, he was probably the only one who could beat me in a sprint, which was probably why he got to the door faster. He wasn't as tall as the rest of us, but he was the leanest. "D—"

I shoved him against the door, physically putting him there. My buddy raised his hands, but I had a feeling it was mostly out of respect. He could hold his own, just like any of us. We were the biggest dudes on the fucking football field. Wells's head touched the door, lazy bottle-blond all over the place. "What are you doing, man?"

I didn't know what I was doing, but my insides were twisted up enough to justify it. A dull knife slicing at me, *stabbing me*, couldn't have felt worse. "Back off."

Wells's hands lowered the same time Thatcher's shadow

cast over the pair of us. He probably *could* stop me. He was bigger than me but only just.

He chose not to in the end and actually opened the door when I shoved Wells off it. Thatcher raised his hands too, head cocked, dark circles under his eyes. None of us had slept in the last twenty-four hours. He nodded toward the door, his spiked earring dangling. He was giving me his permission to go.

Not that I needed it.

I was over this kiddie table shit, and I didn't care if I could help or not. I needed to know at least what was going on.

I cut a corner but didn't make it far. I stumbled into a tower well over six feet, Ares with his hoodie hood up and his head down. He hadn't seen me at all and didn't stop until I physically put my hands on him.

"Dorian. What?" A disorientation laced Wolf's eyes, his speech lazy, confused even. He started to say something else but stopped at the heavy cadence that fell to a hard stop behind me. It seemed Thatcher and Wells weren't letting me go alone to find someone to give me answers. Wolf frowned at them. "What are you guys doing?"

"We could ask you the same thing." Thatcher tucked his hands under his arms. "Thought you were with your parents, man."

"Yeah, what's up?" I guided Wolf right when a couple cops passed us in the hall. I honestly didn't know why the fuck they were here. It wasn't like they were fucking helping with this situation. They were just as worthless as us kids apparently were. They couldn't move on the hospital without risking a body count, not to mention witnesses. The hospital Sloane was in was a private one, and whatever security it had wasn't shy about flashing what *they would do* if the Maywood Heights police precinct tried to enter that hospital.

My grandfather had that shit all set up, some kind of outside security obviously. Rent-a-cops didn't carry the kind of shit or authority all those men and women had at the hospital doors. They'd been professional, *outsourced*, and not many could do that.

Especially against the most powerful families in town.

There'd been an edge of preparedness I think we'd all witnessed, and though our parents didn't say it, they'd been quick to get Thatcher, Wells, Bow, and myself out of there. I'd been surprised when my god dad and Brielle had actually allowed Wolf to tag along on their trip back. I didn't think they were planning on entering, but they were surveying the area with their resources. These were mostly Knight's and whatever else the city could give them. Wolf's mom was the *mayor*, and even she couldn't get in there.

The irony was had it been any other hospital in town the families would have had no trouble getting inside it. The Mallicks basically owned the others because they were all connected to the one that screwed over their family. Ramses and Brielle's *baby* had been taken from one of them.

So, yes. They owned them.

If someone wanted to control foot traffic, taking Sloane exactly where she was definitely would be the perfect place. Again, there'd been a preparedness there, and I didn't think any of us ignored that.

Wolf's arm was in my hand when I pulled him away. He came with me, but again, he appeared disoriented. "You okay?"

"Yeah. I'm just higher than shit." Wolf squatted down, and I made Wells and Thatcher give him room. Wolf breathed in his hands. "I was just wandering the house. My parents wouldn't let me go back. I..."

"It's okay." I got to the floor with him, Wells and Thatcher too. "Have they called you or anything since?"

"Yeah, I was actually just on the phone with them." His long arms hung over his legs. "We spoke but not about any of that. They wouldn't tell me anything about that when I asked."

That didn't surprise me. They were all shutting us out right now.

Wolf's fists touched his mouth. "They mostly just wanted to talk to me about her." He eyed us all, me last. "They were asking all these questions about her. Personal stuff like what she was into. Things she liked..." His arms surrounded his legs. "I couldn't give them much. I told them you'd know more, D, and they might call you. You know her better."

But did I? He'd been the one to stay with her, *believe her*. I swallowed. "Okay. That's fine."

Wolf's throat worked. "I think they're preparing," he said, his voice so quiet. He scanned us all. "Preparing for a life without knowing her or some shit, and I..."

"Hey. Don't say that," I said, and he pushed me away. He pushed all of us away, getting up.

"But it's fucking true." His words amplified in the hallway, suits stopping, cops pausing. They lined the halls on their phones and speaking into coms. Wolf sneered. "What the fuck are you all looking at?"

Wells cringed. "Bro—"

"Don't fucking *bro* me. You don't know shit, Wells. What this feels like?" He shook his head. "I'm fucking *dying*, and she's out there and—"

I held him, fucking tight until it was hard for me to breathe.

Wells and Thatcher joined.

We locked in, a strong huddle with Wolf at the center. It wasn't long ago I'd been at that center. They'd surrounded me when I'd needed it.

"It's going to be okay," I gritted, forcing myself to keep my own shit together. Wells and Thatcher backed off when I took Wolf's face, making him look at me. "I'm going to make sure this shit is okay. She's going to be all right, and nothing bad is going to happen to her."

I was telling myself this as much as him, emotion thickening my voice.

The same laced Wolf's eyes, and I didn't let go until he nodded at me. I hugged him again, the others too. It took him a second, hell all of us, to stop shaking, but once Wolf did, I had the others guide him back to the lounge. Things would be okay.

I was about to make sure of it.

I found my dad in Ramses's office, one of the bigger rooms of the house, and it looked like some kind of war room when I entered.

For starters, it held the most people, mostly suits in here. Our parents had a team of confidants and trusted friends in their corner. Our families weren't just powerful because of their money, but also because they were decent fucking people and did a lot for the community. Any one of our parents would bend over backward if someone they knew was in need and that was why most of these people were here. Very few of them actually worked for our parents.

I angled through them all, a guy I passed watching the news footage on a small screen. He was taking notes beside it, and he must have been watching recorded clips because Sloane was on the screen.

I'd played this over a few times, her being escorted into the hospital with that fucking goon that my grandpa employed. The man was a hired gun, and he had *my girl* by the arm. I'd let my father know right away who he was, and Wolf had been able to confirm since he'd seen him before too.

If any of our parents didn't know my grandpa was involved with this hospital takeover they knew now with that little detail, and I stared too long at that clip playing. I'd only stopped because my parents had taken my phone and only partially because I'd fucked up. Them and the other parents had been attempting to use it to call Sloane too. They knew I'd been seeing her.

I'd told them that too.

In fact, they knew just about everything, using all our phones at one point to try and speak with her. She hadn't answered my friends' lines or mine, but even before the kidnapping the news mentioned, she hadn't been talking to me.

Don't do that.

Fighting negative head shit was the hardest part in all this. To think she wasn't answering on purpose. We'd had our problems, but the last time I saw her things had been good.

I refused to believe she wasn't talking to me on purpose, and that almost made things worse. The alternative was my grandfather was deliberately keeping her from me and not letting her answer my calls.

I found my dad in the center of all the chaos with Wells's dad, Jax. My god dad stood by my father's side, a receiver to my dad's ear. They'd been the only two to stay in this fortress of manpower the parents had created, and Dad was the best one to man the hub with the other parents preoccupied.

That said something considering his own dad was at the center of it.

Dad had been too silent when I'd told him everything. It had to have been breaking him, but when he'd finally spoken, he'd been my dad. He'd been calm and more than collected when he shouldn't have been.

I almost wished he'd yelled at me.

It would have been better than the *look* I'd gotten when I finally had seen him, the look similar to the one he was giving me now when he noticed me in this room.

A slow shake to my father's head, he held a stony expression that only said one thing.

Disappointment.

My dad was disappointed in me, and when his shoulders

dropped in my very presence, my stomach soured. Few things had been able to cause me to feel ill today. I had held my shit together.

But my father looking at me this way...

He removed himself from the fleet of people around him, Jax too. They were both laid-back, Dad with his sweater bunched at his elbows and Jax in a Grateful Dead tee. My god dad often dressed down. He was cool like that, but Dad never did in the presence of others. They'd both been awake a long time.

Maybe even longer than me. I knew for a fact I hadn't slept, and how could I?

She was still out there.

The thoughts of Sloane escaped when my father approached, still speaking into the line at his ear. He multi-tasked this while maneuvering toward me, but with the intent of his strides, I knew I wouldn't be seeing the inside of this room for long. My father, *all the fathers and mothers*, had been very clear that we kids needed to stay out of the way and especially out of here, the place of their operation. The adults needed room to work.

Hence the kiddie table.

"Son—" my dad started, but I edged closer first. I maybe had one shot at this before he kicked me out of this bitch.

"Can I talk to you?" I asked, his eyes twitching. Maybe at the audacity? Shit, I didn't know. I was fucking bold coming in here. I buried my hands in my pockets. "Please. It's important."

I forced myself to have an iron stomach in front of my father. I hadn't told him everything, but now wasn't the time for that.

I might not get her back if I didn't.

I suppose the cowardice... the secrets stemmed from the potential disappointment from both my parents. Not just my dad. I couldn't bear to think how my mother would look at me after I revealed what I had to. I couldn't have her see me in a way I was already seeing myself. I wasn't just a coward.

I was my grandfather's grandson.

My dad covered his line, his eyebrows narrowed, features hard. He had been about to kick me out but stopped and brought the phone up to his ear.

"One second, LJ. It's Dorian." Pulling the phone away, he eyed me. "What is it? Have you heard from her?"

He knew I hadn't heard from Sloane. His people had my phone. I shook my head, and he went back to his call.

"He said he needs to talk to me," Dad continued, frowning. "Give me two seconds. Just keep working on Judge Perez. Do whatever you have to. We've got to get into that hospital."

He hung up the phone on who I knew to be my god dad. I hadn't seen LJ here, but I knew both he and Billie, his wife, were trying to get here. I'd heard the adults talking about it. The two had to drive all night from where they were since they couldn't catch a flight.

Everyone really was coming out for this. Out to help one of us when LJ was more so my Dad's friend than the Mallicks'. Of course, our parents were all good friends, but some had closer ties.

That didn't seem to matter as my dad guided me out of the room. He'd given his phone to Jax to handle any incoming calls, my god dad lifting his hand to me with more than a tense expression etched on his face. Jax was hardly ever serious.

Everyone was today, and with my dad asking LJ to get involved, I had a feeling that meant the parents weren't really working inside the law. If they were trying to do that, they'd speak to Brielle, *the mayor*, or even Jax, whose dad was a congressman.

Nah, LJ was the guy the parents went to in order to get shit done. Legally or otherwise. I wasn't certain of LJ's background, but I did know he had contacts both underground and above. Whatever he was into, whether past or present, made people move for him.

"What is it?" Dad braced my shoulder but released when soft steps touched behind me. He angled his body in that direction, and next thing I knew, he was leaving me.

And my stomach tightened more.

Mom… *my mother* had her jacket on, a thick blanket and a thermos in her hands. Dad instantly went to her, and though I had too, I had a rigidness to my steps that slowed me down.

She wasn't supposed to be here. She's not…

But here she was and with my father.

"Em, why aren't you at the hospital?" Dad cuffed Mom's arm in a delicate hold, and she placed her hand on his. My parents together were a fucking perfume ad, that glamorous Giorgio Armani shit that was basically fucking flawless.

Timeless.

My parents had an air about them that commanded people, and only some of that had to do with how visually stunning they were. I took all that from them and more, priding myself on it and even used it to my advantage in the past. I'd felt entitled to it.

And look where it had gotten me.

I had the weight of secrets and loss the equivalent of my goddamn body weight. I used the most beautiful elements of my parents for bad, not good.

And here I thought I was the good guy.

I knew my place in all this now, waiting while my parents greeted each other.

"Getting some stuff for Brielle," Mom stated after Dad embraced her, touched her. She squeezed his hand. "Tea and blankets. Hoping maybe I can get her to sit down."

Brielle hadn't before she'd left, the loudest voice before Ramses had forced her to take a step back. She'd been trying to lead everything, acting like the mayor instead of the grieving mother she was before Ramses suggested they go to the hospital with Knight and his team. Like always, Wolf's dad played the peacemaker. He had to be dying inside too just like Wolf.

He was just better at hiding it.

Everyone had to be breaking at this point. I mean, they'd all been here when the initial kidnapping had happened, all the parents grieving right along with the Mallicks. Us kids had been spared for the most part.

At least in the worse ways.

Those wounds obviously still remained, and we never had to know Pilar to *feel* her. She was everywhere. In Brielle's beauty…

Ramses's heart.

I swallowed, my parents coming apart.

"Dorian wanted to tell me something." Dad placed me on the spot, his hand on my mother. "He said it was important."

"Important?" Mom exchanged a glance with my dad, and though she'd been better at hiding her disappointment at several revelations lately, I noticed her heavy sigh. Her hold tightened on her blankets. "What happened? There's something else?"

Fuck.

"That can't possibly be the case." Dad's hand warmed my mom's shoulder before facing me. He frowned. "Because that would mean our son's *still* lying to us, *keeping things from us.*" He shook his head, his fingers folding into blond hair. He sighed. "What is it, Dorian?"

It was like he knew, right? He did know because he knew me. They both did. I wet my lips. "Remember when I told you Grandpa threatened me? Threatened Mom?"

I had told my parents mostly everything. It'd been necessary. We all needed to get Sloane back, and I'd dished everything I could to make sure that happened. They knew about my visits to Grandpa Prinze this summer.

And they knew why.

My grandfather helped with the Mayberry situation, helped me with *Charlie*, and though my parents hadn't been happy, I think it did fill in some blanks for them. Blanks about how it had all gone down. They even knew how he'd tried to teach me a lesson by blowing the whistle that led to my arrest.

They'd been so quiet during that.

None of it'd been good, but the urgency had been there to move. Move to try to help the Mallicks, and everything *I'd* personally told them hadn't led to any repercussions yet.

I had a feeling this was for lack of time, my father's hand folding into his hair again.

"We remember." Dad eased my mother into his side, his nod subtle. "It's the reason why cops now have to follow your mother *and you* every time you leave."

Ouch.

"Not to mention the authorities being here around the clock." Dad waved his hand to them. "This is the evidence of that. So yes. We remember."

I cringed, and Mom squeezed her eyes.

"Dorian, if there's something else you need to tell us. *Tell us.*" Mom's lips thinned. "This isn't a game. Pilar's life is at stake. Who knows what your grandfather could be doing to her. What he's been doing," she gasped, and my chest tightened. She took my hand. "If you haven't told us everything, now is the time."

They did know almost everything. They knew about Sloane, her brother. They knew Grandpa Prinze's ties to them. How he was their guardian and taking care of them.

But they didn't know this.

"I didn't feel like I had a choice," I started, all this fucking hard. I lifted a hand. "Dad, he threatened Mom."

Dad's throat flicked, the only indicator anything I said affected him. He'd been so good about it, hiding his feelings, hiding his pain. His chest rose, a large and full breath. "Dorian, for your safety, *Pilar's*, and everyone else involved here, if you know something else about my dad, you need to say it."

This wasn't about his dad. It was about *me* and what a fuck up I was. I didn't regret what I'd tried to do.

I regretted not being able to finish the job.

I regretted not being able to *end this* and the possibility of Sloane getting hurt because of it. I opened my mouth, but even when I did the words wouldn't come out.

My mom lowered to the floor, leaving my dad. Placing the blankets and thermos down, she held my hands. It was like she felt she needed to. Like I was her scared little kid, her little boy. "What is it, baby? Just tells us. Your dad and I won't hate you."

He'd promised that before, and I knew he didn't, but his disappointment almost felt worst. I admired my father so much.

But I'd lose him with this.

He waited too, patient with his hand on my mom's shoulder. He didn't give me his hand, and his fingers flexed at his side. It was like he wanted to come closer but was fighting himself. Like he wanted *to comfort me* and always had in the past.

Today, I appeared to be on my own. At least, when it came to him. It was graduation day.

And this was me walking across the stage.

"I tried to poison him," I said, but I didn't whisper it. I straightened. "He threatened Mom so I tried to poison him."

Dad didn't flinch, nor did mom. Dad's mouth parted. "With what?"

"Something lethal." I didn't go into specifics because I didn't feel that was exactly what he was looking for. I assumed he wanted to know the severity. I expelled a breath. "It didn't take. He survived."

"Baby, let's get this straight." Mom breathed out the words, her hand to her mouth. She glanced my way. "Are you saying you tried to kill your grandfather?"

"He isn't just saying it, Em." Dad panned my way, Mom moving to his side. She let go of my hand. She let go *of me*. He stood tall. "He tried to do it. Our son tried to kill my father."

"It didn't work—"

"Obviously, it didn't, Dorian, but you tried to do it." Dad angled away, his hand covering his mouth, his face. "My son tried to kill my father."

It was like he was trying to tell it to himself, sink into it, believe it. I stepped forward. "Dad—"

"And now he's out there with *the daughter* of your mom's best friend with no doubt some sick vendetta against you." He raised and dropped his hand. "He could be holding her because of you."

I swallowed. "I know."

"And you just kept this to yourself. You keep *keeping* things to yourself. Things like Charlie that have serious consequences for not just you but other people in your life. People who care about you, *love you*."

"I know, Dad."

"I just don't understand. I don't *get it*, Dorian. What has your mother done, what have *I* done to ever warrant such behavior? To warrant you continuing to shut us out."

"You haven't done anything." I started to move, but Dad still had his hand up. He wasn't looking at me, Mom's hand to his chest. I cringed. "I didn't tell you because I was…" Weak. Foolish. "I thought I was doing the right thing. I thought I had it handled."

"Well, you didn't." His head angled my way. "And now a girl's life hangs in the balance."

But it wouldn't. It *couldn't*. I was going to make this right. I *had* to make this right. "Dad, if you just let me—"

"Let you what," he started, but Mom said his name. Dad

didn't get angry. In fact, he wasn't even raising his voice. There were cops and suits moving past us, and none of them looked our way at all because, to most people, my father didn't give any obvious tell he was angry.

But I knew my dad's anger. He didn't have to raise his voice. The heat rolled off him, thick, weighted.

And it made me sick I was the reason.

I kept doing this to my parents, hurting them. "Let me talk to Grandpa." They'd taken my phone, and if they'd let me, I already would have tried to contact him. My parents had been quick to shut me out, though, said their people would handle contact with my grandfather.

I hadn't even gotten to voice that contact should be me.

I could end this *all* if they'd just let me.

"He wants a relationship with me, Dad," I said, both my parents turning away at this point. "That's all he wants, and if he is holding Sloane," I paused, knowing they knew her more so by another name. The guys, Bow, and I told them her name, of course. The parents just didn't know her by it. She'd always been Pilar to them. "He'll let her go. I know he will, and he didn't even want to hurt Mom. He just threatened that, bluffing."

"Manipulating, which is what my father does to get what he wants."

"Royal." Mom's word was hushed and nearly like medicine. I watched my father's body visibly relax at the sound of his name, his wife's hand on his shoulder. "Perhaps we all need a moment."

He glanced my way, starting to say something, but the door of the war room opened. Jax came out of it, easing through the traffic in the hall.

"Royal, we need you back in there *now*," he said, completely overlooking the tension in the hallway. He ignored my mother and me when he normally wouldn't. "It's your dad. He made contact."

What?

"Says he needs to talk to you. Says it's urgent," Jax continued, and with that, he was gone, my parents behind him. I think the only reason no one stopped me was because the rush to get into that room was priority.

It was dead silent.

The room, which normally held the hustle and bustle of attorneys, the authorities, and other representatives of the family, stopped, and in the center was one suit, a guy holding up a phone. I recognized the phone as my dad's, and as soon as the guy gave it to him, the man sat down at a station. This same guy put a headset on, easing in front of a laptop. He then waved to my dad to move on with the call.

I suppose the guy might be trying to track the call, but we all knew my grandpa was most likely at the hospital.

Wasn't he?

I guess we couldn't confirm that. We really didn't know, and the moment my parents did realize I was there in the room with them, they attempted to wave me out of it.

I didn't budge, couldn't. Even if I wanted to, I didn't think I could physically move. I was stuck.

I wouldn't leave.

CHAPTER
FOUR

Dorian

My god dad came over to me, his hand up when my parents wouldn't do anything but look at me. Jax put his hands on my shoulders, waving my parents on. I wasn't leaving, and it seemed he thought it best just to be with me in that moment.

Maybe my parents felt the same way because my mom's attention traveled to my dad next. He raised that phone to his mouth, the call apparently on speaker, and the seconds in which he didn't say anything amplified in this quiet room.

"Dad," he said, the word foreign coming from him. I mean, he was *my dad*. So yeah, hearing him call someone else that was weird. Dad's jaw shifted, tight when the muscle feathered along his jawline. "Any idea why you're holding an eighteen-year-old girl who's been missing for the past eighteen years?"

Straight to the point, my father, and when Jax refused to breathe behind me, I realized we were both doing the same thing. We were holding our breath.

And we were doing it for my dad.

We all knew his history with my grandfather. Maybe not everyone in his room, but the people closest in his life. This wasn't easy for my father, this conversation.

Some static occurred on the line, movement. Wherever Grandpa was, things were going on, moving. "Royal." The word amplified in the room as much as the silence. "Thank you for speaking with me."

If my dad had a tell for what it was like to speak to the abuser during his youth, he didn't give one. He merely glanced down when the man beside him, the one behind the computer, lifted a paper.

He's at the hospital was written across the paper, big and bold, and my father took his attention back to the call.

"And I'm sure you want answers," Grandpa continued, deep and smooth as my dad's voice. Hearing them together was crazy, trippy. They probably hadn't spoken to each other since before my birth. Grandpa had been in prison before. "I'm here to give them, but to start, the *hold* you speak of was merely a security precaution."

A lazy smile touched my dad's lips, but I was sure he'd found nothing funny. He angled the phone toward his mouth. "Holding her against her will and keeping her from *her family* was a security precaution?"

"All due respect, son, you're not her family, and as far as the Mallicks, she didn't know they were. Until she did, it didn't seem appropriate for, to put it bluntly, an army of strangers to come and get her."

Dad sneered.

"As far as holding her against her will, this was not true." He sighed, a bit of agitation in the old man's voice. Was my father getting to him? "I've actually been trying to get her back to her family, *her real family,* since she's come into my care."

"Well, please. Enlighten me and everyone else in this room because no one else knows what's going on but you." Dad raised a hand toward the room. "Because how it looks is, you have a missing person in your custody. A missing person *my kid* tells me you've been lying to. At least about your identity."

I stiffened, my god dad bracing my shoulders.

Dad angled in my direction. "He's also been telling me how you pursued a relationship with him behind my back and without my authority. One he more than clearly cut off after his mistake, so from how it's looking, at least on your end, it's not good. Especially when it seems one of your final meetings together didn't end so well. For him, or for *you*."

He'd changed the words up, danced around what had actually happened but probably only for my benefit. This room was full of strangers, friends, and Dad hadn't wanted to put what I'd actually done out there.

He didn't want to tell anyone his son had attempted a murder.

My parents kept eye contact with me, both of them, and though it was hard, I didn't look away. I had done what he'd said, and I owned up to it.

Even if it was late.

Another sigh from the old fucker on the phone. "I'm sure you think you know what's going on, and yes, things do look a certain way. It was unfortunate what happened with Dorian and me and completely my fault in that regard."

My mouth parted, my dad's too. I didn't think either of us had actually thought he'd admit that.

"Pursuing a relationship behind your back was wrong, and I make no excuses for that. I was the adult in the situation, and I should have put a stop to it when he came to me. I'm sure he explained to you why."

"He did." Dad's tone was stiff, rigid. "And he knows what he did was wrong, but that doesn't excuse some of the things I've heard you've done to him. Nor does it make anything right about what you're doing now to Pilar Mallick. You're holding her and the fallout of what happened between you and my son—"

"Aren't related whatsoever. Pilar Mallick, who goes by the name of Noa Sloane, was simply my ward and a bad decision made by a man I called a friend." Grandpa paused. "A man who's now dead after we pursued him."

Mom looked at my father. We all did.

"His name was Godfrey Sloane. His wife Marilyn. Godfrey used to work for me—"

"We know," Dad said. "We know all about that. The kids told us who Sloane's alleged parents were, and it wasn't hard to figure out the connection to you. He used to work at one of our plants, *work for you.*"

"Yes, but I'm sure your team also knows he left the company shortly after the initial kidnapping when the child went missing. My people looked into this too. Godfrey and his wife had issues having children. The pair lived not far from Maywood Heights. I'm sure Sloane was the perfect opportunity for them. They skipped town not long after, went off the grid."

"And the man just so happened to give the baby to you after his demise, which was apparently false?" Dad eyed the room. "Quite coincidental."

"I'm sure you know it's not."

I blinked, my dad and more than one person in the room twitching too.

Grandpa's sigh was once again heavy. "You know my history. It's the same reason I've given your family *space,* something I've been doing for over a decade and at your request despite you sending people to watch me over the years."

Dad frowned, and it was news to me he'd asked Grandpa to stay back. He hated his dad.

I suppose it shouldn't have been news then.

Even still, it was, and my father cleared his throat.

"I've been doing everything you've asked of me with the exception of most recently when *your son* came to *me*, son," Grandpa said. "But even still, that doesn't excuse my history and who my old friend Godfrey believed I was."

"Which is?" Dad asked, and there was silence on the phone again, rustling. Someone's voice came in, hushed, hurried. I heard mention of the words *must hurry* and others, which had the people in the room jotting things down, police, detectives. I couldn't hear much clearly, but what had been said definitely made people uneasy. There was lots of shifting, and my mother touched my dad.

"Someone who did something terrible in the past," Grandpa said, surprising me. "And I don't expect retribution, nor your forgiveness. I'm just saying that's who Godfrey believed I was. He trusted me to take care of someone who clearly wasn't his own, and when I found that out, one thing he probably didn't expect was for me to try to reunite the girl he and his wife had taken with her real family. In fact, I'm sure that was the opposite of what he believed because not only did he come back, come back to *kill her* and cover up what he'd done…"

My mom gasped, and Dad froze. My stomach twisted the fuck up too, and my god dad noticed.

Jax's hands tightened on my arms in a firm grip. It wasn't unknown my relationship with the girl we were all speaking about. I introduced her to Brielle as my girl that day at school, so of course, the other parents knew that detail too now. Sloane was my girl.

And I loved her.

I think sharing that with her might have pushed her further away in the end. She hadn't been shy about letting me know she hadn't trusted me in the past.

A sharp chill racked my fucking body, my grandpa speaking again.

"He would have had it not been for Lucas, my head of

security. We found Sloane and Godfrey in a warehouse in the end. The man had been about to blow the place to kingdom come. He faked his own death and, after he took care of Sloane, planned to take his actual son away. Bruno Sloane, Noa's kid brother, is actually biologically his."

"And how do you know all this?" Dad shot, his teeth bared again. "How could you possibly know all this?"

"The man detailed it, son. All of it." Hushed voices occurred in the background once more, and I was sure I wasn't the only one straining to hear them. Someone was trying to get word in to my grandfather about something. "He'd been staying in a motel. The motel called the hospital after seeing Sloane's story on the news, a story *I leaked* to help find Godfrey in the first place."

That sharp chill cut across me again, my parents exchanging the same look. Dad covered the phone, and with the way they weren't speaking to each other, they clearly were at a loss for words. Before I knew it, my mom of all people was taking the phone.

"You really were trying to get her back?" she asked, and no one attempted to keep her from doing this. Not even my dad. Though, his jaw had clearly tightened. He didn't want this, this exchange.

But hell if anyone could stop my mother from doing anything she wanted to do.

"And speak quickly, Callum," she said, her voice rough, low. "You talk now because I swear to *God*, if you're lying, I'll come for you myself."

"Em." Dad took Mom's hand, but even still he waited patiently. Perhaps he wanted to know the answer too.

"I've been a lot of things. I have done and *was* a lot of things, but I am not this man my old friend believed," Grandpa said, and I noticed he didn't acknowledge the change of voices. He had to have an indicator this was my mom though. He had to know. "I'm not, and I truly have been trying to get Noa back to her family. Back to your friends. I only apologize for how long the process was taking. We were still trying to collect evidence and unearth a lot of things Godfrey attempted to cover up. It was a tedious process, and one I thought best to keep quiet until at least we'd concluded and had all the evidence. We were reaching the end of that process when Sloane was taken."

Which explained why he lied to me about knowing who she truly was… I guess. He told me none of this in Sloane's kitchen that day when I ran into him.

And from how it sounded he knew he was talking to my mother, mentioning her friends and all that. I started to come forward, but Jax cut me off.

"No, kid," he said, so serious. I wasn't used to it. Not from him. He leaned in. "Just no. Let them handle it. Her handle it."

But how could I just stand here, my mom talking to the man who, well, did something so terrible to her, *her sister.*

"I understand your distrust… especially yours with who I assume you to be," Grandpa started, both my parents too still. "But history, at least for now, needs to be set aside." More hushed tones broke the conversation, my grandfather and someone else. Several someone elses actually. They all spoke for a few moments before he returned this time. Grandpa forced a harsh breath into the phone. "The girl's been missing for over an hour now."

"What?" Dad took the phone now, my mom willingly giving it to him, and this time Jax didn't make me stay. I was at my dad's side now, my mom grabbing me.

"I mean, she's gone. She and her brother," Grandpa huffed. "They somehow escaped the hospital together."

"What do you mean somehow?" My dad asked my question. "You've got that place locked down."

"I do, with the exception of hospital staff. They come and go as they please. Noa was dressed in scrubs from her ordeal.

Godfrey covered her in gas and tried to set her on fire this morning."

"Oh, God." Mom's words were laced with a thickness that had her covering her mouth. An extreme and violent nausea hit me to the point where, if my mother and I weren't virtually holding each other up, I would have fallen to my knees.

"Dad," I said, my dad's hand coming to me.

Dad's throat jumped. "I advise you to speak quicker, father. You said she's missing. Is she injured? Seriously hurt?"

He looked at me, the movement in the back of the call amplified.

"She's experienced no serious injuries. Bruises here and there. She could be in the hospital, but with the way she's dressed could have just as easily slipped out. Especially if they got Bru, her brother, scrubs as well."

"Must have slipped out." Dad pushed his fingers over dark blond. "Any idea why someone you saved and *provided for*, according to the kids, would want to run away from you?"

"Probably because I told her the truth."

"What?"

"I told her the *truth*, son. I told her about me. Who I was and why I think Godfrey trusted me to keep his secrets."

My mouth dried.

"I told her my history. With the town, yes, but also with her grandfather. Her biological one."

My hand gripped my shirt, my legs fucking wavering. I rubbed at my chest, but no matter what I did, I still couldn't breathe.

"And as it sounds like Dorian explained, she didn't know my true identity. She didn't, but she does now."

She does now.

"That being a part of her transition back, back to Mallicks, wasn't a part of the plan. I hoped to get her set up, tell her the truth about her identity, then remove myself from the equation. I believed that was the right thing for all involved, and I'm sure you understand why."

The illness didn't leave. Sloane knew the truth?

Leaning against the desk, I managed to remain standing, and I noticed my father held eye contact with me. Perhaps I looked as sick to my stomach as I felt. Sloane knew the truth, a truth *I* should have told her. I hadn't told her about my connection to my grandfather.

You're the liar. You.

"I planned to release a statement to the press after my people made contact with the Mallicks. I told her that too," Grandpa continued. "She reacted as well as you could expect. All of this was a lot, and she was quite silent. In fact, she didn't really speak at all, and after, she simply asked for some time alone. Her brother stayed, and my people and I left. We gave her time."

Too much time, as it sounded.

"She was gone when we got back, and it'd be nice if we could work together to find her. Right now, my team is scouring the hospital and the surrounding areas, but it'd be nice if they didn't have to worry about yours coming through the hospital with battering rams. We were going to attempt to talk to them, but I thought reaching out to you first was best. You could make a call and uncomplicate things in that regard."

"I'm sure you have it all figured out, Dad," my father said, but he was snapping his fingers. He did first to my god dad. "Get Ramses on the phone."

"On it, brother." Jax left me, on his phone, and my mother grabbed Dad's hand. She mentioned going back to the hospital, but when I attempted to go after her, Dad snapped his fingers in my direction.

"You stay," he said, then directed a cop over to me. "Make sure he gets back to his friends."

What?

"Dad." I came over to him. "I need to be out there. The guys and I can—"

"No," he challenged, and when a cop touched me from behind, I pushed the fucker off.

"Dad. *Please.*" He couldn't keep me here. I needed to look, look *for her.* "You have to let me go. I have to look for her."

"You've done enough," he volleyed, and in that moment, my father shot me an irregular look. It was one completely foreign to him. He was always so patient with me. Even when he had no reason or right to be. He always was.

But not today.

Today, and in this moment, it felt like we lost something, the pair of us, and covering his phone, Dad wet his lips.

"Go," he said, just one word before he was getting back to things. The cop didn't have to escort me out after that.

I went by myself.

24 hours since the news broke…

2 days since the news broke...

1 week since the news broke...

The present.

CHAPTER
FIVE

Dorian

"How are you doing today, Dorian?" Dr. Singh asked me, her head tilted. She'd barely looked up from her notepad today, which meant nothing good for me. "Are your nights getting any easier?"

Meaning was I sleeping.

Since the answer was no, I shook my head, and *her head* went down again. Some days I wondered if all the epically fucked-up shit I gave her on the regular could be made into a volume of encyclopedias, a manifesto of a fucked-up youth…

At least, that was what I'd call it.

I'd been seeing Dr. Singh off and on since my grandparents died when I was a kid. My parents had signed both Charlie and me up, and I'd kept going mostly for Charlie. He hadn't wanted to go but seeing me had kept him going so I had.

I had to admit, over the years it'd been nice, the check-ins. Dr. Singh had been there for all the milestones. The first time

I'd tried weed, then later, the harder stuff when I'd been a fucking idiot enough to try it. That phase hadn't lasted long, but she'd been there for it.

She'd been there for the parties and even the conquests. I'd bragged to her when I'd lost my virginity.

Like a fucking tool.

We had this doctor-fucked-up-client privilege thing so I knew she wouldn't tell my parents about any of the things I told her, and Dr. Singh had actually been a bit of a release. I could unload all my shit, then go about my business. I could *live my life* doing all the fucked-up things I wanted to do, and ironically enough, despite telling her all my shit, she really didn't know shit.

At least where it mattered.

I'd kept all the personal stuff close to the cuff over the years and hadn't even seen her since Charlie had died. I hadn't needed anyone poking and prodding into my life.

Not that I had a choice now.

Dr. Singh continued to scribble on her notepad, her salt-and-pepper braid over her shoulder. We spent a lot of time like this, her writing, me sitting. She often tried to offer advice I never took, nor did I allude I would. Never stopped her from trying to, though, and I knew me being here made my parents happy. They saw therapists themselves, thought it was healthy.

I shifted on the couch, biding my time. We had forty-five minutes, and we'd only eaten up maybe ten.

"How are you doing with your attachments?" she asked me. She pushed her glasses up into her hair. "Letting go of the things you can't control. I know you've had trouble there in the past, and I think it's important to really work on that now. During this time?"

During this time.

I fought myself from smirking, my hands open. "Please. Help me. *Save me.*" Daring her to, I leaned forward. "Because believe me, if anyone had the fucking remedy for my life, I'd take it right now."

Dr. Singh had no reaction for my passive-aggressive shit, never did. She just continued to write, and I cursed. None of these behaviors would get me off her chair.

Nor make my parents back off.

They were the ones controlling shit right now, controlling me. These sessions *weren't* optional. I threaded my fingers together. Dr. Singh wanted to talk about my grandfather next, so needless to say, the next thirty-some-odd minutes were deathly silent. I didn't want to talk about my grandfather.

And I definitely didn't want to talk about Sloane.

I was on my phone when I came out of the therapist's office, and if I'd thought Ronald, our butler, had given me a chance to breathe by taking off, I'd been wrong. He was right there outside the room when I exited, a smile on his face and his hat on his lap. Standing, he held the expression. "How did it go today, Master Prinze?"

He knew how it went. I was here, wasn't I?

If that wasn't an indicator for how shitty my life was right now, I didn't know what was.

Because I was respectful of our family butler, I kept silent. I saved all the attitude shit for Dr. Singh, and it wasn't Ronald's fault he was forced to babysit me.

It's yours like everything else.

The self-deprecation I kept to myself too, swallowing hard. Ronald waved us on, staying close. I assumed he'd already done recon on the area since apparently, I was the president's kid these days.

Our butler may be older, but he was also ex-military. He was security just as much as he was traditional household staff and had been assigned my personal keeper as of late. Not only had I lost access to my ride, but I couldn't physically go anywhere without Ronald or a cop in tow.

My parents would justify these changes with having

something to do with my grandfather, and though maybe some of that was there, I'd be hard-pressed not to know they were keeping *me* controlled as much as protecting me. They were still looking for Sloane, and they were attempting to keep me out of it.

And any breeches held consequences.

The last had gotten me Ronald, me sneaking out, going rogue. Since I didn't sleep, I spent pretty much every waking hour doing one thing, and my parents were completely aware of that.

They weren't dumb.

Ronald got us to the house in silence, never one to prod. That wasn't his job. He was there to protect me, as well as get me from point A to B. In this case, that included my weekly therapy session, but that hadn't been the consequences of a breech. Regular sessions with Dr. Singh were the result of my parents' disappointment, their *fear*. I'd tried to kill my grandfather, and now, I was sitting on a shrink couch every week.

My parents were scared, *scared for me*, and they probably should be.

I was scared for me.

I was scared of *what I'd do* if something didn't change soon.

If we didn't find her...

A burn rolled like tight heat in my chest, my head lowered as Ronald cruised one of my father's sedans past the gate into our neighborhood. The familiar news vans were there, all of them attempting to snap pictures and calling my name. Thatcher and Wells had similar activity outside their houses, and at Wolf's house, it was difficult to get on the block.

I shielded my face from them all, people here for the story, and that was all. Once word had gotten out that Sloane and I'd been a thing, I especially had been slapped across the papers and internet search engines. I was now the boyfriend of the missing Mallick girl. I was *Pilar Mallick's* boyfriend.

Not the kid with his fucking heart ripped out.

I didn't know where Sloane was. For *an entire week*, I'd been left to wonder if she were alive or dead. I'd been left to wonder if she was even here, or if she'd skipped town entirely. She'd somehow gotten out of that hospital with her brother.

And the rest of us were left to simply wonder.

The restless nights began that night, no sleep ever coming to me. I spent all my mental energy either looking for her or thinking about her, but it wasn't like I could do much.

My parents, *the families*, had my buddies and me under close surveillance. They made us sit on our hands while they moved pieces and talked to people. Maywood Heights was in a city-wide search, and the details of that my friends and I were kept out of. We weren't allowed to move unless they said we could.

So, we moved without them.

I was facing the consequence of that now, my butler never more than a breath away these days. He was nice about it, and as a friend of the family, I doubted he minded, but he was always *there*. He was my own personal keeper, and I really had no control.

I forced myself to at least look okay about that once I got inside. Ronald told me my mother wanted to see me, so I fixed my fucking face enough to make it seem I was good today. Being good got rewards, and maybe they would even drop the therapy sessions.

I ended up finding both my parents when I went looking for my mom. The pair were in the kitchen, talking, but they stopped in my presence.

This wasn't surprising, speech halting around me. My parents may be at home full time these days, but that didn't mean they were speaking about anything they were doing. I was being shut out, black-balled.

And my father could barely look at me.

Mom had been better about it, better at *hiding it*, her disappointment. There was a reason they both were forcing me back into regular sessions with Dr. Singh.

"How was it today, baby?" Mom eased off her barstool, Chestnut at her feet. The family dog bounded over to me, and Mom smiled a little. "Progress?"

It'd only been a week, but Mom clearly was trying to make conversation with me.

Dad too waited for this response, interested, but that didn't surprise me. He did care, cared about me.

But that didn't mean I hadn't fucked up in his eyes.

He'd been begging me to talk to him, pleading even about my problems and everything when it came to Charlie. I hadn't listened then.

And now here we were.

I ran my hand through Chestnut's fur, playing with her for a little while. I didn't know really what to say. My default was lies in the past, lies about how things were and what I was going through.

My silence was very telling.

It caused both my parents to sigh and my dad to put his hands together.

"Well, I at least hope you're giving it a fair chance." Dad swung a rare glance over to me. His eyebrows knitted in tight. "It will only help you."

I begged to differ there, but I wouldn't today. "I'd like to be helping you."

I was working on honesty. Being honest instead of gut reacting.

Dad panned away. "I think we both know that's not happening."

"But I can help—"

"Like sneaking out at all hours?" My father cocked his head. "*Going missing* with your friends and making your mother and me worry when you know our attention is needed elsewhere?"

We had a few times, Thatcher, Wells, and me. We'd even recruited some Court kids, everyone ready and willing to help us. They'd been at late hours and outside of the city's searches with the local law enforcement and city volunteers. We'd only left Wolf out of it because we'd been forced to.

His parents had him on lockdown even worse than us if one could imagine.

Wolf wasn't leaving unless his parents knew about it. They were worried about him, worried about him spiraling. We were too, but we knew our brother. His energy was better spent looking, but again, his parents weren't easing that tight grip.

I guess they'd already lost one kid.

I couldn't breathe thinking about that, and it crossed my mind more than once that maybe Noa didn't want to be found.

I mean, she'd left, hadn't she?

One better, she hadn't contacted me after she'd left. If she were scared, overwhelmed, she should have done that. I didn't know the reason exactly why she'd left, but I did know I hadn't been a part of the decision. She hadn't *come to me.*

Even still, that hadn't stopped me from trying, and with Wolf tied up, us guys had attempted to do our own thing. We kept our searches local to the city for the most part, but also left its boundaries to knock on doors and ask questions in neighboring towns. The last evening's search ended me up with Ronald. I'd come home and run into Dad.

He'd been coming to check on me.

He hadn't said as much, but it'd been obvious. He'd left without saying a word, and the confrontation had just added to the epic shit, me continuing to disappoint my parents, my dad.

"Wanna know the way you can help, Dorian? Help your mother, me, and everyone else?"

My head shot up, my father's eyes on me.

They narrowed. "You can *help* by going to your therapy sessions. You can *help* by taking care of you and letting us all do what we need to do to find Ramses's and Brielle's daughter." Dad's legs crossed at the knee, his arms rested on them. "It's bad enough we're already having to deal with my dad being in the mix of all this, and it'd be great if you were a factor none of the adults have to worry about on top of it."

"Are you working with Grandpa?" I asked, pretty much ignoring the last part of what he'd said. My dad wasn't working with Grandpa.

If he was, the world would know.

A lot had changed in simply a week, and one of them had been my grandfather essentially coming out. He'd held a press conference the day he reached out to my dad. He'd detailed who he was, his connection to Sloane and Bru, and his place in all this. He'd told the truth.

And no one had been surprised more than me.

I didn't trust my grandfather, not for shit did I trust him, but I couldn't deny that he'd put himself in front of the firing squad. This town hated him as much as the Legacy families. He and Wolf's grandfather, Ibrahim, were essentially black-listed after they'd helped Wolf's great-uncle Leo.

Even still, he'd come out, and, in that announcement, he'd offered to help the families in any way he could. He'd said he would, but only if they wanted that too. He'd keep his distance if they didn't.

Needless to say, I hadn't heard another word about him.

The families, my parents, were clearly doing their own thing.

"The lines of communication are open," Dad said now, his hands together. "His people give us everything they gather. Though, it's not any more than we have."

I didn't know what they had, but I did know Sloane *wasn't back*. That told the truth more than anything. They didn't know where she was.

My mouth dried. "Would it help if Grandpa were maybe brought in?" The two could join forces. I really didn't trust my grandfather, but we should be doing everything we could do. "I just think that—"

"You think, huh?" Dad got up, my eyes at his level. We were pretty much equal in size, my father and me, but even if I were larger, that wouldn't matter. My father commanded and intimated the fuck out of anyone I'd seen come into his presence. He and my god dads were a force, a team of influence and affluence.

It only helped that they were great people.

They were, each and every one of them, but when tested, they didn't play around.

I stayed silent, but I meant what I said. We should be working with my grandpa. We should be doing everything we can, and I wasn't sure how much of a threat they actually found my grandfather these days. Sure, they made sure I didn't leave the house without Ronald or a cop, but I was ninety percent sure that had to do with me. They wanted me to stay out of things, and lately, I was looking more guilty in their eyes than anything Grandpa had done.

This was a hard truth and one I hated to admit. It was true, though, as shit as that may be. Grandpa had been helpful, and I was the one going behind their backs.

I was the fuck-up.

"Like I said, the lines of communication are open, son." Dad took his jacket off the bar. "We haven't cut my father off from his hand, and in regard to that relationship and *my decision* on how to handle it, that has nothing to do with you."

Understood, I nodded.

"In any case, your mom asked to speak with you," he said, bending down and kissing her cheek. "I'll be in my office."

"Okay." Mom's gaze followed my dad's exit, and it seemed they had more to talk about. I bet they did. Though none of it did ever have anything to do with me. My parents had made a stance here, and they weren't breaking it. I wouldn't be helping, and that was that. She took my hand. "Ramses asked to see you, and it'd be nice if you could stay over there tonight."

My mother didn't have to ask, of course, and Ramses didn't have to ask me to come by. Thatcher, Wells, and I had pretty much lived over at the Mallicks' this week.

I noticed Mom said Ramses had requested to see me specifically, though, and that didn't surprise me either. Every time I was over there, he wanted to talk, talk about Sloane…

Knowing the specific reason for the request, I told my mom I would.

"Ronald knows to go with you," Mom said. She held my face. "Your dad's right. You can help us all so much more by taking care of you, and that isn't just therapy." She cupped my cheek. "You know you used to talk to us."

It felt like so long ago, those days. My parents and I never had the deep conversations, but we did used to *talk*.

It used to be easy.

I didn't know why it seemed so complicated now, but I knew that definitely had something to do with me.

My mom ended up leaving me with those words, and after throwing some water on my face, Ronald took me over to the Mallicks.

We had to fight through the paps and media to get close.

The Mallicks had gates, but Wolf and his family weren't in a secure neighborhood like mine. Being the mayor, Brielle always wanted herself available to her constituents. The mayor's house wasn't open by any means, but it was like the White House in the sense it had gates but could easily be seen from the street.

I ducked my head again, avoiding flashes and questions. This had become old hat for me, and oddly enough, Wolf's house was as quiet as mine today when I finally got inside. Normally, they had people lining the walls and the reason was obvious there. Many people wanted to help them.

People were mourning for them.

I wasn't mourning, *refused*, and if I knew anything about the girl we were all looking for, she was keeping her head low. She was *thinking* because she was a fucking thinker just like me. She thought too much sometimes.

Also like me.

We had way too much in common, Noa Sloane and me, and I thought about that as I sought out Ramses. I found him in his office, alone and on calls. He was always on calls. These ceased immediately when he saw me, and he waved me inside.

"Hey, kid," he said, getting up, and the way he charged over to me, one would think he hadn't seen me in days, weeks. Like this wasn't something we did every day.

Like he didn't ask me the same *question* every day.

There was a reason Ramses asked to see me specifically, and if we didn't see each other, my god dad always called me or texted. This had become our routine, something I'd come to dread because every time I was forced to give him the same answer to his question. Every *day* I had to break his fucking heart, and that killed me.

But it always destroyed him.

I had to see his face change, and if we weren't in front of each other, I heard the disappointment in his voice over the phone. Ramses wore his stress well. The guy was a rock and was always trying to make people feel good.

Even when he was drowning within.

He never let me see that side of him. At least, not before this. He was so good at hiding his pain, but in these quiet moments with just the two of us, I got let in a little. I *saw* the grieving father.

I saw his fight against the current.

Like the rest of us, my god dad hadn't appeared to be sleeping much. Dark rings underlined his hope filled eyes, and when I asked about Brielle, he told me something that, unfortunately, had become as familiar to me as our conversations.

"She's back at the office," he said. "Plan to join her tonight."

Brielle didn't leave the office. At least not these days. Pretty much all the chaos surrounding the search for Sloane had moved there, all the families and city officials operating out of there. It gave the Mallicks back their home so that was good.

Not that they were here much outside of Wolf and us guys.

Of course, we all had security too, people to keep an eye around, and the kids out of things. Really, Bow was the only one getting to do what she wanted to do and was making way more progress than we were. She'd been running local searches, and the parents were *letting her.*

Probably because she listened to them.

She was out scouring the town with local search parties while us boys were under lock and key.

"So, anything today, um..." Ramses started, and I was surprised the conversation hadn't led with this. It often did even before we said hi. His head lowered. "Have you heard anything?"

Again, the same question every day. Had I heard anything, *heard from her.*

"No, sir," I said, and I think the only reason I had been given back my phone was because I did know Sloane. They all knew she didn't have a phone right now, nor her brother. Grandpa had told them, and that was one of the few things they'd told me. Her phone had gotten destroyed, and Bru had given his to Grandpa's team after the media had been harassing them.

Even still, the parents hoped she'd reach out to me. They hoped because I let them know what we'd been, how we had something, and *they believed* she'd contact me because of that connection.

She never did.

Sloane had left me as much as she'd left this town, and there was so much fucking irony in that. I'd left her once *selfishly* and to my own delusions.

I suppose this was penance.

My stomach rolled from the reality as much as I watched that change occur across my god dad's face. He brought a hand over it, brief about it, but that didn't matter. Our meetings were taking their toll. All of this was so fucking shitty. Ramses Mallick was one of the best people I knew. He was so good, kind.

And all this was gutting him.

I saw the wear and tear every day, and after the check-in, Ramses told me to go see Ares. I planned to do that, but I stuck around for a beat. I watched him on calls, one of the rare parents to actually let me do that. The parents had started their searches outside the city, but the extended ones were being done remotely. They were talking to people, getting information. The whole world knew Noa Sloane was missing at this point, and the families had her face on every screen. They needed the world to see her.

They needed to find her.

The last call was clearly Ramses talking to Brielle. He told his wife he loved her and would see her soon before getting up, and when I asked how they were doing, he simply hugged me.

"We'll find her," he said to me, a hard and unyielding hug. "We will, and we won't stop until we do."

How ironic he'd been telling me this, and if the emotion hadn't fucking choked in my throat, I would have manned up and told him that. I would have given *him* this hug, but then, he wouldn't be my god dad if he would have let me.

He was always taking care of everyone else.

CHAPTER
SIX

Dorian

When I found Wolf, he was in his parents' garage.

He tossed paint at the wall.

My buddy was covered up to his arms with red and black paint, the canvas in front of him bleeding. He'd literally punctured holes in it, and the paint he threw gave the illusion of a canvas that seeped a blood red, the combined color choices only helping to give it that distinct tone.

Wolf ran his hands through it, smearing it out. He'd illustrated eyes, which bled from puncture holes. The guy was covered in sweat and looking just as untamed as he did on the field.

I wondered how long he'd been out here.

I treaded cautiously into my friend's space. Saying he was going through it right now was an understatement. I knocked hard. "Hey."

Not even a flinch from his direction, but he did remove his hands from the canvas. He was playing rock music and shut it off without looking at me.

I suppose I was welcome.

The Mallicks had a sink in their garage, and Wolf used it to scrub his arms. He had paint everywhere, his jeans, his hair. It'd probably be on his shirt too had he been wearing it. He tipped his chin from the sink. "Dad tell you where I was?"

He hadn't. I came over to him, leaning against the wall. "Followed the tunes."

He always played them when he worked, kind of like a code for us to stay the fuck out. When Wolf was playing music, we texted him, let him know we were here, and *he* found *us*.

A lot of things had changed, and I wasn't letting my buddy close himself off. None of us guys were. I folded my arms. "Wells and Thatcher coming over?" I hadn't heard from them but figured they would. Like stated, we'd been all spending pretty much every night together.

Wolf's parents had pulled him out of school this week, and though the rest of us hadn't been, we just got up in the morning and went. Ronald usually came by to get us.

"Uh, yeah," he said. Hands clean, he shut the faucet off, and I tossed him a towel. Once he finished drying, he draped it over his shoulder. "They texted. They're bringing pizza or something."

I nodded, pushing off the wall when he left to clean up the area. I noticed he didn't appear high today, which was good. We all did and continued to do our fair share of weed together, but we typically spent more hours sober than not.

Lately, we couldn't *not* find Wolf baked, and I thanked fucking God my buddy had never touched the harder stuff. He might use that now, needing the release. I nudged him. "So, I was thinking tonight we could all just..."

"Whatever you want," he mumbled, and finally did grace me with his face. With all that hair down, I wasn't making out much, but my friend didn't look right. He looked *worse*, which was saying something. As far as I knew, he was still able to sleep. At least a little.

There was so much vacancy behind his eyes today, and when he caught me looking, he brought his head down again. He picked up a paint can, and I started to say something, but the can in his hands went flying.

It hit the canvas.

If the piece looked like it'd been bleeding before, it was gushing now, a thick and violent ooze from the paint in the can.

A gore of red and black.

Wolf said no words about it, simply standing before it. He braced his arms. "My dad talk to you?"

He always asked that question. Every day his dad asked *me* a question, I got one from his son too. I buried my hands in my pockets. "Yeah."

And that answered another question, one he wondered too. Had Sloane reached out to me, but one better...

Had she mentioned him.

He knew the answer before he even asked the question. If I had heard from Sloane, there wouldn't be a wonder. He'd *know*.

But that didn't stop him from asking.

Wolf left my side, continuing to clean up, and I followed his steps. "Buddy—"

"I'm thinking about going out on my own," he said, my brow jumping, but his expression remained unchanged. He was completely serious, a sigh in his voice when he scrubbed his hair. "Just doing my own thing for a while, and maybe hitting up some places she might go."

"Places like where?"

"I don't know, D. I just..." he started, his fingers working. "My parents are treating me like I'm a fucking mental patient, and I'm becoming one the longer I'm here and not doing anything. I'm losing my fucking shit, so yeah, I have to go do something. She's out there, and we're *twins* you know so maybe it will," he paused, lacing his hands above his head. "Maybe it will come to me. Where she is, I mean. Twins are supposed have like a link, right?"

Yeah, but as far as I knew, not supernaturally.

I wasn't giving my buddy what he wanted to hear because he threw his hands up at me, leaving. Crossing the garage, I got his arm. "I just don't think you should go out on your own." He'd done that before, done that so many times, and it wasn't good. "Maybe we just need to listen to our parents. If they keep having to worry about us, they're not able to do what they need to do."

I was aware my father's words were coming out of my mouth, and though I didn't completely feel that way, the last thing I needed was my friend, my *grieving* fucking friend, to be going out and chasing *a thought* he had about a twin link. He needed to be here.

He needed us.

We all needed each other right now, and it was all I had to keep my own shit together every day, to be there for him, his parents, and everyone else when I felt like fucking breaking.

My jaw clenched. "Buddy, listen to me when I say you need to be here with us." I let go of him. "And say you do go out. You do that and she comes back, and we don't know where the fuck you are." I lifted a hand. "How do you think that would make Ramses and Brielle feel?"

"I didn't ask for your permission, Dorian," he said, his voice even, but his eyes cut. "And I'm only telling you because I'll need your help to cover for me."

Of course, he was. I'd always covered for him in the past, and it was stupid then like it would be now.

We all enabled each other. Wells and Thatcher lying for me when I'd gone after my grandfather. All of us lying *together* to keep shit from our parents. I shook my head. "I'm saying just give it a chance. Let our parents handle this."

"But they aren't, Dorian." He cringed. "They haven't found her, and I can't just not do anything."

I knew the feeling. I *understood*, but I also knew what not listening to our folks had done in the past. We'd all fucked up.

"I'm going to handle my business," he said. "She's my sister, and I'm going to find her."

But he wouldn't find her. He hadn't in the past.

And he wouldn't now.

All him doing what he wanted to do would cause more chaos, and I literally couldn't handle another fucking thing. It would drive me over the edge.

I'd break.

"You can't leave," I whispered, throat flicking. My voice had gotten fucking tight, and I swallowed that shit away. "You can't, and I'm begging you to let our parents handle this."

This was the hardest thing I could ever fucking say or do. Not searching would *kill me*, but I couldn't worry about Ares too. He couldn't go AWOL, go off the grid *too*. I knew for a fact I wouldn't be able to handle it.

I was already hanging on by a thread.

I was dying inside just like he was, and he knew that. It might not be in the same way, no…

But it was there.

The absence of Noa Sloane was affecting both of us, and I needed him to be here right now. I needed that for him, his parents, and to give me and the other guys peace of mind. I wasn't the only one not sleeping and laboring each night. Wells, Thatcher, and I were up at all hours.

My gaze clashed with my buddy's, his throat working too. Color charged his face. "I can't wait forever."

I didn't expect it. I think it was a matter of time for all of us. We could only sit on our hands for so long. "I know but just give it a little time."

"How long?"

I didn't have the answer to that, shrugging. "Just give them a chance. A fair one."

His head lowered. I thought he'd fight me more, but when he nodded, I finally got to fucking breathe again.

In silence, the pair of us cleaned up the garage together, but I knew my friend. He was letting this all be squashed, but only for now.

This wouldn't be the end of this conversation.

CHAPTER
SEVEN

To: noa.sloane@windsorprep.edu

From: dorian.prinze@windsorprep.edu

Subject: Today

So, I don't know if you're getting fucking emails, but at this point, I'm desperate since you're not talking to me. I don't know if it's because you don't want to, or you can't. I'd like it to be the latter, but I know us.

I know you.

I don't know if you're okay. I don't know if you're *good*, but I'm a hopeless fuck so here we are. I can't give up.

I refuse.

I thought a lot about what I'd say to you if I knew you'd see this message. In fact, I thought about it so much I've rewritten this email about three times. I honestly thought it'd be a bunch of fucking angsty shit where I bleed my heart out and just hope to hell you'd get back to me. It started that way the first three times until I settled on this. I know exactly what I'd want to say to you if I knew you'd read it.

I'd tell you about your dad.

Your father, Ramses Mallick, is my god dad. I have a total of four and out of all of them, he's the one I've never once seen lose his cool. The man's patient to a fucking fault and literally takes anything that comes at him with a smile on his face. I wouldn't mistake that for weakness, though. All my godfathers are badass and would be quick to knife a motherfucker if they deserved it. They'd do it to protect their family, and what's nice and unique about your dad is he'd never even have to lift the knife.

He's just that badass.

Your dad's a talker, a peacemaker. He could make his greatest enemy fall to his feet, but the thing is, it'd never be with a threat. Ramses is just a good dude, kinder than shit, and is quick to pull the shirt off his back to help others. He's a fighter and a lover, and your mother, Brielle, wasn't an easy case from what I understand. In fact our parents joke *a lot* about how Ramses had to pull out so many stops to prove to her they could be something great. He fought for her, and he won, struggle be damned. Wolf is a lot like his mom, your mom.

But I feel like you're a lot like your dad.

I could go on and on about how and why, but I'd like you to come back and figure that out yourself. Your dad, Ramses, asks me every day one question. He asks it knowing the answer. He asks it despite *the pain* he knows it will cause him. He wants to know if I've heard from you, no more, no less, and even though I tell him no every day, he still asks. He doesn't give up.

Like I said, he's a fighter.

I have a feeling he's going to continue asking me every day, and I look forward to the day my answer doesn't suck anything out of him. I look forward to the day I'll give him life instead of taking it from him.

Anyway, that's all I got for now. That was today.

Tomorrow, I'll tell you about your mother.

CHAPTER
EIGHT

Dorian

Thatcher's sister took over our lunch table again today, and though I appreciated what she was doing, I didn't appreciate the ass-kissing bitches she brought with her.

And that was a catch-all term.

The guys, in fact, were the absolute worst and were quick to attempt to talk to Thatcher, Wells, and me instead of paying attention to Bow, i.e. the reason they were *there*. Thatcher's sister had a peer group (mostly student council and other academy kids) who ran their own searches around Maywood Heights. They were looking for Sloane and her brother just like the city officials, and I think the only reason the parents let that fly was because they were escorted by local law enforcement.

These were also one of the few activities the guys and I could take part in where our parents didn't blow a fucking gasket. We could help look for Sloane, but only on their terms, and Legacy's participation in the search party had fuckers coming out of the woodwork across the campus to help. They wanted to find the long-lost Mallick girl.

Ass-kissing just came with the territory.

These fuckers were wearing *shirts* now. Slogans like *Team Dorian + Sloane* and other nonsense splayed across both girls' and guys' backs when Wells and I entered the lunchroom that day. Thatcher was already at our table. He and Bow's search party groupies were inside today with the weather changing.

Things were getting cold.

I tried not to think about what that meant, things getting cold. We didn't know where Sloane was, but that didn't mean she and her brother were chilling in a forest somewhere. There were other places they could be, shelters…

I tried to think like two kids needing their space, but I couldn't imagine the two had many resources. I mean, my grandpa had been providing for them until recently.

Wells pounded Thatcher's fist, our buddy looking grateful as shit to see us. Thatcher had his collar popped, his tie loose, and about a million chunky rings on his knuckles to accompany his Court ring. Thatch touched ours together. "Bout fucking time," he said, stealing a slice of pizza off my tray. It was mine and Wells's day to cover lunch. He leaned forward. "I'm about to beat a bitch."

A circulation of our table told why. We normally had groupie bitches, but usually, they were Court. They were part of the brother and sisterhood Legacy partook in.

Lately, it'd been a damn free-for-all. People were all over the place and trying to get a piece of us, a piece of me. They claimed to want to help, but they spent more time all over our jocks than actually listening *to Bow* who was at the head of the table. She was conducting some kind of meeting, but as soon as Wells and I arrived, the little attention she had shifted to us and Thatch. We got the normal song and dance of phony-ass concern. They wanted to know how we were faring and holding up.

They wanted to know if we had news.

The thing was, none of this shit was genuine. These people were benefiting off us, *our popularity*, way more than we were getting anything from them, and that pissed me the fuck off. These people thought this was a *joke*.

Which meant they thought my life was one.

The only thing keeping me in check during these ass-kissing lunches was the fact Bow was running them. They obviously weren't doing much, but that wasn't the point. This was something she clearly felt she needed to be doing, her own way of dealing with the fact that Sloane was missing. No one respected that more than me, and I supported anything she wanted to do. She was my sister just as the boys were my brothers.

But her meeting couldn't wrap up quickly enough.

The end of it got the boys and me the usual attention, some girls actually *crying*. They were apparently overcome with emotion regarding Sloane's absence.

"I can't imagine what you're going through," one of the chicks said to me, the one crying. She rubbed her nose. "You and Wolf? Will he be back to school anytime soon?"

I got *that one* a lot, girls offering to swing by and bring our buddy cookies.

And other things.

They weren't shy about asking me to pass the message regarding their company along, and the last time one had suggested it, I really did almost lose my shit.

Bow had had to intercede.

She did the same today, telling the girl she'd see her tonight. I guess they were doing another search this evening, Murphy's Park from what it sounded like. That was the last place I wanted to be, some history there, history with Sloane and Bru.

I simply directed my gaze frontward as Bow guided the

chick away. Thatcher's sister had her arms full of flyers, and the guys and I helped her get the rest of them off the table.

"Thanks," she said, but mostly to me. She'd been hesitant to talk to me, shy. Thatcher's sister may be more soft-spoken in general, but she wasn't shy when it came to telling things like it was. Lately, though, she'd been tiptoeing. "We're conducting another search tonight. Murphy's Park if you want to come, Dorian."

I'd heard that, but besides not wanting to fucking go there, I didn't see the point. They'd already searched the park, her group, the authorities...

I didn't want to tell her any of this was pointless. For all we knew, Sloane wasn't even here in town anymore.

Don't do that pessimistic shit.

"I'll be there," I said, head lowered. I shoved a fry in my mouth, but Bow wasn't leaving.

"How have you been?" She put her flyers down. "I heard the parents saying you hadn't been sleeping so..."

It was nice my business was all out there, and I was sure that'd all gone through the parental network just like anything else.

Thatcher and Wells stayed silent across the table, and I panned away to smile at Thatcher's sister. "I'm good. Like I said, I'll be there tonight."

She nodded, leaving things at that. She took her stuff, and with her gone, I had Thatcher clear the table. All that had remained besides us were Court people at this point, but I needed to talk to my buddies alone.

"I'm worried about Wolf," I said, getting right into it. I leaned in. "He's talking about going out on his own. He mentioned shit last night before you guys got there."

When Wells and Thatcher arrived, we'd all gone into cheer up Wolf mode, so we hadn't been able to talk. At least, candidly. We'd eaten pizza, played videos games. There might have been a little porn involved, but I'd done homework when all that started. I didn't want to look at other girls.

They weren't any others.

Noa Sloane had everything, my mind and my fucking *body* now. It was fucking frustrating as shit, and if I wasn't so worried about her, I'd be pissed at her. I could probably nut off to a *picture of her* at this point before any kind of time spent with the best porn. She had my heart and mind.

Wells had been texting before I spoke, Thatcher too. They both immediately stopped, and Thatcher pushed my tray over. He'd acquired it and eaten half the fucking food. "What? Like before? That shit *before* when his parents caught his ass in California?"

Needless to say, none of us had forgotten that time. It'd been scary, *for all of us.* "I don't fucking know. I just know if we don't find her soon, he's going to do something stupid, and I might be right there with him." I was beyond hiding feelings at this point. Emotions. "We've got to do something."

"What? You know our hands are tied." Wells cuffed his arms, his jacket off and laying across the lunch table. He pulled fingers through dark roots, a sharp contrast to his normal blond. Seemed like he was growing it out. His jaw shifted. "Why didn't he tell us about her? We might have been able to prevent this. All of it."

I thought about that too, how all of this could have probably been prevented had Wolf just *told us about her.* If he'd told anyone about her. I shook my head. "I gave him reasons to doubt her." He hadn't trusted her or was at least trying to figure out if he could. He'd mentioned that, and even though our friend hadn't shared exactly why he'd kept things from us, I had a big feeling it had to do with me. "It's my fault. I thought she was caught up in shit involving my grandpa. Wolf was trying to prove he could trust her, I think. He was trying to help me. He was…"

Wells tapped my shoulder with his fist. "We don't know

Wolf's reasons, and even if they had something to do with you, whatever, man. It's not important."

But it was. It was everything. I squeezed my arms. "He's going to go rogue. I know he is, and I'm about to lose my shit too. I just don't get why she'd fucking *leave*." She ran again instead. She ran *from me* again. I placed my fingers to my mouth. "I just don't get it."

She had to know the chaos it would cause and the fury that would arise in me.

I mean, I told her I love her.

She was physically cutting me apart on the inside and, little by little, driving me to do something stupid. Something like lie to my parents again, which was the opposite of what I wanted to do. I really wanted to regain their trust, but the fact of the matter was more could be done. My grandfather had offered to help, and he should be.

He owed her that.

I still didn't trust my grandfather, but like shit with Charlie, I was willing to milk that fucker for all he was worth. If Grandpa wanted to help, he should be fucking helping.

I might just go to him again if something didn't change soon, and the thought made me ill. I didn't want to lie to my parents.

I didn't want to lose any more of their respect.

"Maybe she just needs time."

Wells had been about to say something and me too actually. I didn't know what he'd been about to say, but we both stopped since Thatcher had spoken. Thatch had a fist to his mouth, his gaze studying the table.

I sat up. "What are you talking about?"

"I'm saying what I said." Thatcher lowered his fist, shrugging his big shoulders. "There's probably a reason she left, and maybe she just needs to work that shit out."

My buddy was never one to have, well, emotional intelligence. In fact, out of all of us, he was probably the one with the least amount. He spent a lot of time fawning over his own ass, so needless to say him coming to bat for Sloane and supporting her potential reasons for taking off was surprising the shit out of me.

With all eyes on him, Thatcher's jaw shifted. "Maybe we just need to give her time. She might come back on her own is all I'm saying."

"The fuck are you talking about?" Wells dropped an arm over Thatcher's chair. "It's been a week, bro."

"Yeah, and she still might come back." He opened his hands. "She might if we give her time."

"Yeah, well, it doesn't sound like Wolf's going to be giving that to her. He's not, and I won't." I pushed the rest of the food toward him. He could have that shit. "I'll get at y'all later."

I got up, grabbing my jacket. Thatcher had his hands laced behind his head, and Wells was frowning at him. He socked Thatch in his arm before he got up too, joining me. If Sloane needed time, she would have been back by now, and I'm not just going to sit on my hands. I would work on things that weren't in my control.

But not today.

CHAPTER NINE

To: noa.sloane@windsorprep.edu

From: dorian.prinze@windsorprep.edu

Subject: Brielle

Your mother's name is Brielle Mallick. Her name was Brielle Whitman-Quintero before that. She's mayor of our town and like a mom to me. I have a few of those outside of my own, but out of all my god dad's wives she's the most scary.

You'll see why in a second.

I had a nightmare once. Long story short, I'd gotten high off some shit I should have stayed the fuck away from. I'd only done it once, and that night I'd done it was the only one I touched the stuff.

Again, you'll see why.

Honestly, I think the nightmare was because I was just scared.

I was scared I tried that bullshit. I was scared even more I liked it, but what scared me the most ended up happening after I had the nightmare.

I stayed at Wolf's house that night. I didn't want to go back to my own house after getting so high. I snuck in through his window and tiptoed across the hall to my own room. I told you I have a room at his house, and he's got one at mine too. Speeding up, after the nightmare I wandered the house. I was freaked the fuck out and just needed to mellow out.

I ran into your mom.

She knew right away something was wrong with me, and because I can't keep shit from her, I ended up telling her exactly what I did that night. I'd been at a party, and things had gotten crazy. The only reason Wolf hadn't been there was because he had a huge test the next day.

(Your brother is a genius by the way.)

I'll tell you more about him later, because now, you're about to see why your mom is so badass. She not only got me to admit what I took but is the sole reason why I never ended up taking what I did again. You see, she had this stash of the stuff I took. She had it right in her home office and showed it to me.

I was shocked. I mean, what I'd taken was some pretty hard shit, and she just had it there, you know? It was fucking weird, but she said she was saving it for a day like that night. A day where she caught her son on that shit, and she could have this come-to-Jesus moment with him.

It ended up being with me.

Brielle told me she'd never taken the stuff, but it was there for the two of us to take together now and in that moment. She said she would take it *with me* and even offered me the first hit.

I told her no, of course. That was crazy, and the very *thought* of her taking something like that made me sick. It was one thing for me to do it, but she couldn't. It was so addictive. Anyway, after refusing, she put it away, then looked at me from across her desk. She looked at me like a mother and told me to remember that if I thought about doing that dangerous shit again. She told me to remember that feeling of help-lessness.

She told me to see her face.

I did after that moment, and I have been introduced to the stuff on more than one occasion. Those times probably won't be the last, but I know with more confidence than shit I won't be touching the stuff in the future. I did see your mom's face during those other times. I saw it every time, and I didn't like the powerlessness.

It made me sick just like that night.
So that's your mom, little fighter. Basically, as cool as shit, and she's here in Maywood Heights waiting for you. She's actually tearing up the city trying to find you. Don't make her get to the point where she's got to burn it down because she will.

Because that's Brielle Mallick.

CHAPTER
TEN

Dorian

I skipped my next therapy session and instead got Ronald to take me to see my dad. Our butler hadn't been happy about it. He had orders, but I guessed, since the destination was to see my father, he didn't put up much of a fight.

My father was at his office today, Prinze Financial. Our family owned several banks, but only one held my dad's office. He typically wasn't in much these days, busy with the search and everything, but he did dedicate one day a week to help out at the office. He had plenty of faces on the company, so he didn't need to be there.

That was just my dad, though, and the office was open to me when I came. Outside of Reed Corp. and Mallick Enterprises, my family's bank took up the largest real estate on the block. Thatcher's and Wolf's dads were in real estate, moguls just like my dad. Wells's dad, Jax, was too, but in his own space. Besides his burger franchises, he held businesses in other culinary sectors around the globe.

My father hadn't expected to see me when I arrived at the top floor of the city skyscraper, but that was a given. I was supposed to be at therapy today.

In a gray suit, my dad was rushing out of his office with several people, but the party stopped upon seeing me. Dad cut around them, his hand raised, and he immediately noticed Ronald flanking me. He directed a look to him before me. "Why aren't you at your session?"

Everyone in the office had grown silent, Ronald too. I was sure he'd hear this for not taking me where I was supposed to be, but coming here wasn't his fault.

"I need to talk you," I said, and right away, my dad spoke to the other suits with him. I recognized them from his board of directors. Our family name was on the bank, but the Prinzes did answer to others, shareholders. My family maintained the majority stake, and I had my own shares as well. I'd get even more over time, and I had to get through school first before I could start getting involved.

I'd caught my dad in a busy moment, clearly. His time was valuable, and though I didn't want to waste it, this was important. He must have felt that way too because he dismissed the others, and Ronald left last. Our butler closed the door, waiting outside it.

Dad glanced through the glass walls toward the people waiting for him. "What's going on? You okay? We were just about to head to a meeting."

I bet he was. Again, his time was valuable. "I want to talk to you about everything with the search."

"What about it?" Dad smoked out his glass walls, giving me his full attention. He sighed. "You're still not getting involved, son. And you know, as soon as we know something, we'll inform you."

I trusted my father. I really did, but I also knew my friend was hurting. Wolf was threatening shit, and I wasn't doing all right either. "I want to work with Grandpa."

It took a lot for me to come here today, to actually talk to my dad instead of going behind his back, but I was taking a chance here.

I didn't want to lie anymore.

It physically made me ill, and I literally couldn't take my dad or mom being any more upset with me. If I was going to go to my grandfather, I wanted to do so with his blessing.

Right away, my father severed our gazes. He looked at everything but me in his office in that moment. "We've been over this."

"I know but—"

"We've been *over* it. We have, and I won't repeat myself. You know my position when it comes to this, so stop pushing it."

He wasn't *listening to me*, ignoring me. "Dad, you asked me to talk to you. You did, and this is me trying to do that right now." Like I said, this was the hardest thing I'd ever had to do. Normally, I did listen to my dad.

Which meant something that I wasn't right now.

I could count on a hand how many times I'd actually defied my father, and I think he knew that as well. I hadn't before everything with Charlie.

His attention shifted in my direction, at least listening.

I decided to speak quickly.

"I understand why you don't want Grandpa involved," I said, swallowing. "I do, and I don't expect you to work with him."

This really got his attention, his arms folded.

"That's why I'm begging you to let me," I rushed. "I want to take on that burden, so you don't have to."

This was hard for him, which was something I completely understood. My grandfather was a son of a bitch.

He'd *hurt* him.

The two had a history I'd only heard whispers about, and I think my father had actually only talked to me about it once.

The other conversations I'd snuck up on, intimate conversations between him and my mother. My father wasn't open much with his feelings, and once he and I had talked about it, he buried it. He'd wanted to let me know about those whispered conversations I'd stumbled in on, said he felt he owed them to me.

His chest raised with a large breath. "What do you mean, Dorian?"

"I mean, contact can be through me. Like I said, Grandpa wants a relationship with me. I don't think he'd hurt me, but you can have Ronald go with me. Hell, you can have a whole fleet of cops come, but I need to do everything I can to find Sloane. Wolf's really not doing well, and I..." My voice shut down, tight and my throat raw. "Just let me do this *please*. I'm coming to you, but I'd never make you work with him. I won't, so let it be me."

My father unbuttoned his jacket in that moment, his hand sweeping over his head. He stared at me for a long time, and next thing I knew, he was directing me to sit down.

We sat on his leather furniture, him on his easy chair and me on the loveseat. His lips pulled together. "I know you want to find her." He lifted a hand. "Brielle talked to me about that day you introduced Pilar..."

My mouth opened, and his hand lifted higher.

"Apologies. Sloane." He sat back in his chair. "She talked to me about that day you introduced Sloane to her. I know she means something to you and probably more than you're willing to share with me right now."

I hated he assumed that, but he did because he knew me.

I was a lot like him.

It was hard enough for me to feel what I was feeling. Let alone talk about it.

Dad pulled a hand over his face. "And even if we were working with my father, you have to know you'd never be the one to do it, son."

I said nothing, Dad's sigh heavy.

His hands came together, and before he could shut me down again, I leaned forward. "I don't care if it's me. I don't care about any of that, but I'm begging you to let our people work with his. I'll do anything you want. I'll go to therapy, and I'll be happy about it. I swear to God I will, but we just need to be doing everything we can."

It was like I was a fly on the wall in the moment, looking at myself pleading with my dad. It was like I was outside of myself. I wasn't *acting* like myself.

"You talk as if we're not," he said, his expression tight, serious. "Like we're not doing everything we can."

My mouth dried. "That's not what I…"

"Because we are." His chin lowered, nod firm. "We are, and as I've stressed before, the lines of communication are open. Our people are in contact and your grandfather knows to contact us if he has anything."

My father got up then, and after he unsmoked his glass walls, he waved Ronald inside. Dad took his phone out of his pocket. "I'm going to call Dr. Singh. I'll let her know you'll be coming *late* because Ronald's on his way with you."

I got to hear that exchange when Ronald arrived at my side, and when he asked if I was ready, I knew where I was going next.

I mean, Ronald heard my dad as much as I had.

Dad tapped off his phone when he was done, his head cocked, eyebrows narrowed. "I understand this is hard for you," he said, and I noticed a tightness in his voice. He ended up running a hand over his mouth before looking at me. "But I'm begging you to do what I ask. You need to let me handle this. *Be your dad* and take care of you and our friends. They're my family too, and we are all doing every-thing we can."

I hated that what I said came across that way, and I did think he was doing everything *he* could do. That was why I wanted to take on the burden, protect him and deal with Grandpa.

I only nodded to my father because he needed me to. He was walking along his own ledge here.

We apparently all were in our own fragile houses.

CHAPTER ELEVEN

Dorian

I passed Thatcher in the locker room.

He was rubbing oil down his abs.

I lifted my eyes to the rafters but didn't give him shit about it. He often was one of the last people out of the building after practice, vainer than shit. He was one of the few dudes who kept a mirror in his locker, and Wells and the rest of the football team were long gone by now. I'd only stayed late for some time in the shower, the heat getting me out of my head a bit.

I was in there a lot lately.

We didn't have long until the end of the season, but Wolf was out for the remainder of it. His parents would have let him play, but he'd had no interest. He'd never been as passionate about the sport as the rest of us.

Everything going on now in his life obviously took priority, but I, unfortunately, had to be here. I was still the captain and people relied on me. It also gave my brain something to do so there was that.

Thatcher studied me on the way to my locker, and after he finished his abs, he tossed the rest in his inky hair. That shit was basically black it was so dark brown. His lips pulled together. "We all at Wolf's tonight?"

We always were. I opened my locker. "Yeah."

"Cool." He lingered for a beat before recapping that bottle in his hands. "I was hoping to talk to him tonight. Try to convince him out of that shit about leaving. You know that's not good, and I'd like you to help me. I already talked to Wells, and he's down for it."

Normally, I would be too, but after that talk with my dad didn't go so well, I didn't know how I was feeling.

"I'd like your support on this, D. I know how you feel and how this is for you, but..." He tapped a locker. "Wolf doing shit like that isn't good for anyone, and we got to think about him."

I swung a glance his way. "If he went anywhere, I'd go with him." I'd already decided this basically.

Thatcher angled a look down before scrubbing into his slick hair. He raised a hand. "You *both* need to stay. The parents are already going through shit, and who knows how close they are to finding Sloane. Just help me keep him here for a little while. Please?" He shook his head. "We got to be supporting him right now, don't you think? Keeping him calm and not going rogue."

I honestly didn't think I was the best one to do the job right now considering my place in all this, my personal stake. I was in my head just as much as Wolf.

I had no words for my friend, so I just got dressed.

"Just think about it, okay?" Thatcher pushed before throwing that bottle in his locker. He tugged on a shirt, then closed it. "You know, out of all of us, he listens to you the most. We all do."

I knew they all did, which was what scared me the most. I shouldn't be the voice of reason right now.

And I was sure they knew that just as well as I did.

It was something that none of us would talk about, and that mostly had to do with me because I didn't want to talk about it. I had a job to do, and it *was* being the voice of reason.

I finished getting dressed after my buddy left the locker room, and when I eventually left it, I was surprised to find someone else in the place of Ronald. Our family butler parked in generally the same place to get me after school or practice, but he wasn't there today.

My father's Tesla sat idle in Ronald's spot, and when I walked toward it, Dad got out. He was dressed for the office without the tie and jacket and was probably downtown with everyone else today at the capitol building.

Noa's search was still operating out of there, and that was where all our parents spent the most time. Dad rested an arm on the top of his ride as I sidled up to it. His head tilted. "Practice go okay?"

About as good as it could. I nodded, and he angled a nod for me to come with him. He never surprised me at practice and definitely didn't these days. He didn't have time for it.

It made me worry about what this impromptu visit was about, but I did get in the car with my dad.

"I hope you don't mind, but I'd like to take you some-where today," he said, strapping in. "Gave Ronald a break so we could go."

"Where?" I strapped in too, but I noticed we didn't move after I did. My dad just kind of sat in his seat.

He tapped the stirring wheel. "I've been thinking a lot about how you came to the office." He hooked an arm on the wheel. "And I'm sure that was very hard for you. Coming to me? I know I don't make it easy sometimes."

My dad could be stubborn, but I got it. I mean, I had lied to him.

I'd dug my own grave with him.

My parents didn't trust me, and they had good reason. I

was literally just talking about going on my own again, so yeah, I got it.

Dad's head shook. "You and I are a lot alike, Dorian. We both have reactive personalities. We react first, then think about the consequences later, and in my case, I had to think about why I said no so quickly to you. No about your grandfather, and why I've been saying no instead of really thinking about what good could come out of working with him to find Noa."

I angled in his direction. "I know why you said no." My grandfather was a bastard, point blank. All of the things he'd done recently only stressed it. "I get it."

"I don't think you do," he said, his head tilted. "My issues with your grandfather… well, they're deep, but they're also in the past and something I did take the time to deal with. It took a long time, and it wasn't always pretty, but I did deal with it and not wanting his help didn't have anything to do with that. Our history?"

I didn't understand.

My dad moved a hand down his jaw. "I think it just triggered me that you went to him instead of coming to me when it came to everything with Charlie," he said, my lips parting. He frowned. "That you chose that route instead of trusting me."

I sat up. "I went to him because I didn't want to hurt you. You? Mom?" I swallowed. "I just had suspicions about Mayberry, and I wanted to protect you guys. Mom was already going through so much and…" My jaw shifted. "I just didn't want to hurt you guys when I didn't even know something as fact."

And he had to *know* that. I didn't trust Grandpa more than him. I didn't trust that fucker as far as I could throw him.

"I know, son." Dad brought his hands together, nodding. "But you have to understand that doesn't stop how it felt. How it *feels* to know your kid went behind your back to someone else regardless of the fact that person happened to be my father."

"Dad—"

He raised a hand. "These are things I have to deal with, but they're not enough to keep your grandfather out of the fold. I've set up a meeting with him today, and well, I'd like you to go with me."

I blinked, his hand lifting higher.

"I want you to see for yourself everything that is going on, and after, I'd like for you to drop it. There will be no more sneaking around and definitely no more lying." Dad's lips turned down. "Your grandfather is going to be a part of all this, but only on my and your mother's terms. We were up all night talking about this, and the only way *this* will happen is for you to follow some rules. One is you are never to reach out to your grandfather directly. There's no need for it, so it won't happen, and you're definitely not going to see him. You may be right that he doesn't want to hurt you, but you having any type of relationship doesn't sit well with me or your mother. It was all I could do last night to convince her that this meeting should happen."

"Why is it happening?" I asked. "You working with grandfather doesn't have to have anything to do with me."

That was something he'd made clear in his office.

Dad started his car. "Because again, you're like me. You won't drop this issue until you get some closure. My dad has agreed to meet with us today to talk about a collaboration, but your presence is only as a spectator. You agree to that, and you can be a part of the initial conversation."

It was sad he felt he had to do this for me, and I hated that he was right. I needed to feel like I could control something, *anything.*

I nodded quickly, and Dad sighed again. He got us moving, and we were silent for the most part. We were going to see my grandpa.

And I was going to see him with my father.

————

The meeting my grandfather and dad had set up ended up being at the house my grandfather had purchased in town. Thatcher, the guys, and I had found out he'd purchased a property in Maywood Heights, and though my grandpa had yet to explain that, I was surprised my dad had agreed to meet him there.

I didn't when I got there.

My dad had half the cops in the city there to meet us, and even one of my god dads was present.

When LJ had made it into town exactly, I didn't know, but he and his wife Billie had shown up pretty early in this thing. He was there now outside my grandfather's mansion, standing with the fleet of police when my dad rolled up in his Tesla.

"Hey, brother," LJ had said to him when he got out, then hugged me. "How you holding up, kid?"

As well as I could, hugging him tight. It was always good to see him. I started to let go, but he didn't let me right away.

"This is taking a lot for him, so have his back in there, all right?" he said, pulling away. Dad was shaking hands with the chief of police, and LJ squeezed my shoulder. "You be sure to be his support. I'm going in there too, but you need to stand by him with me and especially listen to him."

I didn't know what had been said before I got here, but Dad had told me I was a spectator today. I would listen, and I knew this was going to take a lot for him. I mean, how couldn't it?

This was Grandpa.

I didn't want to be putting my dad through any of this, and it tore my stomach up just thinking about *this*. My father and grandfather in the same room.

It shouldn't be this way.

I really wished my dad would just let me do this myself, but I knew that wasn't happening. I could possibly keep myself out of the equation here and not go, but then my dad would worry about me sneaking around. It was a lose-lose situation either way. This meeting was going to happen.

After speaking to the police, my dad hugged my godfather.

"The police got everything secure, brother," LJ mentioned, letting Dad go. "Got people both inside and out. Your dad made it easy."

Yeah, he was being super agreeable here, super *helpful.*

I didn't know how to feel about that, but I guessed nothing. He owed us all at least that, and I stood by my father.

"Remember our agreement," Dad said to me before waving his hand to the police chief. He wasn't the one who'd arrested me. I'd found out later that'd been the county sheriff and thank fuck for that.

Today, I was surrounded by allies, and the Maywood Heights's police chief himself personally escorted my father, me, and my god dad up to the house. LJ flanked my dad and me, and where LJ had my back, I would have my dad's. I'd listen to him today.

It was the least *I* could do.

We passed a lot of security on the way inside of the estate that took up like half a city block, and I found out some of the people were our own as well. My dad had hired private security on top of acquiring help from the police force, and my grandfather's goons were actually few and far between. The dudes were definitely there. They had their fingers to their earpieces and looked ominous as shit. They were actually the ones directing us through the property, but for the most part, *my dad and LJ* had the most guys, security.

I didn't know what that meant either, never knowing my grandfather's games. It could be a show of trust or just him being arrogant, but I didn't think my dad would ever have his people hurt anyone. Them being here was just for our safety.

This place was busy.

Everywhere I looked, there were folks clustered in rooms, people in front of computers and large screens like this was some intense government operation. They were passing off files and talking both above and to each other. Did they work for my grandfather? A part of his business?

Dad seemed surprised by all this chaos too, and I noticed LJ lean in and tap his shoulder.

"Our guys tell me your dad's been doing his own search-es," LJ said. "This is it. Our people inquired about all this when they allowed us in to post our men and comb over the area."

What the fuck?

I scanned around. All this was for Sloane?

Again, Dad appeared surprised by this, his blond eyebrows dashing up half his brow. He flattened his tie. "Nice he's being of some use."

He'd mumbled this, but it was audible enough for me. Dad passed a look over his shoulder, and I made sure to stay in his sight. I wasn't trying to be a bother today.

"Glad you could come." When my grandfather made his grand entrance, it wasn't much of one. He'd been chat-ting with more of these people, all of them in a cluster when Dad, LJ, and I were escorted into the room. This was one of the biggest and nearly the size of a small movie theater.

Grandpa appeared to be at the heart of the show after what he'd said, still with that ridiculous-ass cane. The ruby on top alone could probably put more than one student through a full year at Windsor Prep.

My grandfather liked to show off, money he still had despite not being an active part of Prinze Financial. Sure, I bet he still held a nice part of it, but I didn't know the details there.

I just knew my dad was in charge now, and I watched him, not at all rigid in my grandfather's presence. I was quite sure he hadn't seen his father in years.

But not once did he show it.

No weakness, or really anything else displayed on my dad's face. It was as if he had no emotion for my grandfather. His expression was passive, calm. His chin raised. "Well, we should be doing everything we can."

"I agree." Grandfather tapped that cane across the home's polished tiles, coming closer. If anything, I stiffened and noticed LJ place a hand on his jacket. It wouldn't surprise me if my godfather was strapped. Hell, Dad might be too.

If only for me.

Once more, my dad didn't act threatened, and he put a hand on LJ's shoulder. "I'm sure you remember LJ."

"Mr. Johnson and I reacquainted ourselves before you got here, son," Grandpa said to Dad, and LJ's smile quirked right.

"Yeah, I'm the one who patted him down personally." LJ's grin was high, and Grandpa's head lifted.

"I remember, Mr. Johnson, and whatever makes you all feel more comfortable." Grandpa raised a hand. "I just want to help and thank you for openness. I believe working together is our best bet in finding Sloane."

"Well, you can thank Dorian for that." Dad's attention didn't leave my grandfather, but he did place a hand in my direction. "As discussed, he is merely observing today. He knows this, and now, you do too."

Grandpa's attention shifted, falling wide on me. "Even still, I'm glad you've allowed him to be here. I didn't handle things well there, and I'm sure you know this."

I wasn't sure if this was an apology for the threats he'd made to me and my family, but that might be the closest I could ever get.

I wasn't allowed to talk to him.

I wasn't allowed to do anything but observe, and this was made even clearer when my father edged in front of me. He cut all direct eye contact off, at least from my grandfather to me.

"Might we get on with this then," Dad said, and that was exactly what my grandfather and his team moved on to do. Grandpa had everyone escorted into a quieter room, one cut off from everything and everyone.

Well, everyone but my father and all the people who'd come with us. Him and his team filled up a good portion of the room, which had been fashioned into some kind of conference room. There was a long table and chairs. Grandpa and his people took one side, and those who could fit on Dad's took the other.

LJ and I surrounded Dad, security around us. The men on both my side and across the table began speaking right away, and I shifted my focus from one to the other. People chimed in like popcorn over a fucking fire, and it took all I had to just keep up. Everyone here knew exactly what to talk about.

They were all clearly well-acquainted with this topic.

I wasn't surprised to hear this on my dad's end. They'd been working tirelessly to find Sloane, but Grandpa... yeah, that was surprising.

It sounded like he'd been working on this just as hard as us.

"I'll be starting to pull my men in closer to the city if that's okay with you, son," Grandpa said. "I feel their services are better here than wide with the intel your people gave us this morning."

To my surprise, my father faced me. "We know she hasn't gotten anywhere via any services offered to the public. Knight had some contacts that took care of that. Airports, buses, trains, and even cabs and rideshares are all out. She hasn't used any of them, and from what your grandfather told us today, she wouldn't have had a lot of money to anyway."

"She used her credit card once at an ATM to get cash the day she left." Grandpa slid a document over. "Took out five hundred dollars. Bru never used his, and though I can't be sure how much they had on them before they left, I do know they mostly used their credit cards when they were living here. I've also acquired their vehicles. Bru's Audi and Godfrey's Chevelle have all been picked up by my men, and from what we know, the kids never got the chance to use them. We were able to get to the cars first, so there's a strong possibility you're right, Royal."

Right about what?

My attention shot to my dad, and he edged closer.

"There's a strong possibility she's still in the city," Dad said, and my heart fucking stopped.

It crashed.

She was in the city? But how could she be? We'd looked everywhere. The town and *I* had looked everywhere. My friends and I had covered a lot of ground long before my dad caught us.

"She's got the most famous face in the world right now," Grandpa said, sighing. "If anyone saw her… Anyone tried to *help her*, I think we'd all have heard about it. Especially with the reward her parents have posted."

I think we'd all heard about that. The Mallicks had posted an amount they probably felt was low, but to anyone outside of our world it would have been life-changing. If someone had seen Sloane, no one would have kept that information to themselves. They had far too much to gain by selling her out.

But I didn't understand this, any of this. If she was still in the city, why hadn't we found her?

Why hadn't I?

The talks moved on after that, me staying silent while the adults continued to talk. They were combining forces. This was something I'd wanted, but chilling thoughts surfaced again. My grandfather was right. Sloane had the most known face in the world, not just in this city. If she didn't get help and was *still in this city*, she was lying low.

And doing so on purpose.

CHAPTER
TWELVE

To: noa.sloane@windsorprep.edu

From: dorian.prinze@windsorprep.edu

Subject: Wolf

Ares Mallick is one of the smartest people I know. He's the one I go to when I don't know something. He's the one all of us go to. He's top of our class and probably could have gone to any STEM school in the goddamn country if he'd have chosen to. In fact, had he not been such a modest shit, he might have taken up one of their offers I know he's gotten in the past. He's brilliant, beyond it.

And even he couldn't find you.

You know, your brother used to look for you? When we were kids, he drove himself crazy trying to find his twin. It was his days, his nights, his weekends, and his life, and it went on so long I'm not even sure of when the searches began.

I just know how they ended.

I wished you knew the person Ares was before he realized he couldn't find you. He was still dark. I mean, how couldn't he be? He'd lost a piece of himself in never having known you, but he's always known about you. Your parents, Ramses and Brielle, were very open about those few days in the hospital they got to be with you before you were selfishly taken from them, but no amount of recollection from his parents could ever really let him know you. I mean, even they didn't.
Like I said, I wish you knew the person Wolf was before. He wasn't the wolf. He was still Ares, and your brother. He had hope, but I'm afraid he'll never get that now.

Things are so much worse now.

I found out something today. It's something about you, and I'm not sure how I'll be able to tell your brother. It would hurt him so much worse, and I can't fucking do that to my friend. He's *my* brother, and he doesn't deserve that truth. *Your truth.* He doesn't and nor do his parents who are some of the most wonderful people I've ever had the pleasure of having in my life. I love them like I love my own goddamn folks.

I just don't understand.

I'm trying to get it, Noa. I'm *trying* to be patient, but things are getting deep here, and now, I'm spiraling worse than my best friend. I've left a lot of things out in these emails. I've left out *us* and ignored things. I ignored what I told you before you left. I made myself. No matter how bad it cut, I did, but I can't ignore it now. Please help me understand you and what you're doing. I mean, a few words from you can keep my world from leveling completely.
Because that's how much you mean to it.

CHAPTER
THIRTEEN

Dorian

I shouldn't have gone to Sloane's place. I mean, there wasn't a point.

It wasn't like she was there.

The house my grandfather had purchased for her had been searched many times. The authorities had combed it, and it had remained a high priority sight for a while. It was the most suspected place she would go if she was out on her own and needed a place to lie low. She wasn't there, and that'd been ruled out pretty early.

Even still, I cruised toward that area, in my own car today. Dad had actually given me back my keys after that meeting with my grandfather.

He said he trusted me.

I didn't even have to go anywhere with Ronald anymore, but I did have rules. If I went anywhere, my folks had to know about it, and I had told them I was swinging past Sloane's today on my way home from school. I'd told them I just wanted to drive by and take a look.

Of course, my father stressed that the area had been searched. My mom too. I knew what they were telling me, and I knew what I knew myself.

My chest felt all locked up rolling through the hills, anxious and tight every inch I traveled. I mean, what was the point in finding Sloane if she didn't want to be found?

What was the point in loving her if she didn't love me?

I hurt *everywhere*, heavy and weighted. If I did find her today, I didn't know what I'd do. I didn't know if I'd yell or fucking kiss her, *fuck* her *raw* until she cried out and bled for me. Until she bled for what she'd done.

And continued to do by being gone.

I ached and was beyond pissed about it. I was ravaged by obsession, warped by pain, and I think the only thing keeping me on this path to actually check her house and not hit up my father's liquor cabinet was because I kept thinking about that last email I'd sent her. I wouldn't send her any more, but I couldn't forget the topics. All this was bigger than me, and I had to find her for my family.

Even if she didn't want me.

I drove slow on purpose, and that was for my safety more than anything. I was sober as shit, but I was so fucking in my head I worried I'd wrap my ride around a goddamn tree. Because of that, I rolled along real slow, but reacted quickly when Sloane's gate opened.

I recognized the car coming out of it.

Myself and my friends had the newest rides at our school. With the exception of Bruno Sloane coming to Windsor Prep recently, we did have the newest, so saying I knew the Audi coming out of the gate was an understatement.

Thatcher had his arm out of his car, immediately turning right and the opposite direction away from me. His engine charged the air as he peeled off, and I shifted gears after him.

What the fuck?

My friend hadn't told me or anyone else he'd be coming

through here today, and by that I meant he hadn't told us, his boys. Of course, my friends all knew Sloane might still be in town. They did with the exception of Wolf.

I hadn't known how to break it to him yet that his sister was a lot freaking closer than we thought. That she was but still wasn't surfacing. I actually planned to explain it all tonight, and Wells and Thatcher had agreed to be there as emotional support when I'd texted them.

What the hell?

Thatcher obviously hadn't seen me here today. He'd peeled out of that bitch quickly, and I nearly lost him when I drove after him. Thatcher tended to like to drive fast, so that wasn't surprising, but the rate he was burning those tires was even unusual for him.

I kept an eye on him as he rolled through town, and I couldn't really keep up since he was going so fast. We had a few cars' distance between us at all times.

Me: Hey. Where you at?

I tossed my phone on my seat after texting him, able to see him ahead but not clearly in traffic. We had about a block and several cars between us now.

Thatcher: At home, why?

The fuck?

I started to text him again, but the light changed, and I needed to keep him in my sight. I left the phone on the seat and decided to keep chasing. He had no reason to be lying right now to me, and instinct had told me when I initially saw him, he might be trying to check the house out like me. He might have just wanted to help by combing the place for Noa and thought he was or something.

That was starting to not feel like the right conclusion as I continued to tail him, and when I eventually did get closer, I stayed back. If he was lying, he was lying for a reason.

I stayed vigilant, giving us a couple blocks' radius when cars became few and far between. My buddy appeared to be keeping his focus on speed because he charged the fuck through town all the way to the last place I thought he would.

He ended up at Windsor House.

Windsor House was headquarters to the Court, but needless to say, none of my friends or myself had been going there for meetings or to hang the fuck out. We'd all been busy. Busy with everything and trying to help one of our own keep his shit together. We'd been trying to help Wolf, and that didn't involve sneaking over to Windsor House when one of us claimed to be at home.

But that was exactly where Thatcher went, keying in his entry code before the iron gates let him in. I stayed back, watching him before I too did the same. There wasn't a lot of traffic coming and going out of the place since there were no meetings or anything today.

The property had pretty much been a ghost town. I mean, half the town was looking for Sloane and helping the Mallicks. Most people were downtown at the capital, or at least the most powerful were. We all looked out for our own around here, and power usually lined the walls of Windsor House.

Today, the widespread property usually packed with guys and girls playing Frisbee and just chilling out was empty. I followed Thatcher mostly by sight from there, but I assumed he'd be parking in the garages. I remained back to let him do that, then parked behind the building. I got out in enough time to see him going into the clubhouse with something large on his back.

A bag.

It was nice and thick, but I couldn't see inside it. The door closed behind him, and I waited a beat before following.

There were a couple of dudes in front of the fireplace once I sprinted inside, others around and playing chess, but no Thatch.

"Where's Thatch?" I barked, and backs immediately

straightened, eyes wide. I hadn't been here in weeks. "He came through here."

I saw him, and right away several fingers pointed toward his route.

"What's up, Dorian?" a guy asked me, but I ignored him, following my buddy's trail. I didn't see Thatcher until I hit one of the halls.

He was picking something up.

A paintbrush... one sole brush with a long handle and thick bristles. He was getting it, and I stopped, tucking myself around a corner. Peering out, I caught him looking around the hall.

He panned the area for a second before stuffing the brush inside his bag, and at this point, I didn't let him get a wide berth from me.

I stayed on his fucking *ass*.

Thatcher took the stairs, ending up on floor six in the end. This place had so many fucking rooms and corridors, and it was easy to get lost in this bitch. I had a time or two when I'd been a kid. This old castle was even older than the home I grew up in. It had hardwood floors that creaked like a bitch, and I followed every one of Thatcher's creaking steps.

I followed him right up to a door.

I let him go inside that door, hanging back again. My hands flexed, my fists knuckling, but I waited each of the seconds it took my buddy to come out of that room. These were all bedrooms up here, places where Court members could stay. The Court often had events and out-of-town members and their families typically made use of the rooms when they came back for whatever the society had going on that day.

The room Thatcher went into should be empty, though. Most of the rooms up on this level were. There were newer rooms, better ones, that were refurbished on the lower floors.

Perhaps he knew that.

I held my breath but did wait until he came out of there. He had no bag once he did, rubbing his hands on his ripped jeans. He tossed fingers through his hair before he shifted on his Chucks away from that door.

He ran into me.

We physically collided, my friend a huge-ass mother-fucker, but I caught him by surprise. He hadn't expected to see me standing there, and because of that, I held the upper hand.

He was the one to stumble back, his head darting up, and the dude puffed the fuck up. He had his fists raised like he was going to hit something, *hit me*. One of my best friends was jumpy today, and that was obvious.

"Dorian." Slowly those fists lowered, his face red, body still charged to hell. He was breathing like he'd run a mile and his driving held consistent to that. He pocketed his hands. "Hey, what's—"

I shoved around him, his hand coming to my arm. He physically tugged me, and I shoved enough force into him to send him across the hallway.

Again, my friend was frazzled. He held size over me and a technique on the field that shouldn't have thrown his footing for shit. Thatcher Reed was panicked for some reason.

And I was starting to see why.

I didn't want to see it, think it. But when I charged toward that door again, he got in my way.

"Dorian, no." He had his movements together this time, a quick hand on my chest and his body in front of mine. "Wait. Just—"

"I saw you, fucker." I threw his hands off me, then darted a finger at him. "I was on my way to her house and *saw you* leaving."

His eyes flashed, his hands high.

"I stayed on your ass," I said, getting closer. "I saw you come here, and I saw you drop a *fucking paintbrush.*"

His hands remained steady in front of me, like he was dealing with an animal instead of his friend.

He wasn't far off.

Thatcher wet his lips, but he wasn't speaking fast enough. "Let's talk downstairs."

He had to be joking, right? I closed distance, and he put hands on me again.

He got my arms. "Please. Just let's talk first."

"Get the *fuck* out of my way."

"I will, buddy. But I need to talk to you first." He faced the door behind him, his expression tight when he came back. "You just gotta understand something first, okay?"

There was nothing *okay* about this. In fact, this appeared to be the deepest betrayal I think I'd ever felt. It came from him, my brother and one of my best friends.

My head shook, slow. "You need to get out of my way, Thatcher." I was giving him one more chance, *one more* before I broke each and every one of his fucking limbs.

Friendship be damned.

He was damning our friendship right now, and I couldn't even describe what he was doing to his friendship with Wolf. This was betrayal in its purest form if he had going on what I thought he had going on behind him.

Behind that door.

He'd had a paintbrush. He had been at *her* house, and when he'd gone in that room, he'd come out with none of it. My friend wasn't a fucking painter.

Let alone painting with what was most definitely her stuff.

Thatcher raised another hand to me, and this time, I got him by it. Working him around, I slammed his fucking body against the wall until his face touched it. Framed art fell and crashed at our feet, glass exploding as I pressed Thatcher's face into wallpaper. He didn't plead or call out despite how close I was to forcing his joint out of the socket.

"Dorian—"

"Shut the fuck up." We weren't talking. There were no words he could say, and I was so close to breaking my friend's arm.

I would have had the door not opened.

The sight of another surprised me enough not to damage my buddy's throwing arm, but it wasn't the someone I expected to see. Bare feet hit old oak floors, and when Bruno Sloane pulled me off my asshole of a friend, I couldn't have been more surprised.

"Dorian, what the fuck?" Bru shot, checking Thatcher, and the dude was in his motherfucking bed clothes. He had lounge pants and a Windsor Prep T-shirt on. All of it was too big, and I was pretty freaking sure both belonged to my buddy who was currently working his arm. Bru looked up from Thatcher. "Have you lost your mind?"

I hadn't.

But I was about to.

I forced both of them out of the way and went into that room. If Bruno Sloane was here, his sister wasn't far behind.

His sister…

She was that to him. That'd never leave, and no one expected it to. Least of all me. I understood that love and care for someone who wasn't necessarily biologically related to you.

She wasn't here.

The room was empty, bed messy and food boxes on it. There was also a game controller there too. It'd been left idle, and the television said *game over* on the screen above the fireplace. Someone was clearly living in here, staying here.

I headed toward the next room.

Some of these older rooms had connected suites and were typically only used when the nicer ones downstairs were filled. My buddies and I (like a lot of the Court) stayed at Windsor House quite often. Sometimes, a guy or girl just didn't feel like going fucking home, like I typically didn't after ragers when I was high off my ass and didn't want to run into my parents.

I charged into the hallway that connected the rooms, faintly hearing words called to me. I was pretty sure they were Bruno's and Thatcher's, but I didn't fucking care.

"She's not here," I heard Bru say as I hit the other end of the hall. I threw open the door, and my heart fucking stopped.

It was the easel.

It had a step stool in front of it and paints at the feet of it. The whole setup was positioned to face the balcony, but the doors were closed, and the shades were drawn.

That hadn't stopped the person from painting though, *her* from painting. The easel held a canvas that had a partial rendering of Windsor House's back gardens on it, pastel colors.

Soft.

I stared at it, and a peek through the curtains definitely let me know those back gardens could be seen from this room.

This was her.

I picked it up, and the bag Thatcher brought had been left by the easel. It was unopened, and the bed in the room was made. In fact, everything in this room was pristine unlike the last. There was no trash or anything, but she'd been here.

I could smell her.

Her light aroma suffocated this room, drowning me, and the painting's existence only proved the point. I put it down the same time steps hit the room behind me, and when I whipped around, both Bru and Thatcher were fighting their way into the room.

"I told you she's not here," Bru stated, breathy as shit. I must have been going pretty fast, and Bruno had obviously not been on the field in a while. "I called her. She's not coming back."

"The fuck do you mean?" I crossed the room in two, maybe three strides.

Bru hit the wall on the fourth.

I pinned him to it, and I had to give it to the kid.

He put off he wasn't scared.

On the football field, I often saw fear, and more than my fair share, when others came across me or any of my boys in the halls at school. People knew Legacy could do anything we wanted, take anything. Fucking with us wasn't a good idea.

And Bruno Sloane was fucking with me.

"Dorian." Thatcher's warning came from my side, but I noticed he didn't act. He stayed in place. He had no right to intercede here.

I mean, he was obviously a part of whatever this was.

"I heard you guys fighting," Bru said, and though he blinked, his voice didn't waver. The dude was scared, for sure, but he wasn't openly trying to let me see it. "You and Thatcher. I heard you fighting, and I called her. She walks the city to get air sometimes, the back roads, and wears a hoodie. Anyway, I called her with one of our burner phones, and she's not coming back if she knows you're here." He shook his head. "She won't. I know her."

My mouth dried, air physically sucked out of the room, my chest. "What do you mean? Why wouldn't she?"

Bru eyed Thatch, and I noticed my friend put his hand on my shoulder. He was cautious, just like outside.

"Let him go, Dorian," Thatch said. "Please."

I did let him go, but I didn't give Bru space. "You're saying she's hiding out." I paused, my voice tight, thick. "You're both hiding out, and she *left* because of me?"

"Nah, man. I'm not saying that." Bru fixed his shirt. Dude was fucking swimming in it, and it had to be Thatcher's. Bru tugged it down. "But I do know all of this is *a lot* for my fucking sister, so if she decided she needed a break, I was going to give her that. Be with her."

A break...

My chest touched Bru's, my hand raised slow. "You know how many people are suffering for that break?"

"Dorian—"

"Shut the *fuck up*, Thatch," I shot, sneering at him. I'd deal with him fucking later. I jabbed a finger in Bru's chest. "Your sister's actions have consequences and have hurt some of the people I care about the most. People I'd fucking die for."

"Well, I'd die for her," he said, making me blink. He nodded. "And I've spent too much time in this town trying to please you and your friends instead of sticking up for my sister, and that's something I'm not doing again."

"You're going to call her." I bared my teeth. "You call her back and make her *come back*."

"She won't." His arms moved over his chest. "She'll know you told me to."

Because apparently, she didn't want to see me, and I didn't care what he said about that earlier bullshit. She didn't want to see me and ran right after my grandfather told her the truth. Sure, my grandpa had been lying to her too, but not like I had. He'd taken care of her, always.

And I hadn't.

I'd lied to her, and who knew what she believed about the details of those lies. For all she knew, I could have been lying to her the whole time about her identity just like my grandpa. I mean, she knew at least Wolf knew. She found all that shit at his house, and if he knew about the details surrounding her identity…

That typically would mean I knew as well.

That thing was happening again. Where I couldn't breathe and was fucking suffocating. Pulling out my phone, I left the room, and Thatcher was hot on my heels. He gripped my arm. "Dorian?"

I worked his hand off me, shooting a finger in his face. "How could you? Do this to me? Do this to Wolf!" I got him by his shirt again, scanning his eyes. "Why would you do this to us?"

My voice broke, my body heavy. I was shaking to *fucking hell*, but I wouldn't let him go. The impulse to kill charged my veins, but the rage channeled to mostly myself. She might not have run at all if not for me.

"D." Thatcher swallowed, his face red again. My buddy kept blinking, his hands cuffing my wrists. "I was afraid of what she'd do. That she'd skip town and then none of us would know where she was. She said she only needed a few days. Just some time to—"

"Time to what, Thatch? She's been gone for well past that, and you fucking knew about it!"

I'd lost count of the days she'd been gone, more than a week but less than a month. Either way, it was more than a few fucking days.

Thatcher cringed. "I know."

"How the hell did this happen?" I asked, and Thatcher laced his fingers over his head.

"She came to Bow for help."

"Bow?" I stepped back, and Thatcher nodded.

"That first day she went missing," he said, his shoulders sagging. "The day all of us were out real late at the Mallicks? Anyway, when I eventually came back home, I ran into her and Bru creeping outside my house. They were waiting for Bow. They wanted her help, but I saw them first before they could find her."

What?

"Sloane said they both just needed a place to crash for a few days. She said she just needed some time," Thatcher stated, my heart racing. He'd said that shit at the lunch table that day, that she'd needed *time*. His Adam's apple flicked. "It was only supposed to be for a few days, and she said she just needed time to clear her head. I got them set up. Food and shit and put them up here."

And in rooms no one had checked. Windsor House had been searched, of course, but clearly, not as thoroughly as it should have. Maybe the police hadn't felt the need. Only Court had access to the place and Court affiliation usually meant loyalty.

I couldn't look at my friend, backing away. "You kept this shit from me, Wolf, his parents, and the families…"

"I had to, D. You didn't see her that first day. She—" He wet his lips. "She looked fucking *broken,* and I care about her too."

I blinked, and Thatcher's fingers tightened over his head, dark hair gripped under his knuckles.

"Of course, I do, man. She's one of us, and even outside of that, I've always been cool with her. She needed help, *pleaded with me.* She's Wolf's sister, bro, and it was better for one of us to know where she was and help her than to let her go off on her own and to who knew where. If I'd have blown the whistle on her, she would have gone running. Point blank. She already did."

"Did Wells know?" I asked, and he grabbed his arms.

"He does, but only recently," he stated, frowning. I stiffened, and he raised a hand. "We mixed up phones yesterday at practice. He saw my thread with her and freaked." He shook his head. "Hasn't talked to me since then."

Because he was pissed, understandably so, and had I seen him after showers, I probably would have noticed.

"Don't be mad at him. He told me I had to tell you guys by the end of the week, or he was doing it himself." Thatcher cringed. "I was going to but gave Sloane an ultimatum first. She needed to stop with all the cloak and dagger shit because I wasn't doing it anymore. I gave her the time she asked for, and she agreed. She seemed fucking receptive, and I thought she was going to say something and end this shit."

But she didn't. She hadn't.

And she left anyway.

That was on him, and though I'd done a lot of things... *fucked up* pretty much everything in my world, one thing I wouldn't have done was what he had. I tapped a name on my contacts, then pressed my phone to my ear.

Thatcher's mouth parted. "Who are you calling?"

"Wolf," I said, and he shouldn't be surprised. "And doing what you should have done in the first place."

Thatcher said nothing, the phone ringing in my ear. It went to voicemail, and I cursed. Wolf had been painting a lot and probably couldn't even hear his phone with all that music he played.

I tried again and this time walked away from Thatch. I'd go to Wolf if he didn't answer.

"I couldn't rat her out, Dorian," Thatcher said behind me, and when I turned, he cringed. "She couldn't leave again, and you know that. We both know what it would have done to Wolf, yes, but..." His hands threaded above his head once more. "I know what it would have done to you too."

I had no words for him because, in that moment, I heard Wolf's voice on the line. He asked me what was up, saying my name, and after facing away from Thatcher, I answered him. I answered him and told him what I needed to say. I told him the truth and was somehow able to speak it.

Even after Thatcher spoke mine.

CHAPTER
FOURTEEN

Sloane

I didn't know how to make a fire, but I figured I should try.

It was going to get cold tonight.

It was *already* cold considering night had fallen, and this stupid hoodie wasn't going to do much.

Get it together. You're going to be fine. It's going to be...

Swallowing, I continued to root around for tree branches, weeds, and anything I could possibly make a fire with, my sight guided by my burner phone's light. If I didn't have that, I had the lighter I always kept on me. I had one on my key chain for the times when I did have a little cash to cop some weed.

These days, I hadn't really been smoking any at all, and I had a big bundle of leaves more than any branches I could find for a fire. There weren't really any trees out here. The concrete channel Ares had brought me to that one time only had wet trash and other debris. I figured it'd be a good place to camp out with all the pipes and all that.

The graffiti wall did have a few trees down the hill,

though, so after grabbing a bunch of what I could find, I headed back. I couldn't start the fire on the hill. Someone might see, but I planned to stay as close to the wall as I could. I liked being there for some reason.

Sniffing through chilled nostrils, I hugged the leaves and shit and made my way. I kept my hood down, snuggling into the heat I had but it made seeing pretty shitty.

Had I been watching where I was going, I would have seen him.

I hadn't *seen* anyone outside of my brother and Thatcher Reed without the use of a screen for a long time. It'd been long enough where the presence of another definitely threw me, and not only did I drop everything in my hands, ice immediately locked on and froze my entire body. Limbs wouldn't move. *Legs wouldn't run.*

And sight took hold.

Palms up, a man came out of the shadows from behind the graffiti wall, but even before he got up on me, I knew who he was. Thick curls tucked under a backward ball cap, his letterman jacket on, but he was *tall* and something I always took note of because I was tall too. I had a vantage point way over most girls, and I usually stared guys in the eye, even if they held a few inches over me.

But this guy, this boy I always had to look up to, and even more so than the dark prince.

"Don't run," he said, and I noticed I did have a leg out, arms up. I was mid-sprint and didn't even know it. Ares patted the air. "Please don't run."

I blinked, staying there. I wasn't reacting how I thought I'd react and did think if I saw him again, I would run. He'd *lied* to me.

But for some reason I stayed still as he gained closer, each step deliberate but cautious. His throat worked. "It's just me."

It's just him.

I even looked to see, studying the corner he'd come out of.

I'd been on the painted side of the wall when he'd come through.

The side we'd tagged.

Of course, it hadn't been just us. He said his dad and him had…

"No one else knows I'm here," he stressed and even pulled off his hat. His curls fell out of it. "I swear it's just you and me."

My breath accelerated, air supply short, chest tight. "How did you know I was here?"

When Bru had called me, I'd just *run* and had no thoughts at all where I was going. He'd tried to ask me where I'd go, but I'd hung up. I had left and come here and totally hadn't known where I was going until I'd arrived.

Ares shifted on his shoes a beat, and where he stood, breathing appeared to be hard for him too. He took a large one after I spoke. He faced back to the wall. "I thought if it was me, I'd come here." He pressed his hair down before sliding his hat back on. "Lots of pipes and places to hide so…"

That made sense.

"I guess I just had a feeling too or… or something." He wet his lips. "I don't know. I felt like you'd come here. Like I said, I would."

I nodded, messing with my hands. He started to come closer, and I raised mine.

He did too.

"Sorry. I won't— Fuck." He bit his lip, nostrils flaring. Large puffs of air clouded around him, and there definitely wasn't a lot of light going around. Besides the shitty lighting coming off the channel, there was just the minimal light pollution from the city below the hill. His hands lifted higher. "I'm not here to do anything, and I haven't told anyone I'm here."

He hadn't?

"D called me after he ran into Bru, and I just hopped in my car. Started driving." His jaw shifted. "I just want to be here, okay? No pressure, and you don't have to come back with me or anything like that. Just..." He swallowed. "Just let me be here. Be here with you."

I didn't know what to say to that, but definitely hadn't expected that tightness to hit my throat. He just wanted to be here, and for some reason, I wanted him to be and what the fuck?

"Okay." My voice cracked, like I was on the verge of fucking tears and what the fuck *again*.

Ares's hands lowered. He took a step back, letting me past.

We sat at the wall.

We parked it there together in the low light, my legs out and his up. I gauged time between looking at them and at him, though he stayed facing forward.

How did I not know?

How did I not *see* it, our similarities? Besides us both having pretty crappy attitudes the majority of the time, this guy basically had *my face* if I was *a boy*.

It was my face.

I mean, obviously we weren't identical, but we both had angular features, straight noses and wide eyes. Ares had also been in a lot more physical altercations than me. He had a scar under his eye and along his jaw. They were faint, but they were there and possibly because of football.

This is wild.

He was like an inverted version of myself, masculine features where mine were softer. Then there were the more obvious things, our height being one of them.

We had the same *hair*.

Though Ares had put his ball cap back on, his dark, almost black curls still nearly touched his shoulders. These days, I definitely wasn't straightening my own, and we even had a similar curl pattern, thick and untamed if one let it get to that point.

Ares's lengthy fingers tapped his jeans, rips at the knees showing the same honey-gold complexion like myself. He braced his chunky Court ring, like Dorian's just without the rubies for eyes.

"How's your cheek doing?"

Our gazes clashed after what he said, and I apparently hadn't been the only one looking at the other. He had his knees up, arms out. He pointed toward me. "Your face? Is that okay?"

I touched my cheek, no pain, but my own altercations hadn't healed completely yet. I'd hit the floor in that warehouse, the warehouse with Godfrey. I hugged my legs. "It's fine."

He said nothing, still *staring* at me. Me and this dude even had the same *eyes*, tawny colored like a doe's fur. I suppose a buck in his case. His hand locked around his wrist. "What about over all? I..." Lengthy fingers gripped his cap. "I heard you had some bumps and bruises."

I suppose he had.

The world knew my story after all.

Those physical scars were basically gone today, all evidence of that day *gone*, but how could it really be?

The mental wounds still there, I turned away from him, pressing my face to my knees. "You said no one's coming," I stated, arms shaking, so fucking chilled by all this. "Why?" I thought he'd bring an army if he found out where I was.

They had before.

Silent, Ares left me to hear my own words fade off into the air.

He touched me.

Or at least he tried to. I whipped around, and he had his hands up. The jacket he'd been wearing was in his hands, and he held it up. "I was just going to… you know." He pointed toward me. "You look cold. You were shaking."

I was shaking and only partially from the cold.

His lips moved. "Here. Take it."

I did, putting it on, and the wash of heat surrounded me. Ares's jacket was heavy, and the Windsor Prep W was stitched on the chest. Lined with a silky material, I hated how comfortable it made me feel. How it reminded me of other comfortable times, late nights and laughter in his garage when we'd painted together.

Or watched late night TV.

That time we'd binged *The Office* and eaten so much junk food I thought I would pop still lingered in my mind. He'd come to my rescue that night, been there for me. I closed my eyes. "Why are you here by yourself?" I asked again, turning. We locked eyes again, and I swallowed. "Why didn't you tell anyone? Why didn't you tell…"

I couldn't *think* his name, let alone say it. It was like my brain was rejecting it or something, and that remained consistent. Whenever I thought about his friend lately, it triggered things in me.

And the reason these days were obvious.

If Ares knew what I'd been about to say, he didn't mention it. His gaze fell to the hill. "You ran before," he said, his attention flicking up. "But you didn't with Thatcher. You trusted him."

My breath left in short puffs, heart racing.

"I figured having your back obviously worked for him so…" He shrugged, his expression hardened. He brought a hand down his face. "Figured it was my best bet. Didn't want you to run."

He shook his head after that. Like he was rejecting thoughts too. Maybe he was. This was obviously difficult for him.

"Why did you run?" he asked, and this was far beyond us

just *being* beside each other. He didn't have a right to ask me any questions.

Not after what he'd done.

And he couldn't deny that shit. The evidence had been *there* and in my friggin' hands when I'd gone into that home studio at his house. My jaw worked. "How long did you know?"

His chin tipped, head cocked. "Is that why you did?" He leaned forward. "Because I lied? Lied to you?"

I was glad he was admitting it.

I didn't answer, and he sighed. Raising up, he touched his back to the wall.

"Not as long as you think." His gaze swung in my direction. "I didn't know who you were when you first got here. Honestly, it was a fucking fluke how it happened."

I scanned him, watching as he scrubbed his hands down his face.

"A fucking miracle." His attention latched onto me again, pointed, heavy. He frowned. "Remember that party I had? That day I mean?"

Of course, I fucking did. He *lied to me then* too.

He blinked, pulling that cap off and running a hand over his curls again. He returned it backward on his head. "Of course, you do. I made a fucking fool out of you."

It was really crazy how my thoughts really did align with his. Like we were always kind of on the same wavelength, and I'd noticed it before this when we'd worked together closely.

Trying not to think of those similarities, I sat there, and Ares braced his long arms around his raised legs.

"Well, before the party, I saw you looking for something." He chewed his lip. "Remember that? How you were on your knees looking for something?"

I shrugged. I guess I did. Honestly, I'd forgotten about it. I had seen a flash of something, but he'd made me feel like an idiot for being on the floor.

He reached toward me, and when I sat back, he raised a hand.

"There's something in the pocket." He directed a finger. "In the jacket? You can get it."

Eyeing him, I tugged the pocket over, feeling around until I did feel something. I pulled it out, and it took me a second to see what I was looking at. Metal, whatever it was had been tarnished to the point where it wasn't recognizable as, well, anything. It had a layer of age and distress, and with the channel's low light, I couldn't really see what the object was until Ares shined his phone light on it.

But when he did…

My heart stopped, like fucking stopped, full stop. I definitely recognized this thing.

It looks like his.

It resembled Ares's emblem, the one he'd worn when we were painting. It looked exactly like it, but it was older and dented.

My thumb running over it, I looked up but only to see the same one in front of my face.

Ares held another, this one dangling from that familiar chain he always wore in his garage. His was newer, or at least nicer. He swallowed. "The one you're holding is the one I found on the floor that day I saw you in the hall." He cleared his throat. "I looked under the lockers after you left."

He tugged his off, giving it to me. I was able to compare the two then, and they were completely identical.

I ran my thumb over both of them. "I don't understand."

"I didn't either." His back touched the wall again. "As far as I knew, I only had one. My parents gave mine to me when I was a kid."

That's what he'd said to me in the garage, that he got one as a kid.

"But I should have been the only one," he continued. "Dad told me he had it made out of this old, archaic-as-shit necklace Court guys used to give their girlfriends. They called it a 'Court Kept' necklace or some bullshit. Only guys were members back then, and it was a way to claim their girls."

Jesus, that was archaic.

"Right?" Ares laughed a little, apparently the pair of us on the same wavelength once more. "Anyway, I don't know why it was never given to my mom. Maybe because it was archaic. I know he got it in high school, and they didn't meet until my dad was at college so…" He angled forward. "Basically, I was the only one supposed to have it. It was unique. Obviously, since Dad made it out of this thing he used to have. He had that old necklace melted down and actually did it himself. He's into metalwork. Don't know if I mentioned that."

I stayed quiet, watching him.

"He said the old necklace was special, that it meant something else, but now, it was for me because I was theirs. His and Mom's." He put his hands together. "They gave it to me when I was like real little. I've had it for forever."

I stared at the two, all that meaning there. What he'd said was so beautiful, wonderful.

"But I hadn't seen mine in years," he said, and I looked up. He nodded. "I used to lose it all the time, and it meant so much I had my mom keep track of it. The day of my party, I pocketed that one I found, then texted my mom after. I wanted to know where mine was so I could compare them. I hadn't seen mine in a while, you know, so I wasn't completely sure they were even the same." He focused on me. "I also asked her if another was made. I figured there could be a possibility because I was, uh… well, because I was a twin."

My throat dry, I squeezed the emblems. "What happened?"

"Well, nothing at first. My mom's not much of a texter, and both my parents were out of town that day." His breath was harsh, labored. He gripped his legs. "She didn't call me until late. Told me where mine was and confirmed there'd been two. She said my sister Pilar had the other one, and both were on our baby blankets before Mom and Dad made mine into a necklace."

I rubbed my chest, my throat.

"I bet I've seen that photo a million times. Us. *Me and Pilar* in those blankets." He faced me, his mouth turned down. "But I never put two and two together. *That my necklace* came from the blanket and her charm obviously came from hers." He pressed his hands to his face, his mouth. "I just hadn't put it together, and even after my mom told me the connection, I didn't believe what I had was *Pilar's*. I mean, how could I? I couldn't." He studied the sky. "It didn't make sense, and it definitely didn't that you found it."

I sat up, struggling to.

"No sense *at all*," he continued, looking at me. "You looking for it in that hallway, *my hallway* in my school didn't make sense. Pilar's would have been on her baby blanket." His jaw tightened. "She was taken in her baby blanket so no, that didn't make sense."

I'd heard how I was taken, the details. The news had talked all about it, and Thatcher had given us a room with a TV. The baby had been swiped, right from the hospital, and in the middle of the night. She'd been taken from a family and only been a newborn. She'd been in the NICU because she'd been sick.

"I found my necklace after the conversation with my mom." Ares stared at the ground. "She told me where it was. It was easy." His words sounded haunted, his eyes appearing the same, and I think he was cold now the way he squeezed his arms. "I compared the two and…"

"Ares."

His attention shifted, on me again. "It still didn't make

sense, and I wouldn't believe it." Emotion hit his voice, his eyes. His nostrils flared. "I spent so long looking for her."

I noticed he didn't say me, but I didn't blame him. I was sure a lot of pain came with that search.

And I had heard about it, his search.

That topic was for another day, another thought, and I definitely couldn't think about it now. This was too much for *me* now.

I covered my mouth. "Is that why you poked me?" I asked, and though he didn't look at me, I knew he heard me. His back straightened, his jaw tight. "That day in the hall at your house? You poked me, right? Got my DNA?"

The news talked about that too, how the families had DNA evidence, and it didn't take me long to put together how they'd gotten it. I thought Ares had stabbed me with something that day, a prick to my leg.

"I needed evidence," he said, glancing my way. "I needed the truth, and even after I had it, I still didn't believe it." He scanned me. "No matter how obvious it was."

He didn't even have to elaborate on that. *His own friends* had said how much we looked like each other, acted like each other. "You've known that long then? Since then?"

"Not long after. Found out the DNA results that day Bru did the haze."

I closed my eyes. That day had been a mess, and I recalled Ares acting weird that day. He'd texted me out of the blue and had been *weird*. He'd been weird about Dorian.

Dorian…

Chills covered my body again. My face touched my knees.

"I was going to tell you." His whole body shifted in my direction. "I wanted to tell you so bad, Sloane. I swear to God—"

"Why didn't you?" I shot, eyes cloudy, voice strained. "You knew that whole fucking time, and you said not one word, Ares. You didn't say a goddamn thing to me. You didn't… You didn't..." Tears blinked down, and I couldn't finish. My throat was raw, and I couldn't see. "He didn't tell me either."

I barely heard those last words spoken myself. I didn't want to hear them, feel them.

He lied. They all *lied.*

Everyone in my life lied to me, everyone I cared about the most. Everyone I *trusted,* and especially Dorian Prinze. His lie had been the worst.

Because he'd gotten the closest.

The anguish of that truth shook my entire body, and it took me a moment to realize how close Ares had gotten.

"He didn't know," he said, locking eyes with me. His held a shine to them, one he squeezed away before hunkering down with me. "I told no one. Not my parents." His Adam's apple shifted. "Not the boys. Not D."

Not D.

"He didn't know, Sloane." Ares brought his hands together. "The night you found that file, the file *I'd* made about you, was when I told Dorian, Wells, and Thatch. They didn't know before that, and my parents found out not long after. I told them too. Basically, right after."

He didn't... know?

I didn't understand.

"Why?" I ached, my insides searing. "Why did you lie? Why did you do that?"

"Because I fucked up." His breathing was harsh. "I fucked up because I was *scared,* and though I knew who you were, I didn't *know* you. I didn't, and I needed to protect my family. My parents, the guys and their families..." His shoulders sagged. "And you too."

This didn't make sense, any of it.

Ares rubbed his mouth. "The only thing I knew about you was the company you kept." He glanced my way. "You were hanging around with that Callum, and I didn't know if you were trapped. You could have been up to shit with him and trying to screw our families. Up to shit *with him.*"

With him.

I closed my eyes, the chills enveloping me again. I wished I didn't know what he meant. I wished I didn't know *the truth.*

But I did.

I knew so many things now. Because so much had changed, so many truths revealed.

"Callum..."

"You mean Dorian's grandfather?" I asked, and Ares blinked. My throat worked. "Callum Prinze?"

The words rang in the air, loud, vibrant.

But then so much silence.

They ghosted off into the night and completely froze both of us.

Ares leaned forward. "He told you then?" His legs lowered. "Told you the truth? He said he did."

He'd spoken to him? "He talked to you?"

"He reached out to the families, yeah. He said he told you the truth, and you ran after." Ares's hand gripped his wrist. "Before tonight, I thought that was why you ran." He rocked a little. "But now, I'm feeling like a lot of that had to do with me. Me and my lies."

Lies. Lies. Lies.

So many, and they all made me sick. People *lying* to me.

"Did he ever hurt you? You or Bru, or..." He studied me. "Anything like that?"

He felt the need to ask, and that made sense. I hated it made sense.

How had this become my life?

How was I here and in a world where people told you lies, and truths weren't the norm?

"Sloane, *please* if you don't tell me anything else just let me know he didn't hurt you. Let me know that you were okay, and that he never—"

"He was honest with me," I said, nodding. "And from how it sounds maybe the only one?"

My words surprised him, Ares's mouth parting, and they surprised me too. I'd had a lot of time to myself at Windsor House, the Court's headquarters, with Bru. *At lot of time* to find truths and discover what were the lies. Thatcher had given my brother and me a laptop to use as well as a room with a TV, and I used it to decipher what was real. Callum had told me many things before I'd left, many dark and disturbing things, and I went to the computer to flesh it out.

The internet only confirmed what he'd said.

He hadn't told me a lie about who he was, not one.

I wished he had.

"I know about it all, Ares," I said. "The murder cover-up, the cruelty…" I held onto his jacket, needing the warmth so bad. I glanced his way. "How he helped our family?"

Our family…

I was suddenly in a world where people hurt each other, and families protected each other to the point of madness. Where terror and horrible acts reigned supreme and darkness flapped its ugly wings. This was *my legacy.*

This was my family.

It was Ares's too, and though the Mallicks weren't the only parties involved, we'd started this. The news articles said *the Mallicks* were at the helm.

Ares put his hands together. "Our great-uncle and grand-father," he said. "Yes."

And that was all he had to say, that truth out there too. Our great-uncle had murdered someone, and our grandfather helped cover it up. He'd gone to someone to help him, and that someone hit real close to home.

He'd been taking care of Bru and me.

"Great-Uncle Leo is still serving time." Ares adjusted

against the wall. "I've never met him, and he'll die in that place." His expression cut. "For what he did, he'll die in there."

For what he did...

I knew about that too, of course, all of it.

"As far as Grandpa, I've never met him either. Though, he's out of prison now." Ares's head lowered. "He stayed away my whole life. Like D's..."

My eyes shut tight, the tears blinking down.

"He's his grandpa," I gasped, rubbing my nose. "Callum is Dorian's grandfather." It'd been the first time I'd spoken the words aloud and since they'd been originally spoken to me. "Callum Montgomery is Callum Prinze." It was like I needed to hear the words again to believe them. "And he covered up the murder of Dorian's aunt."

His aunt Paige, his mother's sister.

Holy fuck.

Nausea surfaced and not the first time. I'd thrown up many times since I had gone out on my own. During restless nights.

After nightmares.

Sickness threatened to grapple hold again, and I hoped I could hold it down.

"Yes," Ares whispered, his gaze pointed, focused on me. "He really did tell you everything."

Callum had told my brother and me the truth, told us *all of it,* and each gritty detail was only confirmed by those internet searches. My guardian had told us facts, and though he'd spared us the specifics, that hadn't mattered.

I'd still asked for the trash can.

I'd thrown up literally everything to the point of stomach bile that day, and Callum had rushed everyone inside the room. Doctors had come, nurses. It'd only proved to smother me even more. I'd needed out.

And he'd given that to me.

Callum had given us the room after I'd thrown up, and my brother and I had taken the first opportunity we could to leave it. It was all too much. It was...

"I know D didn't tell you," Ares said, his hands coming together. "About his grandfather. I know he didn't tell you who he was and that he knew him, and that probably looks really bad, but you have to understand where he was coming from. D and his grandfather..." Ares huffed. "It's some complicated shit. The fucker has stayed out of his life just like mine, and there's a reason for that. You know about that murder cover-up, and Callum Prinze did that shit to his own *family*. Dorian's dad was dating his mom at the time."

Christ.

"Callum Prinze has done some fucked-up things, and none of us could trust him."

Which meant they couldn't trust me? "What do I have to do with any of that?"

"That's the thing. We didn't know. Like I said, *I* didn't know and..." His expression fell, pained. "I was scared about the possibility of that, but I was more scared for you. I was scared he was having you do things, causing chaos on his behalf and possibly hurting you in the process."

"I wasn't."

"I know." He rubbed his legs. "It took me some time. Time to know you and..." His jaw moved. "Even outside of that, he never hurt you, right? Never did anything to make you feel unsafe? You or Bru? Please just let me know that so I don't go fucking crazy."

He hadn't. He didn't.

He'd only been kind.

I closed my eyes, my own pain rupturing again. "He was only good to me and Bru," I said, lifting my head. "And he didn't even have to tell the truth."

In fact, he hadn't even been going to. He'd said he didn't want to be part of this and what Godfrey did.

He'd just wanted to right a wrong.

"But I know now that was weak of me. Selfish."

His words lingered in my memory, some of the final ones before my world collapsed even more than it'd already had. He'd been the one person who'd been honest with me.

"What do you mean?" Ares asked, and I nodded.

"He didn't have to tell the truth, or at least his place in it." I rubbed my hands. "He told Bru and me once he found out about what Godfrey did, he'd planned to keep his part in bringing me back here quiet. Said there were other factors, which he later explained was his history here."

He'd said he couldn't come forward. There was too much history here and him coming around would cause pain.

He'd said it would bring pain to his family.

"He said coming forward would hurt his family," I said, Ares's eyebrows narrowed. "And he felt a sense of responsibility that my dad…" I bit my lip, still getting used to that. "That Godfrey had come to him to care for us."

Callum had said Godfrey thought Callum would keep his secret if Callum had ever found out, and from what I knew about Callum, him and his history with that town, that made sense.

"So why did he then? Come forward?" Ares asked, and I dropped my legs.

"He said he realized he'd only been trying to protect himself, and he shouldn't do that anymore." He'd admitted that too.

Ares blew out a breath, his head shaking. "He's done some fucked-up shit, Sloane. A lot of fucked-up shit and…" He studied the ground, his head lifting. "Helping you or not, I'm sure it helps him. Whether it's to clear his guilt, guilt about shit he's done or whatever." His eyebrows narrowed. "He's messed up a lot of peoples' lives, his own family's the most."

I did know this and was so aware of it.

I mean, he'd told me himself.

Ares left me with those thoughts. We were silent for a while, and when he pulled out his phone, my head shot up.

"I'm not calling anyone," he said, somehow knowing what I was thinking. He pressed a button, and his phone went dark. "My family can track my phone as well as the guys, so I shut it off." He pocketed the thing. "I meant what I said. I'm not setting the dogs on you. I just want to be here, and if that means a while, that's what it's going to be."

Putting his legs out, he crossed them at the ankles, the frown on his face evident.

"I'm going to earn back your trust," he said. "So as long as you're here, I'll be here too."

I didn't know what to say about that, so many questions in my mind. I faced him. "But your parents. I mean..." I stopped, my jaw moving. "You can't just ghost."

He couldn't ghost them.

I didn't even want to.

I didn't know what I wanted. I was so confused. I just knew up until a month ago I'd been something else.

I'd been *someone* else.

Now, I was being told I had a whole other life. My brother, Bruno, wasn't my own, and I had not one living parent but two. I had a family, and an interconnected web of other families. I'd seen the Prinzes, Reeds, and the Ambroses on the television too.

I'd seen them fight for me.

"If you're here, I'm here," he said, swallowing. "I'm not going to make you do anything you don't want to do, and I'm not letting anyone else do that either."

And then there was him and probably the closest link of all. We were *twins*.

I was a twin.

I didn't know what that meant. It'd just been Bru and me for so long.

"Can I ask you something?" He whispered the question, his body incredibly still. "How did you know Pilar's charm…" His head shook. "How did you know that charm was under the lockers? Have you been here before? In Maywood Heights? You had to have."

But I hadn't. I never. "I've never been here. I don't know how it got there." My finger scratched my wrist, restless. I used to wear the charm there on a bracelet *my parents* had gotten me.

At least, I thought they'd been my parents.

I just had a scar in that place now, and I had no idea how I'd gotten that either. It had happened a long time ago when I'd been young.

Why can't I remember anything?

Maybe I'd just been too young, and there'd been no chance at all to remember anything.

Ares's lips came together after what I said, and though I thought he'd ask another question, he didn't.

Taking them off my lap, I gave Ares back both charms. I didn't know the answer to his questions, and God I wished I did.

Ares's hand closed around them both, and after pocketing them, he faced forward. He folded his arms, and when he closed his eyes, I knew he was serious. He was going to stay out here with me in the cold.

"He really didn't know?" I asked, and his eyes open. "Dorian. He didn't know about me. Who I was?"

Ares told me he didn't, but there were just so many lies.

Ares head tilted. "If he did, he would have blown the whistle on that shit. *Instantly.* He would have called my parents for me. Fuck, he did call my dad and made me tell the truth. The truth about you."

What?

"You would have known, Sloane, and he would have told you himself had I refused. As far as keeping quiet about

Callum, D didn't have all the information. He didn't know who you were, and had he, I think he might have done a few things differently."

But Ares didn't know that. Not really.

"If he's part of the reason you ran, he shouldn't be," he said. "The secrets and shit was me, and D and his gramps are complicated. I'm sure he'll talk to you about it if you ask. Just got to give him a chance."

He was always trying to be the peacemaker, and it made sense he believed what he did, about me running, and I probably would have come to that conclusion too had I been him.

It's not that simple.

I was cold again, my head lowering. I zipped Ares's jacket up, and stared at the city with its twinkling lights. I sat next to my twin brother, my eyes closing. They were itchy and hot.

The tears that followed only made it worse.

CHAPTER
FIFTEEN

Dorian

Wolf: Where are you guys?

Me: On the way to your house.

Wolf: Wells and Thatcher with you?

Me: Thatcher is.

Thatcher: Yeah, and why the fuck aren't you picking up your phone, Wolf?

Wells: I'm on my way too. Was eating dinner with the parents. Wolf, what's going on? We're worried.

Me: Hence why we're coming over. We're not stupid. We know you shut your shit off, and we can't track you?? We're on the way to your house, and your ass better be there when we get there.

Wolf: I'm not there.

Wells: ???

Thatcher: Where the fuck are you?!

Me: Wolf…

Wolf: I snuck out, and chill the fuck out that's why I'm texting. Can you all make your way over to Windsor House?

Me: We can. Why?
Wells: ???
Thatcher: Dude, what's going on?
Wolf: Just meet me there.
Wolf: I'm on my way.
Wolf: I found her.

CHAPTER
SIXTEEN

Dorian

Wolf's texts had been cryptic as shit besides the little information he did give.

And he didn't answer anymore after that.

He left us to wonder. He left *me* to wonder, and I didn't like that shit. He found her? How? Were they together or…

I didn't like not knowing whatever my buddy was doing here, and I drove faster than I probably should have all the way back to Windsor House. Thatcher said some shit about it, grabbing onto the dashboard and being dramatic. He did *not* have a say in what the fuck I did right now, and the only reason I hadn't killed him was because he was my brother, and I might have regretted that shit later.

What the fuck's going on, Wolf?

I texted him as much as I called, but he answered nothing. His final text simply told us to meet in the rooms I'd told him Bru and Sloane had been staying in, and when Thatcher and I got there, Wells was already there. Bruno was with him, of course, and the dude had been pacing the fucking floor. He also stared at me the moment I arrived.

He hadn't stopped, going between that and messing with his phone. He basically would only check the front before pocketing it in a huff, so I assumed he was either checking the time or seeing no one was trying to contact him right now.

Not even his sister was answering him.

I wanted to kill that fucker too *with my hands*, and Wells made sure he and I were on opposite corners of the room. There were couches in the big suite Bru had been crashing in and Wells sat with me while Thatcher took the easy chair near Bruno. We all basically surrounded the door, and I had a feeling Wells's decision to babysit me *on the other side of the room* was because of fucking Thatcher. They hadn't really talked to each other since we all got together, and clearly, there was still some tension there. I wasn't happy with Thatcher either, but that last shit he'd said had gotten to me. The shit about knowing what Sloane running again would do to me.

I hated he was right, but I wouldn't admit he was right. Not about this. This wasn't about me.

It's not.

I pushed my emotions away, staring at the door. My gaze clashed with Bru's on the way back, and when he shook his head, I sat up. "Got something to say, man?"

I literally was taking back all the good shit I'd said about him in the past. He'd been a decent dude up until now, and I got he was trying to have his sister's back, but what he'd done was really fucking shitty. He knew she had a family here and was one of us.

He fucking knew that.

He knew she had a twin brother, and he chose to go all silent and shit knowing this entire town was going crazy looking for her. They had a TV in here, so they knew what the fuck was going on. Bru crossed his legs. "I don't have anything to say."

"Seems like you do." I pocketed my phone. Wolf wasn't answering it anyway. "So say it."

"I wouldn't." The advisement came from Thatcher. He gazed up from his phone. This was probably solid advice my friend was giving Sloane's brother, but that didn't stop the dude from cocking his head at me.

"I just hope he'll relax is all. When she gets here?" Bru swung his head in my direction. "Dude looks like he's going to punch something, and things are already tense with my sister."

"I said *I wouldn't*, bro." Pocketing his own phone, Thatcher grew two sizes next to Bru, and that said something. My friend already wasn't fitting in the chair he sat in. "Make no mistake. I helped your ass out, but I will always be with my boy here. He wants to kick your ass, I'll let him, so I'd watch what you say to him."

I didn't need Thatcher coming to my defense. I could handle my shit, but it was nice to know where he was right now.

And I did know he'd always have my back.

Like Wolf recently, it seemed a few of us were keeping secrets in regard to Sloane, and if I had a secret to keep, one she entrusted me with, I didn't know what I'd do.

Yeah, you do.

He had been trying to protect her and have her back, and no one got that more than me. The need to protect her. The need to keep her safe…

"Let's just all relax." Wells lifted his hands. He was always the more laid-back one out of all of us. He looked at me. "You okay?"

That was him asking if I was going to punch something. I shrugged, and with a sigh, Wells glanced at Thatcher. "You okay over there too? If shit starts hitting the fan, and I get a shiner, I'm not going to be happy about it."

I smirked, and Thatcher did too. If Thatcher and I got up to shit, Wells knew he'd be in there too. Fucker had our backs, and even if he was mad at Thatcher, or any of us, he would stand up for that person. We were all just that close, and I noticed my friends nod at each other before they both went back to their phones. Their beef wouldn't last long, never did.

"Guys?"

We all swung our gazes to the door, Wolf easing inside.

He wasn't alone.

We all got to our feet when a girl in a jacket behind him surfaced. She was in *Wolf's* jacket, the hem hitting her toned legs, thighs bare and exposed. The jacket sleeves touched her at the fingertips, and she tugged the hood of a hoodie she wore beneath down. Dark and wavy curls fell out of it, a thick wave of brown-black, and I swallowed.

Cookies.

A wash of them hit me, like Christmas morning and birthday parties. Like happiness, sadness, and everything in between. I'd clearly forgotten what she smelled like, what *she tasted* like, because all that came back the minute she was in the room with me. I was reminded about each flick and taste of my tongue, and the hints of soft scent that came off her skin while I did it. I was reminded how I hadn't *had it.*

And how I hadn't had her.

Her face was different, not thinner or anything, but tired, weary. Subtle shadows underlined her eyes, and she had a bruise on her fucking face. It was yellow and faint, but it was *there*, and before I had time to react to that, her goddamn brother crossed in front of me.

"You okay?" Bru asked her, and I stopped myself from reacting and doing the first thing I wanted to do. That thing included taking her away from here, away from everyone and even Wolf. It included keeping her with me and not only making sure she was okay, but keeping her, claiming her.

A subtle squeeze to my forearm let me know I wasn't fighting off those urges by myself. Wells *and* Thatcher surrounded me, and while Wells had my arm, Thatcher had my shoulder. They were keeping me here.

They were helping me fight.

I had a tendency to go blind and do shit I probably shouldn't do. Things like punch Bruno Sloane in his fucking face just to get to her.

"I'm fine," Sloane said to Bru, and that was when Wolf stepped in. He hadn't left her but had snapped the door shut quickly behind her. With him being there, I really got to look at them both beside each other, and how the fuck I hadn't seen their twin connection until now, I didn't know. Maybe I hadn't wanted to see it or was just too blind to, but they definitely shared some distinct features.

She looks so much like Brielle.

I hadn't seen that either. She was like the younger, taller version of her from her hair to her golden skin. The height thing obviously came from Ramses.

How is this possible?

I knew the facts, but still this was fucking crazy.

And I couldn't move.

My buddies weren't even holding me now, but I was stiff as a rod in Sloane's presence. I hadn't seen her in so long, and with me not moving, I noticed Thatcher approach her. He had his hands in his ripped jeans, his shoulders shrugging.

"You good?" he asked her, taking her by surprise when she jumped. She'd been talking to Bru, and Thatch obviously surprised her. He rubbed his neck. "I mean, are you okay? Are you all right?"

She noticed she had an audience in that second.

She noticed me.

Her dark eyes fell on me, sweeping over me. She did that

a lot when we were together, and I used to fuck with her for it.

Not today.

Today, we were looking at each other just as much. That jacket did nothing for her, but it couldn't hide the shape and curve of her legs. Nor how it caught on the shelf of her large tits and gave me sight of those *fucking* legs. She may have been stressed. She may have been tired…

But she was still fucking beautiful.

The girl took my goddamn breath away as cliche as it sounded, and I physically wavered when she stopped looking at me to pay attention to Thatcher. It was like I'd been caught in the force field of her, trapped and suddenly let go.

"I'm okay," she said to him, her attention shifting between me and him *again*. She was giving herself away and obviously finding it hard to focus too. She scrubbed into her hair. "I'm sorry I ran off. Really sorry. I shouldn't have done that to you. We had a deal, and I messed it up." She sighed. "It was fucked before that. I took advantage and probably shouldn't have had you keep the secret in the first place. It was wrong, and I'm sorry for that too."

I was surprised she was saying this. I think we all were, and especially Thatcher. He'd gotten in some real hot water for that shit, and that was just with us.

The parents didn't even know yet.

Ramses and Brielle didn't know, and once Thatcher's own parents found out he'd been keeping secrets… from all of us, I was sure he'd hear it just as much as I had from mine when I'd kept things to myself. My god dad Knight was fucking *scary* and none of us were trying to do shit to piss him off.

This was obviously a consequence Thatcher had been willing to make for her. He gripped his arms. "Nah, you shouldn't have, but I'm glad you're okay."

The two stood there, then out of nowhere, Thatcher leaned forward and swallowed Sloane's little body up in a hug. More awkward than shit, the hug was stiff, my buddy not the best at fucking hugs, and Sloane hadn't been expecting it. She had her arms out, and I think we all held our breath that Thatcher had, well, just grabbed her. I mean, she'd been running from the world, running from us.

But then, she laughed.

Her arms came around him slow, her laughter soft, vibrant. I'd forgotten about that too, her laughter. She didn't do it a lot, and I had a habit of pissing her the hell off half the fucking time. Her expressing her joy was extremely rare, so when I did get it, I made note of it.

I relished in it.

Her hugging Thatcher ended up being just as awkward as him hugging her, and my buddy kept that shit quick. My buddy was as allergic to his emotions as I was. He crossed his arms after. "Just happy she's here, and I don't have to keep that shit quiet anymore," he said to the room, apparently feeling he needed to make a vocal announcement. He edged out of the circle when Wells approached, and Wells shook his head at him.

"Forgive him," Wells said, his eyes lifting. "What he means is he's glad you're here, and that's it."

Behind him, Thatcher's expression fell. "I said that."

"Yeah, in your own douchey way." Wells lifted his hands before tucking them under his arms. He faced Sloane. "I'm glad you're back too, and that you're safe." He smiled a little, glancing between her and Wolf. "I just can't believe it. Can't believe you two. This is crazy."

He didn't have to elaborate. Seeing them here, *together*, was crazy. Wolf had just been looking for her for so long.

Wolf was present for all these exchanges, but I noticed he remained quiet during it all. He'd just been watching Sloane like he himself couldn't believe it.

"Still trying to wrap my head around it," he said before

glancing over the group. His sight fell on me, and when Wells noticed, he tapped Thatcher's shoulder.

"Maybe we should give them all the room," he announced, but if they were, they didn't need to give me any allowances. If Wolf and his sister needed a moment, they should have that, and the way Bru was keeping a watchful eye over the situation, he'd probably be a part of it too. He should get time.

That was his sister too.

Regardless, none of this had anything to do with me, and I tried to make myself believe that as I approached. I noticed Sloane hug herself when I did. She got all locked up.

She got tense.

I tried not to let myself feel anything about that when I stared down at her. I nodded. "Yeah. We probably should. The guys and I can wait outside. Give you three time. You, Bru, and Wolf." Each word tore at me, *fucking aching inside me.* I swallowed. "I'm glad you're back too."

I was glad, and to the point where I thought I'd physically crumble if one more moment went by where she was in one place and I was another. I'd been *drowning* before she walked through that door and on the verge of killing Bru for what he'd done by going off with her. I'd been about to kill Thatcher for keeping the secret, and he was my goddamn friend. I'd felt like I was dying before Wolf sent his text that he'd found her.

I still felt that way.

I almost felt worse, and seeing her lock up tighter after what I said didn't help.

"Thanks." The word tight on her lips, she dismissed me to speak to Wolf. "I need to talk to Bru about what we talked about anyway."

I didn't know what they spoke about, but I'd definitely been dismissed.

You did it first.

I hadn't wanted to, but I didn't want to stand in the way either. The three should have time, and it was too late to take it all back when she walked away.

She took Bru with her, the two going off in the direction of her room, and right away, the four of us shifted. Wolf started to go that way, but I waved Thatcher and Wells in that direction.

"Keep watch," I told them. There was no way out of Sloane's room, but I think an eye on her would give us all peace of mind.

The two nodded, leaving, and though they followed, Wolf continued to stare that way. I didn't blame him. I was fighting the urge myself.

"Where did you find her?" I asked, trying not to fidget, but madness was brewing inside me.

Why did you say that shit to her?

I thought I'd bleed out my heart to her when I saw her but ended up saying all that stupid shit.

"Remember how I told you I took her to that graffiti wall?" Wolf said, his focus still in the direction of the hall. They'd all disappeared down it, but that didn't seem to matter. "How I took her there to tag that one time."

He'd mentioned it to our parents and with good reason. It, along with her home, had been one of the places searched the most after she'd gone missing. There were lots of pipes there that someone could lay low in and searching places Sloane was familiar with made sense.

"Well, that's where I found her." Wolf grabbed his legs, releasing a breath. I wondered if my buddy had been holding it the whole time. He stood up. "I thought about where I'd go if I needed a place to disappear quick. She ended up being there."

I guess he'd been right about the twin link thing. Damn. "What did you guys talk about?"

"A lot." He swallowed. "I told her everything and how I

found out who she was. Told her why I kept things from her too. That didn't really go over well, and I think she might have run because of that. Because of us?" His eyes lifted. "Sounds like your grandpa actually told her the truth about everything. He didn't lie to her about, well, anything."

The dread hit me. "What do you mean?"

"I mean, she knows what he's done and the Mallicks' place in it." He glanced back toward the hall. "He told her the truth, D. She knows who he is."

"And that he's my grandfather."

My buddy swung his eyes in my direction, his nod firm. "Yes, but I explained why you kept that from her. I explained your relationship with him is fucked, and you couldn't trust him, and because of that, we weren't sure if we could trust her. Until I could, I had to keep all that under wraps too. Who she was and all that."

I had a feeling that was why he hadn't told anyone about her.

So, this was my fault, all this. It started with my fuck-ups even if he had his own.

"And she ran because of that." I couldn't breathe, stomach tight, locked. "She ran because you and I lied to her."

"She didn't say specifically, and I told her you didn't know who she was." His head tilted. "I really messed all this up. If I'd been honest with her and everyone else… fuck." He pulled his hat off, bending it. "I fucked all this shit up. It's by the grace of God she let me bring her back here. I thought we'd be out there all night, but out of nowhere she said she wanted to come back here." He righted, expelling a breath. "She said she wants to meet my folks."

CHAPTER
SEVENTEEN

Dorian

I had to take a second after what Wolf said. Sloane wanted to meet his folks? For real?

I had him sit at this point. He wasn't looking right, and I needed to take a seat too. Sloane knew everything.

Sloane knew I'd lied.

Of course, I'd suspected I might have been a factor in why she'd run. Especially after I'd realized she not only had a phone with which to contact me if she needed help, but also that Thatcher had given her and Bru a laptop to use. The pair had had internet access.

Which meant she'd gotten my emails.

She'd gotten it all, but still hadn't reached out to me. That meant something, and with what Wolf was telling me now…

"She said she wants to meet them," he continued. He still had his hat in his hands, wrestling with it. He stared toward the hallway. "I'm sure that's what she's telling Bru."

Well, that was good news. Great news. "Well, then we

should call Ramses and Brielle then." Fuck, bring her over there now. "We can get this all going."

"But what if it's too soon?" He was fucking the shit up out of his hat, and he tossed it on the couch. "You didn't see her face when we were talking about all this shit. She looked *horrified* when we were talking about the fucked-up things my grandpa and great-uncle Leo did." His pained expression twisted my stomach. His head shook. "Your grandfather may have helped, but it was *my family* who asked the favor. That family is also hers. This *legacy is* hers, and who knows what she thinks about it."

I knew what I would. I knew what I did. There were monsters residing in our world, and I didn't have clean hands either. She had a right to fear us and definitely had a right to fear me.

I'd done some dark shit.

"My parents have been through so much." He held his arms. "If Sloane runs again, I know it's going to break them. I don't know if she's really ready, but even if she's not, I can't keep this shit from my folks."

He wouldn't, and I couldn't. We couldn't keep our parents out any longer, and I refused. "We're not keeping anything from them. We'll call them up. Call mine, Thatcher's, and Wells's too. We'll tell them the truth but convince them all to give Sloane at least a night. It's late anyway, and she should have that. Just one night before everything changes."

I didn't know what I was saying, but I did know what I was doing. I was still fighting for her.

Because I still loved her.

I was willing to fight *our families* who I knew would come crashing through the walls of this place if they knew she was here, but I didn't care. I didn't want her to run again, and maybe if she didn't, we could keep her here.

I could keep her.

Wolf's head was shaking before I even finished what I said. "You know they're not going to stand for that."

I did know that, and it'd probably take all four of us to make them see the light, but we had to try. "Well, we're just going to have to convince them. If we don't want her to run again, we have to do this delicately."

"That's why I went to her by myself." Wolf's knuckle brushed his nose. "I guess Thatcher had something. I figured if he got her to trust him that way, I'd try it." He smirked a little before looking at me. "I still might kill him, though."

"Only if I get the first shot."

Wolf laughed, sitting back. "Before the families come, you should probably talk to her. I told her none of this was your fault. The lies and shit, and it sounds like your grandfather was actually trying to help her."

I'd believe that with cold hard evidence but wasn't trying to think about that now. We needed to focus on what we'd say to our parents, and I would talk to her. I just didn't know when.

Let alone how.

CHAPTER
EIGHTEEN

Sloane

I closed out my academy email account.

I'd been reading the messages too many times.

In a huff, I got up, then headed to Bru's room. He was up and watching TV.

I could see why.

I stiffened where I stood upon seeing Callum, *Dorian's grandfather* Callum. He stood at the front of a large home, wide with thick columns, and he had about a billion microphones in front of his face.

Still in his bed clothes, Bru angled around, waving me to sit with him. He must have heard me come in.

I joined him but was slow about it.

"He's been making announcements all morning," Bru said. "Ones about you."

Ones about me.

I stayed completely still when the news people calmed down enough to let him talk.

"We've heard from representatives from the Mallick family," he said, nodding. He wore a suit, but it was barely 7 AM. "And it's true what you've heard. They tell us Pilar Mallick has been officially found, but other than that, we know no more than you. Thank you."

Shocked, I sat back, watching as Callum retreated back up the steps and into that big home he'd stood in front of. My brother flicked off the news, then rested an arm on the back of the couch.

"Looks like they know," he said, his eyebrows narrowed. "And he's right, the press do too. The news stations have been talking about it all morning. I guess the family reached out to them all and told them you've been found."

I leaned forward, breathing into my hands. This was news. Especially because last night Ares had come in and said he'd give me a night. He said the evening had already been enough, and since it'd been late, I should just stay put. We were supposed to talk about everything today, and what I'd ultimately decided. I wanted to meet his family.

I needed to see who I was.

Of course, no one had been shocked more than me that he'd wanted me to take that night, and if the family knew about me now, why weren't they here? I feel like they would have been up here like they had the hospital.

"Are you sure you're ready for this?" Bru frowned, angling in my direction. He was swimming in his clothes, things Thatcher had gotten for him to wear. Thatcher had gotten me stuff to wear too, but they'd been Bow's things and way too small. He said his mother wasn't much different in size, so he ended up thrifting me some stuff after I told him my size. Bru's head tilted. "Once all this starts, there is no putting it back in the bottle."

All this was already starting. It had been for a while now, but I'd just been too scared and confused to be a part of it.

"I need to meet them," I said. The words still foreign in

my head, they felt even weirder coming out of my mouth. "It's going to be fine. I'm going to be good."

He looked at me for a while, and though he nodded, I knew my brother. He wasn't okay if I wasn't okay, and I hadn't been a lot these days. He sat forward with the remote. "Did Callum reach out to you via email? I saw you on Thatcher's laptop earlier."

I had been on there and definitely not in a productive way.

If my brother saw what I'd been reading *again*, he didn't say anything about it, and he did know about the emails. He'd caught me reading them before. It was something we didn't talk about, and I definitely didn't want to talk about it. Especially after last night.

Someone else hadn't wanted to talk about them either.

Dorian hadn't wanted to be vocal at all really, and that'd been okay with me. Knowing about who I was or not, he'd still lied to me. "No, I haven't."

"Figured." Bru folded his hands. "He reached out to me. Said he was just checking up but he didn't want to bother you. Sent me an email."

"What did he say?" I asked the question with my breath unsteady, trying not to fidget but I couldn't help it. We'd found out so many things about him, both of us. They'd been things he had told us himself, but still…

There was just so much darkness.

"Not much." Bru rubbed his hands. "Sounded like he was just extending a hand, and that he was around for us. Also that he was sorry for, well, everything." His head lowered. "He's reached out a few times, but I haven't responded. Probably should have told you about it, but I didn't want to stress you out."

It was funny how things had changed. Bru was always trying to take care of me these days.

"I just can't believe he lied to us. Did all those things." He shook his head. "I just don't know how to feel. He was so cool and took care of us."

I got what he was saying, and if I was being real, I was feeling conflicted too. He'd been the only one I could trust, and he had taken care of us.

But he'd just done so many dark things.

I didn't know if those occurrences were of the past, a history of a man who'd done the wrong thing and, today, *had* tried to be different. He'd only been kind to my brother and me, and with my own family history I'd learned, I wasn't so sure if it was fair to damn him.

I wasn't sure if things were so black and white.

These were thoughts and things I'd have to deal with, and I added them to the laundry list I seemed to be compiling these days.

"I want to respond and at least tell him we're okay." Bru's jaw moved. "Only if that's okay with you, of course. I don't know if we can trust him, but I at least want to thank him. He was just so cool with us."

It seemed my brother was conflicted too, and he had been closer to Callum than I had. I rubbed his arm. "You don't need my permission."

"I don't, but this is all fucking crazy, especially for you, and I need to know you're okay." He sighed. "I'll only talk to him if it's good with you."

I appreciated him doing that, and I told him that right as someone knocked on the door. I got up to answer and definitely wasn't prepared.

The dark prince had bags on his arms.

Two dark duffels hung off broad shoulders, his head snapping up. He pulled tendrils of his golden tresses out of his eyes, and though he'd knocked, he'd distanced from the door like he hadn't expected it to open. "Hey."

One word. One stupid freaking *word*, and my body ceased

to function. I had thought I'd slam the door in his face the next time I saw him.

He'd been so cold.

The chill had physically emanated off him, and what few words he had said had come off completely passive aggressive. Like he was pissed *at me* when he had no right to be. I hadn't been the one who'd lied and definitely shouldn't be punished for it.

But I was being punished, consumed by him. I wanted to yell at him, but all I was doing was *staring* at him. His slouchy tee hit hard against his firm body, his denim jeans tapered at his waist and hugging thighs the size of about two boys his age. He had them cuffed and bunched above his military boots, but it never seemed to matter what he wore. He was still ridiculously beautiful, and here I was in shorts and an oversize tee, fully clothed but exposed.

Naked.

I felt bare in front of him, stripped down to nothing more than feelings and girly emotions. He kept doing that shit, and I hated I couldn't *breathe*.

"I brought you some clothes." He presented the bounty in front of me, one bag, then two when he lowered them to the floor. He righted to towering height. "They're your own clothes. I had Thatcher run over to your house and get them this morning. Don't know why he didn't do that the first time."

Probably because he didn't want to get caught doing something that could connect him to anything having to do with me and where I was. I'd been thrown yesterday when he said he was going to get my own paints and other gear for me from my house. I'd been making do with the craft store stuff he'd picked out for me, but it hadn't been ideal. He'd known that, but I'd never told him he had to get my stuff.

I had a feeling the gift was going to be his last-ditch effort to get me to come clean, and I did hate he had to keep my secret for me. I'd gone to see Bow about it first, but he caught me before I could find her.

I suppose I probably shouldn't have gone to ask her in the first place. All this stuff and what I was going through was my burden, not theirs.

Bru cut in beside me, and when he witnessed me, the bags, and Dorian, he frowned.

"Morning, Prinze," he said, cold himself. He definitely knew how Dorian was and the lies the dark prince had told me. I'd cleared up some of them last night before we'd gone to bed, but I couldn't do them all. I mean, there were still lies he'd told me. Bru angled a look down. "What's this?"

"Clothes." Dorian's attention didn't leave me, and a wash of molten lava seared through my soul, my flesh. He glanced at Bru. "Your own clothes. Had Thatcher get them."

"Hmm." Bru didn't leave my side. "Well, thank you."

He was dismissing him and definitely being rude about it. Honestly, he was probably doing the job I should be doing.

Then why don't you do it?

Probably for the same reason I couldn't stop looking at him.

Dorian pushed his hands into his back pockets. "Well, breakfast is ready. We got it all set up downstairs on the first floor, and you don't have to worry about anything. I had the house cleared so no one will be bombarding you or anything."

He had?

"We'll talk about stuff so, yeah." Dark eyes eased in my direction. "Hope the clothes help."

He walked away, but I wasn't sure he would have had my brother not been standing there.

"Tool," Bru muttered under his lips. He picked up the bags. "But at least he got us clothes."

I suppose there was that.

I had a thought after Dorian left Bru and me to get dressed

that maybe the dark prince had wanted to talk to me. I mean, he could have easily sent up Thatcher or Wells, and bringing my stuff actually sounded like something Ares would do. He'd been the last one to leave last night, but it hadn't been him at the door today.

I wasn't completely sure I was ready to talk to Dorian, but I wasn't sure I would have much of a choice. We'd need to talk eventually and…

Ares waited outside the elevators when Bru and I eventually came down, and it was so freaking weird to see him and Bru today. They acknowledged each other politely, respectfully, but they both had this weird territorial dance about them when they tried to establish who would take which of my sides. Clearly, they were adjusting to whatever this new relationship was between us as well. I mean, they were technically both my siblings.

"Y'all sleep okay?" Ares asked, walking backward down the hall. "I see you got your clothes."

I'd chosen jeans and a nice top, Bru something similar. I nodded. "Great, thanks."

"Great." He looked at Bru. "How about you? You good? Sleep well?"

He was trying here, and Bru shrugged.

"Fine," Bru said before glancing at me. His look said it all about how weird this all was, and though I agreed, I gave him a reassuring nod. This would be weird.

Especially for me.

I could smell all the food before we even got into the large kitchen deep in the heart of Windsor House. I'd never really gotten to explore the large castle, so seeing the expansive kitchen ready and able to serve Maywood Heights's elite definitely didn't disappoint. It had large windows that let the sunlight in, marble countertops, and probably about six or seven fridges. I didn't know much about Windsor House except that people in the Court got to use it. I assumed it was some kind of a country club.

Wells, Thatcher, and Dorian sat at a table with all the food by the windows, but they weren't by themselves. Two women sat with them, one significantly smaller than the other. I recognized them both, but only the smaller one leaped out of her chair.

"Sloane!" Bow Reed's chair actually toppled over she left it so quickly. She rushed at me, and when she grabbed me, I grabbed her right back.

She was shaking.

"Oh my God." She hooked her little arms around my neck, and I realized I was shaking too. I was and, for some reason, couldn't stop it. Bow braced me tight. "Are you okay? Are you okay?"

I hugged her back, hugged her *hard*, and I had my eyes closed. It was like realizing you were missing someone once you had them back, or maybe it was just the connection.

Maybe I just needed the hug.

I felt myself seep into it, squeezing her. "Hey, little rabbit."

"Hey." Again, she was shaking when she let go, but she didn't release my hands. She had her academy uniform on, and that was something I hadn't missed. School. She shook my hands. "Oh my God. Your face."

She touched it, and I raised a hand.

"It's fine," I said. "I'm okay."

"You swear?" She squeezed my hands, her round cheeks flushed. "How can you be okay? You're not okay."

I wasn't, but I was trying. "I'm fine."

Whether she believed me or not, I didn't know, but right away her arms came around me once more.

"I can't believe Thatcher didn't tell me about you." She let go, looking at me. "He said you came to look for me first."

I had because, out of everyone, I didn't know who to trust. Bow and I had our history, but she'd never lied to me.

She'd always been a friend.

"You're my friend," I said, trying not to fucking cry, but Bow already was. She wiped away her tears, and when I helped her, she laughed.

"I am your friend." She pulled a handkerchief out of her pocket, and this girl would have one of those. She had another one of her shiny broaches on where a tie might go, her hair up in a little brown bun. She wiped her face. "I'll always be your friend. You're my friend too."

Oh my fucking God.

I blew out a breath to keep away the tears, and it took me a second to realize we had an audience. The boys at the table had all gotten to their feet, and the woman who was with them was behind Bow. She waited patiently, and I'd only seen her on a television screen. She'd been with her husband, son, and the rest of the Legacy families. She'd been at the hospital and come for me too.

Dorian's mom.

Even if I hadn't seen her with him on the television, I would have known. Especially when he came to stand beside her. He completely dwarfed her in size, but they had the same eyes, a dark and alluring ebony that sucked you inside them.

And in my case, never let go.

I tried not to pay attention to her son, as he approached with his mother, and besides the eyes, he did have similar features to her. They were subtle and not quite like how Dorian resembled his dad, who I'd also seen through the TV and previously. His softer features came from her, the woman fairer in complexion and with hair nearly as dark as mine and Ares's. She wore a pair of bib overalls, and sported a messy bun, Converses on her feet. Honestly, if I didn't know this was his mom, I might have thought she was a young hip aunt or older cousin.

"Mom, this is Sloane," Dorian introduced, and suddenly, our circle opened. Ares and Bru, who'd stood behind me, came forward and immediately found places at my sides again.

Ares took hold of the right. "My twin," he said, and I glanced at Bru. He had his hands folded, seemingly unaffected by what Ares said, but I could imagine this was different for him. I mean, it had always been him and me.

Dorian's mom took inventory of the three of us standing there, her attention bouncing back between Ares and me on the last rotation.

"I can tell," she stated, her smile quaint, kind. I'd seen glimmers of it within Dorian's own features, but it was like he fought it more often than not. When he was kind, it was always through action, and he never made a big declaration about it, like when he'd brought my brother's and my clothes this morning. Dorian's mom glanced back at Dorian. "Pregnancy test?"

I blinked, having forgotten about the trick I'd played when I'd first arrived. I'd sent Dorian's mom a pregnancy test to fuck with him.

Dorian's lips parted, as well as the rest of the room's. News of the pregnancy test scandal had definitely gotten around the halls of Windsor Prep. Dorian rubbed his neck. "Uh, yeah."

So, she knew about me and, well, us. Or at least *that*.

Honestly, I didn't know what the dark prince and I had anymore. There'd been so many lies, and I could imagine he'd never had to tell his mom we'd been something. Dorian himself had introduced me to Ares's mom once.

My mom.

My brain was still trying not to reject things, and I swallowed in front of Dorian's mom. "I'm sorry about that."

Her smile widened, her head shaking. "You know, it never ceases to amaze me how much my son is like his father." She adjusted the bag on her arm. "Or I guess like his parents. His dad and I didn't get along either. At least not at first."

The pair of us eyed each other long enough I ended up severing the connection. It was just too much.

Mom shouldered her son before facing me. "And don't apologize, honey. It's okay. Really."

I nearly felt things were okay upon standing in front of her. There was something so soft and pleasant about her.

She placed a hand on her chest. "My name's December, and I guess I'm here because all of us adults decided to listen to our children. At least, well, on this issue." She glanced at all the kids in the room. "This is a delicate situation, and I'm here on behalf of all our families, I suppose." Her head tilted. "Your father, Sloane, is my best friend, and he and his wife are two of my dearest."

Ares gripped his wrist, his attention falling on me. I wasn't quite sure if I remembered being informed that Dorian's family and, well, ours had such close ties. I knew they were friends, but all the Legacy families were friends.

I suppose all the kids couldn't help but be so close to each other then, their parents close.

"I'm here as a neutral party because we all do understand how delicate all of this is. Delicate for you, Sloane, and your brother Bru." She smiled at him, obviously already having been told about him. "The parents were very quick to take things into our own hands in the beginning of all this and honestly hadn't thought about how that would affect either of you. I'm sure it's scary, so I'm here. Like I said, a neutral party."

The boys had all braced their arms, and Bow had the biggest smile on her face. She rubbed my shoulder, squeezing, and I could have cried.

I can't believe they did this.

They'd all managed to speak to their parents, and I didn't realize how much that would make all this easier. Easier for me.

Beside his mother, Dorian had his hands in his pockets,

but as soon as our gazes clashed, his averted a little. I wondered if he disagreed with all this.

Stop focusing on him.

I couldn't focus on him, not now. I might break if I did. I couldn't think about another damn thing.

"And if you don't mind, I'd like to speak with you in private, Sloane." December gestured toward Bru. "Your brother can come too if he likes. I just have a few questions for your sister."

Bru directed his focus to me, and I lifted a hand. "I'm okay. You can go."

"We won't go far." December waved toward the table filled with all that food. There was quite a spread there, pancakes. Bacon.

I had to cross in front of Dorian to get to it, and he opened his mouth like he was going to say something but stopped.

He directed the others out of the room in the end. They headed to a connecting room that had couches and a few TVs from what I could see. The majority of them ended up sitting on the couches, and I noticed Ares angle around, Bru too.

Dorian stayed by the archway, but when his mom tilted her head at him, he nodded. He left too and eventually, joined the others on the couch.

I didn't know what that meant. Especially when she smiled after.

"I suppose I first want to start with an apology." December laced her hands. "The adults really didn't think about how our abrasive measures would affect you. It took our kids to see it, and though we didn't want to listen, we realized they were right about that."

She didn't have to apologize. I understood.

"And I want to lead with no one wants to make you do anything that you don't want to do or would otherwise make you feel uncomfortable. You're eighteen, and you're completely in control of what happens from here. Even if you weren't, no one's going to force anything on you." She frowned. "All Ramses and Brielle want is for you to feel safe. That's priority, and we all feel that way."

My heart squeezed, my nod firm.

"And with that being said, I have some more difficult questions." She braced her hands. "As you know, Dorian's grandfather has been involved with your care and the well-being of you and your brother."

My lips parted, hers too.

"So I have to ask if he ever hurt you. You or Bru. We've talked to the kids, and they said that you explained he hadn't, but…" Taking her purse off, she placed it on the table. "I have to ask. He's been helping with everything surrounding the searches. *Appears to be helping* and claims he's always had your and your brother's best interest in mind, but we have to ask. The kids also explained you know the history there, so I'm sure you get why I'm asking."

I was sure this was difficult for her, asking me this. He'd hurt her family, her sister. I played with my hands. "He's only been kind to me. Never hurt Bru or me."

She acknowledged that, her head bobbing twice. "He was informed you were found this morning and has agreed to distance himself now that you and Bru have been safely found. He stated he was going to offer this to you both anyway after he helped you get back to Ramses and Brielle."

"He was. He tried." I ran though. "None of this… any of this was him. Everything was all Godfrey…" I swallowed. "Marilyn."

"And did they ever hurt you?" The question was even, her attention focused. "And if you can't answer that… if you don't feel comfortable speaking to me about that, it's okay. We can find someone appropriate to talk to you about anything delicate."

That wasn't necessary. I could talk about them.

"They were my parents." My voice strained a bit. I looked up at her. "I loved them."

I had, and I felt sick about it. I mean, I loved my kidnappers. What the fuck?

"That's okay, you know." December placed her hand on the table. "That's all right."

It's all right.

"They didn't hurt me," I forced out. "They did nothing like that. I had a normal childhood. My dad had a lot of depression but—" I shook my head. "Godfrey had a lot of depression and anxiety, but he was fine. Just sad. Sad a lot."

I guess I got that now.

"Okay." December laced her fingers. "Well, I guess I just have one more question, and that's if you've ever been here before. To Maywood Heights? There's obviously a proper investigation going on as far as your kidnapping, but I'm asking for Ramses and Brielle. Ares explained how he knew it was you with that charm. I think we're all wondering."

"I've never been here before." At least, that I knew of.

December's smile was sad, the only tell that any of this might have been difficult for her too. I wondered if we ourselves had met before, when I was a baby and all that. Odds were, she had if she was so close with, well, my dad. Mom too. "I suppose what happens next is up to you. You don't have to meet Ramses and Brielle. You can continue to live here, but we will have a team of security coming through. The press are monsters, and though my husband's father appears genuine, we'd like him to not have access to you or Bru. He's explained he's Bru's guardian with him being underage, but again, he's agreed to step back and allow us to take care of you both. He says it was always supposed to be that way anyway."

My heart squeezed, a tight twinge. He'd never been overbearing and always helpful. He'd always given us freedom, but I got the need for security too.

God, this was all so fucked.

The families didn't trust him, and I did get that. There was a history there, one beyond me and my understanding, and I got it.

Like my brother and his conflict, mine was there too, but I wouldn't disagree with the Legacy families' decision. I needed the distance as well. If anything to think about all this.

"Like I said, Ramses and Brielle just want you safe. Happy." Her smile lifted higher. "They're willing to wait as long as you need. We all are."

I had a feeling they were.

My heart ached again. "I want to meet them. I think Godfrey and Marilyn have stolen enough time." They had. They'd taken *everything* from me, and they weren't going to get any more.

"Okay then." December's voice was soft again and so kind. It made me feel like I was staring into a looking glass of what her son could be.

That was if he let himself.

I glanced up to see him easing into the archway again, and when I did, his mom angled around.

"Hey." He lifted a hand and was almost awkward about it. He rubbed his hands, one palm running over the other. "Everything okay? Guess I'm just making sure."

Because he needed control, didn't he? Always, because that was who he was. He didn't need for me to be okay, but himself. I looked away, but December smiled.

"Almost done, baby," she said, making him nod. He left, and another smile tugged at his mom's lips. "I tell you my son has me wrapped around his finger. All of us." She slid her purse into her lap. "He and the other boys were somehow able to convince the parents not to come here last night and hold off until morning to do anything."

So, the dark prince had been a part of the decision?

"But it was my son who suggested clearing this place out

and letting you live here." Her eyes warmed. "Said it'd be a good middle ground. A compromise for all of us and would give you more options that we all felt comfortable with."

I didn't know what to say about that. I mean, what could I say? I studied my hands. "Thank you for the option." And I really did appreciate it.

I more than appreciated it.

CHAPTER
NINETEEN

Sloane

I actually put on makeup that afternoon, powder and foundation. I didn't want to see that ugly bruise anymore, and I definitely didn't want Ares's parents to see it.

My parents.

I obviously was still trying to wrap my head around this, and it might be something I struggle with for a long time. I'd had two different parents for so long.

Forcing out a breath, I took one last look at the place I'd been calling home for a while. I was going to a new place today.

I was going to my house today.

Again, I tried to wrap my head around going to what had always been Ares's house. I was going to live at his big-ass mansion with Bru and, of course, Ares's parents.

Your parents.

I entered Bru's suite, expecting to find him. I was ready to go, but he wasn't in there when I stepped inside.

Ares sat in the middle of a made bed, but he got up when I entered the room. He pressed his hands down his jeans. "Hi."

"Hey." I eased into the room. "Where's Bru?"

Like he realized it was unusual he'd been sitting in here by himself, Ares glanced around the room. He directed his thumb toward the door. "He took the bags downstairs. I asked if I could speak to you for a second before we take off."

I nodded, and Ares and I both took up residence on the couch. Another thing I had to wrap my head around was just *being* with him. We had this close tie but were essentially strangers. We'd also been pretty shitty to each other when we first met, so yeah, this was different.

He rubbed his hands, the sleeves of his letterman jacket pushed up. "So, uh, it's a big day." He nodded. "Just kind of wanted to go over what's about to happen."

I'd been pretty much briefed on that. Before Dorian's mom had left, she said she was going to contact the Mallicks. Everything was getting set up there, set up for Bru and me to leave here and stay with them. I leaned forward. "Okay."

"Of course, everyone wanted to be there. Thatcher and Bow's parents, Wells's." He adjusted in his seat. "They all want to see you along with Dorian's god dad LJ and his wife, but the parents all discussed they'd hold off. Give you some space for a little while."

I'd met Thatcher and Bow's parents, but it'd been under different circumstances.

"My grandparents... my mom's parents and my dad's mom and her husband wanted to meet you too, but they're going to hold off for the same reason. My grandma Evie, my dad's mom, got remarried, but my grandpa Jimmy is my grandfather. I've known him my whole life, so yeah. He's my grandpa."

I understood that. All of this was a lot.

"I guess I just want to stress that there's still time to hold off. On a meeting, I mean?" His lips turned down. "My folks will understand."

I'd been told this by more than one person after I'd decided. They all wanted me to be comfortable. I appreciated that, but it was time. "I told you. I'm good. I'm ready."

"Okay." He sat back, releasing his breath like he'd been holding it. "I guess I just have one other thing. D's parents are going to be there. Royal, and December you met. Maybe they all thought that'd be a good buffer for you. Especially since you already met December." His jaw shifted. "D wants to be there too, but he won't be if you don't want him to."

I hadn't seen him since I'd come upstairs to get ready. "He asked you to talk for him? For him to me?"

"No, but I offered." His head tilted. "I know things are tense."

I was sure he knew everything, my life an open book.

"I told you this before, but the lies really weren't his fault."

I raised a hand. "If he wants to, he can be there." I wouldn't try to stop him, and with all those people there, we probably wouldn't be talking much anyway.

We wouldn't have to talk.

Another thing I was trying to wrap my head around was what his mom had said. It'd sounded like he had really fought for me. Me and my comfort.

But he'd been so cold before.

Maybe he was having his own conflict, but I was beyond trying to figure it out. I had so much on my plate already.

"That's the thing. It doesn't matter what he wants, and he knows that." Ares dropped an arm on the couch. "I'm not speaking for him, but I know he wants to be there. He does, but he doesn't want to be a hindrance either. He wants to support you, but won't be there if he knows his presence would make things worse for you."

This sounded consistent with what his mom had said about fighting for me and making me feel comfortable.

Why does he do this stuff?

The boy was like a brick wall, hard to get to, but once you did…

"He should be there," I finalized, making myself say it before I cancelled the thought in my mind. "Tell him it's fine."

We still had so much between us, but I'd be lying to myself if I didn't admit I wanted him there.

That I wanted his support.

My heart ached for it, just like my soul ached for what we'd been. My insides screamed for it, and I feared we never would get it back.

How could we?

So many lies had been said, and he hadn't trusted me before. That made it hard to trust him, and for obvious reasons. Trust was so, *so* important.

Ares studied me. "Okay. I'll text him. He's already gone ahead behind his mom. He was going to meet us there but leave if I said anything different."

I glanced away.

"Do you have anything for me then?" He opened his hands. "Any questions before this all starts happening, I mean."

I didn't have any questions, but I was glad he brought this up. I pinched at my sweater. "I know I'm your sister, and that you're my brother…"

"Your twin." He lifted a finger, chuckling. "And I get that's weird. It's weird for me too. Fuck, I've been looking for you, and it's still weird for me."

I knew he had. Someone had told me once.

I held my arms. "It is different. It's different for me, and it will be an adjustment, but I'm more concerned about Bruno." I shook my head. "I don't want him to get lost in all this, and I guess I'm asking you as a favor to help me make sure that doesn't happen." I nodded. "I want him looked out for. Taken care of."

His life had been upheaved too. He'd lost his real parents, found out they were kidnappers, and now, his only remaining family, he found out wasn't his own. He was being forced to move into a home full of strangers, and though he was being brave and putting on a tough exterior, I worried about him. I worried *for* him.

"I got his back, little," Ares said, and I rolled my eyes about the name. He chuckled. "Seriously, I do. I owe the kid. He looked out for you when I wasn't there, and I'll never forget that."

My heart squeezed. "Thank you."

"No problem."

"And enough with the *little* shit." I tossed a pillow at him, which he caught. Fucking *football players*. "I heard through the grapevine I'm actually older than you." Thatcher and Wells had been joking about it at breakfast.

Ares rolled his eyes now. "By five whole minutes, yes. But you're still little." He grinned. "The name's not going anywhere so get used to it."

I suppose I'd have to, wouldn't I? We were in each other's lives.

And it looked like that wasn't going away.

CHAPTER
TWENTY

Sloane

There were news vans and press outside of Ares's house, but the security kept them back. There were people in suits stationed outside the wide property, and they waved Ares's blue Hummer through the crowd.

"They haven't left since everything went public," Ares said, navigating. The shutters went off like popcorn, but with the dark tint of the Hummer's windows, the press probably couldn't see much.

Not that the fact stopped them.

They banged on Ares's car, but like stated, the security kept them back. They called my name and his, and considering Ares had a wolf (his football namesake) painted on the front of his ride, I was sure all these people knew he was in here, local press or not.

There were so many, and easily twice the amount of news vans that'd been stationed outside of Dorian's house recently. After the Mayberry scandal with his uncle had surfaced, his gated community had held a similar amount of attention.

But it was nothing like this.

This was *insane*, and thank God for the security. They kept the press away enough for Ares to navigate himself, my brother, and me inside. We'd all said goodbye to Thatcher, Wells, and Bow at Windsor House. They'd wanted to come too, of course. Especially Bow.

But like Ares had said, only a few people would be there today. The parents... *his parents* thought it'd be better that way.

Your parents.

Apparently, those plans included Dorian Prinze, who was there at the property when Ares pulled around back. Ares had to considering the media circus outside, and Dorian was stationed between two security personal, sitting on the steps of a back veranda, which gave views onto the property through wide windows. The dark prince got up, and the people actually sitting on the veranda did too. There was a man and a woman behind the glass, one blond, the other a deep brunette.

His parents.

They both came outside and joined their son, Dorian's dad just as striking as his mom. Dorian may have had his mother's eyes and softer features, but he had the angular jawline and strong disposition from no one else but his father. The two were like clones, the older version in a thick sweater with his arm around Dorian's petite mother. She had a jacket on, warming her arms, and waved at the car when Ares shut it off.

Ares immediately got out, but when I started to, Bru pushed forward. He'd been in the back seat.

"Prinze is here?" he asked, frowning, and I forgot I hadn't told him. Things had been moving quickly.

Unstrapping, I angled a look back. "He wanted to be here, and his parents are friends with Ramses and Brielle."

I hadn't been told what to call them yet, but I assumed

their names. Mr. and Mrs. Mallick felt weird, all of this just another thing I had to wrap my head around.

"I get them wanting to be here." Bru unstrapped too. He dropped his arms on the seats. "But it's Prinze, and he lied to you."

I knew he had, and I also knew we hadn't talked about it. "I said it's okay he's here, all right?" And I didn't want him arguing about this with me.

I was already arguing with myself about it.

The activity outside had ceased, and though Ares had gotten out of the car, he hadn't gone to talk with anyone. He was too busy with his sight focused in the Hummer. His head tilted at me, and I waved him off. We were fine in here.

Again, that was so *weird.*

It would take some adjustments being under the protective eye of Legacy. Especially when another watchful gaze appeared at Ares's right side. Dorian too was looking in here.

"Just as long as you're fine with it," Bru said, backing up and getting out. There was so much more I wanted to say to my brother, but I didn't. I'd never gotten a chance to really go over anything with him before he'd left to take the bags down this afternoon. He needed to know he had control in this situation too and should always talk to me if he needed something. I really didn't want him getting lost.

Promising myself I'd make sure that didn't happen, I did get out, but not on my own. Security ended up opening the door for me, and I thanked the woman who got the door. Ares joined my side then. Dorian was in between his parents, a perfect mashup of their beauty and poise.

The dark prince was nervous. He kept wiping his hands on his jeans, but when no one said anything, he stepped forward.

"Dad, this is Bru and Sloane." He gestured between us. He stopped on me. "I suppose you both already met my mom."

He fidgeted again when his mom came forward and took my hand.

"I hope the drive was okay with all that madness," she said, obviously referencing the press. After Bru and I got out of the car, Dorian's dad dismissed the two members of security we had, so they could do another walk-through of the property just in case. I'd heard him. She placed her other hand on mine. "Hopefully some of that will die down soon."

"Yeah, hopefully."

She smiled at Bru. "And good to see you."

Bru took her hand, shaking it. At this point, Dorian's dad waited, patient, with his son by his side. A smile graced his dad's lips during the exchange, and when his wife introduced him, he offered his hand as well.

"Nice to meet you, Bru," his dad said before his gaze fell on me.

"Royal, this is Sloane," December said, her hand cuffing around his arm. She leaned in. "Ares's twin."

"Definitely can see that." Royal directed a look between the Legacy boys, his lips turned down at them both. "And you kids missed that how?"

I'd give them credit that it wasn't obvious. I mean, we weren't identical, but if the fact had been put out there, people definitely wouldn't be surprised to know.

Hindsight was twenty-twenty, I guess. At least, in their case. The boys ended up shrugging, and when Royal offered his hand, I took it.

"Nice to meet you, Sloane," he said, his shake short, polite. He definitely didn't linger, and that might have been for my sake. These people all probably thought I'd run if given the chance.

You had before.

My gaze fell on the dark prince. In fact, he hadn't looked at anyone but me since I'd arrived.

December was hugging Ares, her hands on his face when

she came away. I'd heard during breakfast she was his godmom, and that made sense if Ramses was her best friend.

"Where's Mom and Dad?" Ares asked, and December returned to Royal's side. Royal put his arm around her, hugging her close, and I realized I'd never really seen exchanges like that growing up. Marilyn had died when I'd been so young.

"Inside. Brielle was pacing so…" December studied Royal, whose smile was tight, pleasant but tight nonetheless. She placed her hand on his chest. "Ramses thought it'd be a good idea for her to get a hot tea. Take a break. He took her inside to make one for her, and we told them we'd come get them both when Bru and Sloane got here."

Ares had mentioned sweet things his dad did for his mom before.

They sound so nice.

The guilt did sit heavy that I'd run from them. In running from everything else and every*one* else, they'd gotten caught in the crossfire.

December faced Dorian. "Baby, can you go get them?"

Dorian started to, but Ares cut in.

"Let me go," he said before glancing at me. "Will you be okay?"

"She's with us, honey. She'll be fine," December said, and once Ares got that, he took two veranda stairs at a time up to the house. I hadn't been to the back of the house aside from the garage, and it was crazy. The large home kissed the sky, the home's gardens and widespread landscape so lovely back here.

Of course, security strode through it. People with their fingers to their earpieces who smiled pleasantly at us over hedges. That was all my fault, all this because of me.

Chaos.

Forcing my breath to steady, I swallowed and stayed close to Bru.

"Maybe we should get our bags," he said to me, but Royal lifted a hand.

"We can take care of that. Son?" Royal waved Dorian after him, and though Dorian went, he took a beat. He was *always* taking a beat and looking at me while he did.

And why did my breath stop?

It did, and it steadied nearly immediately after. Like one subtle acknowledgment from him was enough to remind me of something, and no matter how much I ran from it, I couldn't deny it. He was *here*.

And he was here for me.

He and his father came back from the trunk with Bru's and my bags, and though Royal reunited with December, Dorian took my empty side. He said nothing, just standing there, but when that veranda door opened and three people came out of it, I grabbed his arm. I grabbed my brother's hand too, but...

I squeezed the solid muscle, shaking when Ares arrived with two people behind him. The three were making their way down the steps, and for some reason, I couldn't let go of the dark prince.

"Don't be scared," he whispered, and our gazes clashed, eyes locked. He hooked his arm, allowing the death grip I had on him to stay. He smiled slow. "They're more nervous than you."

I couldn't breathe again, swallowing, and suddenly, we were moving. *Dorian* was moving me closer to the three people making their way down the stairs. I didn't let go of him, nor did I let go of Bru.

Bru squeezed my hand, and he may have noticed my hand on Dorian too. If he had, he didn't say anything, and the only thing I was certain of was two facts. One was that Ares Mallick looked exactly like his dad and mom.

And I did too.

Ramses was tall and even more so than his football-playing son, his hair a wash of thick curls that were rich in dark color. They were way tamer than his son's and a lot shorter, his shoulders broader, but the two definitely had similar features. Ramses had his hands on Brielle's shoulders, the woman wearing a sweater dress under an ivory trench coat. She looked so official, *the mayor*. Her honey-gold complexion was only slightly fairer than Ramses's, and I wondered about their ethnicities.

I guess I wondered about mine.

Air intake became harsh again, the woman so lovely. Her brown-black hair was bumped under and rested on one of her shoulders. She had silver hair, but just a strip of it on one side, which seriously made her look like a superhero. I recalled having that thought before when I'd initially met her at school, but that meeting had been different. I hadn't known I'd met *her* at the time.

My mom.

"Sloane and Bru, this is Ramses and Brielle." December introduced us, and I noticed her voice had changed. It was thick with emotion, and when I glanced at her, I noticed a sheen coated her eyes. She blinked it away quickly before facing the Mallicks. "Ramses, this is Sloane and her brother Bru. Brielle, I know you met at least Sloane."

She had, but again, it'd been different.

We looked at each other, and I could tell we were both studying the other. Had she known then? At least, some part of her?

Neither of us said anything in the moment, maybe too shocked to. I didn't know why she didn't say anything, but I'd been in complete dismay. I noticed one of Ramses's hands leave his wife's shoulders in our silence, and he directed it toward my brother.

"Bru," he said, and I was happy for that buffer. It was like I couldn't make my mouth work, and it was possible Brielle had the same problem. Ramses smiled at Bru. "Welcome to our home."

He placed his other hand on top of my brother's, and his voice cracked. It was only slight, but I noticed. It was also enough to cause Brielle to place her fingers to her lips and December to squeeze her husband's arm.

"Thank you for having me," Bru said before shaking Brielle's hand too. She said something similar to what Ramses said. Her voice didn't crack, but it sounded raspy.

I was still frozen before her, before them both, and a hand came over mine. It gripped the hand on his arm, and a reassuring squeeze followed.

"They're more nervous than you."

I couldn't see Dorian. I couldn't *look* at Dorian, but I knew he was there.

It proved to be enough.

I was able to let go of him and my brother to approach Ramses and Brielle, and I recognized so many of my own features between them. Especially Brielle. She was older, but each sweeping angle of her defining features I definitely recognized in the mirror, her nose button-tipped and her lips like two soft strokes of a paintbrush. She wore a red lipstick, and whenever I did, I looked exactly like that.

"You and I have met, Sloane," she said, nodding. "Though, of course, I didn't know. I..." She glanced back at her husband, her fingers touching her mouth again. She shook her head before facing me. "I'm happy you're here, and that you felt safe enough to come."

I did feel safe. I felt overwhelmed, but safe. My throat constricted. "I'm sorry I ran."

"Oh, honey." She took my hand, and I thought I'd *die*. A wave of emotion crashed over me, and I held onto her. We held onto *each other*, and I think we both needed to in that moment. She squeezed my hand. "We're sorry. We're *all* sorry.

We hadn't been thinking about you or your brother, and had we been, things probably would have been different."

They shouldn't blame themselves for *me*. Me running wasn't their fault and something I still had to deal with. I wanted to run now.

I'm chaos.

I closed my eyes, trying not to shed tears. I was a fucking mess.

"You've done nothing wrong, sweetheart," Ramses said, and out of the two, he appeared to wear his emotions the most. At least, in the moment. He was blinking a lot, and though he kept everything in like me, his struggle was clear. He placed his hand on top of mine and Brielle's, and when he grabbed Ares, I thought I would cry.

Ramses hooked an arm around his son, my… brother. Ares had his arms braced, but when his dad grabbed him, Ares pushed an arm around him. Ramses pressed his mouth to Ares's head. "We're all going to be okay, all right?" Ramses said, then glanced at Bruno. He smiled at him. "All of us. We are *all* going to be okay and get through this."

Bru nodded at Ramses, and when Bruno breathed out a harsh breath, I knew this was difficult for him too. Ramses waved him into the circle. He *welcomed* him.

So kind.

The words of a dark prince touched me again, one that wasn't so far away. Because in this circle, his parents touched Ramses and Brielle, their hands on their backs, but their son went another place. Dorian had one hand on Ares.

But the other was on me.

CHAPTER
TWENTY-ONE

Sloane

It was an emotional day, an emotional night. Ramses and Brielle gave Bru and me a tour of their home, and that was nice without Ares's partygoers. They had a beautiful home, and after, we all sat down to dinner with the Prinzes. I got to hear my birth story there and how I'd been sick at the hospital. I'd been underweight and hadn't adjusted as well as Ares had when we'd been born. He'd been underweight too, but his organs had been more developed. Because of my issues, I'd required more care. I'd spent a lot more time *away* from them, and during that period, I'd been taken.

And that was it really.

It was such a simple story, but so complex for all those involved. Godfrey and Marilyn had ruined my life, and now, I carried their namesake. I mean, I went by *Sloane*. It was all so fucked, and that was when things kind of got emotional. It was hard for Ramses and Brielle to tell the story, and eventually, that was when the Prinzes would sway the conversation. They were a good buffer, kept things light, and Dorian was *so* much like his parents. His dad carried a strong air about him that made you just want to respect and listen to him, and his mom, well…

She was lovely.

He was like the perfect mashup of them both, and it was nice to have him there too. He talked to Ares mostly, but cut in when he saw the empty spaces in the conversation. The ones where Bru and I couldn't speak when we were asked about anything related to our parents.

His parents.

My brain was going to have to do a lot of reprogramming, and gratefully, I didn't have to say a whole lot. The adults in the room just seemed content to have me and my brother there, and I did get to talk to Brielle's parents, as well as Ramses's. The couples called in separately via FaceTime, and I got to find out that I was Syrian on Ramses's side, Mexican and Puerto Rican on Brielle's, and European on both. It was wild to find that out, and emotional too. Ramses's mom was crying while talking to me, and that was hard. It was *all* hard, and this was day one.

Maybe tomorrow would be easier.

The adults got Bru and me set up in rooms near Ares's, and we did eventually say goodbye to Royal and December. December ended up giving me her line just in case I needed it, and both offered to be around if my brother or I needed anything at all. I got that a lot from everyone today. If I needed something, they were all there for me.

I guess I did have a lot of support.

I was told I'd get to meet the other Legacy parents too at some point, but *at this point*, I was exhausted. I said goodnight to Bru, and after, I attempted to find my room, but there were so many rooms in this house. So many, in fact, I missed mine. I ended up reaching for the door to a bathroom as someone else was opening it.

The dark prince was shirtless.

A muscled torso and broad physique swallowed up the door frame that surrounded it. He was coming out and had a thick terry cloth towel bunched and tucked under his bicep. His feet bare, we just about collided, nothing but a pair of low-riding jeans sitting on Dorian's defined hips.

"Sorry," he edged out. Out of the bathroom and in front of me, he loomed large above. He blinked. "My bathroom is out of towels so…"

He tugged the one from under his arm, lifting it, and my mouth parted. He was staying here?

"You're, um," I paused, backing away a little. He was too close. "You're staying here."

I hadn't been told this.

His nod firm, he tucked the rolled towel back under his arm. "Uh, yeah." He tugged the door closed, then pointed back. "Did you need in there? I assumed your room had a bathroom."

It did.

If I could find it.

"I'm kind of lost," I admitted. I scratched my ankle with bare toes. "Big house."

It was a big house.

But I guess not big enough.

It wasn't enough to avoid him, or how much space he did take up. He stepped forward. "I can take you there. You're just down the hall from Ares, right?"

Down the hall was like a mile in this place. "I'm okay. It's good for me to get to know the house anyway."

His mouth came together, but even after another firm nod, he didn't move. He tapped the air with his towel. "I'm just here for Ares and, I guess, Bru." His jaw shifted. "The parents thought it'd be a good idea, and Thatcher and Wells are somewhere around here too. Probably with your brother and Wolf."

I hadn't asked, and he could come and go as he pleased.

"Not sure how long I'll be here, and Wells and Thatcher are only staying the night. Or, I guess, just Wells is." He braced the towel. "My god dad, Knight, really gave it to Thatch for everything. The secrets and all that, so he's going to be heading out soon."

I cursed internally. His secret was actually mine.

"He's grounded for basically eternity." Dorian cuffed his arm, and I shook my head.

"I didn't mean to get him in trouble." I hadn't and hated that I had. Things had just gotten so messed up.

So much pain. So much… madness.

There was so much, and I was at the heart of it. All of this *me.*

Chaos.

I blinked away, overwhelmed again, and it took me a second to notice Dorian had closed a little space. It was enough for me to notice how his hands wringing that towel roved his shoulder muscles, a flush over his tan skin. "You shouldn't feel bad about that, and I get why he did it." He wet his lips. "I didn't at first, but I did once I thought about it. He did that for you, and you trusted him, and I'm sure you felt not a lot of that was going around."

I hadn't. In fact, I'd trusted no one and definitely not Dorian himself.

"I know I would have done the same. If you gave me a secret, I mean." An edge to his voice, he glanced away before looking at me. "I guess, we have a lot to talk about. You and me."

My heart raced, pumping, clenching. A door opened down the hallway, and I noticed we both did something.

We stepped apart.

The pair of us had gotten dangerously close, but Ramses entering the hallway took all that away. He came down it in a dark sweater, his hands together. "Everything okay?"

We both nodded, as Ramses joined us both. He had his

hands in his pockets at this point and took a second to glance between myself and the dark prince. He eyed him. "This isn't going to be a problem with you being down the hall from each other, right?"

The question was one hundred percent directed at Dorian and something totally a parent would say.

A dad.

A flutter touched my chest, and though I hadn't gotten to talk to Ramses one on one, I wanted to. He seemed so nice. Both of them.

Dorian worked his fingers through his hair. "No, sir. I was actually just saying goodnight to Noa."

Noa…

Only he called me that, the muscle inside my rib cage squeezing again. Especially when that dark gaze fell on me. "Goodnight, Noa."

"Goodnight."

And with that, Dorian left us both. Shaking his head, he muttered something to himself. I couldn't hear it, but he seemed to be chastising himself about something. He'd said we had a lot to talk about, and we did.

"Irony is something else." Ramses had his hands tucked under his arms, his smile on Dorian. "I was pretty much in love with his mother in high school."

I had to do a double-take, thinking I didn't hear him right, and Ramses chuckled.

"The universe obviously had other plans," he said, his smile on me now. "It's a good thing too. Otherwise, I would have missed out on meeting the love of my life."

It was hard not to see that today, the amount of love and affection he gave Brielle. It matched the amount of thought and attentiveness he gave her, but she hadn't been the only one to receive it. He'd said we'd all get through the chaos of this situation, and he'd extended that to my brother. He'd made sure to look out for him, and I hadn't even asked.

He'd just done it.

"Thank you for what you did today," I said, his head tilting. "For what you said to Bru and including him." He had done that, *all day* he'd done that. There wasn't a moment where Bru hadn't been invited to be a part of the conversation, and Ramses had stayed at the helm of that. He included him. No questions asked, and he wasn't even his own.

Ramses pocketed his hands. "You both are so important to this family. Important to Brielle and me." His voice thickened, and it was hard to watch him struggle. He seemed to be the peacemaker in the craziness today, the one with the reassurances, but he had his own battles. I mean, how couldn't he?

He'd lost a child too.

"I want you both to feel welcome," he said. "Things are difficult for you both, and it's important you two feel safe."

I swallowed, nodding. "Thank you."

"No ask is too big, all right?" he continued. "If you or Bru need anything at all, you let Brielle or me know. We'll get you anything you need. Do anything you need."

He really was nice, kind and so quick to make sure others were feeling good. He did, and to the point where it felt like he was ignoring even himself and what he was no doubt going through like the rest of us.

"But I feel like you're a lot like your dad."

The dark prince's words struck me in that moment, and I shook my head before I did something stupid. Something like cry or worse, and I'd been doing so good today. I'd managed not to cry at all in front of strangers.

I'd managed not to cry in front of him too.

Dorian being there today had done so much for me, and my emotional reserves only worsened in front of Ramses. Ramses rubbed his hands after what he said. Like he didn't know what to do with them, and I wanted to thank him for something else. He and Brielle had had so much patience with me today. They'd give me *space,* and there were moments like this where I noticed it. Moments where it looked like it took every fiber of their beings to resist and give me that space.

When all they really wanted to do was something else.

I felt like some of that was in me too. Like there was a compulsion within me to run to these strangers and cry my eyes out, both for them and with them. Unlike myself, they actually remembered me…

Where I'd been fortunate enough to be spared.

I eventually did find my bedroom that night, and because I hadn't expected anyone to be there, I know I had tears in my eyes.

She saw them.

Bow Reed was sitting on my bed, beaming, but she stopped when she saw me. She stood. "Sloane?"

I suppose she'd been asked to be here like the other Legacy boys. I could assume anyway.

God, they all really do care.

"It was supposed to be a surprise," she said, looking around. She put her hands together. "I asked if I could stay the night. Is that okay?"

It was more than okay, but I couldn't seem to find the words. I just wanted to *cry*, finally cry, and she came over.

She didn't say a word, and when she saw my tears, she hugged me, her little body just holding me, which probably looked hilarious. I was so much taller than her.

"It's okay," she said, letting me sob into her hair. She touched mine. "Is there anything I can do?"

She was already doing it.

She just didn't know it.

TWENTY-TWO

Dorian

"Yeah, I can get you what you need." Thatcher swiveled around in the computer chair, legs stamped out, fingers folded. He opened his hands. "But why are you asking me to."

Hacking into any database wasn't a thing for my friend, not at his level of technological experience. Knowing the ins and outs of how online security worked from his dad's security company gave him that, so getting access to a few digital records wouldn't be an issue.

But of course, that wasn't why he was looking at me the way he was now.

Pushing the sleeves of my academy jacket up, I leaned forward. "You and I both know justice hasn't been served." I nodded. "I need to know any and all players involved in Noa's case."

I was aware the parents were conducting their own investigations surrounding Sloane's kidnapping. They could do that, and what I was doing wouldn't interfere with it. I just needed my own answers.

I needed my own closure.

Thatcher shifted weight between his feet, his chair moving. I'd caught him and the tech lab in a rare moment where either him or Wells weren't boning a chick. In Wells's case, I usually caught him with dudes more. He'd been hooking up with a couple teammates recently, guys who were closeted and weren't as in touch with their sexuality as himself. I was pretty sure his hookups both knew about the other, but who knew. Thatcher and Wells tended to go through them, Ares too but not as of late. He'd had his mind on other things.

Gone, obviously, were those days for me, long gone, and I got nothing but Thatcher's sigh in front of me.

"And what will that do for you besides drive you fucking crazing?" He had his jacket draped over the computer desk, and he pushed his arms through it. Leaving the collar popped, he crossed his arms. "I think you're channeling, my guy. Things are fucking shit right now, and you're needing something to control."

My friend thought he knew me, didn't he?

Thatcher frowned. "Of course, I can get you Sloane's adoption records." Thatcher clicked around, putting the monitor in front of him to sleep. "I can, but I don't see the point."

He didn't see one, but I did.

"I mean, what are you going to do?" he asked. "Hunt every fucker down that had anything to do with Sloane's kidnapping? It's crazy."

I didn't ask for his opinion, and what I did or did not do with the records had nothing to do with him. "I need to know who was involved in this. You can't just adopt a kid who's been *kidnapped* without knowing a few people." And if those people were out there, they needed to be found. "Noa deserves justice."

"Yeah, she does. I agree." He threw fingers through the dark wave that normally fell over his eyes. He let go, and it sprung back, earrings in both his ears today. "But we both know that's not what this is about. You're going stir-fucking-crazy because you haven't talked to her, and now, you're asking me to do shit I don't want to do."

I didn't like what he had to say.

I didn't like even more that he was right.

I hadn't talked to Sloane, but it wasn't because I didn't want to. She had so much more shit to deal with right now, and as far as us… us…

I *needed* this right now, and I needed him to help me. I needed to feel fucking useful for once instead of the fuck up I was and continued to be in her life. "I need less of your opinions right now and more of your help."

"Yeah." He shook his head, expelling a harsh breath. "I'll get you what you need by the end of the day."

Good.

"But I think you should at least talk to Sloane about this." He grabbed his bag off the desk, standing up. "These are her records you're looking into, and this secret shit isn't looking good on any of us."

He would know, wouldn't he? And though I hadn't killed him for what he'd done, I still wasn't happy about it. I started to say that, but then the door opened, and my buddy angled around.

We weren't alone anymore.

"Thatcher?" A head eased into the lab, a body following. It wasn't rare for girls to just find their way in here. This entire school knew what Legacy got up to behind these walls, and often, they just wanted to get in on it. Another hookup in here be damned.

That wasn't the case today, and I got up, two things hitting me. One, I was glad we hadn't been disrupted like a second earlier.

I was already in hot water with her.

And two, no matter how many times I saw the little fighter and was around her and breathing her air, it never *ever* got any easier to be around her. We'd eaten at the same dinner table multiple nights this week, and I still felt my insides crumble every time. I couldn't touch her, hold her…

Sloane hadn't known I was in here with Thatcher, because when she spotted us both, she nearly backed up. She'd started school again with her brother this week. Ramses and Brielle hadn't wanted them to get behind, but they had given them an option for homeschooling.

The two obviously hadn't taken it, and her brother was somewhere on campus too. It'd been an adjustment for them, and I think everyone else at the school. Especially since security had been amped up to help with the press.

Brielle was still here too, acting headmaster until she or any of the adults saw differently. From what I'd heard, the school had hired another headmaster, but they were on standby. We were all obviously making accommodations here.

"I'm sorry. I didn't know," she started, flustered. She tugged up the sleeves of the big Windsor Prep hoodie she wore, the thing covering her down to her thighs. If I had it my way, she'd wear nothing but those fucking hoodies that ate her up, making her look small and reminding me of how she'd looked in my clothes. I'd given her stuff to wear at Wolf's party one time and nearly nutted myself. "I didn't know you were busy. I just wanted to talk to you for a second."

Her sight fell on me, and Thatcher came forward. I think we were both thrown to see her. Especially that him being here had brought her to the lab. "What's up?"

He looked at me after he said it, and Sloane apparently decided retreating was pointless. We'd both seen her, and she acknowledged me with a nod when she came in, but I think only to be polite.

How had I let shit get so fucked up?

"I guess I heard that you got in trouble," she led in with. She glanced at me. "With your dad and keeping what you knew about Bru and me a secret."

Of course, I'd told her this, and Thatcher rubbed his neck.

"Nah, it's okay," he passed off. His hair sprung back after he passed a hand over it again. "My dad's cool. He just needs some time."

Yeah, he was really passing shit off. From what I'd heard, my buddy wasn't only grounded but my god dad was getting him in the boxing ring again. They never spared themselves, but Knight beating the shit out of a trainer three times a week was enough to keep anyone from wanting to fuck up again.

"Even still." Sloane put her hands together. "I wanted to say sorry again and ask if there's anything I could do? I could talk to him if that helps." She sighed. "I just feel bad. You were only trying to help me."

I shouldn't be surprised she was offering this. Not with what I knew about her. *This* was Sloane, the little fighter, the protector.

I rubbed my hands, and Thatcher raised his.

"Seriously, it's fine," he said. "My dad's intense, but with a little bit of time, things will level out."

A hint of hope touched my buddy's voice, but he was right. My god dad burned hot, but when it came to his kids, his wife, and the rest of us, he had a soft spot. All our dads did, and his was no exception.

"Okay." Sloane worked her hands, her nod quick before she bowed out. Thatcher looked at me after, and before I could change my mind, I entered the hall after her.

"Sloane?" She whirled around, and I stopped in front of her. "Can I walk you back to class?" I didn't want my friend to be right about something, but he was.

The lies had gotten us nowhere.

It had Sloane analyzing me with resistance, hesitance. She folded her arms. "Why?"

It had her asking me that.

"Wanted to ask you something," I said, honest. She had her free period right now, so it'd be a good time. "Do you mind? It won't take long."

Please say yes.

Her chin lifted, but when she nodded, I said a silent prayer. Together, we headed off, but we didn't do so alone.

About half a dozen security was in the hall with us, men and women from campus staff yeah, but others too. I recognized the private security firm that was working for our families.

They had probably followed her all the way over to the tech lab.

A lot had changed since Sloane came back, and added security had been one of those things. I was sure she believed it was just for the press, and the families were leading all us kids to believe that too. They wanted to keep us safe and from the prying eyes of the world, but there were also other things here. They still didn't trust my grandfather, and I knew for a fact they didn't want him around Sloane or her brother. I'd heard he stepped back and had no plans to interfere in their lives, but that didn't matter. They didn't want him around them, me, or any of us, and the short alliance they'd had with him seemed to be one of the past.

I wasn't in a position to argue with them, nor to find their concerns unfounded. My grandfather very well could be being honest about his role in the Sloane kids' lives, but I was the last one to give a shit about that. I wanted him away from them too, from her.

Garret and Harrison, two of the families' security, nodded at Sloane and me. None of the security was supposed to impose on our lives, but that didn't mean any of them were giving us any privacy.

"You wanted to ask something?" Sloane pretended not to notice, a few paces ahead of me. She had her hands in her hoodie, but she couldn't not notice when a member of security waved at her. She waved back, pleasant about it, but I could tell it unnerved her. All this shit was a fucking lot.

We rounded a corner. "This security shit is just the parents," I said, tipping my chin to some of them. "Maybe there won't be as many when the press lets up."

I hoped there wouldn't be, but again, who knew. As far as I knew, my grandfather was still in town, and until he wasn't, I didn't think a lot of things were changing.

Sloane acknowledged this, her head bobbing once, but when we cut another corner, I pressed a hand to the wall. This made her stop too, and I got a full blast of those fucking cookies. I didn't know if she wore that scent in her hair or if it was her damn fabric-softener sheets. I just knew I loved it, would kill for it. "How have you been?" I didn't mean to ask her that and definitely had no right to ask her that. I tucked my hands in my pockets. "Everything at home with Ramses and Brielle okay?"

I'd been there pretty much every night, but I wasn't with them every waking moment. I wasn't supposed to be. They needed their time.

Just breathe. It's the right thing, right for them and her.

In my own mental headspace, Sloane eased out of the one she shared with me. Her butt touched the wall, her hands behind her. She shrugged. "We're all adjusting."

She was like a shell of the person she'd been before she'd left, my little fighter still in there but so far away. I leaned closer, but more security strode through the hall, and she gave me cheek. *Motherfuckers.*

I backed off then, and the way Sloane's breath expelled,

this seemed to be desired. She crossed her arms. "What do you want, Prinze?"

A dagger couldn't have cut deeper. She'd definitely sounded like Bru when she said that. "I guess I just wanted to ask your permission about something." More security came through, and I gave them my back. Just because they weren't to interfere with our lives didn't mean they weren't snitches. Eyes for our parents. I had no intention to keep what I was looking into from them, but I at least wanted to talk to Sloane about it first. I angled in her direction. "I'm asking Thatcher to look into your adoption. Your records specifically."

"Why?"

"Because there are other people in all this." My lips turned down. "Lawyers, caseworkers, who knows. I'm sure Godfrey needed help to cover up a kidnapping."

Her expression pinched at the name, and I hated that shit, that the name held so much power over her. If that prick who had taken her wasn't dead, I'd kill him myself. "I'm sure he did, but why are you looking into it?"

"Because someone needs to." My jaw shifted. "Now, I don't know what the parents are doing, but whatever it is, what I'm doing won't interfere." I got close. "I just want your blessing. I'm not going to sneak around, and me looking might not even result in anything." I forced out a breath. "But if I do find something, I'll give it to the parents. Anything I find I'll give to them."

She said nothing, blinking. She glanced away. "Why are you even asking me? You don't ask."

She laughed a little when she said it, a sad, choked laugh. It broke my fucking heart, a million goddamn pieces at our feet. I'd done this shit to her.

I'd done so much shit.

I had once told her we were perfect, that in our flaws we were magic, and she was wrong that we shouldn't be together. I still believed that, but I was hanging on by a thread. I kept fucking hurting her, and her being in pain was destroying me.

"You do whatever you want," she said, easing away from me. Her fingertips bunched the sleeves of her oversize hoodie, her head shaking when she walked away.

I took a step. "It wasn't about you." She stopped, her head turning, her back straight. I took another step. "Me not telling you about my grandfather? It wasn't about you. Never was."

This was the truth, my issues with him and lack of faith in her had nothing to actually do *with* her. It was something I'd always known, and even if I wasn't in therapy, it didn't matter. I *always* had the answer, and it'd never been her.

I crossed the hallway over to her, coming around. She wouldn't look at me, but I didn't fucking care. "My grandfather is a psychopath. He was before I was born, and even if he claims not to be one now, he was back then, and as far as I'm concerned, that's enough for me to never trust him."

I hadn't even talked to my therapist about this shit.

I didn't care, and she was going to listen to me here today. She *needed* to hear this, my truth. "My hate for him, my distrust, was never about you. It's not, because you are *perfect*." I closed space, and her head lifted. "You're goddamn beautiful, Sloane. You're gorgeous, and it was never about you. It was always about me, because you are perfect and you always have been."

She was like fucking light, air and the heaven to my darkness.

The ease to my pain.

She was everything wrapped into one, and if I'd listened to that for a goddamn second, we wouldn't even be talking about this right now.

I wouldn't be bringing her to tears.

The chirp in the hallway was deafening, walkie-talkies. Security stopped as Sloane pressed shaky fingers under her eyes.

"I need to go," she said, more than aware of the eyes on her. "I don't care if you look into my adoption. I just need to go."

She just about clipped a security woman on her way out, and the woman extended a hand to her. She asked her if Sloane was okay, but Sloane merely waved her off. My little fighter left, stalking away.

She was always so good at running from me.

CHAPTER
TWENTY-THREE

Sloane

It took me a second to find him and another to ditch security. He was going to pay for making me fucking cry in the hallway.

The audacity.

We'd had ample opportunity to have this conversation, and none of it had involved me being a blubbering mess in the middle of the hallway. He'd had time to talk to me. Plenty of fucking time.

He hadn't gone back to class.

Dorian was sitting on a weight bench when I finally fucking found him and was naked from the waist up. He was lifting a barbell the size of like three of me, his muscles roving, his breath labored. He reset the weight with a clank, and when he sat up, I accosted him from the front.

I straddled the bench in front of him, grabbing the barbell behind him. He was going to look me in the fucking face and tell me what he had to say.

"Why wasn't it about you?" I snapped, really fucking

snapping. I had the most popular boy in school… the captain of the *football team* and jacked to the freaking nines, between me and a damn barbell. This boy could break me in half.

He wasn't. He just *looked* at me, hands on his thighs, smelling like sweat, boy. Drops of perspiration misted his brow and muscled torso, his pecs flushed and cheeks red. Why the fuck he was in here instead of back in class, I didn't know.

I wet my lips, a visible tremor in my arms as they hovered above his shoulders. He had two legs stamped out, our knees knocking, and his head between my forearms. Our faces were inches away from each other, but I couldn't back down.

I refused.

"Why wasn't it about you?" I ground out and on the verge of fucking tears. We were going to have this conversation, but it wasn't going to be in the damn hallway in front of everybody and God. I'd already gotten enough stares being back. "You say I'm perfect, and you do these things for me…" My voice ached, cracked. "Things like being there for me the other day when I met Ramses and Brielle, and your fucking emails…"

I broke then, a tear, and Dorian's reaction to that was his nostrils flaring. His hands gripped his thick legs, black shorts I guessed he'd changed into under his hands.

"You make accommodations for me. You fight for me." Stop *fucking* crying. I blinked tears away. "I need you to tell me why not trusting me was about you. I need you to fucking say it, Dorian."

I didn't know why I needed this. I didn't know why I was *here.* I just knew he had me crying in the middle of that hallway, and I was so sick of the pull he had over me.

Consideration moved over his face, his head down, his blond tresses thick and clumped with sweat. He'd been in here long enough to exert a fair amount of energy. "Because I've always known the answer."

"What?"

His fingers weaved through his hair, the sides cropped short. The latter was hard to tell since he always wore his hair loose and with little to no product. It just *looked* that way, his hair perfect all the time. He pressed his hands together. "About you," he said, glancing up. "I've always known the answer about you. I've always known your character and who you are. I know you're a good person, Noa. I know you're perfect."

I gripped the barbell, trembling again.

"So yes, me not having faith in you and my distrust of my grandfather had nothing to do with you." His throat flicked. "It was always about me and my issues. It was about *me* and my refusal to trust my gut and believe in *you*. I've always known the truth." He shook his head. "But my fear... fear of loving you and giving you myself completely..."

A sound escaped my throat, my breath heavy.

His nostrils flared again. "It's what made me do the wrong thing. Ares is right. I didn't know who you were. I didn't, but that doesn't matter. I still did the wrong fucking thing when it came to you, and that's because I love you so fucking much it scared the shit out of me."

I let go, backed up, and he stood up. He towered over me, a mountain to my peak.

"You are so goddamn perfect to me." A roughness touched his voice, his knuckles tight at his sides. "Everything about you is perfect to me."

I backed up again, angling away. "You're wrong," I said, making his eyes flash. "You're wrong. I'm fucked up, and you fuck me up."

"Noa—"

"No. Let me fucking finish." I put my finger in his face. "You fuck me up so bad, Dorian. You do, and I do stupid things too."

Confusion laced his ebony eyes, his head cocked. I probably sounded like a fucking basket case.

I was a basket case.

I couldn't breathe at this point, grabbing my legs. I studied the rubber mats on the floor. "I'm chaos." I was nightmare fuel, literally. I created all this destruction in my wake, and it didn't matter what I did, I still hurt people. I'd hurt him and his family and...

"Sloane..."

I needed fucking *space*, my hands up. "I've created so much pain, Dorian," I said, my voice rough now. "And I know it's not my fault. I know I was kidnapped, and things happened outside of my control. Yes, I know that, but it doesn't change what I've done."

"What?" he asked me, concern lining every inch of his handsome face. I hated it. I loathed the accommodations he constantly made for me and how mature he was being. It made me look even more foolish. I *didn't* have my shit together.

I wasn't perfect.

"I found out the truth, and the first thing I did was run," I said, swallowing. "I ran because I knew what my being back would do. I knew how many people it would hurt." I blinked, crying again. "Your grandfather caused a lot of pain, Dorian, and I knew what him being around would do. He hurt *your family*, Dorian. My family..."

He got closer, and I stiffened.

"He was talking about doing this press conference and telling the truth, and all I could see was how that would affect your parents." I braced my hands. "How it would affect Ramses, Brielle, and Ares..." I looked up. "And you."

He was the first one I'd thought of actually.

He'd fucked me up so bad.

His expression fell after what I said, his hands out, but I didn't let him get close.

"The flood gates were going to open up, and I panicked. I ran, and I don't know why," I stated, crossing my arms. "To deny the inevitable or what the fuck ever." I was cold now, shivering. I hugged my arms. "I just knew a lot of people were about to be hurt, and I was about to be the reason."

He did make me do stupid things, but it wasn't just him. Him and this town and all the connections I'd formed definitely helped. Bow, Wells, and Thatcher and their families would have been just as affected as the Mallicks and Prinzes.

Because they were all family.

They were and shared each other's pain and hardships. They had *peace* before all this with me.

"I did the wrong thing," I said. "I ran, and I made people hurt even worse." I put my hand on my chest. "That's on me."

Dorian started to reach for me, *to comfort me*, and all that did was spring more madness within me. I didn't want his comfort, or anything else.

"And through it all, I'm still mad at you." I laughed, honest to fuck feeling manic. I gripped my hair. "I'm angry you lied to me. I'm hurt you didn't trust me while, at the same time, angry at myself for feeling that way because I do get it and why you did what you did." God, I really did sound fucking crazy. My head shook. "But what I think angers me the most is how mature you're being about all this. You are, and I know you're only being that way for my benefit. You're looking out *for me* when I know you're fucking angry too."

I knew this because I knew him too, his character. We were *both* fucked up, and that was one of the things that was so nice about us. He wasn't perfect, and neither was I. We were both equally and utterly stupid the way we handled shit sometimes.

We were beautiful.

I hadn't seen it before... beauty in the chaos, but that was what we were.

"You're mad at me," I said, stepping up to him. "You're furious, and I know you are. You're just as angry at me as I am at you. You're not perfect, Dorian. You're fucking flawed just like me, and I need you to start acting like it before I lose my mind. I feel so *alone*. Alone here and in my head, and I need you. I need us. I—"

My rant ended under his mouth, his teeth biting my lip, his hand around my throat. He tightened his hold, and I gasped, his mouth sealing over mine.

"I am fucking mad at you," he growled, his hand shoving under my hoodie. He ripped the dress shirt beneath open at the buttons, his hand gripping my breast, and I trembled. "I'm mad at you for not fucking trusting me. For going to *fucking Thatcher* and not coming to me."

He unleashed my breast, ripping the lace clean off me. He worked my hoodie off and once he did, he pinched my nipple so hard tears sprung from my eyes.

"I'm mad at you for leaving me," he rasped, his mouth on my cheek, my neck. "I'm mad at you for not loving me."

A boulder to the chest, my body *shaking*. I tried to look at him, but he wouldn't let me.

He was too busy stripping me naked.

My shirt came off in tatters, my bra the same. Soon, I had nothing on but my tie, skirt, underwear, and shoes, but I didn't know how long those would survive.

The dark prince picked me up, a literal toss over his shoulder. I held on, kissing and gripping his back, tasting his skin. God, we were messed up because this was completely turning me the hell on. I bit him, and he grabbed my ass so hard I knew I'd feel him there for weeks.

He slapped it as if to make sure.

"You're going to feel every moment you were away from me," he said, my panties gone when he pulled them off. I thought he'd put me down, but he put two fingers in his mouth, his index and middle finger, then his thumb. His thumb he shoved directly into my ass while he used the other two to coax and play with my clit.

Stars hit my vision, the cry rough from my throat from the invasion in my ass. I'd never tried anal or anything, and I think I'd only had my own digit in here on the rare occasions when I played with myself.

"You're going to feel me," he promised, biting my ass before removing his thumb and putting me down. His face had completely reddened, his hair tousled and his body flushed. He appeared completely mad, and the smile on his lips only accompanied it. His shorts tented, he stroked himself through them. "I'm going to fuck you until we're both weak, and even then, I won't stop."

He bit my mouth as if a prelude to that, his body hot and slick with sweat. Solid muscle hit my body, unyielding with its force as moisture pooled between my legs. He played with my lower lips while he pumped himself, his dick hitting my mound. "You're not going to forget me again."

I hadn't forgotten him. I never had.

How could I?

I hadn't forgotten what he'd said to me before I'd left. I hadn't nor had I been ignorant to see what had underlined each of those messages, how he'd always told me about everyone else but left out things about himself or us. I knew how he felt about me.

I knew he loved me.

I could feel it with each kiss and taste, with each aggressive move when he whirled me around and bent me over that weight bench. He kicked my ankles apart there, shoving his shorts down.

"You're going to feel me and how you make me weak," he gritted, shoving his cock inside me. He hadn't bothered with a condom and thank God I was on birth control. I cried out beneath him, and he roared. "And how I don't care because I love you so fucking much."

His thighs jutted forward, a harsh slap against my ass. The weight bench heaved forward and only caused Dorian to press more of his weight on me.

"You do make me weak, but I don't care, Noa," he said, hard in, slow out. "I love you."

I held his hand, and what he saw as weakness, I only saw as strength. He was the strongest person I knew and way stronger than me. He was strong enough to admit to me how he felt and had since the very beginning. He'd *always* been honest with me about that.

Tell him.

He roared as he came, my walls clenching when I flooded around him too. I cried out, using my arm to hold his weight and mine.

"I love you too," I gasped, tears springing from my eyes. I looked back at him. "I always have. Always."

It was like the words fell out of me, seeping from an open wound. I did love him, and I always had.

I'd been scared.

It wasn't easy to love Dorian Prinze. Because with that love came so much more. He had such potential to hurt me.

Slowing behind me, Dorian lifted my jaw. His hold tight, I couldn't look away even if I tried. He dampened his mouth. "Always?"

Emotion lined his rough voice, and it contracted my throat. I nodded. "Always."

Fear was a weighted thing because even as I said it, I was scared. He could shatter us.

He could destroy me.

Because that was how much power he had over me and how much he meant to my world. He told me he wasn't going to let me forget him.

If only he knew, he never had to try.

His lids lowering, Dorian sealed our mouths, his kisses breathless, his tongue light. He hugged me to him. "I love you," he said, his tongue sweeping, voice cracking. "Fucking always, little fighter. Fucking *always*."

He rocked behind me, still inside me. He didn't let me go under his mouth, and I was foolish enough to never want him to again. He could hurt me.

I just didn't care.

CHAPTER
TWENTY-FOUR

Dorian

"I have to say, Dorian, I wasn't quite sure where we'd be at this point with our sessions," Dr. Singh said. "But I'm happy to say it's a good place. A great place."

I panned away from the downtown office window, snow flurries on the other side. It was the first snow of the season.

Dr. Singh smiled at me. "In fact, I'm comfortable in saying the frequency at which we hold our sessions can definitely be reduced. I'm happy to talk to your parents about that if that's what you'd like, as well as your progress."

I was eighteen, and technically, my parents couldn't make me go to therapy. The proposal had merely been strongly suggested by my parents. Basically, that meant I had to, and though Dr. Singh couldn't share the details of them, she was allowed to tell my parents general things if I gave her permission. She was well aware my parents were making me see her. They'd booked the fucking appointments.

She closed her notebook. "You've been doing so well, and

I'm happy to talk to them. It's really amazing how far you've come in such little time."

Had it only been a month or so since we'd really started diving deep into these sessions?

Had it only been a month or so since she'd been back?

I glanced out the window again, trees covered in light snow. "I'd like that. And you can talk to them. That's fine." I knew she'd be general about it and always had since I'd been seeing her.

"Of course, we're not done here." Our gazes clashed when I looked at her. She placed her hands on her notebook. "I'm merely going to suggest to them that you be allowed to be in charge of your own care." Her head tilted. "I think you've realized how important it is and do feel you'll make the right decision as far as the frequency of our sessions go."

This was a test the good doctor was giving to me, and *I* was happy to say I was about to fucking pass that shit. I smiled. "I want to get keep seeing you, and regularly this time."

It'd been sporadic before, and I'd been bad about it.

"Good." Her legs crossed, her glasses above her head. "I worried about all the changes in your life recently, but you seem to be doing so well with them. Actually, you've been thriving despite them, and it's so good to know things are going so well with Noa."

Noa...

"She's bringing out the best in you." She leaned forward. "And maybe you should consider talking with her about the summer with your grandfather. You said you haven't yet. It might be time, I think."

My attention broke away from the window. It'd wandered again. I was thinking about what I was going to do once I got out today. How I was going to go see Noa. I swallowed. "Doc?"

"You know how important trust is, Dorian, and you have mentioned it's been an issue with the two of you before."

It had, but it was no fault of hers. I'd given her reasons.

"I think you should trust her to be able to handle what happened that summer with your grandfather." The doctor pulled her glasses down, a tight concern on her face. "And well, what happened after."

My legs crossed, they were rocking at this point, restless. What had happened after had been fucked and had ended with my grandfather on the floor.

I'd poisoned him.

"I know it's hard, but me suggesting this is for you. It's your journey. Your *healing*, and you need to be able to talk about this with her like you do with me, your parents, and your friends. You need to let Noa in, Dorian. You said you care about her, and it'll only help you."

But that was the thing. I didn't just care about Noa. I *loved* her, and I was aware of that fact just as much as I was something else.

I hadn't been the only one to say it.

She'd said she always had, *always*, but something had obviously held her back from saying it before. The potential reasons why scared me, and I thought a lot about that after my session with Dr. Singh. Things had been going well with Sloane, and in fact so well I forgot sometimes. I forgot she hadn't told me she loved me at first, and the reasons why now seemed moot. Especially after that day in the weight room. I'd gone in there to wear my fucking body out after our tense conversation, and after she'd come in, everything had changed. She did love me.

The rest didn't fucking matter.

Of course, it did matter. There had been a reason why she'd hesitated the first time I'd told her, but it was easy not to think about it. Add that to the fact that *I* wasn't ready to talk about that summer with my grandfather in general, and what Dr. Singh asked me seemed impossible. I wasn't ready to talk about it, but that had nothing to do with not trusting Sloane. I still had fucking issues, my own shit and things I still had to work through.

Sloane initially keeping her love secret from me only further made me want to bury that summer with my grandfather (and what had happened after) deep in my therapist's office. She'd already been gun-shy about me.

This shit was just hard.

It was also the reason I was still seeing my fucking therapist, and I tucked our latest session away when I pulled up to the Mallick house. A few straggling paparazzi were still at the gate, mostly local press. Since there were fewer prying eyes, the security detail had significantly gone down. There was only one at the gate today.

It was really refreshing, and I knew it was for the Mallick family too. I knew it was for *Sloane* because that shit had gotten annoying in the rough of it.

There weren't constantly people around us now, and the press were starting to forget things too. Sloane and her brother and the ordeal from mere weeks ago were starting to fade away in the eyes of the press, and everyone on the other side of it was starting to move on too.

I saw that in the backyard.

I came up on the throes of a race once I got out of my car, smirking when I got to the mini gate that separated the garage from the yard. Thatcher, Bow, and Bru were in a huddle beneath snow flurries, Wolf, Sloane, and Wells in front of them. Wolf and Sloane were hunkered down, a knee to the earth in a pair of windbreakers, and Wells stood ahead of them.

Here we go again.

Coming to find them all this way wasn't uncommon, and I unlatched the gate, coming inside. I strode over as Wells counted Wolf and Sloane off.

"Three. Two. One…" Wells smirked, grinning. My buddy had a fucking down coat on with a furry collar like he was on a damn runaway. His tongue out, he dropped his arm. "Let's get it."

Wolf and Sloane shot off in a run, and I sprinted, happy for the person who made *fucking leggings*. They made my girl's ass look ridiculous, and I got a nice little shot after she took off after my boy. Wolf got ahead of her pretty quick, and being an asshole started jogging backward.

"Come on, little," he called. He raised his hands. "Why the fuck we been training?"

Sloane had started going with Wolf and me in the morning during our sprints. We rose at the crack of dawn to stay loose. We both played other sports in the spring season, Wells and Thatcher too.

Sloane claimed she was getting up with us just to hang out, but these little sprinting exercises between the two of them had started not long after that. It seemed her competitive spirit matched her twin's.

"You fucking asshole!" she roared, pumping her wiry little arms. She looked like a not-so-fast gazelle, and it'd take her a bit if she really wanted to keep up with Wolf. He was one of the fastest motherfuckers on our team, and those long-ass legs of his only helped.

Chuckling, I caught up with the group who started walking after them. Bow, Thatcher, and Bru clapped and cheered after the two, and when I got to them, I did the same.

"They really at this shit again?" I asked, dropping arms over Bow and Thatch. Wolf passed the flag that signaled the end of the race, the little fighter a good length behind him, and I cringed.

"We tried to talk her out of it," Bow said, cringing too. She clapped hard. "Woohoo! Good job, Sloane!"

Thatcher and I laughed, but I forced myself to stop once

Sloane finished the race too. She'd fucking kick my ass if she caught me laughing.

"You fucking *cheat*." Sloane shot her finger at Wolf as the three of us made our way over. Wells caught up too, joining us all. Sloane frowned at Wolf. "You're like on 'roids or something."

The little fighter was having a hard time catching her breath. She had her head basically between her legs when we all got there, and I shot my shoulder into Wolf. He could have stood to go a little easier on her.

This only made him chuckle louder, roaring at this point. He tucked his hands under his arms. "I'm not on steroids. It's called genetics, and you got the same ones, so really, you got no excuse."

They did both come from a family of runners. Both Ramses and Brielle jogged too and actually went out well before we did in the morning.

"Whatever," she said, but I managed to distract her when I picked her up. I tossed her over my shoulder, and she squealed. "Dorian! Fuck! Put me down. What the fuck?"

Oh, I'd fuck her all right. Nice and good before the night was over. We'd both been growing accustomed to me sneaking into her room after dark.

Things really had been good between us, nice. They'd been *easy* and getting a handful of my girl's ass was a great release after spilling my heart out to my therapist for an hour.

When I did put her down, I grabbed her face. "Hey."

"Hi." She could never stay mad at me, and we clacked teeth when I bit her juicy bottom lip. She held on while I wrapped arms around her head then proceeded to make out with her in front of, well, any fucker who wanted to watch. This got groans from everyone but Bow who proceeded to shyly look away, and my middle finger was for the peanut gallery around her.

Like clockwork, Sloane's came out too for my boys. Her

brother Bru had started playing on his phone, so the finger was definitely for Wolf, Wells, and Thatcher.

I had my tongue down her throat when my buddies decided to give up. They hit me on the back before starting their own race, which consisted of Wells climbing on Wolf's back while Thatcher tried his hand at beating him. It was enough to make Sloane and me pull away from each other to watch that stupid shit. Thatcher lost, of course, but it didn't stop them all from dicking around.

"How was your session?" Having Sloane's focus on me was a place I always loved to be, her arms around my waist, her legging-covered ass under my hands. She grinned. "Everything go okay today?"

She knew about my sessions, and I was very open with her about them. I just didn't go into details, but she never expected me to. No pressure.

Things had been so fucking cool with us, which really made me consider talking to her about what Dr. Singh had advised. I did trust Sloane, but I also had my own shit. I rubbed her ass. "Great. Dr. Singh's actually going to talk to my parents and suggest to them I take over the decisions regarding my own care. She even wants to reduce our sessions. Says I've been doing well."

Her brow raised, and my heart fucking *stopped* when she smiled at me. She looked like a proud fucking parent, and I was the good boy. It made me want to please her for days, forever. Her smile widened. "Whoa, that's amazing, Dorian."

It was pretty amazing, and when I said as much, she hit me in the back.

"I take that back." She pulled away, and I tugged her back. She laughed. "No, seriously. I'm proud of you. I know it's not easy for you."

It wasn't easy, opening up to anyone not easy. I wet my lips. "She also wants me to talk to you about something."

By the hand, I guided her away from our circle of friends

and family a bit. Bru was in the race now, and he didn't appear to be as closed off as he had been. We all had gotten along before this, and though he wasn't trying to have long-ass conversations with me, we were civil.

I think we were both trying for his sister's benefit, and no one really noticed when I took Sloane off to the side.

"Okay," she said, her hands cold. Neither of us were wearing gloves, so I put her hands under my jacket to warm us both. "Everything okay?"

That was a tricky question. I mean, everything was okay in the technical sense, and my grandfather had kept his promise to keep his distance. He hadn't interfered in any of our lives, and it was like things were normal again.

I didn't even know if he was still in town.

I didn't *care*, and I think I wasn't the only one. It hadn't mattered. We'd all been able to find some peace after all that and dredging up all this shit right now... shit about my past with him felt like a step in the wrong direction. My jaw clicked. "Everything is good, but she does want me to talk to you about something. It's about something that happened. Something in the past."

She was silent now, her breath coming in short puffs. Her hands warmed against my abs and shot blood straight to other places. Places that had me wanting to kick this conver-sation. She blinked. "Is it bad?"

It was fucking terrible, all of it. I couldn't believe I'd gone to that fucker about Charlie and everything that had happened after was just more fucked. I forced out a breath. "It's not good, and if I'm being honest, I really don't want to talk about it."

In fact, my hands were fucking shaking, and next thing I knew, she was pulling hers out. She gripped my jacket. "You don't have to tell me anything you don't want to tell me. Especially if that's between you and your therapist."

How the fuck had I found this girl?

"I want to tell you." I took her hands. "I want to tell you everything, but it's hard, you know?"

"Yeah."

I squeezed her hands. "I will tell you. I will, but I just need more time to be comfortable with it. I just want you to know there is something, but me not being able to talk about it has nothing to do with you."

This felt like a step in the right direction. It also opened the door and gave my mind time to wrap around actually telling her.

"Because I'm perfect, right?" She slid her arms around my neck, and I nodded. She was perfect.

"Right. It's just shit I've got to work through, and I will, but I just wanted you to know there is something. There is, but I will tell you." And I would when I was ready.

I thought she'd have something to say about that, but all she ended up doing was taking my face and kissing me. I picked her up, hugging her, and I got a slap on the head that made me whirl around and nearly deck one of my friends.

"Parents," edged out of Wells's mouth just in time for me to spot Brielle coming out on the veranda. I didn't think either her or my god dad had issues with me seeing their daughter, but that didn't mean they wanted it in their faces. Basically, Sloane and I were keeping what we had on the DL, but I did keep my hand in hers when Brielle poked her head out of the glass veranda.

"Dinner's in ten minutes, so whoever is staying better be at the table in five." She eyed all of us. She pointed. "I mean it. Your butt's not in the seat, no food."

She let the door close behind her, a smile on her lips, and it was rare not to see her with one these days. Hell, who wasn't smiling since Sloane had come back?

It was especially nice to see that on Ramses and Brielle lately. They made accommodations in both their schedules to be around, around for Sloane, Bru, and Wolf. They were home every night and available each morning, weekends free and clear. It killed Wolf's hookup social life, but who was that fucker kidding?

He'd been smiling too.

He even went right after his mom after she came to get us, hugging her. There'd been periods in the past where Wolf definitely knocked heads with his parents, but those days seemed to be long gone. He appeared to be trying to get the jump on his seat at the table, and out of nowhere, Thatcher yelled after them.

"Sure thing, Mama Bri," he called, shocking the hell out of us all. He'd been grounded and strictly told to be home before dark. He extended his arms at us. "What? You didn't hear your boy's no longer *grounded!*"

This had Wolf rerouting back down the stairs. He picked Thatch up and yelled, "Hell, yeah," before smacking Thatcher's ass repeatedly. Wells joined in when he punched at the rest of Thatcher. *Fucking jokers.*

Even still, I joined in too, and it seemed things really were getting back to normal.

Again, it was nice.

CHAPTER
TWENTY-FIVE

Sloane

My brother texted all through dinner again that night. It wasn't like it was a thing, but no one else did it.

Maybe it wasn't a thing *because* he did it.

I admit I was still trying to figure out the ways of the land around here, but texting in front of people was generally rude. Especially when we were all at *dinner*. Ramses and Brielle had gotten us new phones, and since then, that seemed to be all he was doing.

Picking at my food next to him, I allowed it. He'd been really withdrawn lately. Not really talking to me, and when I did see him, he was doing homework in his room. Of course, when I asked about this, all he claimed was that he wanted to actually move on with the rest of his class to his senior year. I did too with mine, but honestly, we hadn't had to do much to catch up in school. Ramses and Brielle got us tutors on top of picking up our tuition.

"What do you think about that, Sloane? Sound fun?"

The entire dining room was looking at me, and that was a

lot of people. Thatcher, Wells, and Bow had stayed after my epic fail in the backyard with Ares. The motherfucker couldn't even give me *one* goddamn win and was arrogant as shit. He didn't have to run backward when he got ahead of me.

"We were wondering what you felt about a gathering to meet the other families." Brielle, the one who'd spoken, exchanged a glance with Ramses on her other side. He had her hand, giving it a kiss before Brielle tilted her head. "Knight and Greer and Royal and December you've of course met, but Wells's family would like to meet you, and LJ and his wife Billie."

I'd heard about them all, so many people in the Legacy bubble. Bow had explained to me LJ was in the parents' friend circle as well.

"And I know you've met my mom and my stepdad James, but not officially in person." Ramses looked at Brielle, his smile widening. "Brielle's parents would like to fly in from Jersey as well."

Because that was where they were from. Brielle was originally from there.

I was still trying to play catch-up in this life and with this Legacy family, but before I could speak, the couple fixed a warm gaze to the person on one of my sides.

"We'd like it to be a little bit of a birthday party as well," Ramses continued. "For Bru?"

When his name called, my brother shot his head up.

Ramses chuckled. "We heard you had a birthday right before you moved here, and it'd be nice to celebrate that."

My brother's lips parted, mine too. Bru looked at me. "Yeah, but that was months ago."

"Believe me. None of these folks need any reason to gather." Ramses laughed, Brielle too beside him. He nodded. "But it'd be nice to celebrate you in all this too if you'd let us."

That was so fucking nice, and I looked at Bru. "That okay?"

I hoped he'd say yes. I mean, he was a part of all this, but he really had been keeping to himself. I tried to pop in on him whenever I could, but he preferred his books to anything else.

Bru had all the attention at the table now, and the dark prince took my hand underneath it. At my other side, Dorian tipped his chin at Bru. "What do you think, bro?"

"Yeah. It'd be fun." Ares put his hands together, grinning. "My grandparents are always asking about you when we talk. Sloane, yeah. But you too. They want to meet you, as well as everyone else. The Reeds, Ambroses, and the Johnsons."

I'd asked him to look out for Bru, include him, and that was exactly what he was doing here.

Wells, Thatcher, and Bow all nodded after he said it, and I grinned while Bru sat dumbstruck. Bru put his phone down. "Okay. Yeah." He faced me, more light than I'd seen in his eyes in weeks. "That okay with you? Meeting everyone?"

It definitely was okay, and only more so that it was okay with him.

———

Dorian dicked me down under silk sheets, his weight on my back, his cock tunneled deep. His hand around my throat, he silenced my moan when he squeezed. "You're going to get us caught, little fighter, if you don't cut that shit out."

His throaty chuckle rumbled into my back, nothing like his weight pinning me down. Pretending I didn't enjoy it, I flipped him off, and he laughed again, managing to keep it as low as the chuckle.

"Fuck you," I bit out, and he grabbed my hand, *biting* it. He proceeded to roll his hips in quick succession, and I clamped my teeth down on his arm.

The roar that came next he didn't keep silent… at least not completely. A gritted "Fuck" rolled from his cocky-ass mouth, and his hips slapped against my ass so hard I thought he was trying to spank me with them.

"Do that again, and you'll feel me in your fucking throat," he warned, jerking me to face him by the jaw. He grinned before sealing our lips, and I held his arm around me, rubbing my nipples against the bed while he fucked me senseless. I was seeing fucking stars at this point. Especially since the dark prince didn't bother with condoms anymore.

Not after he found out he didn't need them.

He must trust me because he didn't even ask me for proof I was on birth control. He'd just taken my word for it. He wasn't the guy he was before, and I wasn't that same girl either.

Things were different with us, closer, and I felt near to him in ways I hadn't felt before I'd left. It was hard to even be *around him* some days, our connection to the point where it completely unnerved me.

It rattled both of us.

We were like *this* all the time, fucking consumed with each other, and I had no idea where I fucking ended and he began. Truth be told, it was all as alarming as it was exhilarating, but I couldn't stop.

I was addicted.

Our tongues flicked, dueling, and tangled as much as our bodies. Dorian laced our fingers as he smacked his hips repeatedly into my ass, and when I came, I saw fucking *constellations.* I bit his arm again, and he wasn't far behind.

My muscles contracted around a pulsating cock, Dorian milking himself in and out of me. His eyes shut tight, he bit my arm and whatever strength I had left to hold him was gone. I flattened beneath his weight, and breathy, he pulled me on top of him.

"Come here," he said, an arm under my ass, the other

cradling my back. He kissed me once as if to say, "Good girl," and I'd say something about that if I didn't like it so fucking much.

Like I stated, *addicted*.

The dark prince held me there, steadfast as he massaged my ass and rubbed my lower lips against him. He didn't stop until he had himself up and down against my clit, but if he was thinking what I thought he was, he needed to get his head freaking checked. *Both* of them.

I replaced my clit against his junk with my knee, and he cursed. I grinned. "You need to go back to your room."

We hadn't gotten caught yet, but I wasn't trying to chance it, and the arrogant fuck he was threw an arm behind his head. He was golden, naked, and looking completely beautiful with just-fucked hair and a cocky expression. He eyed me. "It's late. They're in bed."

He didn't *know that*, and it was already bad enough we were living in sin under Ramses and Brielle's roof. I mean, we'd been fucking for a while, but not under their roof. It was different doing this at their house, and he knew I didn't like it.

"Fucking *fine*." He kissed my nose, getting up and flashing me his muscled ass. I swear to God he'd thrown some of his clothes on the other side of the room just to fuck with me. He tugged his boxers on, then lifted his hands. "Happy?"

I'd be happy once he got his ass out of my room and back into his own bed. His shirt still on mine, I threw it at him, and he chuckled lightly before working it on like a *guy*. He had it all bunched up, and basically unrolled it over himself. The maneuver was pretty much as hot as it sounded, and after he got fully dressed, he ambled over and pounced on my bed.

His second move was to pounce on me, and I kicked at him. He didn't get off until I stopped struggling enough to let him kiss me.

Which I did.

Every time, I did, our kisses slow, hot. They were heaven as much as hell because eventually they did end and he did have to go back to his room.

"Thanks for what you did today," I said, not letting him go just yet. I wrapped my arms around him. "By chiming in with Bru." He'd been the first to sound off at the dinner table tonight, and I appreciated it.

He shrugged. "Wasn't a thing."

He said that, but it was. I flicked fingers through his hair. "I'm just worried about him. He's been real quiet and stuff. Texting a lot." I had no idea who he was texting. His friends before we'd come back had been Legacy.

I suppose he could have gotten other friends at school, and I wouldn't have blamed him anyway. He'd been forced into this bubble, but his place in it was definitely different from mine.

I just worry.

"We're all keeping an eye on him," he said, and my brow jumped. His eyes lifted. "We care about him, little fighter. Just like you."

"Yeah, but it's different." He knew that.

He nodded, confirming that. He hugged his big arms around me. "He'll be fine. I think he's stronger than you're letting him be."

He might be right about that, but I couldn't help myself.

I mean, he was my brother.

No one should get that more than Dorian, those connections tight, and they couldn't be explained. Only felt.

I had a tie that was just as strong to Dorian but was obviously in a different way.

"Love you," he said to me before going to bed, and though it overwhelmed me every time, scared me, I never hesitated to say it back.

"Fucking always," I said to him back. He'd said that to me once, and it stuck.

I liked it.

I liked us way too much. I was past the phase of being attached. I was lost in him and us, and I didn't want to get out. Loving Dorian Prinze *openly* was starting to get a lot easier, and that freaked me out just as much as the ease of saying that I loved him in the first place.

He always smiled after, making my heart fucking leap. We devoured each other's mouths at my door before he finally ended up going back to his room, and I couldn't sleep after all that. Dorian had said to me earlier today he was working through his own issues, things he wanted to say to me but couldn't, and I had my own head shit. I was still trying to let go of the past and my fear about him. I was trying not to be scared of him.

But that was hard too.

We'd had a lot of shitty things happen to us and things where he'd hurt me. I was trying to forget and let go, but the subconscious was a son of a bitch. It wanted to protect itself, protect me.

Yeah, this was hard.

I knew we'd never be able to get to where we actually could be until I let go. I mean, how could we?

I needed a strong drink since I couldn't sleep but settled on a milk in Ramses and Brielle's kitchen. I knew my way around the house pretty well these days, so when I came across Ramses's home studio with the light on, I found it curious. It was late, and he was never in there.

This was something I knew for a fact and had long before I'd come to live here. Wells had stated Ramses didn't use his studio anymore. At least, not lately. Actually, Ares had been using it.

I almost expected to find Ares in there, but when I popped my head inside, that wasn't who I saw. Ramses was in there.

He sat at an easel.

Stroking across canvas with a long brush, he stopped once

he noticed he had company. His eyes warmed. "Not making too much noise, am I?"

He wasn't at all, of course, and when he started painting again, I wagered he didn't mind he had an audience. I came inside and was also curious about what he was painting.

A sunset.

The rays opened up to the heavens on his canvas, rich skies of gold and amber. I knew he was an artist. That was where Ares's got it from.

And you too.

It was kind of hard not to see the similarities on the daily, in this house and in this life. Ramses and Brielle were still giving me space, *time*, but they didn't have to do much to make me feel like I fit in here. We all just had such similar interests. Ramses and Brielle were runners too, and though I clearly didn't have that gene, it might be something I could get into.

Apparently, I had the genetics.

"This is so cool," I said, and he smiled. I looked at him. "I thought you were more into metal pieces, though."

His studio was filled with sculptures, and he noticed me looking at them.

"Usually, yeah." His brush glided along the canvas, full and sweeping. He was so good at skies, and I found that crazy since Ares and I liked to paint the sky too, the world and the universe. He shrugged. "My mind is just taking me here these days. It's hard to fight it when inspiration comes."

He smiled after he said it, and it seemed a lot of inspiration had hit him. He had new pieces all over the room, more sunsets. More skies. None of these things had been here the first time I'd been in here.

I wonder what changed.

Wells had alluded that Ramses had some kind of block that had kept him from creating new work in here. He'd said life had gotten in the way.

I sipped my milk. I had my own life changes, my own struggles that had gotten in the way. Things, at least these days, were feeling more like Ramses's skies. The sun was bright, the world better.

"So, my godson's parents have been missing him," Ramses continued, painting. "Was thinking about suggesting to them Dorian spend more time over there. More specifically, in the evenings and at home in his own space for the night."

I froze, clenching around my milk.

"So he will be doing that, I think." Ramses nodded, his strokes not missing a beat. "*Going home* each night and being in his own space."

Oh my fucking *God*.

"And don't worry. I'll talk to him about that," Ramses said, a smile in his voice when he wheeled back on his stool from the canvas. "Love my godkid. Adore him, but he'll know *all* about that. Like I said, his parents have been missing him anyway."

I didn't know what to say. "I..."

"Mmm." Ramses waved a hand, this conversation clearly as awkward for him as it was for me. "Like I said, I'll handle it, but when he does come back, we should probably all have a talk. We can keep Royal and December out of this, and whatever rules they establish at their house Brielle and I will leave them to figure out." He faced me. "But here, we all will have an understanding. I'm not dumb. I know you kids are eighteen and almost on your way out, but yeah..."

He didn't have to go on, and I waved my hands.

He seemed relieved by this, wheeling back to the painting. This was definitely as awkward for him as it was for me, and I totally wasn't used to having parents around. I mean, I hadn't really.

It was different. It was *awkward* but in a weird way, it was kind of nice.

Mostly because it was normal.

Ramses continued to paint for a while, and I watched him in silence. He knew I enjoyed art as well. It came up quite a bit at the dinner table, and of course, Ramses and Brielle knew I'd helped Ares with his senior project. Ramses had even come by the school to see it, which had been cool. He was actually really prolific in the art community, and that was something that had definitely come up while in my previous seclusion.

I'd researched all about him before I'd met him, Brielle too. I just wanted to know them, but with all my searches, all my facts, it could only give me a snapshot. Knowing them was actually getting to know them and being with them. They were these awkward normal moments.

They were painted sunsets and amber skies.

"Uh, before I forget," Ramses paused, wheeling back. He used a long reach to grab something from his desk, and when he came back, he gave me an envelope.

I nearly dropped it upon seeing what was inside.

"Bocelli tickets?" I gasped, and Ramses chuckled. I pulled them out. "Are these real?"

"Very much so, yeah." Ramses cocked his head. "We're hosting him at one of our Chicago galleries."

I knew Ramses had a few, but this was fucking Bocelli. The dude was like the Van Gogh of this century, and people just didn't get tickets to things like this. I pulled a veil of hair out of my face. "These are like auction only, right?"

And had to cost him like a million dollars. Tickets to see Bocelli's work were always done through auction, and the artist always donated the proceeds to local art programs. Whatever city he happened to show at actually.

Ramses chuckled. "Technically, but since we're showing him…" Ramses opened his hands. "You can take them off my hands then? I tried to offer one to Ares, but he's not a fan."

He was being nice about that. I smirked. "He thinks his work is pretentious."

Actually, there weren't many artists Ares seemed to actually like outside of his own father's work. He talked shit about pretty much anyone I brought up that I said I liked, Bocelli being one of them.

"Yeah. I guess I was trying to be nice." Ramses scratched his neck. "Anyway, they're yours. Maybe ask Dorian. He probably wouldn't mind going."

I knew he wouldn't. He'd actually taken me to see art before. One of Ramses's local galleries actually.

Ramses swirled his brush around in more paint before rolling up to the canvas again.

"Would you be busy?" I asked, surprising, well, myself. I shook the tickets. "I mean, I guess I just thought it'd be fun. Dorian wouldn't mind going, but you know, since you're into all this stuff too." This stuff? Really, Sloane? "I just mean if you're not busy."

I didn't know why I was nervous about asking him. I guess I worried he thought it'd be weird or something.

But when he smiled, I wondered why.

"That'd be very nice," he said, and when I gave him the tickets back, he placed them on the table that held his paints. "And you're right. It would be fun, and I'm honored you asked me."

I wanted to get to know him more, and I knew he wanted to get to know me. Like his wife, I was well aware how much the two were still walking around on eggshells with me.

It seemed this was a step in the right direction, and when I left Ramses that night, I couldn't help but notice the air around him was different since I'd arrived. He was sunsets and lit skies now like his paintings, and no longer just a man trying to hold his family together.

I wondered if *that* was what had changed.

CHAPTER
TWENTY-SIX

Dorian

"What do you mean they're all dead?" I asked Thatcher, the other half of our table barely paying attention. Bow, Sloane, and Bru were going over the plans for his birthday party with Wells and Ares. Ares was at least sort of engaged, but Wells hadn't even bothered. He was on his phone while Ares's attention sporadically drifted to what Thatcher was going over with me.

It was some dark shit, and I thumbed past another page in the folder he'd given me. Thatch had ended up getting me Sloane's adoption records that day he'd promised me, but once he found out I'd told Sloane (and that the pair of us had patched things up), Thatcher had offered to look further into things himself. I called that an act of goodwill and his support for my and Sloane's relationship. The two of us had been very early as far as being on the mend then, and Thatcher had wanted me to focus on that.

There was a reason he was one of my best friends, and I

hadn't minded him looking more into things because I had wanted to work on my relationship with Sloane at the time.

Today, I was definitely invested, and Thatcher turned on his chair, the both of us abandoning our lunches to look at this shit.

"I'm mean they're dead," he said, pointing toward the pages in my hands. We had caseworkers here, lawyers, and government employees. They all had ties in some way to Sloane's adoption and birth records. Sloane as Noa Sloane. Not Sloane as Pilar Mallick. These people on these pages had made things happen whether they'd signed off on documents regarding her adoption or simply aided with the process. Thatcher opened his hands. "They all appear to be from natural causes. The ones I found anyway. These records are old, and some of these people are hard to track down."

From what it looked like, the majority, and only a handful of these people were actually dead.

"This one had heart disease. Died during an operation," Thatcher continued, motioning to a social worker's picture. He gestured toward a lawyer. "This guy died during an operation too. Plastic surgery. Not exactly natural, but he died on the table. A bad reaction to the anesthesia."

I gave him back the folder.

"A ski accident," he continued regarding a government employee. This person's name was on Sloane's birth certificate, had signed off on it. He shrugged. "It's been hard to find pretty much any of these people, but the ones I have found..."

It hadn't been good for them.

"Sounds like justice to me," Wolf cut in, barely looking up from his phone. I supposed the party plans hadn't been that invigorating for him in the end. His attention flicked over. "Anyway, I don't know why y'all are even looking into that shit. I'm sure the parents are."

That was the way he'd felt when I'd brought all this up over a month ago. I wasn't about to look into his twin's records and keep that detail a secret from him either, but once I'd mentioned it, he'd wondered why I was bothering. He hadn't seen the point, and I received that resistance even more when Thatcher did start presenting me with information. Wolf and his family were in a good place. They were in a *great place*, and Sloane was back. He was happy.

So, I got it.

Even still, he didn't question my need for justice, which I still wanted for my girl *and his* sister. I leaned in. "You know why I'm looking into this, and you're right. It seems justice has been served."

"Good. So maybe you can give it a rest?" Wolf stroked his jaw, eyeing me, and I shook my head.

"More needs to be done. Thatcher's only found a handful of these people, right, Thatch?"

Thatch didn't look like he wanted anything to do with this conversation, but I didn't push him to engage. No one wanted to battle Wolf's ass, and I preferred not to either.

I ended up having Thatcher put the folder away, at least until a more suitable time when it wasn't bothering Wolf. This freed me up to lock both arms around Wolf's sister who sat next to me. Sloane leaned back into my arms, and though we all may have been talking about things that surrounded her, she was rarely a part of these types of conversations. Like Wolf, she really didn't care too much about the circumstances surrounding her adoption, and I'd even stopped giving her updates. She was trying to find her happy place too, and I respected that.

Her fingers grazed my arms around her while she too attempted to stay engaged in the conversation about her brother's birthday party. The party wasn't about her, but she was obviously meeting all the Legacy families while there. I think she was just staying involved mostly for Bru's sake, who didn't seem at all to want anything to do with the party planning either. He spent most of the time on his phone while Bow was talking about the details.

He was actually doing that now while Bow was going on about streamers or some shit, but looked up when Forrester, the head of the Legacy families' hired security, came over to the Legacy lunch table.

"Afternoon, kids," he said to our group, and my smile stretched.

"Hi, Forrester. You here to go over the daily changing of the guards schedule with us on this lovely afternoon?" I asked, being a complete asshole, but I didn't give a shit. It'd become a game we all played with the security around here. Sloane and the rest of us were campus royalty while all the security personnel (both hired by our parents and not) were our royal guards. It was a way to keep things light and less stressful. Especially for Sloane, who definitely knew all these changes were about her.

I guess it was *my* way to help, to protect her. I knew all the security around here unnerved her, and anything I could do to make her more comfortable I did.

Forrester cleared this throat in front of us. "Good one, Mr. Prinze," he said, not entertained in the slightest, but he played it off, so I'd give him that. He adjusted his tie. "We don't want to bother you kids, but our views of Sloane are obstructed. It'd be easier to see her if she switched sides of the table."

The man proceeded to ask her, which tugged Bru's attention up from his phone long enough to scoff.

"You're joking, right?" he questioned, but she elbowed his arm.

"It's fine," she said, getting up right away, and I did too. Usually, I'd fuck more with Forrester, but if she was fine on moving, I was too.

We got situated on the other side of the table, and this pleased the head of security. He thanked us, thanked Sloane, before heading back to his gaggle of suits.

"God, this is a joke," Bru continued, while the rest of us kind of started to eat again. He frowned. "The press aren't even allowed on campus and barely any of them are out there anymore."

They had stopped the hard hounding after getting the juicy stuff from the people actually willing to talk about Sloane's returned presence here. That hadn't been Legacy or Court since they were all loyal to us, but a few other kids had spread what they knew. It hadn't been much since they didn't talk to her, and eventually, the press had gotten bored. I'd only seen a handful of them out there today.

Sloane raised a hand. "I told you it's fine."

"It's not, but whatev," Bru stated, picking up his phone again. The kid had been testy lately, and I did acknowledge what Sloane had said recently about him. He'd been keeping to himself, but if I had all these changes and shit happening in my life too, I'd probably be doing the same thing. Bru shook his head. "It's just not necessary is all I'm saying."

I definitely agreed about that, but I wasn't going to be the one to tell the parents otherwise. Not to mention it'd be inappropriate coming from me. These changes were mostly for Sloane, which meant, if anything happened regarding reversing them, Ramses and Brielle would be at the heart of the decision.

Knowing that, I tipped my chin at Wolf, who exchanged a glance between myself and the situation. Wolf braced his hands. "Maybe I can talk to my parents," he suggested, specifically looking at Bru. He shrugged. "You're right. The press has been backing off, and maybe they'll consider scaling back some of the security."

I think we all knew it wasn't just the press that kept the security here. The parents were all still uneasy with my grandfather being around, but even I thought all the added personnel was a bit excessive. We were *all* being watched 24/7 in these halls, and after a recent, awkward-as-fuck conversation Ramses had had with me... the one where my god dad had basically barred me from overnights at his house until further consideration, Sloane and I were finding it harder and harder to fuck without prying eyes around campus. We had to ditch the suits and personnel just to be together lately, so yeah, I could use a little less security.

It blew my mind how in sync my buddy Wolf and I were about that, but I also knew any opportunity he could find to help with the Bru situation, he tried. We all could feel how closed off Bru was, and I knew Sloane had asked Wolf to look out for him.

This suggestion seemed to appease Bru a bit when he nodded, and Sloane definitely appreciated it too. She smiled at Wolf, and it was nice to see them getting along. My buddy had wished for this relationship his whole life, and he was finally getting it.

With the chaos of the security issue figured out, Bow broke the tension a bit. She didn't need to be in charge of Bru's party plans, but she had taken the helm since Brielle was juggling trying to be mayor and working at the school. Ramses had offered to help, but he too was behind on work with how much time he'd been spending at home. With them tied up, Bow had basically jumped at the opportunity. She loved shit like that. She grinned at Bru. "So, I guess all that's left now is cake. What's your favorite flavor?"

"Uh, whatever's fine," he said, his phone back in his hand. I wanted to grab the fucking thing from him. We were all trying to accommodate his ass here. Even I was paying attention. His shoulder lifted. "I'm cool with whatever."

Bow leaned in. "Yeah, but it's your party, and we're not restricted to any flavor. The cake will be multiple tiers. So yeah, whatever you want."

"Bru?" Sloane questioned, frowning, and the guy sighed.

"I mean it. I don't care." He tapped his phone. "Besides, I think we *all* know this party is not about me so the cake should just be whatever the majority wants."

Bow opened her mouth, but whatever she'd been about to say cut off when Sloane lifted her hand.

"What's that supposed to mean?" Sloane asked, but Bru didn't even look from his phone this time.

"Just what I said," he stated. "This party isn't about me. My birthday was longer than shit ago, and Wolf's parents are just trying to be nice."

"Our parents." Wolf had his hair down today, wild and looking as intimidating at shit. He tipped his chin at Sloane. "They're her parents too, and you're very much a part of all this. Sure, they're being nice, but we all do want to celebrate you."

No agitation hit my buddy's voice, and he had been very level-headed when dealing with the whole Bru situation. Bru had definitely been pushing lately, distancing. It was affecting his sister the most, which affected Wolf as well. Wolf had 100 percent been handling the situation with kid gloves, and he had to.

We all did.

We were all doing this for Sloane, and with all eyes on him, Bruno swung his attention to Bow.

"Sorry, Bow. Chocolate's my favorite," he said, then proceeded to gather his things. He got up, and Sloane lifted her head.

"Where are you going?" With a hard sigh, she scrubbed into her hair, and Bru shouldered his bag.

"I'm going to the library to get some studying in before lunch ends," he said, mentioning the other thing he was doing lately besides being on his phone. He sauntered away, and when Sloane started to go after him, Wolf eased out of his chair.

"Let me go talk to him," he suggested, though I had no idea what about. He gripped his chair. "Things shouldn't be tense like this, and it has been."

It had, but that wasn't his fault.

Sloane appeared to be two minds about this decision, but in the end, she sat back down in her plaid skirt. She forced fingers through her hair, and the guys, Bow, and I sat in silence. Eventually, Bow had to get to her next class since it was on the other side of campus. Thatcher and Wells had the same issue as well, but they stayed.

"Now do you see what I mean?" Sloane questioned, specifically to me. "He's not acting right. He's..." She gripped her arms. "I didn't want him being a casualty in all this."

I'd once told her in an email she was like her father, and her saying this... putting others before herself, only stressed the point. My god dad, Ramses, was so giving and always put others before himself.

She really was her father's daughter.

I was about to offer advice on a situation that I myself was ill-equipped to handle, but we were all disturbed when a guy from Court made his way over to our table.

"You guys need to come to the hallway," he said, rushed and ominous-sounding. He didn't specify who, but we all ended up following him out of the lunchroom. We actually made it there before security had a chance to follow.

Had they, they might have broken up what we all walked in on.

Bru and Wolf had a circle around them, the two of them at opposite ends, but only Bru was the one who looked puffed the hell up.

"You know what? You may be my sister's brother, but you're not fucking *mine* so back off," he shot at Wolf, Bru's face red. "I don't need your sympathy, and I definitely don't need your fake friend shit. We both know you were only my friend to get close to my sister."

Sloane's eyes shot open at my side. She said Bru's name, but he only looked in her direction briefly before stepping up to Wolf.

"Don't try to deny it." Bru pointed at my buddy. "We both know what that shit was about when you visited me in the hospital and were all nice and shit. You knew the truth. Meanwhile, you were pulling the wool over my fucking eyes."

People had their phones out, and accused of shit that he and the rest of Legacy all knew was most likely true, Wolf threaded his hands over his head.

"I'm not trying to, and I know how things started." His lips turned down. "I do, but it doesn't have to be that way now. It's not that way now."

Bru spun but didn't back off. In fact, when he came back, his chest touched my boy's, and at this point, I was shoving fuckers out the way to get to them both. A thick circle had formed, and people were definitely more interested in getting this on social media than letting Thatcher, Wells, and me through. I had Sloane by the arm, trying to keep her back, but she was following me.

"Bru, what the fuck?" she called, but this time, he wasn't breaking focus enough to look away. Meanwhile, Wolf had attempted to put space between the pair, but for every space he took, Bru took two.

Wolf raised his hands. "I'm not lying, kid. It's not that way now, and I'm telling you. You need to back off and give me my space."

"Or what?" Bru hadn't given him space, clearly egging Wolf on, and Wolf smirked.

Wolf pointed at him. "Let's not forget the last time you stepped up on me like this, *I let* you." His nostrils flared, eyes narrowed hard into slits. "Now, I'm trying to be civil here, but you throw a punch, I *will* end you."

"Give it a fucking shot!" Bru roared, shoving his hands

into Wolf's chest. Wolf raised his fist, but cutting through the crowd, I locked arms under his. Meanwhile, Thatcher got Bru to back off via the chest, but Bru didn't lower his fist until Wells got it.

"Back off, D," Wolf growled, his voice low, menacing. He didn't fight me, but I knew my friend. I let this dude go, and Bruno Sloane would be a pile of broken bones. A deep rumble hit Wolf's chest. "I got this handled."

I think we both knew that was bullshit.

I put hands on his chest, forcing the circle to break when I pushed him out of it. "Go walk this shit off."

"D—"

"*Now*, Ares," I gritted, and at this point, Sloane finally made her way into the chaos. I'd let her go when I saw Wolf swinging, and though she started to go to Bru, she stopped once she realized Wells and Thatcher had him. They were doing the same thing I had with Wolf. They told him to walk this off, and he started to, but one look at Sloane had him navigating the other way.

I didn't know if he didn't want to answer to her or what, but he shouldered through the circle to get *away* from her.

She took a step after him. "Bruno!"

He didn't stop, and that was about the time security finally made their way into the hallway. Fucking *useless*. They immediately started herding people back into the lunchroom, and Sloane stalked her way over to me.

"You said you'd help," she said, but she didn't say it to me. She stepped up to Wolf. "I mean, what the hell was that?"

That had been her brother goading one of my best friends, but it wasn't wise to cut into this conversation. She lifted a hand at Wolf, and all he did was shake his head at her.

He was choosing to be the bigger man when he walked past her, and when he did, I sent Thatcher and Wells after him. *I*, on the other hand, went after Sloane who was now headed in the direction Bru had left, and I hoped this wasn't a snapshot of the future. Me being lodged between my buddy, his sister, and Bru.

It definitely didn't feel like a good place to be.

CHAPTER
TWENTY-SEVEN

Sloane

"So, does anyone want to talk about what happened today?" Ramses asked, and it was one of few dinners where it was only the five of us. Dorian had been eating at home recently, and Bow, Thatcher, and Wells only came over sometimes. Ramses opened his hands. "At school?"

Though the question had been open to the table, it was directed at Ares. I knew because Ramses's sight didn't leave his son, and neither did Brielle's. She had her arms folded beside her husband, and I was sure security had told her all about what happened in the halls of her school today.

I mean, clearly.

Bru, beside me, was picking at his food. I had tried to talk to him about what happened today when I'd finally caught up to him, but he wasn't having it. I'd texted Ares right after. I'd kind of blown up at him, and he hadn't completely deserved it. All I'd gotten *from him* was a text message bubble for about two seconds before he never actually sent anything.

And here we were now.

Ares, on my other side, hadn't bothered to pick at his food. He simply sat there under Ramses's and Brielle's gaze.

At least, until he pulled the napkin off his lap.

"Can I be excused?" he asked, not waiting for their response. He merely got up, his chair squeaking across their polished, hardwood floor. He walked right around the table, passing Ramses, who angled around.

"Actually, no—" Ramses started, but Brielle put her hand on his arm.

"I'll go talk to him," she said, sighing. She tossed her napkin on the table as well at the same time Bru removed his.

"May I be excused too?" my brother asked, and I shot him a look.

Ramses sighed. Instead of responding, he gestured his permission to go, and Bru took full advantage.

"Bruno," I gritted, but he ignored me. He headed out of the dining room as Brielle was making her way back in, mentioning something about Ares needing a minute to stew. I didn't know what was said, but either she didn't like what her son had had to say to her, or Ares really had asked for some time.

I hoped it was the latter, but despite wanting to excuse myself too, I stayed. I cuffed my arms. "I'm sorry." I didn't know what I was apologizing for, but once again, I was at the base of all this crap. I chewed my lip. "We were going over stuff for Bru's birthday party, and things kind of got out of hand after that."

I proceeded to tell them the fallout and confirmed that security had told Brielle all about the fight itself. They'd obviously talked to students, even though security themselves had arrived late.

I frowned. "And it wasn't Ares's fault. Bru was already feeling weird about the security." I told them about that too, sighing. "Ares offered to go talk to Bru after he walked away, and Ares only tried to deescalate things before the fight happened."

All this only sounded worse rehashed, and I covered my face. Brielle touched hers. "I'm sorry, honey. I didn't realize the security was adding so much tension for you and Bruno." She took Ramses's hand. "I'm sure we can figure out something with that."

"It's not a problem," Ramses continued. "But as far as the fighting, Ares does know better. We'll talk to him."

"Please don't punish him. I…" My jaw moved. "He didn't do anything wrong. He was just trying to help." If anything, I needed to talk to him.

Ramses nodded, but his own tense expression didn't lighten. "And we didn't know Bru felt that way about the party. We can cancel that too if he'd like, but this gathering is for him equally. Even if we weren't celebrating his birthday, it would be. I told you how important both of you are to this family, and I mean that. *We* mean it."

He exchanged a look with Brielle, and I did know they both meant that.

I ended up telling them both I'd talk to my brother, but the party needed to continue. Bru wouldn't want them to cancel it and definitely not because of him. He was just going through things right now.

I did excuse myself to go talk to him but didn't make it past the stairs. Ares sat there, and despite sitting several steps up, his feet still touched the floor with his long legs.

His curly head popped up when I entered the foyer, and I sat beside him.

"I'm sorry I was so hard on you," I cut in first, my hands on my knees. "I overreacted, and it wasn't cool. You did try to help."

"I heard." He rubbed his hands, and I wondered how much he had heard. Probably the whole thing. He leaned back, elbows touching the stairs. "But I overreacted too. Poorly."

We both had, and I shook my head again.

Ares swung his head in my direction. "I'm not asking you to choose between Bru and me, or *us* and him." His lips thinned, his expression tight. "I'm not stupid. I know we'd all lose, and it's not fair for any of us to put you in that position anyway."

I winced. He was being so honest with me, and that was one good thing about my twin brother. When he was honest, he was to a fault.

My twin brother.

I think that was the first time my thoughts actually did that, things between Ares and I so different lately, and I wasn't sure he was so right about what he'd said. Honestly, I wouldn't even let my thoughts go there, a choice between Bru and him...

And everyone else.

"I'm trying to be strong, little."

I glanced his way, his expression hard.

He rubbed his jaw. "But this shit is hard, and I'm fighting natural instincts every day. Ones to step up, *be there* for you above all else." His throat jumped. "Be there for the kid when I got my own shit. When I'm here and in this too." He touched his mouth to his fists. "I'm not asking you to choose, but I am asking you to be patient with me. I'm trying to figure out this shit too and how to work my head around it."

Because he was my brother as well, and he'd been being one to not just me. He had, but Bru and I definitely hadn't been supporting him.

I hadn't been.

Ares had been a way better brother than I'd been a sister to him, but before I could apologize for that, he got up.

"I'm going to take a walk," he said, and I let him because I knew he needed that. The front door closed, and I immediately rerouted on the stairwell. I found Bru in his bedroom, but he was talking on the phone when I came inside. I knocked but he didn't answer. Probably because he was on the phone.

"Hey, uh, I gotta go," he said, sitting up on his bed. We had the same setup, full entertainment system and connecting bathrooms. Ramses and Brielle had been really good to us. He stared at me. "It's Sloane."

My eyebrow lifted slow, my shoulder closing the door. Bru hung up his phone, then tossed it on the bed. I cocked my head. "Who was that?"

Bru closed the book on his bed, a textbook. At some point, he must have been trying to study. His back touched the headboard. "Does it matter?" he asked, and my brow lifted. He shook his head. "I just don't think you knowing will make this particular situation better. What happened downstairs and today."

I sat on the bed, my arms crossed, and Bru rubbed his hands.

"Callum," he said. "And before you say anything about that, you told me it wasn't a problem to talk to him, which I have been." He paused, nodding. "For a while now. I have been."

My mouth parted, really not clear on *what* to say.

Or what to think.

I just knew my body had a physical reaction to what he'd said, and it was one that got my throat tight a little. "Okay."

"Okay?"

"I mean, what do you want me to say to that?" My shoulders lifted. "You've *been* talking to him?" I had said he could talk to Callum, but I thought that conversation had only been that day.

"We've been texting," he said. "Off and on." His eyes lifted, as if to gauge my reaction to that. "Even more recently. I texted him that day I mentioned it. I wanted to let him know we were okay like I told you, but also just wanted to talk. He had lied, and I wanted to hear from him, you know?" He rocked back and forth, his hands on his arms. "He'd been so cool with us. Cool with *me*, and he was my friend."

I swallowed. "What did he say?"

"Took ownership of it like that day he told us everything." He dropped his arms on his knees. "And believe me, I gave it to him. I thought it was bullshit he lied even though he was trying to help. I didn't talk to him for a while after that, but recently, I opened up the dialogue again when he checked on me. He just wanted to see how I was doing, and we talked for a while. A long while."

I moved my legs up on the bed.

"He just gets what it's like, I guess. Being on the outside, I mean." He looked up. "He lost his entire family after what he did."

I figured he had. I mean, he should have. It'd been so wrong, terrible.

"But he doesn't claim things should be any different. These are the cards he drew for himself, and he deserves that shit. He knows."

"Bru..."

He glanced over. "He just gets being on the outs, and I honestly believe he wanted to help us, help *you*. Dad came to him for help, and Callum definitely didn't have to do the right thing. He did, though. He took care of us, and I know what he did in the past. It was completely *fucked*, and I know that." He forced out a breath. "But he did take care of us, and he's been a friend to me, Sloane. He has, and though others have lied to me, he did to help you. He did, and that's important."

His face screwed up, his hands rubbing any and all emotions away from my sight. I maneuvered over to his side of the headboard, but he wouldn't look at me.

"I get what it's like to be on those outs," he said, my heart clenching. "We related on that, but I won't talk to him anymore if you don't want me to. I know it's more complicated for you."

It was more complicated, severely.

I lay my head on his shoulder. "I'm on the outs too, you know?" I said, cringing. "I don't know this family."

"But they're *your* family." He touched my hand. "You can always claim that."

He was right. I could.

I closed my eyes, looping my arms around his. I didn't know how I felt about him talking with Callum. I had a physical reaction but saw his conflict. In fact, I believed I only didn't have my own because I'd pushed that part away. I hadn't had to deal with it because my priorities lay elsewhere. I did have a family.

I had a choice.

"I'm not sure he's that same person, Sloane," Bru said, squeezing my hand. He shook his head. "And he's only been good to us."

He was right. He had. Callum could be plagued by his dark past, but for me, I had to be complicated. He'd hurt so many people in my life.

I squeezed my brother's hand back, knowing what I had to say to him. I really hadn't been a good sister to him either, let alone a friend. I had no idea all these emotions were going on inside him. I'd had suspicions but nothing like this.

"I won't get in the way of you talking to him," I said, because I wouldn't. My brother felt he had few real friends these days.

So how could I take away the one he felt he had?

CHAPTER
TWENTY-EIGHT

Dorian

Sloane rocked with the families today. In fact, she was hanging with the moms and her grandmothers when Wells tugged me to see Thatch. Apparently, Thatcher had something to say to me that couldn't wait.

I waved at Sloane when I passed her and the group, but she really hadn't needed me or any of us today. She'd handled her own and even appeared to be enjoying herself at her brother's birthday party.

Which was a damn relief.

I think after the fight on campus earlier in the week, none of us had been sure how things would be. Sloane and Wolf appeared to have created a semblance of patching things up, but Wolf had pretty much avoided Bru today. That'd been easy since it was basically Bru and Sloane's coming out party. They both met the Legacy families and Sloane's grandparents, two of which had flown in from New Jersey. Everyone had been hella excited to meet her and Bru both, and Wolf hadn't stood in the way of that. He'd been cordial with Bru when they had interacted, but for the most part, they had kept to their respective corners.

This left me to man the task of taking care of my girl, but like I said, she hadn't needed me. She'd been mingling and hard with all the people ready and waiting to see her. She'd already met Bow and Thatch's parents, but the Ambroses and Johnsons were new to her. I'd been there with her when Ramses and Brielle introduced Bru and her to them all, and it'd been nice to see everyone together.

It'd been nice to see *her* with them all.

Drink in hand and arm around my girl for the majority of the party, I hadn't realized that these gatherings felt different before. I wouldn't say they hadn't been complete. I mean, none of us had gotten to know Pilar Mallick, but with Sloane here, I definitely felt the difference.

Her own drink in hand, Sloane lifted her hand at me when I passed her. In the middle of conversation, Sloane engaged with her grandmother, Ramses's mom. Her grandma Evie was basically a six-foot-tall lively blonde who also happened to be brilliant. She'd definitely passed some of that down to Wolf. The brilliance part, and Wolf was in the group too. He wasn't doing too much of the talking, but the fact he was with the women and not hiding out in the garage smoking weed let me know shit was different. Different with him. He wanted to be here and around everyone, and even smiled a bit during the conversation.

He tipped his chin at me too briefly before Wells and I navigated out of the Mallicks' parlor. I didn't see Bru with the group, but he'd been hanging a lot with Ramses during the party. I knew my god dad was trying to help by including him, and this was *his* party.

It was like the guy had forgotten that, that we all did care, but I knew things were complicated there. I'd done my fair share of lying to him too in the beginning.

Wells and I found Thatcher in the hall outside one of the

upstairs bedrooms. He was lounging against it, restless as he adjusted his stance several times. I didn't know what that was about, and as soon as Wells and I got to him, Thatcher shot off the wall.

"Hey," Thatcher said, his hands in his pockets, but before he started talking, a toilet flushed in the hallway. Next thing we knew, Knight, *his dad*, surfaced out of the bathroom.

Knight stopped in front of us, his finger lifting and directing between all of us. "You kids up to something?"

Right away, my shoulders lifted, the guys doing the same. I didn't know Wells and Thatcher's deal, but I'd just shown up to whatever the fuck this was.

"Nah, Dad. We're cool," Thatcher said.

"Better be," Knight stated, before tapping my shoulder, then Wells's. He eyed his son before stalking his way down the hallway, and I chuckled at how my friend had possibly failed to miss his dad in literally a bathroom five feet away from him.

He had, though, clearly. Thatcher leaned in. "I've got to tell you something." His gaze circulated the hall. "It's about Sloane's case. I found a weird connection surrounding one of the lawyers involved. One of the ones Godfrey hired to handle it. I haven't found the guy, but something came up when I was looking into his background."

"Okay." Though, I didn't know what was up with all the cloak and dagger shit. If we found something weird, I'd be telling the parents. I shrugged. "What is it?"

"I found out who he used to work for. At least, one of his previous clients." Thatcher's jaw shifted. "Guy used to work for Ibrahim Mallick."

The... hell.

"And for like a while too, dude," Wells chimed into the conversation. "Thatcher said for over a fucking decade."

"Well, what the fuck does that mean?" I asked, and both my friends lifted their hands.

"Whatever it is, it's not good," Thatcher said. "How could it be? That makes no sense."

It didn't. Ibrahim *Mallick* should have no connection at all to Sloane's adoption.

I mean, he was her grandfather.

"You don't think he's involved, do you? In the cover-up, I mean?" Thatcher had his hands laced on his head, restless again. He grabbed his arms instead. "We gotta tell Wolf."

I agreed and fucking *now.*

The party was starting to wrap up when we all got back downstairs, people and family members saying goodbye to each other. Thatcher's parents were taking off early, and we had to stop to say goodbye to them. Bow must have been staying longer since she wasn't with them, and we all had to say goodbye to the Johnsons too when they took off. They said they had a flight out of town, and Wells's parents, Cleo and Jax, ended up holding onto him to chat a bit before they too headed out.

Thatcher and I were by ourselves by the time we got to Wolf, and he was gratefully coming out of a conversation.

I grabbed him before he headed into another.

"Keep watch," I said to Thatcher, not sure the parents needed to hear what I was about to say just yet. I mean, they would, but I needed to tell Wolf first.

Ares and I headed out to his garage, which got some resistance from my friend. It was colder than shit these days, and we both had to put coats on.

"The fuck's going on?" he questioned once we got inside, bundled up in his collared jacket. "My grandparents are about to leave, bro."

"I know," I said, looking around and being just as paranoid as Thatch. "Thatcher just told me something, and you need to know about it."

Thatcher came in, nodding his chin before eyeing through the window on the door, and Wolf arched an eyebrow.

"You know how I've been looking into Sloane's adoption?" I asked, and Wolf's dark eyebrows narrowed.

"Yeah, and I also said that shit is pointless." He waved a hand at me. "Anyway, I'm going to say goodbye to my grandparents."

I grabbed his arm. This shit wasn't pointless, and he was about to hear it. I wet my lips. "One of the lawyers that Godfrey consulted with to help him with the adoption is connected to your grandfather."

"What?"

"He used to work for him, bro," I said, letting go of his arm. "He did, and that seems really fucking suspect. What if your grandfather had something to do with Sloane's kidnapping?" I got closer, nostrils flared. "What if he helped?"

I had to say, it wouldn't be far-fetched. Wolf's family had no relationship with Ibrahim, and I knew Ramses hated his dad as much as my dad hated my grandfather. Ibrahim Mallick had been cut off after the murder of my aunt, outcast from his family and this town.

Which seemed like real fucking cause for a kidnapping.

Wolf's grandfather could definitely be pulling some kind of revenge plot here, and Wolf's reaction to this news wasn't what I'd expected. For starters, he was merely looking at me, his arms braced, his sigh heavy. He shook his head. "That's not possible."

My brow twitched up. "What?"

"It's not possible, and I should know." His expression darkened. "The fucker's dead."

CHAPTER
TWENTY-NINE

Dorian

I stood in silence, Thatcher too when he came over. He'd completely abandoned his position at the door and appeared just as wide-eyed and shocked as I felt.

Wolf lounged against his Hummer. "Dude's dead and has been for years."

My eyebrows narrowed. "How do you know that?"

"Heard my dad talking about it one day," Wolf said, nodding. "I don't know what happened, and honestly, I don't fucking care. I just know he's dead, and *my dad* seemed pretty relieved about it when he found out. He and my mom were in his study when a guy in a suit told them. Dad had apparently hired a private investigator because my gramps went AWOL one year." Wolf's jaw clenched. "They found out that was because he was dead."

Dead.

Thatcher stepped in. "Well, when did it happen? I mean, that doesn't mean he didn't have anything to do with Sloane's kidnapping."

Thatcher was right, of course, and to that, Wolf had his hands raised.

"I don't know when," he stated. "But does that really matter?" He said this, and I blinked. Wolf frowned. "If that fucker did, kind of sounds like he got his just desserts. Karma is a son of a bitch, and it gratefully took his ass out before he could hurt anyone else."

I wouldn't disagree with that, but still. I pocketed my hands. "Why didn't you say anything? About him being dead?"

There were actual times I recalled him making it sound like his grandfather was alive. The most recent being when I'd told him I was going to ask my grandfather for help with Charlie. Wolf had said that'd be a mistake, and I didn't see him going to talk to his own grandfather for help.

Wolf opened his hands. "It didn't seem like it mattered. The fucker's *dead*, and I think you need to let all this shit go. Shit about Sloane's adoption and everything else. It's adding stress to a situation that's finally not being stressful for once."

His voice boomed in the room, off the walls and the cars. Both Bru and Sloane's cars had been delivered here, and they were tucked in between Wolf's and his parents.

A muscle feathered in Wolf's jaw. "She's finally finding happiness here. We *all* are, and I'm not trying to stress my parents out about more shit. Bringing up ghosts, and things that don't fucking matter. Because they don't. Not anymore now that she's back."

Thatcher and I both closed the distance, but Wolf backed away.

Ares raised his hands. "I don't care about this shit anymore. I don't because I *can't*, and I know she doesn't." He lifted a palm toward Thatcher and me. "Or have you both noticed she has no interest in anything you have to tell her about this adoption shit?"

Thatcher looked away, and I wet my lips. Sloane had other

things, *more important* things to think about. She did, and that left me. It was a burden I took on for her because she shouldn't have to think about any of this.

Not when she had me.

I'd always fight for her, always, and when I had nothing to say about that, Wolf shook his head.

"That's because this shit is hurtful," he said. "She's tired, and I am too. Her transition back is already hard enough."

Thatcher started to say something, but he didn't need to. He was only looking into all this because of me. I held Thatcher back to speak myself. "We know it is, bro. That's why we're handling this shit for you. Why *I'm* handling this shit."

"Well, if you're doing this for me and *her*, then you'd listen when I say it's not helping. It is hurtful, D, and I'm tired of being in fucking pain, bro. I'm tired of things *hurting*, and you should know that more than anyone."

I did know that. I just wanted relief after everything with Charlie.

Wolf was a semblance of calm when he pressed his hands together. He breathed into them. "I'm begging you both to let this go. All our families need to heal and especially mine."

I wanted to argue with that, but *that* was hard. This was his family. This was *her*.

I started to say something, but I never got the chance when the garage door opened. It was the one on the other side of the garage, and the three of us got a view of it from behind Wolf's Hummer.

Bruno Sloane came through that door, rubbing his hands with no coat on. He rushed inside, but he wasn't alone.

I recognized the cane right away, and of course, the old man with it. He wore a wool coat, black and a hat to match. He had a colorful box tied with a sea of coiled ribbon in his hands, also black, and I froze where I stood.

I wasn't the only one.

Behind Wolf's Hummer, *both* my boys failed to move a fucking inch. Meanwhile, Bru and his *guest* remained at the garage door.

"Hey, man. You didn't have to get me anything," Bru said, and his guest chuckled, deep, raspy. I recognized it well. Too many cigars and not enough use of his laughter. The man didn't fucking laugh, so when he did, it came out all raspy and shit.

"What the fuck?" This came from Wolf, his eyes expanded to full width. He charged from around the Hummer. Thatcher too.

I beat them both.

I always had been the fastest, intentional with my speed. When I saw a target, I didn't let it go, and I homed in on the old fucker standing next to my girl's brother with nothing but sheer intent.

Old fucker heard me before he saw me, his fucked-up laughter curbing off. A rigid stance replaced it, and right away, he stood in front of Bru. He held up a hand to me. "Grandson—"

"What the fuck are you doing here?" I seethed, grabbing for Bruno, but the dude fucking *pushed* me. Like actually put hands on me, and I collided back into Wolf and Thatcher because I hadn't seen that shit coming. My eyebrows narrowed at Bru. "What the hell?"

"Dorian," Bru started, coming between the old man and me. "Hold off a second. I asked him to be here."

I wasn't the only one to jolt, and a madness hit Wolf's eyes I'd only seen on the field. He grew two sizes behind me, shouldering ahead. "The fuck?"

Bru attempted to calm the situation down with a hand.

Meanwhile, my grandfather sighed. "Bruno told me the event was over," he explained, his lips pulling together. He faced Bru. "Why did you lie? You said everyone had left for a post-dinner at my son's house."

He had?

What. The. *Hell.*

"Wait a fucking second. You two are talking to each other?" Thatcher asked the question. His hand directed between the two. "You two are talking?"

News to me and definitely to Wolf too. We both had hands on each other, sheer shock, I believed, keeping both of us from moving.

Bru shook his head. "That's none of your business, Thatcher."

"The hell it's not—" he started, and my grandfather backed up.

He handed the gift to Bru. "I think you know I need to leave," he said before looking at the three of us. "I'm sorry. Had I known anyone was here, I wouldn't have imposed myself. I just wanted to give the boy a gift for his birthday. He told me about his party, and I meant no harm."

And yet, he kept harming people, didn't he? *Harming me* by being at my friend's house with my parents feet away. I stepped forward. "Get the fuck out of here."

His reaction to this wasn't much of one. He gripped his cane. "I'm so sorry, grandson." He attention drifted to Bru. "I wish you hadn't lied. It doesn't help the situation."

"He said get the *fuck* out, motherfucker!" Wolf blazed, and Thatcher held him back. Thatch got his arm, but even still, Wolf fought. Wolf shot out his finger. "You come anywhere near my family and my friends again, you'll sign your own death certificate. Just *fucking try me*, bro."

The thing was, he *wasn't* lying. I knew my friend, and I knew how I was too. We'd do what we had to in order to protect our families.

With his attention on us, Bru missed my grandfather excusing himself. Bru started to go after him, but stopped when he saw Thatcher let Wolf loose. Bru redirected his attention to preventative measures then, blocking the door like he even could from one of us.

"Have you lost your goddamn mind!" Wolf spat, damn near foaming at the mouth. He bared his teeth. "Why the fuck would you let him in here? Guide him around security?"

Because that was what would have had to be done in order for my grandfather to get onto the Mallick property. The Mallicks had toned down the security lately, but there were still people patrolling the grounds.

Which meant Bruno *led* my grandfather in here.

I shouldered my way forward. "What's your angle? And you better speak fast because I swear to fucking God—"

"What's going on?"

I whipped around, a little fighter at the door.

My little fighter.

Sloane had a wool coat on, hands shoved in the pockets and a flush to her cheeks. Her hair pinned and lips red, she stepped forward in a pair of pumps that brought her closer to my height. I'd have fucked her in them today too had she let me at some point. I'd offered more than one time to steal her away, the red dress beneath her coat *ridiculous* on her curvy body. Not only did it hug her perfect tits, but the high slit gave generous sight to caramel-kissed thighs. She shrugged. "Why are you guys all out here?"

Bru broke away from the circle with a hand over his head, but he couldn't avoid this situation *or Sloane* when she lodged her away in between us.

"I'll tell you what's going on," I said, taking the initiative. I pointed at Bru. "Your brother was just about to tell us why he brought my grandfather in here a few moments ago."

She hadn't expected this *at all*. She whirled around, her sight immediately clashing with Bru's.

Dude still had the fucking gift.

In his hands was that colorful package, evidence of all this, his betrayal. He lifted it. "I can explain."

Sloane's eyes twitched wide. "What are you talking about?"

"We caught them in here. *Both of them.*" Wolf was calmer now, and maybe only because Sloane was in here with us. He lounged back against his Hummer. "D, Thatch, and I were in here talking when Bru comes in with D's grandpa. Fucker gave him that gift in his hands."

I noticed he'd left out the reason why we'd originally been meeting, but at this point, I didn't fucking care.

Sloane's brow jumped at him before looking at Bru, and Bruno fucking shook his head.

"He was in here, but *I* invited him," he gritted, not even bothering to look at us. "I told him about the party, how it was for my birthday, and we were celebrating."

"So naturally you brought the fucker over." I edged forward, hands cuffing my arms. "Meanwhile, my parents are fucking *feet* away from him." All our parents were. All of them. I opened my mouth to say more, but Sloane had one hand on my chest. The other was on Bru.

"You better explain this," she said to him. Had she not been there, I would've been in her brother's face, looking out for his ass be damned. She let go of me to raise a hand to him. "Why would you do that? You said you were only talking to him."

My brow jumped, Wolf's and Thatch's too. Wolf homed in. "The hell?"

"Why didn't you tell us?" I asked, and she shook her head.

"I just found out myself." She had a hand on my chest again, the muscle inside hitting it hard. "As far as I knew, it was just calls and texts, and no, I didn't necessarily agree with it."

But she'd known about it. She had, and she hadn't told me. I didn't know how to feel about that, and her hand didn't leave me when she faced Bru.

"The communication was something that was his, and I personally didn't feel I had a right to dictate," she explained, speaking to me, but her sight on Bru. Her head cocked at him, her expression steel. "But not *ever* was it okay for Callum to be anywhere near the Prinzes or anyone else's family."

The words only got harder with each one spoken, my heart easing, my breaths too. She did care about this situation. She cared about us.

I mean, that was the reason she'd run.

I didn't have to worry about Sloane understanding why my grandfather couldn't be anywhere near us or have any part in anyones' lives. She just got it and never questioned it.

It made my heart ease more, knowing she did get it. Meanwhile, her brother didn't look like he held a stitch of guilt in front of us.

"He wasn't supposed to be," he said, looking at my boys and me like we'd done something wrong. His sighed at Sloane. "I swear to God he wasn't. Callum wanted to give me a gift after hearing about the party. He wanted to ship it, but the party was almost over. I figured it would be by the time he got here, but he came early." His gaze took to the floor. "I was going to get him in and out. I fucking swear, Sloane, and no one was supposed to see him. Callum wouldn't even have come at all had he known anyone was here. He left as soon as he ran into the guys."

He had left, actually telling the truth.

"You know, I don't get you, man." Ares spoke before Sloane could. Before *I* could. His eyes blazed. "This party was for you. It was, and we are all legitimately trying here. *I am*, and you're spitting all that in my fucking face."

"Ares." Sloane got in front of him, but he ignored her.

His nostrils flared. "You're starting fires. I lied to you. D and the rest of the guys too, and I get that, but last I checked, my mom and dad haven't." He pointed at Sloane. "Who also happened to be her parents, and had D's grandpa been even *spotted* by one of them or D's folks, shit would have hit the fan."

"Mine too," Thatcher said, nodding. "And Wells's."

Because we were family, all of us, and he knew that.

"None of them did anything to you." Wolf eased away from Sloane, angling in front of her. "So yeah, it feels like you're just starting little fires and hurting people who don't deserve to be hurt. People who were good to you when they're going through just as much pain as the rest of us."

I was sure Wolf hadn't meant for his voice to break. He put his fist to his mouth, silence in the garage when he turned away.

Sloane's head lowered, her eyes closed. "Bruno…"

"No, he's right, Sloane."

Her head lifted, and Wolf turned around.

Bru swallowed. "I mean, what else could explain it, right? And you're correct in saying your parents have been nothing but good to me, Wolf. They're great, and I've been an asshole."

Sloane eased forward, but Bru backed off.

"I've been starting little fires," he said, nodding like he was speaking the words to himself. He faced Sloane. "And none of you guys deserve that."

Sloane cringed. "Bru—"

"You don't, Sloane." Bru blinked, rubbing his mouth. He pocketed a hand, his nose red, and I imagine from the cold. He had no coat out here like the rest of us. He lifted a hand toward Wolf. "Guy's right. I've been selfish, and I won't do that to you guys anymore. I'm sure Callum can put me up. He's offered in the past if I needed it."

The guy really had been talking to my grandfather.

And this… this new proposal was definitely *not* what Wolf meant to result from what he said. He started to come forward, but Sloane was quicker.

"You're not serious," she said, twitching. "You don't need to leave."

"Actually, I do." Bru forced out a breath, his swallow shifting his throat. "This situation isn't working for me. It's making me not act like myself, and I really, truly don't want to hurt anyone. Especially Wolf's parents. Your parents." He squeezed his eyes. "I *can't* be here, but you need to."

I didn't know what to say, do. I just knew this wasn't the answer, and if we had a conflict, we could work this out. I grabbed Sloane's shoulders. "Bru…"

"No, Prinze." He was shaking his head before I could even speak. He fingered his hair. "And I am sorry. I know seeing your grandfather was fucking hard, and I'm sorry."

And then… he was moving away, leaving, away from all four of us. He had his keys, and he went to his Audi, the one my grandfather had given him.

He got inside with us all behind him, and Sloane looked horrified, Wolf too. He hadn't meant this, his hands laced behind his neck, and none of us fucking had. The guy had been a little shit but shouldn't be with my grandfather.

Sloane got his door before he could close it. "You can't leave, and you *can't* go over there," she said, eyes red, lashes blinking rapidly. She fought off tears behind them. "I can't follow you if you go stay with him, so I need you to get out of this *fucking* car now."

Her voice radiated in the room, all of us frozen. I didn't know whether to intervene or let him go, and I saw the same debate in Thatcher's and Wolf's eyes. Of course, we could stop him. We could physically pull him out of that fucking car, but what was keeping him from leaving anyway after we did? He could run anytime.

And that would make all of this that much worse.

I didn't want to know what that would do to Sloane. I got her by the shoulders as Bru opened the garage with the opener on his visor.

"You shouldn't," he said to her, then looked at me, Wolf, and Thatcher behind us. He faced her. "You need to be here, and it's important for you to be."

"Bru—"

"I'll be all right," he said. "I swear I will be, and I need you to let me go. I can't be here, but you need to be."

She gasped, not even bothering to fight the tears. She blinked two down. "Bru, *please*. We can work this out. Just get out of the car."

He tapped his wheel instead, shaking his head before reaching over to tug the door closed. This forced Sloane to back into my hands, and at this point, I glanced at Thatcher.

"Go get Ramses and Brielle," I said, and my friend rushed away. I didn't know what I hoped they'd do. Reason with the kid or *something*.

It turned out not to matter when Bru strapped himself in. He started the car and made us watch when he took off into a snow-covered world. He disappeared through thick flurries, his sister leaving my hands but not far. She had stayed, let him go like he'd asked.

But that didn't stop her from collapsing to her knees.

CHAPTER
THIRTY

Sloane

Bru: I made it over to Callum's. And please don't worry about me. I'm fine. He took me in. I'm at his house in town, and I'm good, I swear, so please don't worry. Focus on you and what you have to do.

Bru: Sorry for being selfish.

Bru: We'll send someone for my stuff.

Bru hadn't been selfish, but he had sent someone for his stuff. A guy came over right before Ramses and Royal (Dorian's dad) were about to pile into the car with a fleet of security to go physically get my brother. Bru's text had come shortly before that.

I needed a drive.

I found myself standing outside of Godfrey's Chevelle around midnight, but all I did was stare at it. I hadn't driven the car since it'd been delivered to us, and it felt weird now to.

It was my kidnapper's car.

I physically stared at it for so long I didn't notice when I was no longer alone in that garage.

Not until he took my keys.

I glanced up to brown eyes and a boy who smelled too much like raw heat, his hair fingered through, his letterman jacket on over a thick hoodie. Ramses and Brielle had let the dark prince stay over tonight, but I think only because things had been so fucked up. His lips parted. "You going somewhere?"

This was obvious, but maybe it wasn't. I mean, I was just standing outside my car. I glanced at it. "It's his car. Godfrey's?"

He stared at it too, his expression tight. He pocketed my keys before taking my hand and pulling out his own.

It turns out he wanted to drive.

We drove for a long time, him and me. A soft heat flew through the vents while the dark prince gripped the steering wheel of his Audi, no words exchanged between us. He didn't tell me where he was going, and I didn't ask.

I just let him drive.

At some point, he did the responsible thing by calling Ramses and Brielle. He told them I needed some air, and that he'd taken me to get it. He'd gotten some resistance, but not much before the call ended, and those were the final words in his dark ride.

"Can I take you some place?" Dorian's eyes were on the night ahead, his Audi's headlights flooding the bright snow. We'd only had a few inches earlier today, the evening clear now. He looked at me. "It's not far from here if you wanna go."

I didn't care where he took me, my knees up. At this point, I was just trying not to fucking cry. I mean, I'd begged my brother to come back after he'd left. Called him. He'd ignored the calls, and the texts I'd gotten had been his last.

I nodded, my breath shallow and fucked up. I glanced away so I wouldn't cry.

Dorian took me to a cemetery.

Rows and rows of tombstones filled my vision, the dark prince's path an intentional one. He traveled the paths with the ease of one who'd been here before. Maybe many times.

We eventually stopped.

A large memorial towered ahead, several of them. Dorian got out, and I did too, and together we headed over toward some of the biggest. I saw familiar names on pretty much all of them.

Prinze.

This was obviously his family's plot, and he took my naked hand in the chilly air, guiding me around snow-covered tombstones and memories. I had no idea what we were doing until, well, I did.

Charlie Gregory Lindquist.

"This is Charlie," Dorian said, his breath husky and puffing around him. The tip of his nose flushed, his lips red and doing the same. His fingers danced with mine. "This is my big brother."

The breath stopped in my chest, our fingers lacing when he guided me over. He placed me in front of himself, physically presenting me to the memorial.

"Charlie, this is Sloane," he said, not looking at me. He hadn't once since we'd gotten here. He squeezed my shoulders. "She hasn't lost her brother, but she probably knows a little bit what this feels like so…" He didn't have to say what, glancing down at me. He smiled a little. "This is probably weird. Morbid?" His head shook. "Probably dumb I took you here."

It wasn't dumb. Not at all. I looked at the memorial. "Hi, Charlie."

Dorian chuckled, his hand squeezing his eyes before he put his arms around my head, their weight on my chest, the muscled heat cocooning me. He hugged me close. "I've been wanting you guys to meet."

I was glad he did, my hands rubbing his arms. "I don't like that I know what this feels like." Like I was being carved from the inside out with a dull spoon. I closed my eyes. "I hate that I know what this feels like."

Dorian's mouth touched my head, his breath steady, close. It probably took a lot for him to take me here, and it definitely wasn't the same as what he'd gone through.

It probably felt close.

I hadn't been the only one to beg my brother to come home. Ramses and Brielle had called him too, and though he'd answered them, his words had been what he'd emphasized before he left. The situation wasn't working for him. He needed time, and he couldn't do that here. He told them to tell me he was fine and I shouldn't worry. I'd see him at school, and I needed to worry about myself.

But how couldn't I worry about him?

I didn't know how long we stayed at Charlie's memorial. Could have been minutes. Maybe even hours. I just knew eventually it got so cold I couldn't feel Dorian's arms around me anymore, and that was when he said we should go back. We got in the car to find missed texts from both Ramses and Brielle, Ares too. No one else knew we were gone since it was so late, so yeah, there was that. We told them all we were on our way back, but we didn't leave the cemetery right away. I sat in the heated car with Dorian's arm around me.

"I wanted to tell you Bru was talking to him," I said out of nowhere, playing with his fingers. My lips pursed tight. "I think I was ashamed. Your grandfather was so good to us and a friend to him." I swallowed. "A friend to me."

I looked up to already find him staring down at me. He glanced away. "I get that."

"It feels like a betrayal to think that. Say that," I said. "Bru doesn't think your grandfather's that man he used to be. He trusts him."

And I did too.

Dorian's hand covered the back of my neck, squeezing. "He has only been good to you and the kid, and I do get that." He wet his lips. "He's been there for you."

His voice sounded haunted saying that, pained. I didn't want to hurt him by talking about this, but it was the truth.

"He was someone you could rely on," he said, his fingers brushing my arm. "There is no betrayal, and honestly, I'm thinking the only thing I know about my grandfather these days are facts of the past and other things I'm still not ready to talk about."

He'd mentioned that there was something, but he hadn't said it had anything to do with his grandpa.

I squeezed his hand, and in response, he tipped my chin.

"You would support me," he said, smirking. His thumb touched my lip. "You are your dad's daughter."

This didn't feel like a bad thing. Ramses was such a good guy. He was great.

The dark prince guided me onto his lap, my knees touching his leather seats. He opened my coat, and I gasped when he palmed my breast.

"You make me better, you know?" His mouth touched my chest, his fingers tweaking my nipple through my dress and bra. "You make things not so dark."

He did that to me too, everything about him perfect for me.

"I hate that I love you," he admitted, exposing my breast. His tongue flicked my nipple, and I sucked in a breath. "It should be better than me. For you it should be better."

He hugged me close when he eased my coat off, my dress up. He was rock hard between my legs. He rocked his hips up, and heat pooled between my thighs.

"I'm fucked up, Noa," he said, forcing his fingers beneath

my underwear. He braced my ass cheeks. "But you don't make me that way. You make me so much better."

I tugged him to look at me, his face flushed, expression serious. "You make me that way too."

"I wish that was true." His smile didn't reach his eyes, his fingers sliding into my heat. My breath was shallow as his thumb flicked my clit. "But I'm too selfish to let you go."

He added another digit, past the knuckle and to his Court ring. He slid both in and out of me with his other fingers, and I gasped again when he bit my lips.

"I want you always to see me like this." He sucked my lip in, nibbling. "The guy who makes you fucking come. The one you bleed for."

How could I see him any other way?

"The one who gives you heaven, hell, and everything in between." He shoved my dress up and off, unclasping my bra. He sucked my nipple into his mouth, and when he bit down, tears pricked my eyes. He grinned. "But you love that shit because you're as sick as me."

I was sick because of him, gloriously fucking sick. My hand hit the top of his car, my hips rocking against his jeans. My breast, heavy and weighted, fell out of his mouth with a pop only seconds before he latched onto the other one. He pressed a hand against mine on the ceiling.

"But never your nightmare, Noa," he rasped, his eyes closed as he suckled my chest. "I'll be your hell, but never your nightmare. I can't be your fucking monster, Noa. I can't..."

His voice broke, his eyes wild, when he forced his coat off, then rolled up his shirt. He tossed it off, his thick shoulders roving tight with toned muscle, his abs flexing, his body flushed. He hugged me close between firm arms, and I called out when he slammed his jean-clad cock against me.

He cut off the sound with a firm grasp to my throat, his hand tight and grip unrelenting.

"You can't see me that way," he breathed, fusing our mouths together. He pressed hard. "Your monster. Your nightmare."

He wasn't that way. He wasn't. I shook my head. "I don't see you that way." He'd shown me his darkness, but he'd also shown me that heaven. He was a good person. He just had problems in his life like me.

He said nothing, only kissing harder. He unbuckled his jeans, forcing them down.

"I love you," he said, stroking himself. Lifting me up, he guided his length along my slit. "Even if I shouldn't or I'm not good enough to, I do. I can't stop it. I need to love you. I need it *for me* because it does make me better."

He kissed my chest, my eyes *burning*. I didn't understand why he was saying these things, and I made him look at me.

"You're not a monster," I said, shaking my head. I fingered hair away from his eyes. "You're beautiful." He was my dark prince, yes.

But he was also my saving grace.

I'd seen *his face* when I thought I'd been about to die in that warehouse. It'd been *his grin* I thought of and hoped to God I'd get to see again.

"I saw you when Godfey took me," I said, gasping. "I saw you when I thought I was about to die because I thought I'd never see you again. I did, and that terrified me."

His mouth parted, his eyes scanning mine. He glanced away, but I forced him back.

"I need you with me," I said, guiding him inside me. He closed his eyes, and I pressed our mouths together. I bit his lip. "I need you. I love you."

His hips moved, slowly at first, and mine did too. We held onto each other, breathing each other in and out.

"I need you too," he admitted, his hips slamming harder, faster. He held onto my ass, his abs clenching, sweat rolling down his chest. He sucked my tongue into his mouth while he used the steering wheel to keep me pinned, thrusts powerful but kisses tender.

So tender.

Our tongues moved in a slow duel, my hips slamming as equally hard into his.

"Promise me you'll always see me as this," he gritted, his head shaking. He hugged me, fucking me so deep. "I'm only this for you. The one who makes you come and the one who bleeds *for you*. Today. Tomorrow. Forever."

Forever.

"I promise," I said, my arms gripped around him. I bit his neck, and he roared, his thighs jutting forward in quick succession. Heat exploded in my belly the same time he flooded deep inside me, his body stiff and fingers biting into my flesh. His head touched the seat in a gorgeous tousle, lengthy spools of blond falling back, his eyes closed. He even came beautifully.

His eyes opened, and he wet his lips before kissing me again. He sucked me in, and I drowned within his depths. I didn't know it was possible to love someone so much after hating them. He wasn't just heaven.

He was a miracle too.

CHAPTER
THIRTY-ONE

Sloane

Bru missed Thanksgiving at the Mallicks'. I begged him to attend, but he said he had other plans. Since he'd been at Callum's, he'd been going off on long weekends, ones during which Callum was allowing him to do college visits and basically any other thing he wanted to do. If he wanted it, Callum provided it, and this hadn't been uncommon before Bru had left. Callum had always bent over backward to be helpful, and I appreciated him taking care of him.

I just wished I could have.

The Monday after Thanksgiving break, things returned right back to what they were in the halls of Windsor Preparatory, my brother in his clique and me with my own. Another new change was he'd gotten new friends, getting more and more involved in anything academic, which meant the kids in those clubs too. When we'd first gotten here, he'd been all about the football bros, Court, and Legacy.

Now, he seemed to stay away from anything at all that had to do with any of that, them. If I was with Dorian, Ares, and any of Legacy, I got an awkward wave from my brother or a stiff smile, and when I wasn't with them, the interaction wasn't much better. I asked him how he was doing, and the one or two-word responses that followed only unsettled my stomach. My brother was here, but he wasn't *here*.

"*I just need time,*" he said to me one day. I'd confronted him about the holidays coming up. I wanted to be able to see him and open presents with him. We never did anything big, but we were always together.

He said of course I'd see him, of course we'd meet up, but anything having to do with him coming over to the Mallicks' had been questionable. He said he still needed time for all that, but I'd given him time.

It'd been *weeks*.

I really wasn't dealing with all this well, feeling myself give one or two-word answers in the majority of conversations I had. No one pushed me about anything, but they weren't stupid. I was missing Bru, and every day I felt like I had one toe dipped into two different lives. One was with Legacy, and the other was the one I'd been forced to leave behind. It made me a non-participant in the life I felt I had left, and I knew that the moment I ran into a few members of security outside of Brielle's office.

Forrester, the head of security, was ushering people out of the headmaster's office with boxes in their hands, and when I asked about that, Forrester said Brielle was moving things back to city hall.

This was the building she worked at as mayor, and since I hadn't heard about a move, I passed him, heading inside. I had to pass the freakier-than-shit King Kong bust on my way into the office. I knew the school's mascot was the king, but that thing freaked me out every time I saw it. Even when I'd been a student assistant for Principal Mayberry, I'd found myself giving it a wide berth.

Because I was familiar with the space, I waved to the

headmaster's secretary once inside Brielle's office. I saw her secretary a lot here since I used to be a student assistant, and she didn't bother to announce me to Brielle. She just told me to go ahead inside, and I passed more movers with boxes on my way. Brielle was ushering another in bib overalls when I finally did get in there with her.

"Oh, hey, honey," she said to me, signing off on a clipboard when it was presented to her. She finished, and that person left too. "What's going on? Everything okay?"

It was for once, yes. I'd had so much drama in my life recently, so I wasn't surprised she asked, though.

Brielle came around her desk, her slacks long and brown, her top flowing. She came just to my chin, which was where most people did. She put a hand behind my back. "Aren't you supposed to be in science this hour?"

She knew my schedule, along with everyone else in my life. I nodded. "I was just coming from the bathroom. Saw Forrester and he said people were moving things out of your office?"

The place almost appeared bare through further observation, barely more in here than a desk and chairs.

"Yes. I'm actually headed back to the Mayor's office following the holiday break," she said. "Thought I'd get a jump on things. The school hired someone for the position ages ago. They've been on standby, waiting."

They were waiting for me to be okay, I guess, but she didn't say that. We all knew Brielle was only here for me.

Another man came in and handed Brielle another clipboard. She signed this one too, then instructed me to wait a second while she pointed out to the movers a few things that needed to be packed in the foyer as well. By the time she came back, I was sitting down, and she closed the door. She smiled. "Sorry about that."

"No, it's fine," I said, but did frown a little. I had been neglecting this life and her. She'd been right here, so close to me, but I had never not once made it in here while she'd been headmaster. I messed with my hands. "I wish I would have gotten in here to see you more. I'm sorry about that. I..."

Brielle joined me in one of the student chairs, quickly waving me off. "It wasn't your job to come in here and see me. I was just here to help and make sure you got acclimated okay."

Even still, I couldn't get in here once? I shook my head. "I guess I'm just kind of bummed. I don't really feel like we've gotten to talk."

She'd been working a lot more recently, her and Ramses both. They'd ask me if that was okay before they'd done it, and it had been. I wanted them to go back to their normal lives and not feel the need to watch over me.

They had been, though. Especially with Bru leaving. They'd been worried. They'd been suggesting therapy for me too off and on. I wasn't against anything like that, but I'd never been one to open up to many people. Actually, these days I'd been talking more and more to the dark prince, which had been nice.

He'd been opening up too, giving me more and more details about Charlie. Apparently, the two had really used to go by Batman and Robin to each other, which I thought was friggin' cute as hell. The dark prince wasn't *cute* by any stretch of the word, so yeah, all that was fucking adorable.

Brielle tilted her head. She was probably one of the most beautiful women I'd ever seen in my life, strong. Both seemed to be a prerequisite to be a Legacy mom, which I could confirm now since I'd met them all. How they all had ended up raising so many arrogant pretty boys I didn't know, but maybe they were the soft side to them. All the bros had a softer side, even if none of the cocky fucks wanted to admit it. She put a hand on my chair. "I'm always here to talk with you. That won't change just because I'm going back downtown."

I still couldn't help but be bummed, though. I felt like we'd wasted an opportunity here.

I had wasted one.

She was another one who'd upheaved her whole life for me, but I'd failed to even talk to her even though she had been close.

I noticed a metal bust in a box on her shelf, abstract. It was one of the few things the movers had left to take, and I picked it up.

"Your father—" she started, but then smiled. "Ramses made that for me. He'd fill my office if he could. If I let him. He loves giving gifts."

I knew that about him, still looking forward to the show we were going to together.

And I noticed she'd corrected herself, calling Ramses something else besides my dad. They were still walking on eggshells and trying to protect me. I swallowed. "Do you do art?"

"Oh, no." She took the piece from me when I handed it to her. She made it face me. "If I did this, I probably would have lost an appendage in the process."

I chuckled, and she grinned.

She placed it delicately in the box. "You definitely get all that from him. I don't have an artistic bone in my body."

"Could you tell me how you got into politics?" I brought my legs up. "I'd like to know more." I felt like I knew little to nothing about her.

"Well, not much to that really. I actually kind of feel like I stumbled into the mayor's office." She made a face, which made me laugh again. She put her hands together. "I was in academics before. I'd actually just taken the job as headmaster here when… well, when you were taken."

My mouth pressed together, and she lifted a hand.

"That was hard, as I'm sure you can imagine, and losing you wasn't the first hardship I've experienced unfortunately."

She tilted her head. "I had another marriage before I met Ramses. It wasn't a great one, and my ex-husband and I had a miscarriage during it."

I didn't know what to say. "I'm so sorry."

"I got through it. Though, it was a process. By the time I met Ramses, I was on the way toward healing, and he only expedited that. In fact, he saved my life in every sense of the word. He's such a good man, and every day I wonder how he chose me."

He had similar wonderful things to say about her, both of them so kind.

Brielle's smile stayed strong despite the harder details of her story, unfaltering. I was sure she had done a lot of work to get to this place. Her mouth lifted higher. "When I lost you, I worked a lot. Worked for years as headmaster of the school, but also in the community. My community work invigorated me, and I think truly that was the difference in helping me deal with my grief surrounding the loss of you. I was helping other mothers and fathers who'd also experienced the loss of a child, both locally and globally. I started a foundation, and it was my peers who suggested I run for local office. I thought the notion was crazy, but I did it. I worked in a few positions before, again, my peers pushed for the mayor's office." She opened her hands. "The rest is history, as they say."

She'd had so many horrible things happen to her, but here she was *with me*, and still being strong. "How did you deal with all that? With what happened with me and before?"

"Like I said, it wasn't easy, and though you were gone, I hadn't lost hope you were out there and were safe." She nodded, her eyes glassy despite her smile. She shook my leg. "And here you are with me."

Here I was with her, with both her and Ramses.

Her hand left my leg, and she got up quickly. She headed to her desk. "I can write you a pass back to class. That way you won't get in trouble with Dr. Stone. I know she can be a hard-ass."

She winked after she said that, and I smiled. I got up too. "After you go back to the mayor's office, I'd love to visit sometime. See what you do?" I didn't really have too much of an interest in politics, but I was desperate to know her. She seemed amazing, and I, with my own grief, had been missing that.

She stopped what she was doing, the pass in her hands. She came around her desk. "You would?"

"Yeah, if I could." I played with my hands. "I wouldn't want to impose."

"You wouldn't be. Not at all." A warmth touched her eyes, her voice. She tugged some of her hair back. "I'm actually headed down to the office today. Pulling an early day to assist with the move. You wouldn't like to tag along, would you? I can give you a tour, and it'd be a good time with things being quiet down there."

My mouth parted. "I have a few periods left."

"Oh, don't worry about that. I can have Diane get you out of your other classes," she said, before picking up her line. "After all, I am the headmaster, and I also happen to know your mother so…"

She tossed another wink my way, which made me smile. I'd *love* to hang out with her today. It was time I moved past my own grief too.

It was well past time.

THIRTY-TWO

Dorian

Me: Where are you and Brielle at, little fighter? We're all kinda starting to worry about you.

I think we were past that point, Wolf, Ramses, and me. Brielle had texted my god dad she was taking Sloane out of school for the afternoon, and Noa had confirmed this when she messaged me before school let out. I hadn't had much of a thought about that other than the fact the whole thing was cooler than shit. Sloane and Brielle hadn't been doing a whole lot of bonding since she'd come back, and it sounded like they were headed to city hall to check out where Brielle worked.

I hadn't heard from Sloane since her initial text but didn't find any of that particularly alarming. I figured I'd see her by the time school let out, but she wasn't home when I got there. Wolf and Ramses were the only ones who had been, but even Ramses hadn't heard from his wife. He'd gotten the same message from Brielle that Sloane had sent me about the two going into Brielle's office, but that'd been it.

They should've been home by now.

I had started to worry when, every time I did see Ramses, he was on his phone. He'd been leaving voicemails, his wife's name on his lips, and that was when Wolf and I had started texting people. I hit up Bow first, but she had academic shit after school. She hadn't heard from Sloane, and Thatcher and Wells were out lifting weights at the gym. Meanwhile, Ramses, Wolf, and I were chilling at the Mallick house with little to no answers. It was pushing dinner time, but none of us had heard from either of the women.

"Hey, Jersey girl, where you at? Let me know something when you can, okay?"

Wolf and I gazed up to find Ramses on his phone again, entering the room with his hand in his hair. Jersey girl was a reference only he used for his wife of almost twenty years, Brielle from New Jersey. Ramses hung up the phone, then spotted us, a frown on his lips.

"I'm sure they're fine," my god dad stressed, but he didn't look fine. In actuality, he appeared just as worried as I felt, and Wolf and I didn't even bother hiding our phones when he walked into the room anymore. We'd pretended we weren't texting the shit out of half the town in search of Sloane and Brielle earlier tonight, hiding our phones and pretending to play video games whenever he was around. Ramses cocked his head. "Seriously, I'm sure they're just caught up. They might have gone shopping or something."

I started to say something, but then Ramses was on his phone again. He was leaving another voicemail, and Wolf pushed off the floor before his dad could finish.

"This is stupid. I'm going to go look for them," Wolf growled, but his dad snapped his fingers at him.

"You sit and wait," Ramses stated, covering his phone. Wolf sat with clenched teeth, and only after he did, did Ramses finish leaving the voicemail. Sounded like he was trying Sloane this time. He looked at us after he hung up.

"There's no need to scour the city. They've only been MIA for a few hours."

My god dad was doing a good job at keeping his voice even, but he definitely was freaking out. He'd been leaving just as many voicemails as I'd been sending unanswered texts to my girl. I started to leave another, but my head shot up when a door slammed in the house. Almost instantly, Wolf and I shot up, and Ramses stalked toward the archway out of the living room.

Someone entered first, rushing the fuck inside, and nearly collided with Ramses when he did.

I think we were all surprised to see him.

Bruno Sloane had his keys in hand, his phone in the other, and when he and my god dad almost intersected, the guy just about dropped both. "Ramses. Sorry."

Ramses blinked. I did too, and Wolf angled around the couch. Wolf braced his arms. "What are you doing here?"

Right away, Ramses shot him a look, but Wolf raised his hands.

"No shade. Just an honest question," Wolf said, and I believed him when he said it. He'd felt terrible for the way Bru had ended up leaving, and though it hadn't been his fault, he'd taken responsibility.

I was seeing a lot of change in my friend, good changes mostly, and I had all but put away my research regarding Sloane's adoption. I'd done it out of respect and because he'd asked me to, yes, but also, I wanted to enjoy some of this happy too. Things had also been tense when Bru had left, and I hadn't wanted to aid in that.

Even with what Wolf said, Ramses took a second before letting up his look. He studied Bru. "Everything okay?"

"Yeah, and I used my key," Bru said, raising them. "That okay? Dorian texted. Said you couldn't find Sloane."

I had texted him, but when he hadn't seen her, I'd believed that was the end of the conversation. He had sounded concerned when he'd texted back, but I'd told him once we found her, I'd message.

I suppose he hadn't wanted to wait. I angled around the couch too. "Yeah, I did. We still haven't heard from her, bro. You hear something?"

"Nah, no." He frowned. "When was the last time you heard from her or Brielle?"

"Before school let out," Ramses said, back on his phone again. He put a hand on Bru's shoulder. "Try not to worry, okay? I'm sure they'll both turn up. Why don't you hang with us for a bit until they show? And of course, it's fine you used your key. It's yours and always will be."

And I knew my god dad meant every word of that. He hadn't wanted Bru to leave, none of us had.

Bru nodded at my godfather, but before he could take him up on his proposal to hang out, another door slammed in the house. Feminine laughter followed, and this time, no one barreled into each other on the way out of the living room.

"Hello. Hello. We're home," came Brielle's voice, and Sloane's followed. The two were laughing when we all did get to them at the door, and upon seeing all of us filling basically the entire fucking hallway, the laughter curbed off. Brielle's expression fell. "Everything all right?"

"Bru?" Sloane pushed forward, shopping bags filling her arms. Brielle had about double the same, and it appeared Ramses had been right about them shopping. Sloane shook her head. "What are you doing here?"

I wasn't going to put out there that her twin brother had asked the exact same question and even in the same *way*. It was already freaking me out enough I was going with my boy's sister, but the fact they were twins only added another layer of weird. Honestly, I tried not to think about it most days, and I think my buddy was doing the same.

"Uh, Prinze texted. He didn't hear from you so he texted

me. Thought I'd swing by," Bru said, and addressed, he came forward. His jaw moved. "You guys were shopping?"

"Um, yes," Brielle said, beaming. I hadn't seen her smile that big in a long time, and it only brightened seeing Bru here. She scanned the room, but stopped on her husband when he approached. "I'm sorry. We lost track of time. We didn't worry you guys too much, did we?"

Before Wolf, Bru, or I could say anything, Ramses waved a low hand to shut that shit down. Our mouths closed about the same time he greeted his wife.

"Just called a few times since we hadn't heard from you. Not a big deal," Ramses said, kissing her cheek. He reached for her coat while he directed us to help with the bags. Wolf took the bulk while I got the rest and Sloane's.

"Oh, I'm sorry." Brielle let Ramses take her coat, then hugged her husband. "We were at city hall when Sloane noticed all the shops downtown. I suggested we check them out."

"No need to apologize," Ramses said, an inquisitive look with his smile. She eyed him right back, and I'd seriously never seen Wolf's mom this lively. It'd been a long time.

Sloane held a similar look about her when I grabbed her bags. I kissed her too, which momentarily broke her gaze away from the shock of her brother being here. "Hey."

"Hi," she returned, hugging me when I hugged her. "Sorry we worried you guys. I would have answered my phone if I heard it. The shops were loud and busy with the holidays coming up."

"No, it's fine. Sounds like you two had fun." Ramses had his arm around his wife. He kissed her head. "I was just about to call in dinner. You girls pick."

"Excellent, and, Bru, please tell me you're staying to eat." Brielle grinned at him. "It's been a while. We'd love to have you."

Saying Sloane begged her brother with her gaze was an

understatement, but I think none of us expected him to say yes. I mean, the dude had left.

But then, he smiled. He laughed too, scratching his neck. He nodded. "Sure. I haven't eaten yet, and you're right. It's been a while."

"Great." Surprised herself, Brielle reached for Bru's hand. She squeezed. "You can tell us all your news. How's Thai food sound?"

"Sounds amazing."

"Good." Sloane looked at me, my girl fucking *glowing*, which did crazy shit to my insides. I was finding it harder and harder to not feel the same around her, and maybe Wolf was right.

Finding a little more happy in our lives might not be such a bad thing.

Sloane

I'd been surprised when my brother stayed for dinner, delighted. I'd already been on a high from hanging out with Brielle today. She'd given me a complete tour of city hall, and I got to meet all the people she worked with. I'd *thought* this would overwhelm me, but it hadn't. It'd been good, and when she took me shopping, even better. I related to her in ways I never thought I would.

I'd lost Marilyn really young, a woman who was supposed to have been my mother but I'd never really gotten to know. It was nice to experience that relationship with Brielle, that of a mother and a daughter. Biologically, Brielle was my mom, and I think *that* overwhelmed me most today. It was the realization to know she was my mother and that I could have that.

I did have that.

Things only got better at dinner. Bru actually engaged, and he seemed lighter, happier even. When we were at school and I bugged him about how things were, he was always tight-lipped, but today, he talked about all the fun things he'd been doing outside of school. He'd joined a few science and math clubs, getting really involved with the business ones too. It seemed his time with Callum had been good for him, and that relieved me so much. He laughed and entertained the questions and almost seemed happy too.

He was happy.

It was all so weird considering where we all were only weeks ago, and things only got weirder when I noticed Ares sneak Bru away after dinner. I volunteered to do dishes with Brielle since the guys let us pick takeout, and by the time I saw Bru again, he was laughing, Ares by his side. The two even shook it out before Ares took the stairs two by two up to the second floor.

Bru stayed with me downstairs. I only even ran into them both because Bru texted me he was about to take off. I guess he had a science club meeting in the morning. I'd been finishing up with Brielle and the dishes when I got the text.

Upon noticing Ares leave Bru in such a way, I was curious, though, and I eyed Bru as I walked him to the door. He laughed. "What?"

"*You*, what?" I nudged him, and he shrugged.

"He actually apologized to me," he said, my eyes flashing. Bru scratched his neck. "Him and Prinze. They said it was shit how everything happened and apologized."

It was shit how it had all happened, but I think that was a collaborative effort. I even felt I'd played my own part. I hadn't seen that he needed space.

"I told them it wasn't their fault, though. At least not completely." His eyebrows narrowed. "And I really am sorry for how I left. I didn't want to hurt you. That was definitely fucked."

He'd needed space, and I got that now. He did seem lighter and more at ease. We got to the door, and my toe followed the line separating two polished tiles. "Just tell me you're okay. You seem okay."

"I am," he said, causing my heart to dance. Especially when he smiled. He braced his arms. "And it seems like I'm not the only one. You and Brielle going AWOL freaked the shit out of us all, by the way."

I figured that'd been the case. I mean, why else would Bru show up out of the blue?

"But it seems it was worth it." Bru eyed me, and I laughed too.

I nodded. "She's great. And we had such a good time." I released a heavy breath, stupid emotions always betraying me. I smiled tight. "It was like having a mom. It was nice."

My gaze averted, my brother grabbing my shoulder.

"You do have a mother, and it's okay to have it," he said, but it didn't feel okay. Not after everything that had happened. How did I get to have all this, but he felt the need to run? It wasn't fair. His head cocked. "I think this all just overwhelmed me. This house. This family and this world." His smile lifted. "But all this is you, and you need to experience it."

"It can be yours too, you know?" I questioned, and Bru acknowledged that with a bob of his head. I squeezed his hand on my shoulder. "You are a part of this family, and they want you in it."

"I know that. I do." His eyes warmed. "But I also know I needed to figure out what all these changes mean to me first, which is what I've been doing. It's been great actually."

"You really do seem happy."

"I feel it." He laughed like he couldn't believe it himself. He pocketed his hands. "I do, and it's been amazing. I've been doing all those campus visits, seeing stuff and where I could be in a couple years, which is nice, and staying with Callum has been great. He's not home a lot, but that's been okay."

"Where's he been?"

"You know how he works. Travels?" His shoulders popped up. "Really, it's been great not to have the hover. My head got to clear, but when he is around, we travel *a lot*." He chuckled. "We even went to India to visit one of his airports over Thanksgiving break. Did I tell you that?"

He told me he'd been busy, but that hadn't consisted of international travel. I shoved him. "No. What the fuck?"

"Right? It was fucking sweet, and he's been showing me all kinds of things regarding running a business. It's actually been piquing my interest to go the business route in college." He popped his coat collar. "Can you see me as a business major in a couple years?"

He could be anything he wanted to be. He was brilliant. I grinned. "You'd be an awesome businessman. Though, maybe a little stubborn."

"And who do I get that from?" He leveled me a look, making us both chuckle. He folded his arms. "I really am happy, so you don't need to worry about me. I do think I just needed time, and I'll try to be here for the holidays. I miss everyone. It was just overwhelming, you know?"

I did know that, still overwhelmed, but it was getting better.

"And I hope this isn't a weird ask, but maybe you should swing by too. See what's going on with me and where I'm staying, yes, but also to talk to Callum. He's been asking about you. I think he just wants to know you're okay like he asked me."

His boot followed that same line dividing the tiles, this a tricky ask but not necessarily a weird one. Bru knew things were more complicated for me. Even if I was ready to address all that… see Callum and all that, doing so would open up a lot of things I wasn't sure I wanted to open up.

"He's hurt a lot of people, Bru," I said, and my brother chewed his lip.

He squeezed my shoulder. "You do what you need to do. I just want you to know that's out there, and I get it. He does too."

I supposed there was a reason Callum had been planning for a liaison to continue reuniting me with my family.

"Just don't rule it out if that's something you want, though," he said, his head tilted. "And anyway, I'm glad you and Brielle decided to ignore your phones today and freak us all the fuck out. It was nice seeing everyone and for us to talk."

He brought me in then, a tight hug.

"Thank you for giving me the space, sis," he said, my heart warming. "And I'm so glad you got yours too."

I was as well, all of it the best kind of change.

It was hard to let my brother go back, go away from me, but it was easier knowing we seemed to have the lines of communication open again. I watched him leave at the door, then decided to handle a couple items of business myself. I found Dorian and Ares both in Ares's room. They were blowing shit up in a first-person-shooter game, but they stopped when I knocked.

"Can I talk to Ares for a second?" I asked, and Dorian got up.

Ares twitched. "What the fuck? Am I in trouble or something?"

My eyes rolled to the heavens about the same time Dorian tossed his arm around me. Meaty and weighted, the thing about made me collapse at the knees, and he tickled me when I faked my knees buckling.

"I'll give you both the room," he said, before smacking my ass. He popped a kiss on my mouth. "Come find me in yours.

We'll see how long I can get away with it before your dad realizes I'm in there."

His eyes dancing, he seemed lighter too.

Ares made a gagging noise as Dorian left, which caused the dark prince to double back and flip him off. Ares threw a pillow at him, and dodging it, Dorian chuckled before giving him both fingers.

Ares's eyes lifted. "Yeah, never going to get over the fact you two are fucking." He dry-heaved. "You're my goddamn sister, and I'm sorry but that shit's gross."

"Oh, fuck you," I laughed, crossing my arms. "It wasn't weird before."

"Oh, it was *always* weird. I just didn't know it." He chortled. He shot some stuff on the screen before getting up too. "And believe me. He thinks about that shit too. He's just not saying it. I mean, you're my twin and…"

He dry-heaved again, and I punched his arm. He rubbed the spot, muttering something about me being an asshole, and *my God* we were siblings. It was kind of crazy really how quickly we'd both fallen into the roles.

"I actually was coming in here to say thank you," I said, almost regretting that now. I laughed. "Bru told me you apologized to him. You and Dorian."

"Wasn't a thing." He stretched his long wingspan before tossing his controller on the bed. "And I think we both know he wouldn't have left had I not been such an asshole to him."

The humor fell from his face as he stood before me. I chewed the inside of my cheek. "I think we all have some regrets that day."

"Yeah, but mine are a fucking stack." His lips pulled together. "I told you I wouldn't make you choose, and that was exactly what you ended up doing."

It was all more complicated than that, and I think we both knew it. "Bru needed his time, and it seems to have done him some good. He definitely looks a lot better."

"I noticed that." He grinned. "And though I'm not happy with who he chose to take that time with, I'm glad the kid got some clarity."

Ares studied the floor after what he said, and one person we definitely didn't discuss was Dorian's grandfather. This was for obvious reasons, and as I myself still had a hard time with that, I wasn't arguing about the fact. I'd needed time too, but Bru was right I probably should talk to Callum too. If anything, for clarity.

Bru had had time to make his own conclusions about our former guardian, and I think I'd been too scared to do the same. It almost felt like me doing so would betray this new life I was in, and I didn't want that.

Again, it was complicated.

"Anyway, I'm glad you and Mom got to spend some time together today." His smile stretched. "You seem to have made her day. I haven't seen her smile like that in a long time."

My heart fluttered. "It was nice. We had a good time."

This only made his eyes warm more, and when he asked for more details about the day, I gave it to him. Actually, we chatted so long Dorian started blowing up both our phones. He was wondering why the fuck I was in here and not in bed with him.

This only made Ares gag again, but he dodged when I attempted to punch him again. I started to leave to go to Dorian when Ares held his finger up.

"Wait. Before I forget," he said, bounding across the room in like half a stride. Dude could reach the entire expanse of his big-ass room in like a couple steps. He opened his desk, and when he brought something out of it, it was attached to a chain.

I recognized the emblem from our baby blankets right away, and I thought it was his until he pulled his own out from beneath his shirt.

"I got yours restored," he stated, dropping mine into my

hands. He'd had it shined, the thing completely flawless. His shoulders popped up. "Now, we both have one. I mean, if you want it."

I studied it, then his, which he still held. We both did have one now, didn't we?

His expression fell, his hands raised. "Look, little. You don't have to wear it. I just wanted you to have it cuz it's yours so—"

I hugged him, and he froze. Like literally locked up in my arms. He hadn't been expecting this.

And neither had I.

My throat and eyes burning I hadn't expected either, a frog in my throat. "God, would you shut the fuck up, big."

"Big?" he questioned, and it sounded like he had a little bit of that frog in his throat too. His arms fell around me, hugging me back. His chin touched the top of my head. That was how tall he was. "What the fuck is that? Me?"

He said it with a laugh, a throaty, raspy one that made me swallow.

"Yeah, that's you," I said, smiling. I came away. "Little and big. I've officially decided."

"Little and big," he repeated, like we were cementing it. He watched as I put my necklace on, the same one he wore. We matched, and it felt like our own little thing. Like his Court stuff with the rest of the guys and Bow. We were little Mallick and big Mallick.

And I finally felt like we'd be okay.

THIRTY-THREE

Sloane

Wells: Pizza night. My place tonight, right?

    Thatcher: Yeppers.

    Wells: What the fuck? Yeppers?

    Thatcher: Yeppers.

    Dorian: You fucking idiot.

    Thatcher: *kiss emoji*

    Dorian: *middle finger emoji*

    Ares: Dude, our sisters are on this text loop.

    Wells: And what?

    Thatcher: *kiss emoji*

    Ares and Dorian: *middle finger emoji*

    Me: You guys are all idiots. Hopefully, Bow hasn't left the thread this time.

    Bow: Still here. *blushing emoji*

    Me: Good.

    Ares: We'll see for how long. LOL.

    Thatcher: *kiss emoji*

Dorian: Thatch, stop that fucking shit. I swear to fucking God.

Thatcher: *kiss emoji*

Wells: Anyway, Sloane, you coming tonight? Bru said he had a thing tonight so he can't when I asked him about it at school today.

Bru: I do got a thing. Science club, but it's wrapping up early so I should be there. *smile emoji*

Wells: Sweet!

Ares: Fuck yeah! And Sloane can't. She's going to a boring as shit art thing tonight with Dad. Right, little? *wink emoji*

Dorian: Hold up. That art show is tonight? Awesome, little fighter, and Wolf, shut the fuck up.

Ares: *kiss emoji*

Thatcher: Okay, so that's my thing so…

Ares: Yeah, and I'm taking it. Like I said, little is busy. So it's just us guys tonight.

Bow: Still here. *blushing emoji*

Ares: And Bow. Sorry, Rainbow.

Bow: No big, and that art show with Ramses is tonight?? Ahh! So fun! *heart emoji* *star emoji* *rainbow emoji*

Me: It is, and I'm looking forward to it. And it's fine, Dorian. Ares is an uncultured swine so Bocelli's work would go over his head anyway. *wink emoji*

Ares: The fuck ever.

Ares: Also, where are you at? Dad's getting ready but haven't seen you.

Me: OMW. Have to pick up something first.

Me: It's a gift for Ramses.

———

I didn't expect to see anyone at the house my brother and I had stayed at when we'd first arrived, but it wasn't empty as I approached. In fact, beyond the gate was a fury of activity, movers. Several men and women were in brown bibs, and each one hauled boxes or furniture out of the house into moving trucks parked outside the garage.

The garage was open too, and I parked inside it, sending the Legacy group text one last text. I hadn't told them where I was getting my gift for Ramses, and I wanted to keep it that way.

I didn't think it was a big deal I'd decided to stop by my old place after school to get some of my artwork, but they might. The guys had gotten most of our clothes from there and school uniforms that day I'd met Ramses and Brielle, but everything else my brother and I owned had been virtually left behind. I think, at the time, neither of us had wanted to bring any of it up, and Ramses and Brielle had provided pretty much anything we needed anyway.

This meant I'd been forced to leave behind the majority of my artwork and anything Thatcher hadn't grabbed for me that one day. I'd had lots of constellation pieces still at Callum's glass house, my best stuff actually, and had been meaning to get back here for a while to get them.

I didn't expect the place to be packed, though, people moving in and out. I thought about turning around, but if Callum had sent people to clean the place out, I definitely didn't want to lose my stuff. Like stated, my best work was in there, and I wanted to give Ramses one of my constellation pieces. I knew I didn't have to give him a gift, but I wanted to. Those tickets had been very generous.

Anyway, I thought he'd like one of my smaller pieces, so I went ahead and turned off my Hummer in the garage. I hadn't told Ramses and Brielle I didn't want to drive Godfrey's Chevelle anymore, but Dorian must have because the next day, the car was gone and replaced with the Hummer. The black beast was the same model as Ares's, and I'd wondered if it fit my style until I'd gotten behind the wheel.

The thing ended up being perfect for me, and it was newer than Ares's, so I got to brag about that. He grumbled a little bit every time I did, but I didn't think he was too sore about the ride because he offered to help me paint a statement piece on it like his wolf this summer. He said it was something we could work on together, and I was looking forward to that. We also did work well together.

Grabbing my purse, I got out of the car. I thought maybe I could sweep in and out, get my stuff, but I stopped the moment I spotted a familiar face. Callum's bodyguard, Lucas, was outside with the rest of the movers, and when he noticed me, he approached my Hummer.

I adjusted my bag, trying not to feel awkward. I hadn't seen or spoken to him or Callum since that last day at the hospital.

Since you ran.

Yeah, I tried not to be awkward, and he raised a hand as he got close.

"Good afternoon, Miss Sloane," he said, always so formal. He had a long wool coat on, his breaths puffing in the wintry air. "Can I help you with something? We're actually just gathering up your things along with the rest of the house. Callum had intended to ship everything that was yours to you."

He had? My mouth parted. "I actually was going to grab a couple things. That's why I came. Probably should have called."

Called who, I didn't know. I mean, I guess I could have at least told Bru to mention it to Callum.

"Well, they are your things so feel free to take what you'd like," Lucas said. "I can even have the team load your vehicle for you."

I didn't know about all that. I didn't want the Mallicks or Legacy to know I was here. I thought it'd bother them, so yeah. I pointed toward the front door. "I just need one thing actually. An art piece I worked on."

Lucas raised a hand. "No problem at all. Take whatever you'd like."

I nodded, feeling awkward again. I felt like I should thank him. I mean, he had saved me when Godfrey had taken me.

But I'd always had been an awkward bunny. The moment passed, and I ended up rushing off just to avoid the silence. My feet leaving tracks in the fresh snow we'd had this morning, I only got a few steps before Lucas called my name.

"I just wanted to let you know Callum is here," Lucas said, catching up to me. "He's inside. Overseeing the move so…"

He probably felt the need to tell me due to obvious reasons.

You did run.

I had been running, and Legacy, along with Ramses and Brielle, definitely wouldn't like that I was here with him inside. They didn't trust him, and they all had history with him.

I think they all did know the circumstances surrounding Callum were more complex regarding myself, and I had been thinking about what Bru said. Callum had been asking about me, and he had taken care of me.

I nodded to Lucas before he was called to assist with a question the movers had. I was left in the cold then, my bag on my arm, a chill in my body. Going and confronting Callum probably wouldn't be liked by others in my life, but this was *my life.*

I ended up going inside, and Callum was doing exactly what Lucas said he was. In his dark suit and crisp tie, he directed those around him carrying boxes and furniture.

"That's Miss Sloane's stuff," he said to one, a few of my canvases under their arms. One of the works was actually the piece I'd planned to grab for Ramses. Callum placed hands on his cane. "Be careful with everything. We'll be overnighting all personal items to her."

I swallowed, the guy with my paintings passing me. This, of course, brought Callum's attention my way.

"Sloane." He stepped forward, his jewel-top cane assisting him. He didn't seem terribly reliant on it, and I assumed it was more for stability since he was older. He looked around, and I definitely saw the connection to him and Dorian's father now that I knew the fact was there. Decades separated Dorian's dad and him, but Callum clearly used to be blond and had a similar presence about him.

I supposed Dorian may have some of those mannerisms too. I adjusted my bag. "Hi."

"Hello. What are you…" He stopped when a mover required his attention. He answered their question quickly, politely, before gesturing me to the right and guiding us both out of the fray. "Everything all right? We were just moving your things, packing up the house."

I saw that, my fingers clenching my purse. It was weird now, being within the same space as him, like I was doing something wrong by being here and not telling anyone about it. It didn't sit well *at all*, and I really wished I hadn't come. I didn't want to upset anyone. I…

Perhaps, he knew my discomfort as he studied my body language, a frown on his lips. "Have you come for something at the house? We didn't know anyone would be here today."

"I…" I started. *You're fine. You're not doing anything wrong.* "Yes, I did. Just wanted to grab one of my pieces so—"

I caught the mover guy before he got too far, taking the small canvas from him. When I cradled it, Callum had his head tilted. I felt bad for how weird I was being, but I had a feeling he got that.

How could he not?

"We really didn't know anyone would be here." A mover cut in front of him, his smile small at the man before looking at me. He lifted a hand. "Please. Take anything you'd like. It's yours, and whatever you can't we'll have shipped to the Mallick household."

"Thank you. Thanks," I huffed. "Really. Thank you."

"Of course," he said, his gaze averting. I was sure this was just as awkward for him. He braced his cane. "Well, I suppose I better get back to it. Good seeing you, and I'm glad I got to. Your brother mentions you from time to time, but I've always wondered how you've been."

I'd been well, and extraordinarily so. This was 100 percent due to the changes and people in my life, his grandson included.

Callum's expression tight, he navigated away, and I felt like such a piece of fucking crap. He'd always been nice to us, and I was treating him like shit.

I didn't want to keep doing that to him, treating him that way, and when he walked away so quickly, he let me know he hadn't expected anything from me.

"He lost his entire family after what he did."

"I want to thank you for what you did."

He stopped after what I said, peering over his shoulder until I came around.

I blew out a breath. "When Godfrey came to you, you didn't have to help. You could have kept his secret. Hell, you could have just ignored us or washed your hands of us." I gripped my purse. "My point is, you didn't have to do anything, but you did, so I thank you for that."

The gratitude was stiff, and I noticed the waver in my voice. I didn't know this man, and all I did know was what he'd done for me/what he'd done in the past. The latter, quite frankly, still scared the fucking shit out of me. It frightened me because he had that capability, and I didn't know what kind of person he was now.

I just knew who he'd hurt.

Callum waited a long time before speaking, as if considering what to say. In the end, he passed me a slow nod and a small smile. "I hope life is good to you. As far as Godfrey, he did something wrong, and you kids deserve better than that."

My throat constricted, the frog returning to my throat.

"Anyway, best of luck to you," he said. "The Mallicks... Ramses and Brielle seem like good people. I don't know much about them, but again, Bru tells me things. He has nothing but good words to say, and I want you to know he is very much welcome to stay with me for as long as he wishes. He's not bound or obligated, and I am in the process of drawing up custody papers. I assume you would like to be his guardian."

I would be if that was what Bru wanted. I only hadn't been this whole time due to finances.

That had obviously changed.

A lot had, my breath shallow when I nodded.

Callum did the same, his head bobbing in acknowledgment once. He started to walk away.

"Is that why you did what you did?" I asked, needing to know. "You did it to help? Because Godfrey did do something wrong and you wanted to help us? *Just* wanted to help us?"

I hoped that was the reason. I hoped to fucking God because I wanted to believe him, and what my brother clearly already felt. That Callum was maybe a man who had a dark past, but possibly was trying to be different, *better*.

Callum's lips turned down, his expression serious. "I helped because I know what it's like to lose family," he said, the air leaving me. "I know firsthand how that feels, and I wasn't going to let that happen to you kids, and you in particular."

Of course, he didn't say how he'd lost that family. I braced my canvas. "Why did you do what you did? How *could* you? You and my grandfather..." Finding it hard to talk about this, I rubbed my face.

Callum frowned, and when another mover required his attention, he asked if the guy and his team could let us have the room. They started packing things in the adjoining dining room instead, the noise significantly less when they did. "I can't tell you your grandfather's reasons, but I can guess they had something to do with mine. He was trying to help out your great-uncle, *family*, and I believed I was doing the same with my own. There was damaging evidence linking my son Royal and his friends to that night in question. They had nothing to do with what happened. In fact, they didn't even know about what had occurred until the rest of the world did, but they were known to be in the wrong place at the wrong time. So, in a quest to keep my son's name and his involvement from anywhere near the situation, I made a choice to help your grandfather. I did so behind Royal's back, and ironically enough, it was that attempt to help my son that caused me to ultimately lose him and any possible future I could have had with him and later, his son."

"Am I supposed to feel sorry for you?" I asked, my swallow hard. "Sorry that you lost your family?" I knew it sounded harsh, but that was because it was. I shook my head. "The things you did..."

"Require no sympathy, no." He rubbed his cane. "And I expect none. From anyone. As far as helping you and your brother, it was the right thing to do, and the least I could. I think we both know enough lives have already been ruined on both the Mallicks' and the Prinzes' sides. There are casualties everywhere, and if the next generation didn't have to experience that, well..." His gaze took the floor. "There's been enough darkness in this town, and if I could help at all in rectifying that, I was going to."

My throat shifted, gazing away.

Callum came forward. "I'm truly sorry for you and what Godfrey and Marilyn did. I'm even more sorry that you had to find out what you did about who you were and the legacy your grandfather, great-uncle, and myself left for you. It's been a dark cloud over this city and my family for a long time, and I'm sure one of the main reasons my grandson has suffered the way he has. Done some of the things he's done."

My head lifted, my eyebrows narrowed.

"I shouldn't have agreed to help him when he came to me last summer." His lips thinned. "It only made things worse and fractured any kind of connection we ever could have."

"What do you mean?"

He glanced my way, his eyebrows narrowed. "Dorian. He came to me asking for help last summer. His needed assistance finding that woman, Elaine Mayberry, who had an affair with his uncle Charlie. As you know, she was the head-master of your school when you arrived." His head cocked. "My grandson didn't tell you any of this?"

I think he could see all over my face that he hadn't, and I wondered if Bru had told him Dorian and I were together. I'd denied it before. I came forward. "Dorian asked you for help with Mayberry?"

Callum started to speak, but then his mouth closed. His head shook. "You should probably discuss all this with him. It's not my place, and I don't want to damage our relationship any more than it already has been."

I got that, but what I didn't get was why he'd had a rela-tionship with him at all. Ares had said Dorian's grandfather had stayed out of his life just as much as ours had stayed out. "What did he want your help with exactly?" I asked, pushed. I had no idea they'd been in contact. Let alone last summer with Mayberry and everything.

Callum sighed. "You should really talk to him about this. He might not have told you for a reason and that should be respected."

My throat flicked, and mostly because Dorian and I weren't *doing* this shit to each other anymore. He said he trusted me so no, we weren't doing this shit, keeping secrets. "I want you to tell me."

I didn't have a right to ask this, but then again, maybe I

did. Callum had lied to me too after all, and if I deserved something for once, it was some goddamn honesty.

Callum rubbed his mouth, his head shaking. When he lifted it, he sighed once more. "You know about what happened with Mayberry, but what my grandson has obviously failed to tell you is my part in it all. Dorian couldn't find her at first. The woman went off the grid, and I used my resources to find her."

My mouth parted. "And he came to you last summer?"

"He did, and I was so desperate for a relationship with him that I didn't care that was all he wanted. In fact, I was probably willing to do anything he asked me. Anything just to connect with him." He frowned. "It clouded my judgment, made me agree to help him find her, and ultimately, ended up fracturing things so badly between us. I'm sure you saw that when he pretended not to know me."

I did see that, but why wouldn't he *tell me* all this?

"My grandson has a lot of demons and ones I've unfortunately contributed to. I'm sure I'm the reason they're there in the first place. He carries the weight of what I've done in my past. Has to. How couldn't he?" His lips moved. "He's in a lot of pain, my grandson, and I know I only stoked it more. He never would have done what he had to me had I not pushed for our relationship to extend once he got what he wanted."

"What did he do to you?" I heard myself ask the question. In fact, it radiated in my ears, but I still felt outside myself when I asked it. This whole conversation I felt like a fly on the wall, a part of it while not actually being a part of it.

Callum settled both hands on his cane. "He made a mistake, and I told him I forgive him for it. He's not a bad person. He's just troubled, and he never would have done it had he not felt threatened. He was obviously keeping our meetings a secret from his parents, my son. This was apparent while we were meeting, but again, I was very desperate to connect with him. I hadn't known him his whole life and…"

His jaw moved. "Like I said, he made a mistake, and I did too. I put his back up against the wall. I wanted to keep seeing him and held the secrecy of our visits over his head. I manipulated the situation and ultimately, attempted to blackmail him so he wouldn't discontinue our meetings. I was just so desperate and wanted to know him."

His head lowered, and I swallowed.

"But there's no excuse for that." His head rose. "What I did made my grandson act out of character. I didn't know him well, but I knew him well enough to know he made a mistake. He did the wrong thing, and he did because his back was up against the wall, and he felt like he had to."

He was still dancing around the question, what I'd asked. I squeezed the canvas in my hand. "What did he do?"

But most importantly, what was Dorian keeping from me? What was he *still* keeping from me even after everything? I recalled him saying he had to tell me something in the past, but with all his secrets, who knew if this was even it? He couldn't, for some reason, just be straightforward with me. Honest.

That question hung there between Callum and me, and I wondered if he'd actually tell me. He'd been adamant about Dorian telling me all this himself.

"He tried to poison me," he admitted, my stomach turning, knotting. A wave of sickness hit me, and so much bile filled my throat, I had to force it back. Callum nodded. "I obviously survived, and I have talked to him about it. At least, I tried to."

I didn't know what to say to any of this, let alone what he said Dorian had actually ended up doing.

He didn't. He couldn't.

"Promise me you'll always see me as this... I'm only this for you."

Dorian's words played in my head on loop, those moments between us in his car. The nausea rose, and it took me a second to realize Callum said he'd give me a moment. He walked away, and I was still in the middle of a nearly bare living room. He said Dorian had made a mistake, but a mistake was something someone could work through and possibly come back from. With some work, it might not hang over that person's head for the rest of their lives. *A mistake* wasn't just what Callum said.

It wasn't attempted murder.

CHAPTER
THIRTY-FOUR

Sloane

Ramses introduced me to Bocelli as his daughter that night, his daughter who thought she'd finally been starting to get her shit together.

Instead, I got to meet one of the most prolific artists in the world with a tight smile and a churn in my stomach. Both of which I tried to play off and did so poorly enough I excused myself from the conversation. I told Ramses nerves when he came to check on me, and the rest of the greetings I had with his colleagues were the same. Eventually, I just asked to get some air, and Ramses was nice about it. Especially when I said I had nerves. He let me hang out on the balcony, checking on me whenever he could. Since his gallery was featuring Bocelli, he had to mingle, and I was glad because I hated lying to him about how I was actually doing.

Dorian: How's everything going? Having fun?

Dorian had asked this hours ago, a text I stared at more than once. Currently, my thumb hovered over it, at a loss for what to say. He gratefully hadn't been there at Ramses and Brielle's after I'd finally arrived to get dressed.

The nausea swirled again.

Closing out the text, I hung my head over the balcony but lifted it when someone joined me out there.

Ramses brought a lidded paper cup, two actually. I knew them to be serving hot chocolate inside, and he handed me one when he got beside me.

I took it, pretending to be happy about it. I obviously wouldn't be drinking it since my stomach was still so messed up.

"Surprised to find you still out here," he said, bundled up just like me. He wore a dark suit under his wool coat, and I had one of Brielle's black dresses beneath mine. I'd been afraid any dresses I had wouldn't be fancy enough for tonight, and we were surprisingly close in size. Ramses smiled. "Still nerves? I promise you. All my colleagues just love you in there, and Bocelli was seriously eyeing that piece you gave me."

Ramses had insisted on hanging it in the gallery's foyer when I gave it to him earlier tonight, and it was the first thing spectators saw on their way in to see tonight's featured artist.

I'd been honored when he had done that. Especially when he'd said he couldn't wait to get it home and up in his office downtown. He'd said he worked there the most, and he wanted it to be the first thing he saw when he arrived for the day. He had said that like a *dad* whose kid gave him something he valued, treasured.

It'd actually all brought tears to my eyes after he told me that and made me feel so guilty. I'd been quiet the entire time we'd driven up here and hiding most of the evening so far.

I just couldn't help it, though, forcing out a stiff breath before finally looking at him with a faux smile. I shrugged. "I've never been great at things like this. Better behind the canvas, I guess."

This wasn't a lie, and probably the only honest thing I had told him tonight about, well, me. I kept saying I was fine whenever he asked and just nervous since I was being so quiet.

"I get you on that." His smile stretched. "And it's definitely the same for me. In the boardroom, I'm fine, but put me at one of these things, and I'm all over the place."

Probably because he was passionate about it. Not to say he wasn't at his other job. I knew he was in real estate development, but things were different when an artist was truly in their *space*. If he was anything like me at all, he probably lived his art. Breathed it.

"It is getting cold out here, though," he said. "Might want to head inside. Warm up?"

He said this, and I did let him walk me back inside because I was cold. I thought we'd mingle again once we returned our coats to coat check, but instead we walked the floor.

"Is there anything else I can get you?" he questioned, obviously having noticed I hadn't taken a sip of my cocoa. He studied me. "You seem different tonight. Maybe even a little down."

Holy crap. I really wasn't good at hiding it.

I can't talk about this.

I thought I might cry if I did, and I definitely didn't want to do that shit here. I swallowed. "Can we just sit? Relax?"

"Sure." Taking my cup, he waved me to do just that. There was a quieter area of the gallery, less foot traffic there, and we sat on the leather couches. "This better?"

I nodded, playing things off again. "I'm awkward. Forgive me."

He waved me off. "You've got nothing to apologize for. And this is overwhelming."

I glanced away. He'd gotten me water from a server on the way to the couches, and I held the bottle.

"You sure nothing else is wrong?" He sat back, his head tilted. "We can leave if you're feeling ill or something else."

I wanted to talk to him. I wanted to *understand* all this and all this shit that just kept swirling around me for some reason. I felt like a friggin' magnet for it.

"Can I ask you something?" My throat worked. "Something about our family?"

His expression inquisitive, Ramses leaned forward. "Of course. What do you want to know?"

I wanted to know a lot of things. Like I said, I just wanted to understand. My jaw shifted. "Can you tell me about my grandfather?" I asked, causing him to blink. "Your father?"

Ramses hadn't been expecting this, clearly, when he put his hands together. Being real, I didn't know what I'd say before I actually said it. He pulled his fingers down his jaw. "What, um—" He paused, threading his fingers. "What do you want to know about him?"

This was obviously a sensitive subject and probably just as sensitive as Callum was to his own family. These men had caused so much hurt, and I didn't want to hurt Ramses. I waved a hand. "Never mind."

"No, it's okay. What do you want to know?" he asked, his voice serious. "I'll tell you whatever you need."

"I guess I just want to know why he did what he did," I whispered. I studied the grains in the hardwood floor. "How he could cover up something like that and…"

I didn't finish, and Ramses sighed. His lips tightened. "My dad told me once he believed, at the time, he'd done it for family. He wanted to protect my mom and me, and unfortunately, my uncle too. He was family, so yeah, my dad did want to protect him." He shook his head. "But Dad later admitted he'd done what he had because he'd been trying to protect the family name, *his image* as much as us."

My chest clenched. "Where is he now?" I knew he'd been in prison, but not now. Former news articles and Ares had told me that. Callum had served time too, but he was obviously out.

"That's not something you or any of us have to worry about. I know for a fact fate and circumstance claimed my father's life some time ago. He'd gone missing, and I looked into it. I hadn't seen him in years before that, though, and Ares never knew him. My father vowed to stay away before he was born, and that was something he honored."

"What happened to him?"

"I won't get into the details, but it was an accident, a tragic one, and I was sad to hear it."

I gazed up, his smile small.

"I was at peace by the time I found out, and before everything that happened all those years ago, my father and I had a good relationship. He was strict, tough on me, but there was love there, so yes, I was sad to hear it."

My head lowered, I stayed silent.

"Any particular reason why you're asking about him?" Ramses attention focused on me.

I stared off. "I just wondered what kind of person or… *people* could do such a thing." My lips pressed together. "I mean, we share the same DNA. What's in him and my great-uncle is in *me* and…"

Ramses cut off my thoughts before they could surface, his hand raised. "Uncle Leo and my father both made a decision back then. *They* decided to do what he did and only them. These were both choices they made about the people they ultimately decided to become, and that has nothing to do with DNA."

But didn't it? Obviously, there were choices, yes, but…

Callum had spoken to me about demons today, darkness. He'd obviously done the wrong thing too like my grandfather and my great-uncle's choices.

And why couldn't that be passed down?

It could have been, completely it *could have been,* and that had to be the only thing that explained other things today. Things about Dorian…

"You are not your grandfather or my uncle," Ramses continued, sighing. "Neither is Ares or me, nor is Dorian his own grandpa, who you know is also connected to all this."

I covered my arms, his words chillingly accurate to my thoughts.

"You kids have all unfortunately suffered from those who came before, but you are not them, okay? You're not, Sloane. We all have choices. We all have freewill, and the only thing that determines who we ultimately become is what we do with it."

That was my biggest fear, but not for me. We did all have freewill. We did all have the ability to make choices outside of our DNA.

And I think that was what scared me the most.

CHAPTER
THIRTY-FIVE

Dorian

I snuck into her bed around 2 AM, more than a little pissed she hadn't woken my ass up. I'd texted Sloane I'd come over after pizza night to see her. I'd ended up falling asleep on Wolf's floor it got so late, a video game controller in my hand and my phone permanently attached to my hand like a needy little bitch. I was a needy little bitch. I hadn't heard from my girl all night, and I needed to know how things had gone.

She'd pay for that now, and I worked my way under her sheets. I got a hold of her calves first, flicking my tongue across the skin.

Sloane sucked in a breath. "Dorian?"

Who else would it fucking be in her bed, my growl gravelly. Sloane attempted to toe me away, but my hands slid into the underside of her shorts. My rough palms were greeted with supple skin, and when I moved kisses to her inner thighs, those gasps became moans.

"No, Dorian." She said this, but she had her hand in my

hair, her knees up and making room for my assault against her thighs. I bit her flesh, and she trembled. "No."

"Fuck, yes," I gritted, sucking in her soft flesh. I slammed her knees to the bed. "You should have fucking woke me up."

To show her that, I dragged her pussy to my mouth, her feminine scent assaulting *me*. It made me rock hard in my goddamn boxers and made the anticipation of tasting her insane. Before Noa Sloane, I'd never bothered eating pussy, preferring the view of a readied mouth on my cock.

All that was obviously different now, my hand in my boxers as I hooked Sloane's shorts and panties over. I blew heat on her sex while I pumped myself, and Sloane's thighs hugged my head.

"No," she ground out, something between a groan and a sigh falling from her lips. She pushed at my shoulders. "Dorian, stop. Please stop."

This only egged me on. *No* was my favorite word, and resistance my favorite goddamn thing. It always meant *yes* with us, yes to push harder, and fuck her faster. I flicked her clit with my tongue, but barely got a taste before she was easing away from my mouth.

"I'm fucking serious," she said, working her way out of her sheets. She turned the light on, and when I finally got out from all that fucking bed she had, I found her sitting on the side of her bed. She had her head lowered, her hands gripping the mattress. What the fuck? Her head tilted back. "I don't want to."

She didn't... want to? I pulled my hair out of my face. "Okay."

I said this, but I was confused as fucking hell. The way this girl got at my dick was the way I came for her pussy most days. Things had gotten complicated since I couldn't really stay over here anymore, so needless to say, we pretty much jumped at any opportunity we could find to be together.

The only reason I was over here tonight was because I'd

snuck in through Wolf's window. I hadn't wanted to use my house key and alert Ramses since I technically wasn't supposed to be doing overnights right now.

But that fact wasn't enough to keep me away from her.

I did want to know how she was. Tonight was her big night to spend with her dad. She'd been so excited about hanging out with Ramses and had been talking about it forever.

I edged closer to her, noticing when she grabbed one of her fluffy pillows. She forced it onto her lap, and it wouldn't let me get too close to her, which kind of annoyed me, but I let it go since something seemed wrong.

"What happened?" I asked, not trying to sound like an asshole because I wasn't getting to eat pussy right now, but I did have an edge to my voice. I rubbed my arm. "Did I do something?"

We'd been cool at school today, the last time I'd seen her.

Over her pillow, her slender fingers slid through all her dark hair. It hit her tan shoulders, wavy and brown-black like a midnight sky or a detailed oil painting. I noticed things like that about her now, the subtleties about her that made her unique. I used to just find her beautiful. Now, I worshiped this girl and gave no fucks about it. Noa Sloane did make me weak, but if weakness was what being with her was, I'd fucking take it. I'd level the earth for this girl.

I'd start wars.

Noticing I was in her space, she glanced back at me. Her fingers threaded behind her neck. "I don't know what to say to you right now."

I didn't know what that meant, but it was enough to rock my insides. "What do you mean?"

"I mean, I found something out, and I don't know what to feel about it. It freaks me out, and I kind of wish you'd been the one to tell me about it, so I wasn't so fucking blindsided." She studied me. "You said this wasn't about me, but I think it kind of was. Maybe you didn't want to lose me or something."

I didn't want to lose her?

She was scaring *me* now, and frankly, freaking me the hell out too. I touched her shoulders. "Little fighter…"

"No." With the word, her body eased away from hands and what the fuck? She braced her pillow. "You need to tell me why you did what you did that summer with your grandpa."

Blood pumped in my ears, my body heavy, weighted. She shouldn't know shit about that summer with my grandfather.

I blinked once. "How do you know about that?" I tried to keep my voice level, *even*, but I was freaking the fuck out.

How did she know?

She shouldn't know about this *at all*, and I'd told her I would tell her about it. I just hadn't been fucking ready and…

I wasn't ready for this look she was giving me, and the distance, space. The pillow she'd forced between us was definitely explained now, and the realization forced a slight paralysis in my body that was enough to freeze my lungs along with the rest of my body.

Her eyes closed. "That's not what I asked you."

"Well, that's what I'm asking you." I forced my hair out of my face, feeling my blood pressure literally spike next to her. "I didn't tell you, so who fucking told you about that?"

"Why didn't you fucking tell me?" She shot, pushing at me, and I got her arms. She shook her head. "Why wouldn't *you* tell me? Were you scared? Scared I'd run? Did you not trust me? Because this shit is fucked, but I never would have run from you, Dorian. Not anymore. I'm done running."

She trembled in my hands, gasping.

"I love you," she said, but even with that admittance, her eyes veered away. They fell on my hands holding her, her fists braced into tight knuckles. It was like she didn't know what to do with my hands on her. If she should pull away, stay…

She was straddling a line here, and whatever it was had her pulling away from me in more than one way.

But even with the hurt of that, *the reality* of it, nothing hurt worse than when she finally did look into my eyes again. I saw what ran deep in her dark irises just as easily as I could see myself reflected back to me. There was fear there at the surface, *at the present*, but what was surface level could eventually be gotten over. It was what would remain over time that struck a heavy fear in me.

It was what couldn't be forgotten.

I glanced away from it all. "Who told you what I did?"

"No. You need to answer me right now."

"Who told you, Sloane?" I brought her closer, her face screwing up. "*Please*. Who told you?"

"Your grandfather," she admitted, my blood pressure spiking again. She looked away. "I ran into him when I went to the house today. The house Bru and I had been staying at when we got to Maywood Heights."

"The fuck?"

"No, you don't get to do that." She pushed my hands off her, getting up. Her pillow fell to the floor as she stalked her over to a window that gave views of rich gardens bathed in moonlight. My god dad and Brielle had a state park basically out there and was almost as big as my own backyard and what my grandmother had planted. Sloane hugged her arms. "You don't get to get mad at me. Not when you were keeping something so big from me." She raised her hands. "He said he helped you find Mayberry?"

So, my grandfather had been running his mouth and starting shit. I rubbed my mouth. "Why were you at that house today?"

"Why the fuck can't you answer a single question?" She got in my face, my little fighter here and ready to play. *This* was the shit that made me bleed for her, how she stood up to me and didn't give a fuck, but right now, I was being tested.

She'd had contact with my grandfather, and that pissed me the hell off. Her arms still crossed, she scanned my eyes. "Why did you do what you did? He told me he tried to blackmail you, and you tried to kill him. Poisoned him."

Hearing the words from her didn't feel good, nor how my stomach felt to see the reality of them *still* in her fucking eyes.

It won't go away.

How could it? This shit was too big to forget. It was *forever*.

She ran her fingers through her hair, her sigh heavy. I didn't say anything, and eventually, she looked at me again. "Tell me what was going through your mind back then. I want to listen. I want to hear you. Understand it."

I swallowed. "I don't want to talk about it."

"Well, I do." Her voice broke as she got close to me, daring to. She might not be comfortable in this situation, comfortable with me and what we were talking about but she closed the distance between us anyway. She put her hands on my face. "I am here. I am, and I'm not going anywhere, and you should have trusted me to handle this." She shook her head. "I mean, aren't we done with these secrets? These *lies*? You told me in your email you were trying to understand me. Well, I'm trying to understand you now. You said you trust me, but I don't think you do."

I did trust her. I trusted her with everything. My attention veered to the space behind her, the floor, and anywhere I could look *but* her.

This made her laugh in response, dry, throaty. Her jaw shifted. "You really can't answer anything."

"I want to know why you were at that house and talking to that son of a bitch. How he got in your head and how, for some reason, you can't fucking see that he was manipulating you."

"Manipulating me?"

"Yes," I said, nodding. "He is manipulative. He's a son of

a bitch, and clearly, he's worked his magic on you." I gripped my hair. "Did he tell you exactly how he tried to blackmail me?"

"He said he threatened you."

"He threatened *my mother*," I said, causing her to blink. I smiled, tight, but found nothing at all nice about this moment, nothing *good* about being right and her being wrong. "He threatened her life, then tried to go back on it. Said he didn't mean it and was just desperate to have a relationship with me."

She swallowed. "He mentioned being desperate."

"Well, he was, so yeah, I felt threatened. I was trying to protect my mother and my family."

She cuffed her arms, and I laughed, dry as hers had been.

"And did he tell you about what he did after? How after I did try to poison him, he had me *arrested* to teach me a lesson? By the way, that was what happened that day at the cabin. He fed intel to the cops to come pick me up after I kidnapped Mayberry."

Her head shot my way, and I nodded.

I got close. "Did he tell you how it felt that day I did poison him?" My throat flicked, nostrils flaring. "How before the nerves got to me so bad I hurled my fucking brains out just in *anticipation* of knowing what I had to do? Who *I had to be* to protect my mother and my family?"

She fanned lashes over glassy eyes, her own throat shifting. She took a step forward, but I eased back.

"How about how it felt like I died a little bit after? How I had died and could never get back who I used to be?"

"Dorian…"

I locked up when she touched me, attention veering, averting. I couldn't have her *looking* at me in any way that would make my stomach twist even more.

I couldn't handle it.

"Why were you at that house with him?" I asked again. "Tell me before I lose my mind."

I dared to look at her then and saw exactly what I didn't want to see. I saw sympathy, yes, but also that same thing from before running in her irises' depths. She'd looked at me in many ways in the past, the best when she was hot for me, ready. Later, that erratic burn only ignited when something else deeper developed beneath it. It was what made her *bleed for me* and that love she always said she had for me. It was still there, but something else was too. It was something that killed me and something I always knew about myself, but I hadn't wanted her to see. I'd never wanted that for her and us, but it was there now.

It'd be there forever.

"I literally ran into him. Just by chance…" She shook her head before touching my face again. "I told you I wanted to get a gift for Ramses. I had my paintings still at the house and wanted to give him one of those. Your grandpa happened to be packing up the house, and he didn't want to tell me about anything that happened between you to. I pushed him…"

My gaze clashed with hers. It borderline sounded like she was defending the older fucker.

"He actually told me to talk to you about all this, and that it wasn't his place."

"Yeah, cuz he's just so perfect," I said, pulling away from her. "Your savior, and your friend."

Her head shot back. "No."

"Your provider." I swallowed hard before squeezing the bridge of my nose. "Want to know why I didn't tell you about that summer? Why I wasn't ready to?"

"It's obvious why you didn't. You didn't trust me."

"No, that's the thing, I do. I trust you with *everything*." I grabbed her, bracing her. "I love you with everything in me, but *I* wasn't ready. I wasn't ready for *this* and what I know you'll always see when you look at me."

She scanned my eyes, her lips turned down, sad. "What's that, Dorian?"

That was what I felt was obvious. I touched her cheek, following a line up to her eye. "I knew what you'd always see, and I wasn't ready for that." I outlined each eye, both of them closing. I snapped mine shut. "You'll always see a monster in me, and *I* can't look at that. I couldn't see that shit every fucking day, and you will because you won't forget this. You won't forget what I've done and..."

I mean, how could she? It'd always be there between us, lingering like a silent beast.

She opened her eyes after what I said, and I noticed she averted her gaze. She was right. We probably would get past this. She loved me, and I loved her, but that wasn't the point. *This* would always be there.

She'd never forget.

That was what I'd wanted to avoid, and pardon me, for not wanting to jump in and see that between us every day. We were good. We were finally fucking happy, and I didn't want to let go of any of that.

Of course, these were things I couldn't make myself say and my own insecurities I was still fucking working on. I would have told her; when I was ready, I would have. I'd just needed time, but it seemed I didn't have any more of that.

"Well, it's nice you know me so well," she said, sarcasm lacing her voice. She eased her arms away. "And you could have given me a chance to hear me out before just jumping to what you *think* you'll always see in me." Her head shook. "You should go."

I didn't want to, leave her like this, *us* like this, but fear was a son of a bitch. Maybe part of me did think I'd lose her, and that would have been so much worse than the beast underlying between us.

That fear did make me leave in the end. I wanted to respect her, but that didn't stop me from staying by the doorway longer than I probably should have. She cried after she closed it, cried a long time before I finally did leave. Not so long ago, I used to believe her tears gave me power. It meant I'd broken her, and that flawed logic felt like another lifetime away now. Even then, it hadn't given me power.

It had only deprived me of my strength.

CHAPTER
THIRTY-SIX

Dorian

My grandfather's goons made me wait a long time before buzzing me past his gate. In fact, I waited so long I didn't think my grandpa was going to let me in.

He probably shouldn't, best for both of us. I didn't want to be here at all, but I needed to tell him something.

I hoped it would be the last fucking thing.

I was done with the fucker messing with my life, and the people I cared about in it. He'd gotten between me and Noa now, *Noa*.

"Grandson." My grandfather didn't appear surprised to see me, and I was sure he wasn't. After all, he'd made me wait half a fucking century at his iron gates before one of his lapdogs okayed my way onto the property. I'd been escorted after that, led here today. I stood in what appeared to be some type of parlor when my grandfather finally came into the room of his big-ass house, and now was a good opportunity to see him.

He'd be alone.

I'd skipped school to be here today, my academy jacket and tie on to play up the ruse. I didn't need my parents asking about why I wasn't dressed for school when I saw them this morning, and I also didn't need Sloane's brother around. I had no issues with the kid, but he might wonder why I'd stopped over here to give my grandfather a piece of my fucking mind.

Which I was going to do.

Seeing the old fucker in his smoking jacket, cane in his hand, and calm demeanor about him set off an unexpected fire inside me. I thought I'd gotten over him in the passing weeks. What had happened between us felt like a century ago since Sloane had returned to town and everyone in my life was happy. *Finally* happy.

I shouldered away from my granddad's goons, his pal Lucas in particular. I didn't care if the asshole was strapped. Let him try something. I shot a finger at my grandfather. "You need to keep my fucking name out of your mouth," I blazed. There was more anger… fury than I had believed my body still felt for him. I'd thought I was over this shit. I *needed* to be over this shit. I didn't want to hate him anymore. I didn't want to feel anything. I wanted to be free, but he wasn't fucking letting me. I wet my lips. "I don't know what you're trying to pull, but you did your good deed, so you need to get the fuck out of this town and *stay away from me*, and that includes Noa."

Sloane was mine, and I was hers. We were a unit, and if he messed with her, he was messing with me.

He had messed with her, and if he *thought* he'd ever get in good with me, he had another thing coming. The jig was up, and I was calling him out on his shit.

"I really don't know what you thought that was," I contin-ued, stepping up on him. I noticed that Lucas dude put his hand out, but Grandpa put his hand up. Lucas stayed back, and Grandpa Prinze was going to let me approach. Stupid him. I stopped a foot or two away, the old man's aftershave making me gag. Between that and the tobacco smell that basically wafted out of the fucker's pores, I was holding my breath, but I wouldn't step back. My jaw shifted. "Talking to Noa was a mistake and getting between us an even bigger one."

Grandpa appeared calm in front of me, collected. His head tilted. "I don't know what you're talking about, grandson," he stated, and I flinched. "No one is trying to get between you and anyone. I merely told Sloane the truth, and if that didn't sit well with you, you probably should have mentioned what happened between us this summer first."

I would have told her. I would have fucking told her, but that was between us, not *him* and us.

Grandpa sighed. "I didn't want to tell her. I honestly thought you already had."

"Sure."

"It's the truth." Grandpa lifted his head. "Now, I'm sorry if that caused any discord between you. I really am, but I think you and I both know you're not supposed to be here right now. In fact, we're not supposed to be in contact at all, so I'm going to have to ask you to leave the premises."

He had to be joking. I smirked, but when that Lucas fucker put his hands on me, I shoved him off. This had about half a dozen others on the premises stepping to react, but my grandfather raised his hands to everyone.

"My grandson isn't going to cause trouble here today," he said to them all before returning his cane to the floor. He directed a look at me. "Right, grandson? I think it's time you leave now."

Apparently done with me, he turned, but I navigated in front of him.

"You're full of shit, old man. You know that?" I eyed a goon to my right, then left, deciding to stay where I was at the present. I didn't want trouble. I just wanted to prove a fucking point. My eyes narrowed. "I think you wanted this town *and me* to see you as some kind of savior. You come in to save the day with Sloane and Bru, and what? I might want something to do with your ass? I might not hate you anymore and just throw away everything you did in the past?"

My throat jumped, *loathing* that shit. I didn't know what to make of my grandfather. I'd thought I had him all pegged the moment I'd met him that summer, and though I still hadn't trusted him when he'd brought Sloane back to us, I had wanted to believe maybe some part in him had some kind of soul. That maybe he really had had a shitty situation dropped in his lap with that bastard Godfrey and done the right thing just to do the right thing.

But he was still here. He was and still creating chaos in my life. Why do that? Why be around and still causing mess?

"Let's not get it twisted. I will *never* want anything to do with you," I said, Adam's apple jumping. "No matter what good deeds you do or the people you help, so if that's why you're sticking around, don't. You did your good deed with Godfrey so leave and leave all of us alone."

"I'm helping because it's the right thing." Our gazes collided, his eyebrows narrowed tight like mine. "And all due respect, *grandson,* I don't have to prove anything to you."

"Actually, you have to prove fucking everything to me," I shot, nostrils flaring. "You should be on your damn fucking knees proving to me why you're not a complete and utter piece of shit."

His eyes scanned mine. "Step back, grandson."

"Make me." I dared him. "Now, you may have this town fooled, but you don't have me. I'll *always* see who you really are, and that's a sorry sack of shit who beat my father and fucked with my mother and her family—"

"Dorian!"

I whipped around, shrinking instantly where I stood at the sight of my father.

My father, who was pissed.

Dad had his suit on, the one he'd sported at breakfast. Snowflakes dusted his hair, his trench coat on his arm. He still had his leather gloves on, and a chill had reddened his cheeks. "What do you think you're doing? Step back from your grandfather *now*."

I did and right away, shocked to fucking hell to see him here and even more when he strode over to Grandpa Prinze.

"Thanks for calling me," Dad said, shocking me more. He studied me. "My son knows he's not supposed to be here."

"We had an agreement, son, and I intend to honor it." Grandpa scanned me. "I'm not to have any contact with Dorian."

I blinked, exchanging a glance between the two men. They were in contact with each other. About me?

At least for today, it seemed.

My father put his coat back on, leveling me with a hard glare. "Don't worry. We're going to have a talk about this," he said to Grandpa.

"No harm done, Royal." Grandpa held his cane. His head lowered. "The situation was escalating, but I don't think it would have resulted in anything. I think Dorian was more angry than anything."

"I think we both know what his anger can result in, Father," he said, my grandpa sighing. The two spoke to each other differently than that awkward day on the phone. Like they were both comfortable.

Like my *father* was comfortable.

The ease that the conversation had completely unnerved me, and I could do nothing but listen when my dad advised me to head to the car. He said he'd see me out there, but didn't leave Grandpa right away. What the fuck?

I didn't know what the hell was going on, but walked quickly to our cars. I waited outside of mine, but when my dad finally did come out, he waved me over to his.

"We'll send someone for it. I'm taking you to school," he said, and I didn't argue. I just got inside, and I'd never seen my father so angry. I mean, he usually pushed that shit down.

It emanated off him today, and even worse than all those times he'd found out I'd been keeping secrets from him and Mom.

"What the hell was that, Dorian?" Dad shifted gears, his Audi zipping through town. "Tell me you weren't about to do something to your grandfather."

My adrenaline pulsing, I didn't know what I'd been about to do before he'd arrived. "I..."

"The next words out of your mouth better be the truth and an explanation of why you went behind my back to him again."

"I don't know why. I..." I rubbed my legs, looking at him. "Are you guys talking to each other?" It almost sounded like they were or had at least been in contact with each other.

Dad had even stayed behind to talk to him.

I didn't know what to make of that, but what I said had obviously been the wrong thing to say. My dad cut out of traffic, parking on the side of the road. I'd sent my father to a place he normally didn't go, one where he straddled a line to remain collected. Taking off his gloves, I watched him check himself right in front of me, and I felt so bad. He dealt with anger as well, but he didn't allow it to consume him.

He was so much better than me.

"You're not the one asking questions here," he said, his hand moving down his jaw. "And not that I need to answer yours, but the lines of communication are open between my father and me."

But why? I didn't understand. I shook my head. "Dad..."

"Why did you go behind my back, Dorian?" Dad released a heavy breath. "And why did I walk in on what I did? Why did it look like you were going to do something?"

"I wasn't. I swear to God." At least, I hoped I wasn't. I

breathed into my hands. "He told Sloane about that summer with him, and what I tried to do after. Poisoning him."

Silence beside me, and when I looked over, Dad was rubbing the steering wheel. "He saw Sloane?"

"They ran into each other, I guess. Sloane dropped by that house Bru and her stayed at. Some of her paintings were there, and she wanted to get one."

"I see."

"I guess they got to talking, and it came up what I did." I laced my hands behind my neck. "He had no right. *No right* to tell her that."

My eyes closed, *simmering*. I felt like I was going to punch a fist through one of my dad's windows, which would make shit so much worse.

I didn't, though, holding back when I grabbed my legs. When I looked at my father, he had his eyes on the traffic zooming by us.

"Why weren't you the one to tell her, Dorian?" he asked, shocking me. He nodded. "You should have been the one to tell her. You know that, right?"

I did know that, hard facts. I closed my eyes. "I was going to. I was. I…" I dampened my lips. "I just wasn't ready."

My dad sat with that beside me, and where he'd been unnerved before, he wasn't now. If anything, he looked sad, his lips turned down.

"I suppose I get that, but you should have told her," he said, sighing. "Because you didn't, you gave that power away to someone else."

Like I didn't know that? I kept fucking shit up, and I was getting so good at that. I rubbed my mouth.

"How did she react?" Dad asked, and I sat up.

"How she should have," I said, staring out of the car. "Like she can't trust me. Like… like I'm a monster." I stuttered on the last word, my breath shallow. "I am a monster."

I didn't mean to say it, though I felt it. I was a monster, but I shouldn't have said that in front of my dad.

I knew that by the way he looked at me.

"You feel like you're a monster, son?" he questioned, his hand on my neck. He squeezed. "Why do you feel like that?"

"How am I not? Besides all that with Grandpa, there's all the Mayberry stuff, and I just feel it inside me. I'm my grandfather's fucking grandson, and I feel it."

These were facts, cold hard facts, and Dad knew it. He may have been able to battle his own demons, but clearly, I hadn't. They were still fully fledged within me, alive and true.

Dad leaned forward. "You made some mistakes, but that doesn't mean you're a monster."

"But doesn't it?" I glanced his way, cringing. "I have this thing inside me, and I can't control it. I'm a piece of shit, and I can't even fix the things I want to fix right. I messed up with Charlie. I should have just told you and Mom the truth."

Dad nodded, agreeing. He rubbed my neck. "You should have, but that doesn't make you a monster, son. It makes you human."

Human. Right. I shook my head. "It makes me a head case, and Sloane sees that now. She'll always see that." I rubbed my hands. "I'm a piece of shit, Dad—"

"You're not." He took my face, scanning my eyes. "You're my son, and though you're not without flaws, you are perfection in every sense of the word. Perfection to me, your mom, and anyone who's ever gotten the chance to be loved by you. *Protected* by you."

I cringed, and he shook his head, shook me.

"You are, Dorian. You are a Prinze, and my father may have sullied that name, but you have not. You're going to make that name better, stronger." His throat flicked. "I've worked my whole life to create a legacy for you. A strong one... an *honest* one that you one day can be proud of."

I knew he had. Everyone loved my father, his peers, his

employees… everyone, and that was because he protected them. He protected their interests and never let people get taken advantage of if he could help it.

"You're going to make that legacy even stronger, son, and it's going to be an honor to hand that down to you one day. It will be because I know what you'll do with it. You'll be better than my father. Better than me because I'm not perfect either. I had to overcome my own struggles, and you will too."

"How do you know that about me?" I asked, voice breaking. "I never do the right thing."

"That's because you need to do that to learn *how to*. It doesn't happen overnight. It's a process of trials and tribulations. Sometimes you really have to fuck some shit up to figure out how to do something right."

I laughed, and he did too.

He sat back. "But you will. It's guaranteed, because you're an extension of both me and your mother, and thank God for how much of your mom you carry. You have her good heart, and you've always had that."

"I have yours too," I said, swallowing. "Yours is good too." He might not be quick to say that, but he should. He was one of the best people I knew.

He smiled a little. "That took some work too." His hand moved to my arm. "And it helped having your mother."

I glanced his way, and he patted my back.

"Things will work out between you and Sloane. It will if you're willing to work for it."

"I love her," I stated, no waver in my voice. "That girl owns me, Dad."

I might have been afraid to admit that in the past, but I wasn't now for some reason. Maybe because I knew my dad would understand.

His smile stretched. "Then put the work in, and be kinder to yourself, Dorian. You're still young, and you're going to figure it out. Figure life out."

"Why didn't I just talk to you sooner?" I asked, feeling stupid now. I should have gone to him back then, back before Charlie and everything.

"Because you're me." He rubbed my arm. "So, you're welcome for that."

I barked out a laugh, and he did too, my dad and I laughing just over nothing.

"I'm glad you talked to me, and I'm sorry you felt you couldn't before."

It wasn't his fault. I had my own shit I still had to work out, and that had nothing to do with him.

"As far as before and what you asked about your grandfather, we aren't in contact. Not really." His jaw moved. "My dad knows those lines are open, though, like I said. I did that for you in case you needed it."

I studied him, confused. "For me?"

"Yes. I have no interest in taking up anything with my father personally. I'm grateful for what he did, of course. Helping us get back Sloane and everything he did there regarding her and her brother. My father seems to be trying to be a better person, but gratitude is fortunately all I can give the man. I've made my peace with our relationship, but I don't want to be the reason yours is taken away." His lips pinched tight. "That is, if you want it."

But he'd hurt him, *abused* him. "I don't want anything to do with him."

"You may feel that way now, but you never know how you'll feel in a year, two, or even ten. Somewhere along the way, you may change your mind, and if you do, I want you to have that opportunity. You're eighteen, and I know you could do whatever you wish now, but I know you." His head tilted, smile warm. "You'd never even entertain the idea unless I was okay with it, and me opening the lines of communication with my dad will slowly get me there. I hope, over time, if that day ever does come where you do want to reach out, I'd be okay with that relationship, yours and his."

I didn't know what to say, but I did hug him back when he hugged me.

"I want you to have the world, son," he said, his hand on my head. "And I'm willing to get out of my own way for you to have it. It might take me time, and I know it will take patience, but I'm willing to put in the work."

I closed my eyes, gripping his coat. I didn't want a relationship with my grandfather and couldn't ever see that changing, but I refused to not acknowledge the sacrifice my father was making for me. He'd mentioned my mom's good heart, but he had to know he contributed just as much.

After all, I was my father's son.

CHAPTER
THIRTY-SEVEN

December

"I'll be over here, Mrs. Prinze," Ronald stated, allowing me to move forward on my own. He took a nearby cafe table, and I proceeded onward, grateful for our old family friend. When my husband had suggested we hire a security detail for the family, I'd been a little unnerved. I didn't grow up the way he had, and it was different, but back then, Royal had believed it necessary. Dorian had just been born, and Royal had stressed his father wouldn't be in prison forever.

That, in the end, had been the final decision regarding hiring Ronald, who was ex-military. These days, he fell more into his role as butler and family friend, but today, he was keeping an eye over me and the situation. I didn't feel I'd particularly need him for this meeting, but I had to admit knowing he was close allowed me to feel better.

I'd locked my nerves away in a black box a long time ago when it came to dealing with my husband's father. Those first few years when he had been out of prison, I'd been more on edge, wondering if he'd be around the corner, waiting. There had come a time, though, when I decided I was going to take back my life, and that Callum Prinze wasn't going to take any more away from myself or my family.

After all, he'd gotten enough, hadn't he?

I held to that promise, steady in my strides as I approached his table. He sat inside the cafe, sipping a cup of something that steamed near one of the snow-encrusted windows. He was alone, but he hadn't come alone. The dark sedan parked right out front basically had his name on it. There were two men sitting in the front, their windows down, and they had tipped their billed hats at me on my way inside.

Like stated, the vehicle had his name on it.

The man turned from the window the moment I stopped in front of his table, more than a few eyes on us. We'd missed the lunch rush, but this was a small town. Everyone knew me, and they definitely knew him.

How could this town forget?

He'd cemented his stamp on this city, my husband's father. He'd struck fear and left a legacy. The tides may have changed after he'd gone to prison, but this town *and I* had never forgotten. He'd shattered so many lives, the first his own flesh and blood.

"I admit, I was surprised when your people reached out to me," he said, placing his cup down. "And I have to ask... does my son know you've asked to meet with me today?"

Of course, he did. We didn't keep things from each other. "I think we should just go ahead and get this started. I have something to say to you, so I'd like to say it so we can both move on with our days." And Royal may have known about this meeting, but that didn't mean he liked it. In fact, he'd been adamant about Ronald being with me if he couldn't, and I hadn't wanted my husband to attend this meeting with his father.

This was something I needed to do on my own.

Mr. Prinze opened his hands. "I have no problem meeting

with you, but I'd rather not risk my son's wrath. I want to respect him, and if he's not okay with this…"

"We tell each other everything," I stated, clipped. "So, if we could proceed?"

The man waved to the chair across from him, but I didn't sit. We wouldn't be here long.

Mr. Prinze nodded. "I know you didn't come alone, but you can let your guard know I have no intention of harming you," he stated, obviously mentioning Ronald. He frowned. "And any references made to do so in the past were a mistake on my part. I'm sure Dorian told you that I was very much desperate to get to know him."

I did know that. I quirked a smile. "Yes, I know all about how you manipulated my *eighteen-year-old* son to get to know him better. I know all about that."

Mr. Prinze's frown didn't leave him, his hands together. "I'm not a man without flaws, December. I know what I've done, and these are things I have to live with. I know these decisions have pushed me further and further away from my grandson and my own son, and what I did to you and your family all those years ago was—"

My hand lifted, really not wanting to hear anything of this. I came here to say something to him, and it had nothing to do with his "flaws" or things he "had to live with." I put my hands on the table. "I want to start with saying, I don't care what you have to say. I don't, so you can stop it right now."

He did, his lips coming together. He laced his fingers. "So, what is this meeting about then?"

It was about one thing and one thing only. I'd *never* forget what he'd done to my family, my father… my sister. He'd ruined all our lives back then, and what he'd done with Dorian recently only cemented what I felt for him even more. *I'd lost enough* because of this man, and moving forward, he wasn't going to get any more.

My last year had been hell. I'd lost my little brother via signs I hadn't seen. I hadn't been able to save Charlie. I'd been too unaware about the situation, and had I been my sister Paige, things wouldn't have been that way. She would have seen that Charlie had gone to someone he shouldn't have gone to. She would have saved him.

I channeled her upon meeting with my husband's father because today, I wasn't unaware. *Today*, I was taking action, and this man before me was about to know. "I know you're in contact with my husband," I said to him, nodding. "I know he's giving you a chance for our son."

Mr. Prinze opened his mouth, but I raised my hand again.

"No, see. I'm not finished," I cut, the older man's lips closing. I put a finger to the table. "He's doing this for Dorian, and he's willing to put away all the hurt you caused him, the pain and suffering and everything else, because he's a loving father and husband who gives everything of himself for his kid and his family. He's a fierce provider, protector, and he managed to become these things despite, to put it bluntly, the complete and utter fuck-up his father was."

Mr. Prinze said nothing, his back touching the chair. He started to speak again, but I shook my head.

"This meeting is about one thing and one thing only. My husband's giving you a chance. He is, and that's the only reason you get *one* from me. You got one chance at this, Mr. Prinze. One to be a decent person, and this is your warning to take advantage of that."

He blinked, but just once. "Warning?"

"Yes." I crossed my arms. "Because if you fuck this up… fuck with my husband or my child, I *will* come for you. You may have gotten an olive branch from this family, but you most certainly don't deserve it. This is your warning and your only one. I will one hundred percent come for you personally if you mess with my family, and that is a promise."

The man gave no emotional response to what I said, and I

think that angered me the most, made me sad. This probably wasn't his first threat.

But if he messed with my family, it'd be his last.

In the end, I didn't wait for his response. I'd said what I had to say, said my piece. I strode toward the exit, and Ronald was already waiting by the door. He made no mention about what he'd most likely heard, and I knew he never would. He was in our family too, and he'd support it. He'd even aid if we needed someone outside of us to burn.

I hoped for the sake of my husband's father that wouldn't be the case.

CHAPTER
THIRTY-EIGHT

Sloane

Lunch with Legacy had been quiet lately, mostly on my part. Dorian and I still weren't really talking to each other.

I think he was trying to give me space.

He eyed me while Ares talked to him about something on the other side of the table, the dark prince dipping his fry into ketchup. Generally, he tended to do that, juggling eating, conversation, and staring at me. It was like he was trying to remind me that he was still there and wasn't going anywhere.

How could I forget?

I was well aware of his presence, just as I was about the conversation that'd blown up between us the other day. Gratefully, the Legacy table wasn't just Dorian and me, and lately, the boys had been letting more people sit with us. This kept the constant attention off me, which was especially nice since Bow and Bru didn't always sit with us. Bru typically missed most lunches. He studied a lot in the library, and though I didn't know where Bow was when she didn't eat here, I figured it was more academic stuff. She was a brain just like Bru.

Thatcher and Wells were pure entertainment in themselves. Currently, Thatcher was juggling about five oranges while Wells egged him on, a Court guy under Wells's arm. I think he was seeing the guy, but I wasn't sure. The redhead tended to frequent our table the most when Wells brought others, and the guy clapped Thatcher on with the other Court guys and girls who were eating with us today.

Actually, Thatcher had drawn quite a crowd, and even some of the lunch staff was watching from their serving stations. I think that was why none of us saw Bow coming, a bottle of chocolate milk in her hand. I lifted my hand to say hey when I saw her, but stopped when I noticed her face, her cheeks red. She almost looked like she'd been crying, and she didn't stop for me. She actually walked past my side onto her brother's end of the table.

Thatcher caught the oranges. "Sup?"

Bow threw the milk, the chocolatey drink exploding in her brother's direction, but it didn't hit her brother.

It hit Wells beside him.

The platinum blond launched out of his chair, him, the redhead beside him, and the girl next to him all within the line of fire. Wells had gotten the brunt of it, though, which meant Bow had obviously aimed for him. The chocolate beverage covered Wells's stark blond locks down to his dark roots, his chest completely soaked. His eyes blazed. "What the fuck, Bow?"

Conversation at the table stopped, gasps in the air. Thatcher, who'd been completely missed in all this, dropped his oranges to the table. I believed he'd dropped them mostly out of shock, and Dorian and Ares looked like they were just trying to play catch-up. Dorian frowned. "What the..."

"How could you?" Bow was shaking, her little fists balled.

She stamped one of her Mary Janes to the ground. "Why would you do that, huh? You're such a jerk, Wells!"

My head shot to Wells, along with the rest of the table, and Wells's glare only cut deeper in Bow's direction.

Bow came around to him, like a good solid two feet under him, but that didn't stop her from shooting a finger in his face. "Mr. Shapiro told me what you did, and it was so out of line."

"Hey." Thatcher put a hand out, which kept Wells from making a stride distinctly in Bow's direction. The guy was still blinking down chocolate milk, and his face had shot up about three shades in color. Thatcher faced Bow. "What are you talking about?"

"Talk to your jerk friend," she snapped, making *me* snap back. I'd never seen Bow talk this way about anyone. She shook her head. "Mr. Shapiro said I can't eat lunch in his classroom anymore because my brother's friend is an over-bearing jerk who said I have to eat in the lunchroom here with you guys."

"Call me a jerk one more time, Rainbow." Wells's chest touched Thatcher's hand, the boy snarling. I'd never seen him this way either. He was normally the laid-back one out of the crew. He pointed a finger at her. "And you will eat lunch in here with us because that's where you belong."

Bow's laughter was manic, and at this point, Dorian, Ares, and I had made our way to that side of the table. I didn't know what the fuck this was, but I noticed the boys weren't breaking this up. People even had their phones out, an audi-ence gathering. Around the time some of the few security staff around here started to approach our table, Rainbow Reed did the craziest thing. She raised her empty bottle of milk, then proceeded to throw it. Actually, she launched that shit.

It hit its intended target.

The bottle ricocheted off Wells's milk-stained chest, his

white dress shirt clinging to him at this point. His head shot up, and I watched what could only be described as an animal rise inside him. A growl and he shoved his way forward, pushing Thatcher clear out of the way, who was easily twice his size. He cut in front of Bow, but Dorian and Ares blocked his strides. They literally made a man wall in front of her, which gave Thatcher enough time to gain his bearings and lock his arms under Wells.

"You're taking a walk," Thatcher gritted at him, forcing him when he bucked. It took some maneuvering, but Thatcher got him to walk away with him while Dorian and Ares calmed the rest of the lunchroom down. People were up, talking, and snapping pictures, but they stopped at one bark from the dark prince.

"Show's fucking over," he ground out about the same time I noticed Bow escape. Bracing her arms, she left the room through the doors on the other side of the lunchroom. I started to go after her around the same time Ares and Dorian decided to go after Thatcher and Wells. They said as much as they walked away, but I caught Dorian's eyes before they did.

He tipped his chin at me, a mutual exchange there. He was going to handle his friend while I handled mine, and we said as much with a single look. The two of us got each other.

Not focusing on that, I went after Bow, still fucking confused about what had just happened. All this was super weird, and I did find Bow right away.

She was pacing.

Her fists to her mouth, she was on her way to running a fire trail through the floor when I entered the girl's bathroom. Seeing me, her head snapped up, but she didn't stop pacing.

"Oh my God. Oh my God. Oh my God," she gasped, panicked, shaking. She hugged her arms. "Oh my God. I shouldn't have done that."

My head popping back again, I approached her. "What?"

"I shouldn't have *done that*. I shouldn't have..." Her lips moved, opened and closed like a panicky fish. "I need to apologize. If I don't, it'll make things so much worse."

She cut around me, but I grabbed her.

"Apologize? To who? Wells?"

Her nod incessant, she attempted to move again, but I wasn't letting go.

"Um, little rabbit. He should be apologizing to you." He had no right to tell her who she could eat lunch with. I braced my arms. "And why does he think he can tell you who you can eat lunch with?"

"Because he's a bully," she said, shocking me. I mean, were we talking about the same Wells? The guy was more than laid-back, happy-go-lucky. Sure, I'd seen his dark side, Thatcher's too, but things back when I first got here had been complicated. His or Thatcher's behavior hadn't been justified then, but I did get it. Her tiny fingers gripped her arms. "He's controlling and overbearing just like the rest of the guys. You know how him and Legacy throw their weight around here."

I did, but this was crazy. I mean, Bow *was* Legacy, and the kid sister of the group. "Yeah, but that doesn't make it okay."

"I'm not saying it does, but that's who he is, and I need to apologize because I don't do things like that." She stamped her feet. "He just made me so mad."

God, how was this girl even cute angry? I didn't mean to laugh, but I did. I put a hand on her arm. "One, you're not apologizing. He was a jerk, and two, what were you talking about when you said it'd make things worse if you didn't?"

"I just meant I overreacted so if I don't apologize, it'll make the situation worse," she said, but she definitely was flustered while she said it. She really looked like she was going to cry, and I decided to get her a paper towel before she did. She blew into it. "Thanks."

"No problem," I stated, meaning that. I still felt a little confused by all this and even what she said just now. I felt like I might be missing something here, but right now, the little rabbit seemed like she needed a hug more than anything.

I gave that to her, and she laughed. "Thanks."

"No problem," I repeated, laughing too. She settled down a little, and when I pulled away, I wiped the running mascara away from under her eyes. This caused her to thank me again and made us both chuckle.

"He really shouldn't think he can control you," I said, and she shook her head.

"I just want to let it go, okay?" she asked, and I chewed the inside of my cheek. I didn't really want to let it go, but I would for her. She looked up at the ceiling. "I can't believe I threw chocolate milk on him."

"He deserved that shit and more." I hopped up on the bathroom sink, sitting. "I mean, is this why you don't have many friends? Overbearing shit like this?"

She said nothing, but she really didn't have to say it. I'd stay the fuck away too if I knew I'd be dealing with Legacy shit. I mean, I got wanting to watch over and look out for the girl since she was the Legacy's youngest, but this was a bit much, and coming from Wells? Even more. Like stated, he was the easy going one.

I also didn't understand what the harm was that she'd decided to eat lunch away from them at all. Especially with a teacher, and I knew she was working with Mr. Shapiro on her computer programming stuff. She'd mentioned it a time or two.

"I should get back to class," she said, causing my thoughts to drift. She rubbed her nose. "Thanks for being here."

I got off the sink. "Of course, and hey? Want to stay over tonight?" I shrugged. "We can gossip about how the Legacy boys like to take any opportunity they possibly can to... annoy us."

She knew I had my own troubles. Hell, all of Legacy knew.

When things were good between Dorian and me, the world knew. The same with the bad.

I hoped we'd be okay.

I honest to fuck just needed a night of girl time away from boys, and when Bow jumped excitedly, she seemed to need the same. She said she'd bring some girly flicks but promised me some slasher ones too. She'd gotten to know what I liked over the past weeks I'd been back.

Because she was my friend.

CHAPTER
THIRTY-NINE

Sloane

My night was filled with tubs of rocky road ice cream, a completely cringe chick flick *or four*, and Rainbow Reed's spritely laughter. I had really missed her, busy with what seemed like so many other things, and there was nothing like being in Bow's light. She had an optimistic viewpoint of the world I'd all but been forced to shy away from lately, and though she'd had her own struggles today, she still remained positive. I'd had every intention of bringing up what had happened today at lunch with her again, but in the end, I chose positivity too, and did have a good night. Bow had actually fallen asleep right around the time we started the slasher flick I wanted, but I didn't wake her up and give her a hard time about it.

I merely covered her up with a blanket. She'd fallen asleep on my bed and her doing that made me sleepy too. It'd been a long day for me as well. Before I turned in too, I decided to clean up my room, and as I was disposing our tubs of rocky road in the kitchen, I spotted Ares.

He was sneaking out.

I actually spotted him swiping his phone off the kitchen counter before easing his way through the dark toward the back door. I flicked the light on before he could, and he cursed.

"What are you doing?" I asked, and he closed the door, brushing past me to flick off the light.

"Keep your voice down," he growled, but didn't answer my question. He was obviously going out, had his coat on. He shot his thumb toward the door. "I'm just going out for a bit. I'll be back."

Yeah, that wasn't a good enough explanation, and I stood there while he rolled his eyes.

"Seriously, it's not a big deal, little. Go back to bed and don't wake Mom. She had a late night tonight."

Brielle had ended up wrapping up her duties at Windsor Prep early to head back into the mayor's office. She'd already pulled a couple late nights this week, but that was okay. I didn't mind.

I also had no intention of waking her up, but I wasn't going to let Ares just walk out of here with no explanation. Not to mention, he knew we weren't supposed to be sneaking around. I flicked on the light again, and when I did, Ares just about lost his shit. He shut the light off *over me*, and I cut in front of the door.

"If it's not a big deal, why are you sneaking out?" I asked, basically being *that* sibling. Ramses and Brielle didn't need the stress, and though we weren't restricted from leaving, they did like to know where we went if we did.

If Ares was sneaking out, he didn't want them to know something, and that didn't sit well.

Ares weaved his fingers through his hair. "I'm just going to pick up Wells with the guys."

"Pick him up where?"

"Little..." He said this but laughed a little, hushed, low.

He held his curls out of his face. "Fuck almighty, how are you already making me miss being an only child?"

Socking him for that one, I didn't stop, and he blocked himself, mock pouting.

"If you must know, Wells has been arrested," he said, skirting away from me, but he didn't have to. I stopped punching him all on my fucking own. Especially since he was so nonchalant about what he said. He lifted his hands. "Don't freak. It's really not a big deal."

"How is that not a big fucking deal?" I whisper-shouted, and he shushed me. "What the hell happened? Is he okay?"

Ares patted the air. "He will be if you let us fucking go get him. D and Thatcher are out in my truck. I forgot my phone, which is why I came back inside, and you holding us up more isn't helping the situation."

His tone turned serious, and his next move was to head toward that door again.

I grabbed my coat.

"The fuck you think you're—"

"I'm going," I shot, cutting around him, and he groaned at a volume where anyone else in a decent radius would have heard him. I only hoped Ramses wasn't working late in his studio tonight.

With me in front of him, Ares had no choice but to follow me, and I finished putting on my coat while he trailed behind me.

"Little," he started, but I was already at his tank of a ride, the thing humming outside the garage. I spotted the dark prince in the front seat, but before he could get out into the chilled area, I was making my way into the back.

"Uh," Dorian started before cutting a look at Ares who was also getting in the ride. My twin took the driver's side. Dorian frowned at him, then me. "What's going on?"

I tucked myself in next to Thatcher who took up a good portion of the back. The boy was a man-beast, big in the sense where he was both muscular and tall, so that didn't leave for much room in the back. Upon seeing me, he just about dropped his phone. His lips turned down. "What are you doing? I thought you were hanging out with Bow tonight."

"I am." I closed the door, then strapped in. "She's upstairs sleeping and won't miss me. I'm going with you guys."

Dorian's frown deepened. "Since when?" His tone was curious more than anything. He swung a look to Ares. "You tell her we were going to get Wells?"

"Nah, man. At least not by choice. She just fucking accosted me in the kitchen and bled that shit out of me," Ares huffed, and Thatcher barked a laugh back here with me.

"Of course, she did," he said, returning to his phone. His thumbs dashed across his screen. "She's you but with a vagina."

A punch from Ares, and more than one from Dorian who just about climbed in the back seat with us. I literally thought the dark prince was going to climb over the center console, half his body in the back seat, before he finished with Thatcher.

"Shit, man. What the fuck?" Thatcher gritted when Dorian slapped a final hand against the side of his head. Thatcher basically looked like he'd been mauled by a tiger at this point, his dark hair askew, his face flushed. "The fuck? It's true!"

Dorian raised another fist, but this time, I punched Thatcher. I got him so quick and hard the large boy actually rubbed his arm after.

He grinned at me. "You really are Wolf's sister."

"Shut the fuck up, bro." Ares's head touched his seat, his eyes to the ceiling. "Anyway, yes, I told her Wells was arrested. She wants to come, but this truck isn't moving until you get out of it, little." Ares turned in his seat. "You don't need to complicate things. We got this handled."

"How so?"

"You don't need to worry about it. Just know we got this."

This sentiment seemed to be shared by Thatcher, who nodded, but Dorian still had a well-placed frown on his lips. I expected for him to state the same, but when he strapped in and told Ares to get driving, he had everyone darting a look up front.

"We do have it handled, so it won't be a big deal if she comes," he said, flooring me and everyone else in the truck. He waved them off. "We're wasting time. We need to go, so are we?"

Ares still had his head angled in Dorian's direction, but with a huff, he put his Hummer into gear. Next thing I knew, we were on the road, and I was still at a loss for words.

He was letting me go?

I thought, out of everyone, he might fight my decision the most. We hadn't even had a full conversation since that day in my bedroom.

When you kicked him out.

I'd had good reason, always a thing between him and me and that stuff he said… about me being manipulated by his grandpa…

I hadn't liked a lot of what he'd shared that night. Especially when I found out Callum had threatened Dorian's mom. I didn't think the dark prince was lying to me about that, but there could have been a miscommunication with his grandpa or something else.

I hated I even had to question that.

But I did, and it was because Dorian *always* ran hot. He blew his top at the littlest things, and sometimes, only saw things the way he wanted to see them. He'd shown me this more than once with miscommunications with me.

The whole situation made me sick, and when he'd gone into details about that night he had poisoned his grandpa, the sickness had only worsened. He'd really felt he had to do it, and what that had done to him made my stomach turn.

He thinks he's a monster.

Our gazes clashed through the side-view mirror, and I nearly forgot why we were both here until Ares huffed beside him.

"If Mom and Dad find out I snuck out and took you with me, they will literally light my ass up," Ares ground out, his Hummer cutting through the slush and snow. It hadn't snowed for a few days, and we might not even see a white Christmas this year with how quick it was melting. He studied me through the rearview mirror. "There's really no reason you need to be coming with us to do this."

"And what exactly are you doing?" I asked, the truck suddenly silent. "And why in the hell was Wells arrested?"

This day just kept getting weirder and weirder, and none of these boys seemed to want to say anything about it. Surprisingly enough, the dark prince turned in his seat, and when our eyes connected, it always hit me in a certain way. It made my body flutter, made me *weak*. My mouth closed, and he sighed.

"He hit someone." Dorian scanned the others. "Assault."

The fuck?

"He's in the next county, but Ares knows someone on the force who will let us take care of Wells's bail without getting his parents involved."

Right. Because he's a minor, and they'd normally call them. "Who did Wells hit?"

The boys were silent again, and Thatcher's jaw clicked. I thought he'd say something, but Dorian, once again, did first.

"He just stepped out of line and did the wrong thing," Dorian started, and Thatcher scoffed.

"Fucker deserved that shit, D," Thatcher growled, and Dorian frowned. Thatcher tipped his chin up front. "Asshole got lucky tonight. It could have been me who hit him, and best *believe* I wouldn't have stopped at a broken jaw."

My jaw dropped. "He broke someone's jaw?"

Thatcher's tongue came out, the dual crosses in his ears

dangling. "Yeah, he did. Wish I could have been there and seen that shit."

Jesus Christ.

Both Dorian and Ares shot Thatcher a look that popped his tongue back into his mouth. Whatever was going on tonight definitely didn't sit as well with Dorian and Ares as it did Thatcher.

"It didn't have to come to that," Dorian continued, his expression grave. "He knows that, and all tonight did was get his ass arrested."

"Are you guys going to tell me who he hit?" I was between the seats at this point and just got a bunch of averted eyes. "Come on. I'm here to help—"

"Actually, you're not here to help, and if you want to be here and not back at the house, you'll just let us do our thing." There was nothing playful about Ares's tone, and normally, I wouldn't have let him talk to me like that, but he did have control of the truck.

I sat back *only* because of that, watching as Thatcher went back to his phone, and Dorian proceeded to do what he normally did these days. I got casual glances through the side mirror instead of across the lunch table, and he was letting me be here.

He'd even fought for me to be.

———

The drive to the Corrington Meadows county police department was long and quiet. I didn't ask any more questions because I knew they'd be shut down. These boys were being stubborn for some reason and remained tight-lipped all the way to the precinct. When we got there, Thatcher immediately stepped to get out, but both Dorian and Ares told him to sit with me. They apparently didn't trust him not to do something stupid.

I had no idea what that meant, but it could have been his age. He was younger and tended to come off a little less responsible than the others. In any sense, it was Ares who had the contact inside, and while he and Dorian were away, Thatcher let me know how that came about. My twin brother had apparently fucked one of the cops, but to her credit, she hadn't been a cop at the time. She'd been in college, and they were both at a party or some crap.

Even still, that shit made me thoroughly gag, and I'd try not to give Ares a hard time anymore about Dorian and me. It was fucking weird and just... *ick*. Anyway, sitting next to Thatcher, I moved my thoughts on to Wells, who I hoped was okay. I'd come to care about the joker, just like the rest of these boys. I knew right away when he was released because he flew from the precinct and yelled, "Freedom!" so loud in the parking lot he had cops coming back out of the precinct to check things out.

Dorian and Ares hit him on the head in response, all the boys in their thick winter coats. Wells was jumping up and down between Dorian and Ares when Thatcher and I got out of the running truck, and I'd never seen Wells so amped. He was like *excited* or some shit, and when Thatcher zoomed over and picked him up, swinging him around, he was even more so.

The two were a couple of characters, and I suppose always had been. My hands in my pockets, I stood there, my head shaking.

Thatcher dropped him, fake-punching at him before sliding his meaty arm around him. "You okay, man?"

"Yeah, bro, and you should have seen that shit tonight." Wells locked his hand with his friend. "Dude's nose exploded like a fucking gusher. It was awesome—" His smile wiped away when he saw me, and he let go of Thatcher's hand. His dark eyebrows descended. "The fuck you doing here?"

Okay, so prison Wells wasn't fun, and next thing I knew, he was stepping up on me.

"You're supposed to be with Bow," he gritted, and Dorian tugged him back by the jacket. I realized, at this point, Ares was tugging me. I must have looked like I'd been about to do something because he held on.

Dorian put a finger in Wells's face. "Watch how you talk to her. You're already on thin ice for not listening to us. You didn't have to do that shit tonight, and you're lucky Ares knows people in there."

Dorian shoved Wells for good measure, but I didn't need him fighting my battles for me.

"Whatever," Wells said, and Ares came forward.

"Not whatever," Ares cut in, his hands still on me, and I got why now. I was tugging to get up in Wells's face for speaking to me the way he had. I'd come all the way here because I'd been worried about the asshole, and for what? This? Ares pushed his hair back. "You messed up. You lost your shit, and now, you're running your mouth like a cocky son of a bitch. You continue to do that, and I'm gonna let her go and let you handle yourself while I *watch*."

This made Dorian laugh and surprisingly me too. We noticed right away when we both did, and Dorian rubbed it away before facing Wells. He put a hand on Wells's shoulder. "In all seriousness, you okay? They treat you all right in there?"

"I'm good." He put his hands in his pockets, and apparently without the high of discussing carnage, his glee shifted. His eyes averted, and when he asked if we could leave, I wondered if he really was okay. I mean, he'd hit someone. What the fuck?

This, like other things today, didn't seem like him, and though the others let him head toward the truck, I noticed Dorian speak to him first. The two remained outside while the rest of us got in. They stayed out there for quite a few moments before suddenly, Dorian pulled Wells in for a hug.

I didn't know what to make of that, but seeing Dorian do this and how he always showed up for his friends, I definitely noticed.

He did the same thing with me.

If I needed him, the dark prince would always be there, always. He loved so hard.

Gazing away from the hugging brothers, I exchanged a glance between Ares and Thatcher. "So, is anyone going to tell me what happened tonight? Who Wells hit, and why he didn't have to?" They'd all made it sound like he had an alternative.

Ares merely started his truck while Thatcher raised a hand.

"Doesn't matter," Thatcher said, glancing out the window, and when Wells got inside, Thatcher put his arm around him. He whispered something to Wells, and though I think he tried to keep it low, I heard it. I heard Thatcher tell his friend one single word…

He said thanks.

CHAPTER
FORTY

Sloane

The night with Legacy wasn't over, but they stressed it was for me. They had to pick up Wells's car, which had gotten impounded in all this. Whoever he'd hit had had it towed, I guess, and after they dropped me off, they all piled into their individual cars to get Wells's. I figured I wouldn't hear anything more about any of this until at least morning, so I decided to go to bed. Bow was right where I'd left her when I got upstairs, snoozing away on my comforter. I'd known her to be a heavy sleeper.

After getting into my pajamas, I planned to get a little shut eye myself, but everything that had happened tonight still nagged at me. I decided to wait downstairs for Ares to come back so I could hound him about things, and eventually, I did hear talking outside while I waited in the kitchen.

It wasn't Ares's voice, though.

Tugging the curtain away from the back door, I spotted Dorian and Wells. They chatted, Wells's hands in his pockets. Like before, I couldn't hear what they were discussing, but it seemed to be over when Dorian took Wells's hand and brought him in for one of those bro hugs. Dorian said something more to him but stopped when his gaze flicked in my direction.

My mouth parted, caught. Wells shifted in my direction too, frowning, and he exchanged a glance between Dorian and me.

We were still looking at each other.

It was like we couldn't stop, my swallow hard. I let go of the curtain but didn't bother scurrying away. They'd both seen me, so what would have been the point?

I simply waited, looking again to see Dorian head toward his car. Wells headed in my direction. I unlocked the door for him and was still in the kitchen when he finally came inside. He shut the door quietly behind him while I stood in the kitchen, lit by little more than the light above the stove.

"What are you doing here?" I asked, watching as he took his coat off. I thought his face screwed up a little while he did it, but I could have been mistaken. The room was kind of dark.

He folded his coat over his arm. "Wolf said I could stay the night. My dad's a light sleeper. Don't want him to see me sneaking back in."

I leaned against the kitchen island. "Where is he? Ares?"

"Behind me somewhere," he said, looking rather tired himself. It seemed whatever energy he'd harnessed before was gone. He squeezed his eyes. "D and I drive fast so we got ahead. Thatcher went home after we got my car." He yawned after he said it, shaking his head. He laughed. "Dorian wanted to make sure I took no detours back here, I guess. And to check in. Make sure I was okay or whatever."

Because that was the kind of stuff he did for his friends. I rubbed my arm. Wells hung his coat up at the door, and I stepped forward to ask him more about tonight. I started to, but he cringed, and that was something I definitely noticed since he was like a foot or so away from me now.

As well as the state of his shirt.

Blood red and ripped down the side. His white tee currently clung to him in a soaked crimson and was more than visible since he was no longer holding his coat over the stain. I gasped. "Oh my God, Wells. You're like bleeding."

Instantly, he directed a look down, and when he lifted his shirt, he merely cursed while I just about fainted. The bandage he had over his side was caked in blood, the few strips of tape around it the same.

"Damn it," he said, wincing. He messed with the tape and revealed blood-stained abs, a deep gash in his side, and my stomach rolled. "Fuck—"

"Okay, we need to get you to a hospital."

"No." He waved me off, me panicking way more than he was. "It's fine. I just need a new bandage."

"No, what you need is stitches." I approached, swallowing down the bile in my throat. I'd never been great with blood. I grabbed his arm. "Come on. I'll take you."

"No," he growled, shifting into angry Wells again. I was starting to see more of this darker side he had. He lifted a hand. "I got this. Brielle keeps a first-aid kit around here. I just need to clean it."

He said this, but he visibly paled while he stared at the wound. Something told me he wasn't great with blood either, but when he walked away, I knew he was about to try and fix this himself.

I growled now, grabbing his arm. He started to pull away from me, but I made him follow me into the house. I knew where Brielle kept the first-aid kit, and gratefully for him, she kept more than bandages nearby.

"What you doing?" he asked, his eyebrow arching. We'd made it into the bathroom where I found the kit.

"Trying to fix your ass since you won't go to a hospital." I forced the kit into his chest. "Hold that."

"K." His lengthy digits braced the kit, his shirt basically ruined. Especially since it was ripped. His attention followed me around the bathroom to a junk drawer that held a needle and thread. After I got that, I made the boy follow me up to the dark prince's room. We'd do this in mine, but Bow was in there sleeping.

"Why are we in here?" His gaze traveled when I dug into Dorian's sock drawer. I found the lighter, and Wells's brow jumped. "What are you doing with that shit?"

"I'm going to sew you up myself," I said, and not looking forward to it. I really was squeamish around blood, but I'd be lying if I said I hadn't done this before. I tossed Wells a pair of socks. "You're going to need to bite down on that."

"You're fucking serious?" He eyed the socks but didn't do anything with them. "You ever stitch someone up before?"

I gave him a look like it was obvious. "I wouldn't be doing this if I hadn't."

"K," he repeated, sitting down on Dorian's bed when I told him. I instructed him to take off his shirt too, and he smirked. "Hold up, princess. Usually, I ask for a little dinner first."

He waggled his eyebrows, flashing a more than prominent dimple in his right side. Since he smiled a lot, I'd caught it before. He really could look like a teddy when he wasn't being an asshole.

I rolled my damn eyes, then proceeded to get one last item. I knew the dark prince kept a bottle of vodka in his underwear drawer, and he may or may not have used it to lick off my nipples in the past. He was fucking crazy, and I caught myself smiling a little.

Wells noticed, his grin lazy, cocky. He jutted his chin. "You sure know your way around this room, princess. You and D playing house or what?"

My eyes lifted again. Yes, I knew where his vodka was and his spare lighter. We'd both used the latter to smoke weed in the past. I didn't think we were playing house, though. I'd just been in here a lot.

I shoved the bottle into Wells's chest too. He gripped it, telling me I was bossy when I repeated he needed to take off his shirt so we could do this. Eventually, he did, and his wound looked so much worse when he completely took off the bandage. Actually, he bled so bad that we moved to Dorian's bathroom. I didn't want to get blood all over the place.

"What the hell happened?" I had to use several towels to get all the blood off, the wound seeping from his rib cage.

Wells's smirk was just as cocky as his grin. He lounged against the sink with his long legs stamped out, his eyes closing when his head touched the mirror. "Mmm. Don't stop. That feels nice when you touch me like that." To show me, he grabbed the hand rubbing blood off his abs, and I just about socked him in them. He chuckled. "I'm just joking. D would kill me. Fuck."

I would kill him, and clearly, he was being this way to avoid the question, flirting. Whereas Ares and Dorian just got mean when they didn't want to talk about shit, Wells seemed to like to flirt.

I didn't know how Thatcher was since I didn't spend a lot of time with him, but Wells and Thatcher seemed to be as joined at the hip as Ares and Dorian.

"If you don't want me to help you, fine," I said, literally covered in the boy's blood. I raised and dropped my hands. "Because I won't if you don't stop that shit and tell me what happened tonight."

To prove that to him, I started to go, but he wrapped his lengthy digits around my arm.

"Fine." He positioned back against the sink. He shook his head. "I hit someone, and he fought back obviously."

I knew he'd hit someone, but I hadn't known a stab

wound was involved, which was what this was. I studied the wound. "You were stabbed?"

"Barely a nick, but I didn't see it coming." He cursed when I cleaned it. He bared teeth. "Watch that shit, aight?"

I smirked now. "More than a nick then?"

His eyes lifted, and his hands braced the sink so hard when I put antiseptic on the wound I thought he'd break that shit. He crossed his ankles. "Like I said, fucker got the jump on me, but I got the last laugh." His eyes danced, rimmed with cruel delight. If I didn't know any better, I'd think he did enjoy whatever had happened tonight. "Dude went down like a sack of potatoes in the end. He'll never get his face to look right after what I did."

He cursed again when all I did was touch the skin *near* the wound. I told him to drink the vodka, which he did, but when I told him to put the sock in his mouth for the stitches, he refused.

"D wears that shit. No fucking way."

He was being a total diva right now, but he promised not to scream when I did stitch him up. I didn't necessarily believe him, but I didn't have a choice since he refused to put the sock in his mouth.

I guessed he'd gotten this shitty bandage from the precinct, which definitely showed how much they cared about getting him proper care.

I heated the needle, sterilizing it. "Brace yourself."

He did as asked when he lodged his forearm between his teeth. Immediately, he bit down during that first stitch, and every one after that as well. He was so white by the end of it, I thought he'd pass out, but he stayed standing and, as promised, didn't scream. I'd actually done a good job too, considering I'd only patched up myself in the past.

"Not bad, princess. Not bad," he said, analyzing the black stitches in the mirror. He was so tan any scarring he got probably wouldn't be terribly visible. He gave a soft clap. "I guess you have done this before."

I shrugged. "Girl came at me with a box cutter once in the eight grade," I said, and Wells's lips parted. "Yeah, and when you don't have health insurance…"

"Shit. You did it on yourself." He whistled. "I suppose you didn't get any help from that fucker who took you." He frowned. "D mentioned he had a lot of depression and anxiety."

He was right about that, but *that* was the last thing I wanted to talk about. I crossed my arms. "What happened to you? For real. The guys only told me you hit someone." I lifted a hand. "Do they even know you were stabbed?" Thatcher had picked his ass up at the precinct today and twirled him around. Something told me, if he'd known, he wouldn't have done that.

Wells shook his head, and my jaw dropped. "What the fuck, Wells—"

"They don't know because it's not a big deal, and you're not going to tell them." He put his bloody shirt back on, covering my work. He tugged it down. "As far as who I hit, just know he deserved that shit." His growl was low. "He deserved more than that shit. Dude's a fucking creep, and he'll be getting his."

"What do you mean?"

"You don't need to worry about it. The guys are handling it."

He tried to cut around me, but I stopped him.

"Princess—"

"Who did you hit, and why?"

His head lowered, his arms braced. I wasn't going to let this go, and it was easy going against Legacy when it was just one of them. The four of them together had a tendency to strong-arm.

"You're lucky I like you," he said, his grin teasing. He

lounged back against the sink. "I'm only sad our love story had to end for the sake of my boy." He put a hand on his chest. "So tragic."

Good *God*, he was such a hopeless flirt, shameless. My eyes lifted. "Tell me what happened."

"I hit Shapiro," he said, and I croaked. He smirked. "Yeah, Mr. Shapiro, and dude called the cops on me like a little bitch."

"Why in the…" I was at a loss for words. I mean, *was* he a psychopath? "So, what you're saying is you hit a teacher?"

"Nah, princess. I hit a creepy-ass predator who gets off messing with high school chicks." His eyes narrowed. "Fucker even changed his name because the last school he worked at, he had to resign because he's a nasty fuck who likes getting with underage girls."

My mouth opened and closed. "How do you know that?"

"Because he made a pass at a girl I was fucking." His expression darkened. "Shapiro's nasty ass didn't know that I saw but I did, and since I knew Bow was working with him on some computer thing, that shit wasn't okay."

My brow lifted. "Is that why you told him she couldn't each lunch with him?"

He pushed off the sink. "Like I said, that shit wasn't okay. Of course, that was before I knew he changed his name and his history at that other school. Through some digging, Thatcher found that shit out after he asked me why I threatened the guy." He scrubbed his face. "Dude only doesn't have a record because he somehow got his victims to drop the charges. His history at the other school slipped under the radar too because his family has money and covered that shit up. Thatcher and I wanted to go after his ass ourselves since the law couldn't, but Dorian and Wolf said that wasn't the way to go. They both asked around, and it wasn't hard for them to find a few girls that Shapiro already messed with since coming to our school. The girls agreed to come forward, and Wolf and Dorian made Thatch tell his parents all the stuff he dug up so we could get the cops involved in all this. While they were doing that, I went after Shapiro myself. Dude needed a fucking *beating* if he was even entertaining for a fucking second making Bow his next victim, and I knew the cops wouldn't do that."

I didn't know what to say. "Does Bow know about all this?"

Wells cuffed his arms. "Don't know why she needs to," he said, and I blinked.

"Uh, how about because you might have saved her from something really messed up?" Not to mention she thought what he'd done today was because he'd gone psycho. Hell, I'd thought he'd gone psycho. "She thinks you're just being controlling."

Wells's look was dismissive, passive when he moved his blond locks around. He really didn't care what she believed, but I did.

My lips turned down. "You should tell her."

"No, and neither will you." He checked himself out in the mirror like an arrogant fuck. I usually only caught Thatcher doing that crap. The boy had a mirror in his fucking locker. Wells's gaze clashed with mine through the mirror. "She does belong at our table and shouldn't be sitting with anyone else."

I laughed, shaking my head. "You know, I think she has a crush on you." Though, I didn't understand why. Especially since she said he bullied her.

His hands stopped in his hair. "Well, that'd be stupid of her," he said, flicking his stark white locks forward like he was actually going somewhere. "She's like my little sister, and Thatcher's actual sister." He dropped his hands. "Like I said, stupid."

Jesus. He really was an asshole, but then again...

I'd come to know all these guys since coming here, and

being an asshole and being Legacy tended to go together. The dark prince and I had definitely butted heads in the past.

We butted heads now.

"Thanks for stitching me up," Wells said, a door clicking shut from somewhere in the house. Since we were on this end of it, I assumed that person was Ares. "That'd be Wolf. Probably need to, uh…"

Before he could finish, I went back into Dorian's room. I found a spare shirt, then tossed it at Wells. "If you don't want him to know about the blood."

Wells nodded before swapping one shirt out for the other. He seemed at odds with what to do with the first so I took it, telling him I'd take care of it. I didn't know exactly what I'd do with it, but Ares would obviously be looking for him, so I had more time to stash it.

Wells pounded my fist. "Good looking out, princess."

I laughed. "No problem." I started to go, but before I did, he cut me off.

"I know you and D are having an issue, and though neither of you asked for my two cents on the situation, I'm going to give it to at least you."

Getting my attention, I rested against the door.

His hands eased into his pockets. "It probably looks like he really didn't want to tell you about that bastard Callum, like he didn't trust you, but I know D. He does trust you. He just…"

"Didn't want me to see him as a monster." My stomach soured. "I know."

Wells acknowledged that, his nod subtle. "Anyway, I'm not saying you should forgive him, but he loves you a lot and…" Wells rubbed his arm. "He's hurting real bad. He sees a lot of shit in himself that isn't real, and thinking you'd see that shit too?" He shook his head. "I know he's not a monster. We all do, but that shit doesn't matter when a guy believes it, which he does. It kills him knowing you'd see that, or even the possibility of it."

I knew this too, and I didn't see him as a monster. In fact, he was the opposite to me always.

I couldn't believe Wells and his intuitiveness sometimes. He'd shared his own musings on Ares with me before, and he was really surprising me with how thoughtful and profound he could be. He and Thatcher tended to lack a maturity the other boys had, and Dorian didn't seem like the type much to share his *feelings*. He might not have to with these best friends he had though. They all really were intuitive about each other, as if empaths for one another.

There was so much love between them.

I'd seen that time and time again, another example tonight at the precinct. Thatcher telling Wells thanks after what he'd done tonight, which was something he obviously couldn't do himself. Then there was Ares picking everyone up and using his resources to go into the precinct himself to get Wells out. Dorian hugging Wells at the police station, then later escorting him to our house to make sure he was okay only completed their circle.

Wells probably thought we were done, but I ended up hugging him for some reason. I just felt we'd shared a moment, and it was nice…

Until he sniffed my *hair*.

He borderline moaned after he did, and I shoved him off.

He lifted his hands. "Nothing creepy. Just had to get it out of my system. I mean, I am still in mourning here over our love lost."

He nudged me after he said it, waggling his eyebrows. The boy was a fucking *freak*, but he did have a heart. I'd honor what he requested about not telling Bow about what he and the others did tonight, but I, personally, would never forget it.

Even if it seemed like he wanted me to.

CHAPTER
FORTY-ONE

Sloane

Word regarding Mr. Shapiro's arrest traveled the halls of Windsor Prep like wildfire the next day. Apparently, he'd been escorted off-site when he'd shown up for classes this morning. Campus security had delivered him directly to the cops, and it didn't take long for the entire student body to find out why.

Bow was shocked when I saw her, but I didn't tell her the arrest was all Legacy's doing. She, like the rest of the academy, believed it'd been the girls who had come forward regarding Shapiro that had gotten him picked up and, hopefully, on his way to a lengthy sentence behind bars. The little rabbit was unnerved about what happened, and rightly so. She'd had no idea one of her teachers had been so fucked up. She, as well as anyone else who had classes or interacted regularly with Shapiro, was advised to speak with the academy's guidance counselor. Especially if they shared similar stories as the girls who'd blown the whistle on him. The cops stuck around in case anyone else wanted to come forward and didn't leave until the school day concluded.

It was a crazy day and one where I missed the dark prince during most of my classes. I saw him at lunch, but there really wasn't a chance for us to talk one on one with all the other people there.

And I wanted to talk.

I did miss him, and I wanted to fix this shit. I was tired of fighting and being at odds with each other, and even if Wells hadn't talked to me last night, I would have been on my way to fixing this. Dorian and I were just right, and sure, we had stuff to figure out, but we would.

We always did.

I planned to talk to him after school but forgot about the fact that he took off early sometimes for therapy. Today happened to be one of those days, and I scanned the lot for longer than I should have before I remembered the fact.

Me: Can we talk later?

I waited for his return text while I stood outside the school in my winter coat. I didn't expect him to text me back right away or anything since he had a session but did wait a beat.

That was when I saw him.

Callum... Dorian's grandpa was leaving a black sedan, and the one who shut his door was none other than his body-guard Lucas. Callum had his cane, a gloved hand on his coat while he made his way into the school.

Huh?

This was unusual, him being at the school at all. I knew Ramses and Brielle didn't necessarily want him here, and neither did the other parents.

I pocketed my phone, deciding to follow. I was curious more than anything. I watched them all head inside, the school basically clear since everyone typically left right at the end of the school day.

Bruno, Bow, and Ares were still somewhere inside the school, though. They had clubs and stuff after school.

My phone pinged in the hall, a text from Dorian on the screen.

Dorian: Yeah. Want me to come by your house after my session?

"Sloane?"

My head jerked up, Callum staring at me. He and Lucas had stopped in the hallway, a red tint to their cheeks. I supposed they had both just been outside. Callum stepped forward. "That is you. Surprised you haven't left for the day yet."

I stuffed my phone in my pocket without answering. "Uh, yeah. I was looking for Dorian, but forgot he left early for the day."

Should I be talking about Dorian with him? Should I be talking to him at all?

Things had somehow gotten… weirder than they already had before, what I should say or do unclear. This was even more so the case now considering the things Dorian had said about Callum.

I still wasn't sure I could take all that at face value, but I did know there were some things I needed clarity on. I hadn't talked to Bru about what Dorian had told me, but that was mostly because I wasn't clear on everything that was going on. I hadn't been there that summer, and it seemed weird to put stuff I still wasn't certain about out there like that.

"I see," Callum said, and I took a step forward. "Well, I hope you find him."

"Already did," I told him, pulling my phone out. "I didn't know you'd be around the school."

As if he just realized this, he glanced around, his shoulders lifting.

"I'm afraid you caught me," he said, smiling a little. "I'm meeting with your new headmaster today to discuss donating some scholarships. College ones for graduating students. Just a way to help some of those who may not have resources for that. Windsor Prep is my alma mater, and obviously you kids go here."

That was nice of him.

"Planned to meet with the headmaster after you all left and school wrapped for the day." He rubbed his hands over the cane. "I'm sure you know why."

I did, and that all went without saying. The parents really wouldn't like him being here.

"Anyway, I probably should be going, and I do have that meeting," he said. "And if you're ever interested in a scholarship, they should be available for college freshmen for the upcoming year. I know you have the Mallicks, but I don't know the situation there. If they were paying for you, or if you had other plans with that."

I hadn't gotten that far with them. I rubbed my arm. "Thanks. I might look into it. I don't necessarilywant to assume they'd cover that if I decide to go."

Callum nodded. "Well, if you ever want more information, I have packets at the house. I can have Bru forward anything you like."

"Thank you."

Another nod, and he was off, but I wasn't exactly done. I still felt weird about what Dorian had told me, and it wouldn't sit well until I did get some clarity. Dorian and I were talking tonight, and I wanted to go into that conversation with everything out there. I did believe what he'd told me, but if there had been a misunderstanding between him and his grandpa...

Like stated, I just needed some clarity, and I did need it because I didn't want anything else between Dorian and me. I also wanted the packet of information. "Actually, could I swing by after you're done today?" I asked, causing Callum and Lucas to turn. "I really am interested and don't want to have to rely on Ramses and Brielle."

Callum's cane touched the floor. "I'm not sure that'd be such a good idea. I think your parents would prefer if distance is kept between you and me."

I was aware of that, but it had also been explained to me that I wasn't being kept under lock and key. I had freedom to go to and from as I wished, and I wasn't sure I'd ever get another opportunity to talk with him. I did need clarity, and it wasn't just for my and Dorian's relationship.

It was for me.

CHAPTER
FORTY-TWO

Sloane

"Agnes, if you could bring in some hot tea for Miss Sloane and myself."

Callum's maid acknowledged the request, her nod short before exiting the room. I had basically followed Callum and Lucas back to Callum's house after waiting in the parking lot at the school while they wrapped up Callum's meeting with the headmaster.

Agnes returned to Callum's parlor, a large room with the dimly lit sconces and a fireplace already running. She had the packet of scholarship information along with the tea, and I thanked her for them both.

"Well, then. What questions do you have for me?" Callum asked, declining his tea for now with a raised hand. Currently, he stoked the fireplace, his cane in his other hand. "You mentioned wanting to talk at the school. I'm assuming about the program."

I had mentioned that before we'd left, but no, the subject matter didn't have anything to do with the scholarship. I tucked the scholarship packet into the side of my chair, then guided the tea to my lips. I swallowed. "I kind of just wanted to chat. Casually."

"Oh." He hung the poker by the fireplace but stayed by it when I stood. "What about exactly?"

This conversation was probably completely inappropriate, and I hated I was even here to have it. I chewed my lip. "It's about Dorian."

Callum's head tilted back. "I see."

Placing my tea down next to the china pot Agnes had left, I came over to him. "Everything with that summer is just so out of character for him, and I wanted to understand it."

His hand lifted. "Before we get started, this is really a conversation you should be having with him. I'm already in hot water with him and my son. I don't know if Dorian told you, but he came to see me. Blew up on me for telling you about that summer."

He hadn't told me that, but I wasn't surprised. He was so quick to lose his temper.

"Things between us are already tense." He placed both hands on his cane. "And if I want any hope at all in bringing him around, I have to respect his privacy."

I got that and didn't want to create any drama. Heading back to my chair, I picked up my bag, sliding the scholarship information inside. "I'm sorry for wasting your time."

"You haven't, and I'll tell you anything you want but only with Dorian's blessing."

I nodded, starting to leave.

"I am curious, though," he said, causing me to turn his way. His head tilted. "What exactly were you going to ask about that summer?"

It felt silly now. Odds were, Dorian had blown things completely out of proportion. I tugged my bag up my arm. "He said when you blackmailed him, you threatened his mom. He also said you got him arrested to teach him a lesson after, and that just..." I paused, my hand lifting. I didn't continue, feeling too embarrassed. This was probably all just a miscommunication, and here I was in his house saying such things.

"Just what, Sloane?" Callum asked, surprising me, and I had to say, he didn't look as insulted as he probably should. The things I'd said would insult me.

I eased back into the room. "I guess I was just going to say doesn't sound like you." I shrugged. "And I know Dorian. I know him *a lot*, and he tends to see things the way he wants to see them sometimes."

"This is true about my grandson. He has quite a temper on him." Shifting, Callum gazed out of the window. He had snowy views of an expansive property out there and seclusion like at the glass house he got for Bru and me. His place was in another section of the rolling hills surrounding Maywood Heights. "He's a lot like his father in that regard. Always angry. Vengeful."

That didn't sound like Dorian's dad. He was serious, but never mean, angry.

"My son Royal has always been angry. Angry at me for ruining his life and being so hard on him coming up." His lips pinched together. "It seemed Dorian took away from some of that."

I approached his side, staring out the window too. This family seemed to have so much pain, and I know Dorian did.

"It's a shame Dorian feels the way he does about what happened last summer," he continued. "And you're right. He does tend to see things the way he wants to see them."

It didn't feel right talking about him like this, and I started to say that when Callum touched me, his hand on my arm. It took me off guard, and I jumped, easing my arm away. "What are you doing?"

It wasn't the fact that he'd touched me. It was why. It'd come out of nowhere.

His hand returned to his cane. "I was just seeing something."

"Seeing something?"

His nod was subtle yet firm, and he panned outside again. "I suppose how easy you'll make this. Painless. I've been watching you for a while, Sloane, and though you don't necessarily make things easy, you are quite logical."

"I'm sorry. Watching me?" I shook my head. "What are you talking about?"

"*Watching* is a strong word. More like aware. I'm aware of you, Sloane." He looked at me. "Are you aware of me?"

I didn't know what he was asking me, but it felt *weird*. Wrong. I backed up. "I think I need to go."

My stomach clenched tight, I headed toward the door but stopped when I noticed we weren't alone. Lucas stood at the door, his hands together. He completely blocked the way out, and I screeched to a stop on the wood panel floor in front of him.

"Lucas is merely here for you to hear me out, Sloane." Callum's voice was closer, and instantly, my body locked up, my lungs tight. I wasn't getting in much air, and I didn't know why until a large shadow darkened the wall in front of me. It was bigger than mine, taller. "You hear me out, and you're free to go. I'd never make you do anything you didn't want to do."

I really couldn't breathe now, my swallow hard. Lucas, in front of me, gestured a hand right, but when I didn't move, he crowded me until I did.

"Take a seat, Miss Sloane," he said, making sure I did. Callum remained behind me, and I didn't see him until I did take that seat. He still had his cane in his hand, and though he might need it that didn't make him appear any less intimidating. He was a large man and built just as solidly as his grandson and son.

And I wasn't in the room with just him.

Lucas was here too, and he was just as big. I sat in a chair. "What's going on?"

I made that sentence sound confident as hell, steady but inside I was screaming and even more so when Callum chose not to sit but stand. He did so right in front of me, Lucas behind my chair. I didn't know what the fuck was going on here, but I definitely didn't want to hear whatever this was.

"First thing's first. Hand your phone over to Lucas," Callum stated and casual about it. He strode over to the fireplace, the flames casting shadows over his face. "Wouldn't want any disturbances while you listen to my proposal. I assure you. It suits both of us, and by the end, I hope you'll see that too."

I took my phone out with a shaking hand, basically tossing it at Lucas. While I did, I scanned the room. There were several doors, but they might not lead to exits. There was a window, but we were several floors up. "What's going on, Callum?"

A short smile tugged his lips. "I thought a lot about this day with you. What I'd say." His smile deepened. "But I suppose, what I first want to say is, thank you."

"Thank you?"

He nodded, again not looking at me. "It's because of you I have a future here again in Maywood Heights. A town who, though hesitant, is very much open to allowing me to coexist here, and a family who seems to be on the cusp of doing the same." His head swung in my direction. "My son has actually opened up the lines of communication regarding him and myself, and I have nothing but you to thank for that. He's very grateful for my part in your return, so is the rest of the city. Again, I thank you for this."

I gripped the chair as he came over, the cane definitely just for security. He barely used it on the way over, and when he spotted me looking at it, he smiled again.

"You're wondering about it?" He handed it over to Lucas

before folding his body into the chair across from mine. Lucas handed him a box of cigars then, and after Callum selected, Lucas lit it for him. Thick smoke curled out of the aged man's mouth. "I have a bum leg. An accident and one involving your very own grandfather, Ibrahim."

I said nothing, trying to focus and not die on that fucking smoke. It stunk to high heaven.

"Your grandfather laid low for a long time, quiet," he said, nodding. "Our last meeting together ended up being a café in Sicily. He had a terrible accident there. A bombing actually."

My mouth parted. "What? What are you…"

"As you can see, I didn't come away without my own scars that day." He patted his leg, making me twitch. "Old leg acts up every once in a while. I was a bit slow that day and, unfortunately, failed to get out unscathed."

I was trying to wrap my head around what he was telling me, not believing it. "Are you saying you killed my grandfather?" The words didn't make sense. None of this made sense. "You're the reason he's…"

"Dead." He said it so easy, cruelly. Like this wasn't his first time getting involved with something like this, and he definitely didn't care about that fact. He adjusted in his chair. "Your grandfather wronged me, but it started way before his last day in Sicily."

My phone buzzed, but as it was still in Lucas's hand, I could only look at it flash.

"My grandson probably?" Callum asked, studying me. He gestured toward the phone with his cigar. "You want to answer it? I can wait."

I twitched, the dare in this man's voice evident. Especially since he'd said he didn't want us to have any distractions when he spoke to me.

I stayed in my place, not sure what would happen if I didn't. I didn't know if Callum had a weapon, but I was definitely aware of Lucas's. He was his bodyguard. I swallowed. "Are you going to kill me?"

His brow lifted, slow with the question. He tapped off some ash in an ashtray Lucas provided. "What makes you think I'd want to kill you, or that I'd ever have any desire to do that?"

"I don't know." My voice shook, watching Lucas. He took a new position by the window, but it'd be naive of me to head for the door behind my chair. Stupid. I faced Callum. "Besides the fact you're keeping me here, you just said you killed my grandfather."

And he'd obviously hated him. I didn't know what that had to do with me, but he was keeping me here.

"I did say that," he stated, the admittance clenching my stomach, racing my heart. He crossed his legs at the knee. "But this was penance. I don't do anything unless it's necessary, and I very much want you alive. Like I said, I have a proposal for you."

"Which is?"

"First is that you hear me out." He waved a hand. "And though some of this may be hard for you to hear, painful, I hope, by the end, you'll understand. It'd be wise of you, for yourself as well as your family. You seem to find a lot of people in your life you care about these days. Family and friends."

So that was definitely a threat, the breath coming out short from my lips, choppy. "What is all this, Callum?"

And what, upon me hearing, would be painful.

His silence felt like the prelude to that, and when he puffed out more smoke, I nearly did gag. His smile was small. "You are beautiful, you know that? I can see why my grandson is enamored with you." My stomach soured, and his grin widened. "Surely, you know how beautiful you are?"

"Stop please." I swallowed down the bile. "You're making me uncomfortable."

"I don't want to do that." He nearly sounded genuine. "I do find you lovely, and I want you to see that by the end of the conversation. I admire you, Sloane. You're strong. Resilient. Whatever life has tossed your way, you've navigated those waters and brilliantly." He laughed a little. "How you didn't know you weren't Godfrey and Marilyn Sloane's child, I have no idea. Your adoptive father, though a good man, was very weak and your adoptive mother the same."

"They didn't adopt me. They kidnapped me."

"Actually, it was an adoption, and one I made happen almost legitimately," he admitted, my eyes wide. His head cocked. "Surely, you didn't believe Godfrey, as weak as he was, could have pulled off such a feat on his own. The man could barely get himself out of bed most days, and your adoptive mother wasn't far off from that before her accident. She had such issues having children before Bruno came along and was just as depressed because of it. At least, that was what my people told me from the therapist records we acquired."

I didn't get *any* of this, my palms sweating and dampening the leather under my hands. "You kidnapped me?" The words drifted away from my lips whispered, panicked. "You took me?"

Callum's focus on me didn't waver, his face barely made out through the cloud of smoke that thickened the air around him. His lips turned down. "I told you some of this would be painful for you to hear, and it doesn't please me to see you in pain. I've grown quite fond of you, Sloane. Truly."

My throat jumped, and he set his cigar on the ashtray Lucas, once again, provided. The man actually lifted it for Callum's use, and it seemed Lucas wasn't just a bodyguard, but a henchman in the truest of forms.

Callum's nod of gratitude was small in Lucas's direction, his attention shifting to me. "I didn't take you personally."

"But you had people do it?" My throat jumped again. "Was it even Godfrey?"

"The particulars don't matter there," he said, his voice passive as if it really didn't matter. As if this wasn't my whole fucking life, and he'd, apparently, been the puppet master tugging the strings. "But yes, I orchestrated it. You being with Godfrey and Marilyn served a purpose, and it was something I made happen, yes."

"Why?" I scanned Lucas when he moved to Callum's side again. He simply stood by his charge, his master.

"That unfortunately lies with your dead grandfather, the why," he said, his head tilted. "The origin of which started that day he asked me to help cover up the murder of one of my son's friends."

"Dorian's aunt?"

His eyes flicked my way. "Yes. I wasn't lying to you when I told you my son was in the wrong place at the wrong time. The Prinze name couldn't be associated with any of that." He waved his hand, dismissive. "My son was foolish and got himself swept up in trouble. He needed to be rescued, and fortunately for him, I was around."

He sounded like he had no remorse, *none at all*. "What does that have to do with me?"

"Oh, everything, dear girl." He smiled, the cigar returning to his lips. He drew long and hard off it before pointing it in my direction. "You see, your grandfather was a cheat, and though I wanted to help my son, I valued what your grandfather offered a bit more. He said if I helped him and your great-uncle, he'd give me a sizable stake in his company Mallick Enterprises, a promise, in the end, he never fulfilled despite me holding up my end of the bargain."

His phone rang, and he checked it, as if this conversation truly meant nothing to him. He chose not to answer and after, sat back.

"So, you're saying this is revenge?" I asked and froze

when he leaned forward. The move hadn't been done like an old man, but one with physical power and influence.

And the look in his eyes...

Dorian had told me I'd always see a monster in him, but even with what he'd told me, I never saw that in his eyes. In fact, when we'd talked about that summer, I'd seen nothing but a scared little boy in his ebony irises. I'd seen someone who'd made a mistake and was remorseful. I saw no remorse in his grandfather's eyes now.

Only vengeance.

"It shouldn't have had to be that way, though," Callum said, the words chilling me. He sighed. "But your grandfather was smart and picked up that I'd bribed quite a few of his shareholders out of their shares. Their stake and what your grandfather had promised me would have given me quite a bit of control over your family's company." He laughed a little. "Ibrahim obviously hadn't liked that. He reneged on his promise, had his people tell me why, and though I understood, I gave him one last opportunity to make us square. We were both going to prison for what we did with the cover-up, but he could go an honest man. I said if he didn't make us right, I'd take what I wanted anyway. Take what he loved and make him feel it."

My lungs squeezed, his continued smoking not helping.

Callum wet his lips. "I think back then he thought I meant his company, but I wanted to take everything he loved." He smiled as if recalling a fond memory. "Anyway, I'll never know. I obviously didn't see him after he and I went away to prison. I had people on the outside, though, and had them monitor him, as well as the rest of your family. I saw an opportunity with you and your brother Ares's births, and I took it."

He passed Lucas a look, and out of nowhere, the man pulled a file, paperwork. It was handed to me, but I didn't open it. "What's this?"

"Take a look for yourself," Callum said.

I didn't, feeling there was more games here. I already thought I was going to throw up, and Lucas had to physically open the file for me in the end.

I recognized the paperwork. There was a lot of it, but I did recall most. After Godfrey had initially died, I'd gotten this stuff at the will reading when Callum had been named Bru's guardian. Bruno was a minor, so he needed one.

"You'll recall your signatures," Callum said, a lot of signatures in my face. Callum and his team had had me sign all this stuff that day, things for the funeral he'd said. I didn't understand why he was giving me all this now, though. His lips lifted. "You gave me… everything you own, sweetheart."

I said nothing, my mouth dry.

"Control over all your assets," he continued, sitting back. "You signed everything you own over to me to aid your adoptive father's funeral expenses." A slight laugh escaped his lips. "You were so adamant about helping."

"I…" I gazed down. I had wanted to help. He'd been a stranger, and I hadn't wanted to take anything from him. He'd convinced me eventually, worn me down.

"You signed everything we gave you, but granted, I'm sure you didn't know how much you were worth."

I dropped the folder, all those documents I'd naively signed on the floor.

"What used to be yours is mine now, and thank you for that." His eyes warmed. "Once you turned eighteen, you got access to your own shares in Mallick Enterprises, as well as what your late grandfather left for you, and since you're still technically, *legally* Pilar Mallick you can do that."

"This was about money," I gasped, things suddenly blurry. I fought the tears, the heat in my throat. "You took me from my family over money!" I started to get up, but Lucas moved his hand.

He flashed his gun.

I wasn't in control of this situation, Callum was, and it seemed like for quite a long time. I sat down, and he had Agnes come in. She picked up all the paperwork I'd dropped like a good little servant, placing it on the table between Callum and me.

She stepped out, and I heard the blood pound in my ears, the nausea surfacing.

"I told my old friend I would take everything from him. I left his family intact, but I'm sure it was never right after you were gone."

I ached, rocking in my chair.

"And he was a friend, you know." Callum frowned. "Your grandfather and I had an upstanding relationship. We ruled this city together with some of our closest in the community."

I barked a laugh, a raspy, thick laugh. He made himself sound as if royalty, a king.

Callum leveled me with a look. "You served a purpose, Sloane, and I'm sorry you had to pay for your grandfather's lies. Your grandfather had a debt to pay, and it's unfortunate you were needed to settle the score."

"Why bring me back at all?" I ground out, the gut-churning pain physically causing tremors to hit my body, my hands. I held them. "Why bother with all that? You obviously got what you wanted."

And none of it required bringing me back here. Especially if he wanted revenge.

A smile touched his eyes again. "You are smart, and that's why you're here instead of six feet under yourself."

I jolted, quivering, and Callum put his cigar down.

"Though, heaven help you, that had nothing to do with your late caregivers." His expression tugged at clever, coy. "You could be right where they are now due to their stupidity, but gratefully for you, you had a willingness to survive that by far exceeds them and their foolishness." He got up, goose-flesh hitting my arms. Lucas returned Callum's cane, and the older man used it to navigate to the fireplace. He stoked the flame. "Marilyn tried to take you back here once. Playing the hero."

"What?"

Our gazes clashed, his cold, chilled. "She was a very stupid woman who couldn't count her blessings. She and Godfrey tried for years to have children and racked up the medical debt to prove it. It proved fruitless, and all the medical debt did was make them vulnerable. Godfrey was a good man, though. Loyal, and a fine employee on the payroll. I had my people pay off his debts while I was in prison, with only one caveat."

I studied him, and he stood tall.

"To return the favor one day if I needed." He smiled, again as if to a memory. "He took the money. They all take the money, and eventually, they did have a child on their own. Your brother Bru. I had you delivered to them around that time. You needed a place to stay until you were eighteen and I could take everything your grandfather owed me."

"You said she took me back here?" I asked, and he nodded.

"Tried to, foolish woman," he spat, and I sneered. He shook his head. "She found out your mother Brielle worked as a headmaster at the school and tried to take you there one day. Of course, all that did was get her killed and you hurt. From what I heard, something in the building made you scared. You ran from her and hit your head. Fell and got a pretty ugly scar on your wrist."

I played with it, the scar.

"Have you been here before? In Maywood Heights?"

Ares's question that day by the graffiti wall haunted me. He and Brielle had both asked me if I'd been here, but I didn't remember.

Callum said I'd hit my head, had gotten… scared. I'd had dreams recently of a monster, something trying to eat me, and if Marilyn had tried to take me back to the headmaster's office, something definitely stood out about that location.

The king busk.

The gorilla head was scary there.

Had she really gotten me that close? What had to have been only feet away from my mother? My real mother.

"Got her killed?" I blinked down tears, so much making sense now. I must have lost my bracelet that day, the necklace I wore now.

Callum frowned. "I don't take kindly to deceit, which is what Marilyn did when she decided to go back on the debt Godfrey owed. She became a liability after that." He stoked the flame again, sighing. "And poor Godfrey spiraled after. His grief made him foolish. He ended up taking you and Bruno and disappearing for years after that. I don't know if he was trying to be a hero too or what. Must have been, but my people did ultimately catch up with him."

I glanced down, tears coating my braced hands. He'd tried to help me? They *both* had?

And died for it.

"I told him he had only one way to make it right, and he did decide to do the right thing when it was all said and done." Using his cane, Callum stood before the flames, the shadows on his face dark and demonic but only due to his lack of expression. He didn't care about anything he was telling me. At least, his face didn't. It was like he was a complete sociopath.

And maybe he was.

I obviously didn't know him, *knew nothing.*

"He helped me bring you back here and did pay for it with his life," he said. "Like I said, a good man. He was willing to fall on the sword so I could get what I needed. His debt paid."

So, Callum was in on it the whole time, Godfrey faking his death… everything.

"You haven't said why you brought me back." I stood, noticing eyes on me. Lucas was still here, but I didn't fucking care. I swallowed. "You got what you wanted. My money. *Power*." My voice quivered, laced with emotion. "Why bother bringing me back to my family?"

For that question, Lucas interceded again. He pulled something out of his jacket, giving it to me. It was a picture of me, but one taken without my consent. I was sketching on the old stoop of the last house we'd lived in with Godfrey, my head down, legs out and ankles crossed. I had my earbuds in and had escaped the world.

At least, I thought I had.

"You changed it."

My head shot up, Callum too close. He stood before me, tobacco and aftershave clouding the air around me. He reached out and flicked my hair off my shoulder. I twitched, but that didn't stop him from reaching for me again.

I wanted to gag.

The stomach acid literally shot up into my throat, his fingers guiding down my bare shoulder. I'd taken off my coat and left it with his servants.

I jerked my shoulder away, and he smiled.

"You were supposed to die, you know," he said, my lungs freezing. "But you changed that. You're right. I could have easily gotten what I needed from you, then taken you out."

"But you didn't." I looked at him through watery eyes, his head shaking.

"I did let you live, Sloane. I gave you a chance to be here and back with the people who love you the most. I even let Bruno live. I was going to get rid of him too. Especially after I decided to do what I was going to do with you."

Shaking, I stepped back. "What are you talking about?"

"Why, his illness, of course." He placed both hands on the top of his cane, rubbing the jewel. "I was going to take care of him right then, but ultimately, decided against it." He frowned. "I guess I knew what that would do to you."

He got closer again, and I did gag. Especially when he put his hand on my jaw, the pads of his fingers rough, calloused. With as much money as he must have had, he'd clearly done things with his hands.

Preformed deeds just as dark.

His thumb grazed my lip, but when I attempted to tug my jaw away, he didn't let me. He gripped it, his hold solid, unyielding. He forced me to look at him. "I told you I had a proposition, and one that can make everyone in this situation happy. You, Bruno… You know, he'll do anything I want him to, right? He does because he trusts me."

He did trust him, but only because he didn't know the facts.

"And if for some reason that changes, I can make sure he's neither seen nor heard from again." His fingers bit into my jaw. "Just because I'm keeping him alive for you doesn't mean he has to see the light of day."

He kept saying that, keeping him alive for me and knowing what the alternative would do to me. He'd said I had changed things.

"And if you agree to what I have to say, it also works out for your family as well," he continued. "It does because I won't dissect your family's company piece by piece."

I winced, my swallow hard. "What do you want?"

"For you to keep everything, have everything," he said, his voice tender now, his touch. His grip loosened the same time he guided his finger through my hair. Tears fell from my eyes, but he merely looked at them, scanning my face. It was like he was a fucked-up scientist and I was simply his petri dish. "I need a companion, Sloane. Someone to tend to me as I'm getting along in years. I don't plan to work this hard forever, and I'd like to settle down and be with someone."

The air fell from my lips. "You want me to be with you?" I couldn't even… "Like *with you*?"

I thought I really was going to be sick now, trembling when he lifted my face.

"It doesn't have to be what you think or even physical." He touched my lip. "Though, I'd enjoy that. In all honesty, I can and already do have others fulfilling that obligation. They're nice, but they do come and go. What I'm looking for really is just someone to be there. A constant in my life, a partner and equal. You're young and still have time to be that for me."

I didn't know what would make me throw up the most. He'd given me plenty of options.

"I'd simply like you to be around for me." His hands braced my arms. "A friend and confidant, and if you want more, that's fine. If you don't, that's fine too, and you can take on suitors if you need that. I just want to make you happy."

Like a sugar daddy.

Oh fucking God…

"I find myself enamored with you too, Sloane, and it only deepened when I met you. Before I did, you were just a file of information. Facts, but that changed." He squeezed my arms. "You showed me who you are, your fight. The adversity and challenges you continue to rise above showed me your strength, and I'd like to take care of you if you'd let me."

I didn't know what to say to that. I couldn't say fucking anything, completely disgusted by all this and whatever crazy shit he had to have in his head about me and *us*.

"You're strong, and I find I need that in my life." He scanned my face. "And what's good for you is you'll get a say in what happens to your family's assets. In fact, I'd give you complete control of it. Once you graduate and we go away together, we can make that happen."

He was sick, truly. My jaw moved. "And so the fact that I have a relationship with your grandson means nothing?" My voice quivered. "The fact that I love him and he loves me means nothing?" We did love each other. I *loved him* so much. I lifted my chin. "You'd do that to him?"

"Love is fleeting, Sloane." His hands left me, and I nearly fell to the floor I was shaking so bad. "Like I said. You're young. You both are, and you'll get over it."

I trembled.

"And everything I do is with my grandson in mind. He'll get everything after I'm gone. Control over Mallick included." He smirked at me. "But I suppose, by then, he won't even want you."

The metaphorical dagger shot through my chest, the pain of even the *thought* of that causing me to sag forward.

"You're fucked in the head," I stated, my throat clenching. "You can't possibly think I'd actually—"

"The alternative is, well…" He paused, his head tilting as if almost considering. "The alternative is *you* lose everything you love. Needless to say, I'll make sure your grandfather's legacy turns to ash and all the people in your new life will suffer for it. People like your mom, your dad, and your twin. As far as Bruno, he does do anything I say. I'll make sure he lives a life far away from you, and I can do that since I'm technically still his guardian. I'd not test me here, Sloane. This plan was over twenty years in the making and long before you. You can make things harder for the people in your life, or not, but the decision is ultimately up to you. I'll leave that for you to decide."

He walked off, as if I were nothing, and *this* was nothing. Like he wasn't trying to take any more than he already had from me.

"You did get Dorian arrested, didn't you?" I asked, wondering why. I blinked down more tears. "You did that and threatened his mother?"

The answer seemed clear, and it was so crazy how what

had started as a need for clarity had turned into this, as well as how I'd ever, *ever* doubted the man I loved.

Maybe I'm the monster.

"I didn't get him arrested, Miss Sloane. You did," Callum stated, shocking me. He picked up his cigar. "The tracking devices in the phones I gave you and Bru helped with that, and as far as threatening my grandson's mother, I'll do whatever I have to do to make sure I'm a part of his life." His words were serrated, deadly. I saw a peek at the monster again, and he let me see that. He pointed his cigar at me. "I'd think real carefully about your next moves, Sloane. Because you see, whatever you do next will affect everything in your life as you know it."

I knew it would because lately, that was all I seemed to do. Everything I did affected everyone. It hurt everyone, and I was so sick and tired of it. I wouldn't let anyone else get hurt.

I wouldn't let anyone else pay for my grandfather's sins.

FORTY-THREE

Dorian

Sloane had texted she couldn't meet up last night, but I didn't know why until she failed to show at school the next day. Ares said she'd stayed home that morning, sick, he said, so instead of going to classes myself, I skipped. If Sloane was sick, I wanted to see her.

I wanted to see her anyway.

I didn't know why she'd wanted to meet last night, but if she was close at all to wanting to work this shit out, I was game. I was suffering here.

Badly.

Rolling over to her house, I didn't plan to bring any of that up, though. I just wanted to see her. Like stated, make sure she was okay and most definitely if she wasn't feeling well. I got to the Mallicks about twenty minutes after I left the Windsor Prep parking lot and noticed a few things right away. The first was that both Ramses's and Brielle's cars were parked out front. Like they'd left and forgotten something. The second was that *my dad's* car was out front too.

Weird.

I didn't know what that meant, but I definitely wasn't supposed to be cutting classes and just showing up over here. I decided to park down the street, then make my way over to the property. I knew ways of getting in without being noticed, and I used them, sliding through the side gate to get inside. My next move was to use the tree outside of Ares's bedroom to sneak into the house, but that route seemed to already be in use.

A little fighter shimmied down it.

I literally watched Sloane's jean-clad ass make its way down the tree toward me, stepping back when she broke tree branches on the way down. That climbing shit was fucking dangerous with it being icy and snowy outside. I started to go up after her but decided to hold my hands out since she was almost here. She came off that final branch in jump/fall, but gratefully for her, I was there to catch her. She slid right into my arms, and her immediate instinct was to sock me in my jaw.

"Holy fuck—" She covered her mouth, as if stifling a scream. A flush tinted her cheeks when her mittens came away from her mouth. She gazed around. "What are you doing here?"

I had to admit, that wasn't the greeting I'd hoped for, and though my jaw killed me like a son of a bitch, I was happy I'd been there to catch her instead of letting her fall on her ass.

As well as hold her.

My hands full of her ass, I didn't let go, her cookie aroma all up in my nose. Our breaths puffed around us, and I wet my lips. "I don't know. Why aren't you sick and inside?"

She blinked, as if only being aware of that now. Her hands on my shoulders, she wriggled and apparently wanted to be put down, but I didn't right away, waiting. She huffed. "I took a mental health day. Just came outside to smoke. Ares keeps his weed around so yeah. Smoke."

Nodding, I allowed her to slide down my body and felt every inch of that shit. It'd been too long since I'd had this girl in my arms, in my hands. "Is that what you needed last night? A mental health day?" She had canceled on me, which I'd been bummed about.

I still had Sloane pressed to my body, and we were both aware of that. She eased herself away, and it killed my insides I had to let her. We still had this weird shit between us, and I didn't want to test it. She tugged her coat down. "Uh, yeah."

Nodding again, I pulled my Zippo out of my pocket. I flicked it on for her, and when she didn't do anything, I frowned. "You said you came outside to smoke."

As if remembering that, she patted herself down, but peculiarly, she came away with nothing. She tugged her hair out of her face. "I must have forgotten it upstairs."

So, she slid down a tree and nearly died... for nothing. I shook my head. "You okay?"

"Yeah. I'm fine. I just forgot it, okay?"

She was certainly on one hundred right now, being weird. I'd question it a little more, but things *were* weird between us right now.

She probably doesn't know how to act around you.

She stepped away from me but swung around when I asked her about my dad's car. I shrugged. "Do you know why he's here?" It wasn't that my dad didn't come over to the Mallicks, but it wasn't usually when he was normally supposed to be at work. Really, since Ramses was my mom's best friend, only she came through for the most part when it came to impromptu visits.

"I don't know. I..." She cut a look around, again being weird. "I'm going to go. I need to go for a walk."

"Little fighter—" I got her arm, but she tugged away fast. My stomach clenched. "Hey. You all right?"

"I'm fine. I just want to go for a walk so just leave me alone."

I didn't want her going for a walk. I didn't want her left alone. She started to walk away, but when I went with her, I noticed something.

She hadn't been the only thing to fall from that tree.

I'd missed the black duffel bag, the thing stuffed with shit. She picked it up off the snowy ground, but when she started to go, I worked her around. "Dorian, let me go."

"No." I got her in both hands, my throat tight, my breathing uneven. It looked she was going somewhere, and if she was, she was going to face me with that shit. "Why do you look like you're leaving? Leaving me? What the fuck's in that bag?"

"It's nothing. Just—" She cringed. "Please let me go. You don't understand. I need to go, and you need to let me."

She said she wasn't going to run anymore, so if she was running from me, I wasn't going to let her. My jaw moved. "I know I was shitty to you. I know I fucked things up."

"No. No." She was crying, a flush to her cheeks. "I don't want to leave you, but I gotta leave. I can't be here anymore."

I blinked, not expecting that answer. I gripped my hair. "Well, did something happen with Ramses and Brielle? You and Wolf get in a fight? What—"

"No. I just need to go. I need to clear my head. I just need to get out of here."

She was saying this, but I realized she no longer tugged away. In fact, her hands gripped my jacket, her face pressing into my coat.

"Take me away," she rasped, her arms sliding into my open coat. She meshed our heat together, her own body shaking. "Please take me away, Dorian."

Alarm bells went off in my head, my little fighter burying her face into my chest. I didn't know what was fucking going on, but for some reason she didn't want to be here.

I made her look at me. "Tell me what's going on."

"What's going on is, I need to leave. I don't belong here,

and I…" She started to go, pulling away from me again. "I'm sorry I asked. I shouldn't have asked. It was selfish, but I need to go. Please."

If she was going or doing whatever she was doing, she wasn't going by herself. At least if I was with her, I could control this shit.

And be with her.

Fact of the matter was, the moment she asked me to take her away, I knew I would. She had me like that, always fucking had me.

I'd do anything for her.

CHAPTER
FORTY-FOUR

Dorian

"So, you going to tell me what's going on?" I studied Sloane in the passenger seat, her feet up, her arms on her knees. We'd been driving for over an hour, and she'd said little more than two words to me.

She tugged her hood up, her hoodie under her coat. "I told you I'd tell you when we get there."

She'd said that my family's cabin was the destination. She wouldn't let me go to the one in Maywood Heights, though. She said she wanted to get out of town, and I was only doing this shit because I was trying to restore some trust with us.

I dampened my lips. "I can't keep whatever this is from my parents." My gaze hit the road, my focus hard. I already wasn't happy I hadn't called them yet, but again, I was trying to restore some trust here. If I called them, I knew they'd tell me to turn right back, and I had to in order to keep *their* trust. I'd fucked up a lot of things lately, and I wasn't trying to disappoint any of the people I cared about. I faced her. "I'm calling them when we get there."

She said nothing, never did. Instead, she chose to hide her face inside her hood. Her cheek touched the door, and the way she curled up on that thing, it was like she was trying to get away *from me*, and that shit didn't sit right.

I decided to keep driving.

I'd needed gas *before* this drive so I had to stop once we hit state lines. Sloane said she had to use the bathroom so that worked out. After I finished, I waited by the bathrooms for her. She was acting weird, and I didn't want to risk her running.

I heard her voice on the inside.

Muted, I pressed my ear to the door, but it was definitely her voice.

"Yeah, we're still on the way to his family's cabin, and I don't need to hear it from you, okay?" Sloane breathed out, her voice low. "I'm sorry."

I angled off the door but didn't leave when I heard her flush the toilet. I wanted her to see I'd been listening, and when she came out, she walked right into my chest.

"Shit. Fuck." Her head shot up, a gasp to her lips.

But then she realized it was me.

Almost instantly, her body fucking sagged, my presence relief. I preferred that over anything, but I didn't get why she was so jumpy. I focused on her. "Who were you talking to?"

As if she remembered, she gripped her phone. "Bruno. Before we left the city, I texted him I was leaving with you. Told him I needed time. Needed space. Anyway, I called him just now to let him know I was fine." Her gaze averted, her lip lodged in her mouth. "Can we go please?"

I didn't want to do anymore of this, and since when the fuck did she leave her brother behind in any type of capacity? I pressed a hand to the wall above her, cutting her off. "Since when do you leave your brother anyway?"

"Since I do need space, and if you fail to remember, he got

it once." Flustered, she weaved her fingers through her hair. "And when he needed it, everyone gave that to him."

This was different, and she knew that.

"Let me through. You said you'd take me to the cabin."

I got her wrist, angling a look down. "It's not a good idea for us to just up and leave and not tell everyone. I told you. I'm not keeping this shit from my parents and definitely not yours."

By the grace of God, none of them had realized we were gone yet. Me, probably because I was supposed to be in fucking school. As far as Sloane herself, she was supposed to be sick up in her room.

Her jaw shifted. "You also said you'd take me to the cabin first and let me talk to you about things when I was ready."

Because there were things. There was something going on, and I was only waiting on the details due to fear. Things were shit between us, but I felt like I was making things almost worse by supporting her. Enabling her and whatever *this* was.

Easing her arm away, she adjusted her bag on her arm. "Now if you can't do that, I will find another way. I will, so either honor what you told me or let me go."

She was pleading with her eyes as she spoke, her voice the same. Like she wanted me to leave but didn't necessarily mean it. The dare was evident for me to take a step back, but definitely not for the one up on her end.

I knew she would go. She'd walk her little stubborn ass out into the winter and say to hell with me. Even if it killed her, she would. She was that stubborn, but I was too. I folded a hand behind her neck. "You're going to tell me *everything* when we get there. You hear me?"

I had my own dare in my voice. I dared her to go back on her word. She was using my own fear against me right now, fear I'd lose her if I didn't do what she said, and that was there completely between us. She was making me choose between her and my instincts, and that I wouldn't put up with for much longer.

It didn't matter how much I loved her.

————

The rest of the drive to the cabin was silent and only partially because Sloane wasn't talking to me. The weather got pretty bad during the drive, a snowstorm folding around us. It actually got pretty scary there for a bit, but we managed to beat it in the remaining hours of our drive.

I checked my phone inside, no missed calls or texts. I thought this was good that no one knew we were missing yet, but then I realized the drive through the hills made for some pretty shoddy reception. It was damn near impossible to get any type of contact on these backroads.

There were spots in the cabin that were good, though, and as I looked for them, Sloane stayed by the door.

"I'm going to look for a room," she said, her bag on her shoulder. She'd find plenty of them in this place. This cabin was meant for all the Legacy families to stay at, and most recently, we'd all been here after everything with Charlie.

I lowered my phone. "We're talking when you come back down." And we'd stay here a night, tops. We really didn't have much of a choice, as the storm had followed us here, and I hoped with maybe a night she'd come to her senses. She'd come back with me, back *home* and where she belonged.

Once again, my little fighter's eyes averted from me. She headed upstairs, and the paranoid fucker I was, I stayed by them. She was acting really weird, and I needed to keep an eye on her.

My phone rang.

It seemed I got a little reception by the stairs, and I answered, Wolf's name on the front of my screen. "Hey."

"Hey, man." His voice drifted off, nervous sounding. I

could assume by now he knew I was missing. We shared a lot of the same classes, and maybe he had reached out, but I wasn't getting much reception out here.

I folded my fingers into my hair. "I did something stupid, bro." I dropped my hand. "I let Sloane convince me to take off and out of town. She said she needed some space. We're at my family's cabin out of state and—"

"I know."

I closed my lips, my eyes narrowed. "What?"

"I know you guys are gone. I talked to her. You guys were at a gas station or something."

What the fuck? She'd said she'd been talking to Bru then.

My back up, I shook my head. "Okay, so why aren't you more pissed at me?" He sounded calm, rational. "Does everyone else know we're gone?"

"Yeah." Voices prattled on in the background. Wells and Thatcher. I heard him tell them both it was me on the phone. Wolf blew out a breath. "And I am pissed, but my hands are fucking tied right now. First off, did you make it to the cabin okay?"

I didn't understand what was going on, my eyes shifting. "Yeah, barely missed the snowstorm coming up, but yeah."

More talking, more fucking *chatting* in the background. I heard Wolf tell one of the guys to relay this information to the parents, *my parents*. He said he was texting his own that Sloane and I were okay, but I was the only one who wasn't getting fucking talked to.

"What's happening?" I sat on the stairs, waiting. "Why does it sound like you already know what the fuck's coming out of my mouth but I'm missing something?"

"Because you are, but it's not your fault." His voice lowered, a growled whisper into the line. "Our parents wouldn't let us call you."

"Call me about what—" My phone beeped, and I lowered

it to see my mom's name. I pressed my phone to my ear. "My mom's calling me."

"Good. Then she can explain things."

"Explain what?"

"What you need to know and don't get mad at Sloane. They wouldn't let her tell you either after they realized you both left together."

A buzzing rang behind my ears. "What?"

"Answer your mom, bro. She'll explain everything because if I do…" He paused, growling again. "It's best she tell you, and I need to call my parents. Let them know you both got up there okay."

I didn't know what to say, but it sounded like he wasn't going to be telling me anything anyway. I said bye, then clicked over to my mom. "Mom?"

There was silence for a second, but then a sigh. "Baby, are you okay? Did you make it to the cabin?"

I held onto the wall. "Why do you know I left?" And most importantly, why wasn't *she pissed* I left? She sounded just as calm as my buddy, and I didn't get that.

"Because Sloane let us know once we all realized she was gone this morning." There was some chatter in the background. I didn't know who she was with, but I made out the voices of some of my buddies' moms. I didn't hear Brielle or any of my god dads, though. "Your dad and I were over at her house this morning with Ramses and Brielle. Once we realized she left, we tried to call her. She didn't answer, but not long after that she texted where she was going. That she was with you, and we let you both because we thought it was best. You're safer away from this situation until we have it contained."

My throat worked. "Safer?"

"Yes, now, honey, I need you to listen to me very carefully. First, make sure the doors are locked and the security system is on. We're sending people out to you, but with the storm coming in, they might not be able to meet you until morning. LJ and Billie will be with them. LJ was already working in the area when this all happened."

"When what happened?"

I got my mother's silence then, too much silence. She swallowed into the line. "Your grandfather threatened Sloane late yesterday afternoon. She told her parents this morning, which is why your dad and I were over there. We were all talking about it."

I scanned the room, the floor. "Threatened her how?"

"I won't go over the particulars with you. They're both deranged and disturbing, and I need you completely with me right now as I go over the next steps with you."

Socked in the gut, fucking ill when I craned forward.

"You are to make sure you two stay there, all right?" she continued, the words swirling in my brain. "It's better for you both that you're there, and that you and the other kids stay out of this. We pulled everyone out of school earlier today, including Sloane's brother Bruno. She mentioned your grand-father threatened him too."

"How did he—" I closed my eyes. "Mom, what did he do?"

"Unspeakable things," she stated, the words sharp, cracked. "But you don't need to worry about any of it because the adults are. I want you to let Sloane know that Bru is safe. Him, Ares, and everyone are fine. We have the boys and Bow barred down with a security team outside of the city. The location is remote, and as far as we know, unknown to your grandfather. Myself and the other mothers are meeting with them now. We've been with your dad and the rest of the fathers. They're working on trying to find your grandpa. We believe he's still in the city, but he's making it difficult to find him at the present."

My hand caged my mouth, my heart fucking slamming against my chest. "Mom, I know you don't want me in whatever this is, but I need to know what's going on. I'll stay here. Just please fucking tell me."

I was… shaking, my teeth biting down on my knuckles. If my grandfather threatened Sloane, I need to know how.

"He tried to blackmail her," she said, finally, and I waited for the details.

They came slowly.

Careful, my mom told me things I couldn't even envision, *a nightmare* and with Sloane in the middle of it. Parts got quiet too, real quiet when I assumed my mom really didn't want to talk about those particular things. Things like how it sounded like my grandpa had killed Wolf's and how he'd orchestrated a *kidnapping* over revenge…

And what he tried to do to my girl after.

Mom's voice lowered real soft then, and mine did do. I said not one fucking word while she spoke, and I didn't breathe during any of it. I merely bit my hand.

I drew blood.

It dripped down my knuckles before I realized I was doing it, but the pain headed into the far off reaches of my mind.

"Now, I know you're going to want to do something," she said, finished, but my ears were ringing, my chest tight. "I do because I know you, but you can't. You won't."

I won't…

"You have one job right now, and that is to be there with Sloane," she said. "She needs you right now, and you both need all of us—your parents—to do our jobs too. The adults will take care of this, and we will protect you."

She didn't say how, and probably wouldn't even if I asked her. Instead, she told me she loved me and sent my father's love too. LJ and Billie would be there in their absence, and I was to do my job.

She came from the shadows.

Sloane, her hand on the wall, lingered in the stairwell. She sat, as if she'd been there for a while.

As if she'd been listening the whole time.

My phone was still lit. My mom had hung up, but I hadn't done anything after. Sloane got up slow. "I was going to tell you." She chose this as her first thing to say, as if I hadn't caught her *running* from me. She took a step down the stairs. "Your parents thought it'd be best we come here, though. Texted me that in the car after I responded to them."

Because they'd all been in on it, tricked me. My gaze sliced away from Sloane to the floor, and when she eased beside me, I recoiled.

She cringed. "Dorian, I wanted to tell you."

"That's the thing. You didn't." I put my hands together, my laughter dry, rough. I faced her. "Because if you did, you would have, and long before I caught you climbing down that tree."

She wouldn't have run, which was something she'd said she wasn't going to do to me ever again. She'd told me she was going to trust me, and if she did, I wouldn't have found her trying to leave.

"I didn't want to be a liability," she gasped, her eyes red, wet. She put her hands out. "He was using me for so long, and I didn't want him to even have the option of hurting anyone else."

"So, you run again," I said, nodding. "And when you got caught, you helped my parents manipulate me to keep me out of the situation."

It sounded worse out there, the betrayal worse. In all honesty, I got why the people I loved banded together to do such a thing. They were just trying to protect me, protect her.

It was Sloane's lack of faith that got to me the most, and she didn't trust that *I* could have taken care of her. I got up, and when she started to follow me, I raised my hands.

She played with hers. "I didn't want you to get hurt." There was so much irony in what she just said. By trying not to hurt me, she had. She blinked down a tear. "Please say something."

She didn't want me to say something.

So, I didn't.

Instead, I left her standing there, then proceeded to lock down the house. I was going to keep her safe tonight and do whatever I had to.

Even if she didn't believe in my capability.

CHAPTER
FORTY-FIVE

The dark prince slept with a shotgun in his lap.

But he slept.

He hadn't asked to sleep with me, beside me, but I didn't think he would even if I had asked him. Instead, he took the corner of my bedroom, his ankles crossed, his head touching the wall. The location happened to be where the only window in the room was, and he took it, the gun he'd gotten from the shed out back across his legs. He slept restlessly, sporadic between tugs of the curtain, but when he did, I watched him.

I couldn't help it, I guess.

I used to enjoy watching him in those rare moments when he forgot to leave my bedroom. The morning rays of early sun always hit his hair, flecks of gold bouncing off his feathered locks. It was always messy as hell before he woke up, perfect, and the result of a late-night fuck.

He always teased me when he caught me looking.

There was no teasing now, none of that at all, and this morning, I had to pretend to be sleeping when he ultimately got up. I'd just about vomited last night when I saw his reaction to being tricked.

This morning, I took the coward's way out and pretended I didn't notice when he peered at me from the side of the bed. He'd gotten up, come over, but just stood there, his dark shadow looming largely over the sheets. He lingered for so long, and my body called out to him. That he'd touch me and tell me everything was going to be okay.

But then, he left.

"You talk to Dorian this morning?" I asked Ares what felt like hours later. I ended up going back to sleep after Dorian left but woke up again when my phone rang. I draped my arms over the sheets, watching as my twin brother scowled at me through FaceTime.

"Yeah, I did, and he's pissed like the rest of us." He wasn't lying down and had his running clothes on. I didn't know if he was going for a run, or already had. He sighed. "You lied to him, and we had to lie to him for you."

None of that had been my idea, but his parents'. I'd panicked after I started getting calls from both our parents after they all had realized I was missing. Dorian had been beside me in the car, and he would have known something was wrong if I didn't appease our parents with some kind of explanation.

It'd been the biggest surprise when December herself had texted me to let her son keep driving, that she and her husband felt it was safer Dorian and I were away from the city and together. Brielle and Ramses only backed her up in subsequent texts, and I went into protection mode then, protecting Dorian from himself because I knew what would happen if he found out what his grandfather had done. He'd be the dark prince, and I couldn't risk what came with that. He'd tried to kill his grandfather when he'd threatened him before, and I saw what that had done to him. He thought he was a monster, and I couldn't let him become one.

Especially over me.

"It kept him safe," I said, no regrets. "He can be pissed at me. You can be pissed at me."

"I would be if I wasn't so worried about you." Ares wet his lips before moving a hand down his face. "You okay? D said you guys got through the night all right when we talked this morning. Sounds like the storm gave you hell, though."

It'd been loud, that was for sure, and we'd definitely gotten snow when I looked outside this morning. "We're fine. You guys?"

"Yeah, we're good. I haven't seen Dad, but Mom came through and joined the mothers with us last night. The dads are all still out doing stuff. They won't tell us what."

I didn't know what that meant, or what they were doing to help. Before I'd left, they had asked me to trust them, and it had only taken me a night after Callum had threatened me to know I did need to tell them what had happened.

I didn't know this world, but I had come to know the people who were around me every day. They were fiercely protective, but I was too. I knew they could handle things, but I wanted to protect them as well. I wasn't going to let Callum use me as a bargaining chip, so I had to leave and did once I'd been told Bru was safe. Before I'd run, Ramses and Brielle had said they'd gotten Bruno from school, and he was in transit back to their house. That hadn't left me with a lot of time because I knew others would be notified next.

Dorian would know next.

The dark prince was the one person… *the only* person who could completely break my resolve about leaving. I knew, if I'd seen him, I wouldn't have been able to do the right thing, and that was leave all the people I did care about. I would've wanted to stay, be weak and be with him.

Which was why things were as fucked up as they were now.

I had one toe in and one toe out in my plan to leave and

had ended up betraying Dorian. "How's Bru?" I'd spoken to my brother briefly yesterday when I'd gotten here. I'd called him but getting a read on him had been difficult. His anger had been evident, but he'd looked like he was trying to mute it through FaceTime. I think he'd been doing it for my sake and had spent most of the conversation in a sea of apologies, looking completely guilt-ridden over something that had nothing to do with him. Callum had betrayed him as much as me, and my brother had simmered with anger.

Even if he'd tried not to let me see.

It killed me he was going through that, but it was better I was here. I also knew the families would keep him safe, and he was better with them.

"He's good," Ares said. "He was still asleep when I got up this morning. Him and the rest of the house."

A familiar face came through behind him, Brielle. She too had her running clothes on, and it sounded like they may be going together when he called back to her. The chatter stopped when she noticed I was on the screen, though, and Ares handed the phone to her.

"Morning, honey," she said to me, both of them on the line. Ares hugged her and said he'd be outside with security. It sounded like a team was going to escort them when they went out this morning. Ares said goodbye to me first, though, saying we'd talk later. I waved at him through the line, and Brielle smiled at me. "I didn't know you were up. Otherwise, I would have called."

"It's fine." More emotion hit my voice than I wanted, seeing her, missing her and Ramses too. I'd cried my eyes out between them both when I'd told them what had happened with Callum. "How are things? Is Ramses okay?"

"Yeah, honey. He's good." Her smile was a shaky one, like she was trying to stay strong and struggling. "He misses you. I miss you too."

"I'm sorry for running." I lowered my head, using the

blanket to wipe my eyes. "I keep running, and I'm stupid."

"No, you were scared, and Dorian said how you didn't want to be a liability. He called us."

He did?

"But you aren't one, you understand?" She wiped her eyes now. "Something terrible happened to you. Unimaginable, and we're going to do everything to make sure you and everyone else stays safe. I want you to know that we are handling this, and we will all be all right on the other side of it."

But how could we? Callum had said so many things…

I was scared, scared for everyone. I just wanted it to be *me*, me to suffer. At least, if I left he couldn't use me against anyone else.

"Ramses and I love you," she said, a sheen over her eyes. "We love you so much, and you will be safe. You, Bruno, Ares, Dorian, and the other kids. Callum Prinze is not going to win this. He will *burn* for this and will not bring fear to this family. We are stronger than him, and even more so, because it's not just us. Rest assured, all the parents are working together on this issue to ensure you will have a safe place when you come home."

Her words made me ache, the emotion in them. "I love you guys too. Tell Ramses that. Please?"

I wished he was there, and I could tell him. Somewhere along the way, they really had become my parents and I'd become their daughter, and I know that was why I told them the truth. I hadn't even considered another option. They were my mom and dad.

And I needed a mom and dad.

Brielle did cry then, not bothering to wipe away her tears. She pressed her fingers to her lips, before touching them to the screen. "My love, you just wait for us, okay? Your dad and I are fixing this, and we will make it safe for you to return to us. Whatever it takes, we will."

I think that was what scared me the most. Callum Prinze was a dangerous man, and what if whatever it took…

Left nothing but ash.

———

A fleet of more than one car rolled up to the cabin later that morning, security. Brielle had told me they'd come before we'd hung up so I wasn't surprised. I got dressed, and by the time I got downstairs, the dark prince had already let them inside.

He was hugging one of them.

"How you holding up?" the guy asked Dorian, and I recognized him. I'd met LJ and Dorian's other god dads at Bru's birthday party.

LJ was a tall man, broad-shouldered, blond. He had a sea of dirty-blond locks that, at the present, he wore tucked in a bun behind his head. Coming away, the man folded a hand behind Dorian's neck. "You both get through the night okay?"

I saw Dorian nod, but just barely. A beautiful redhead obstructed my view a little, and I knew her to be LJ's wife Billie. Brielle had mentioned Billie and her husband were coming over with security to be with us.

"Hey, sweets," Billie said to Dorian, hugging him next. The dark prince swallowed her up with his size in comparison, but that didn't matter to Billie. She squeezed him so hard his shoulders bumped like he'd laughed a little.

I hoped he had.

The security team who'd come with them started filling up the house, and when one greeted me, Billie and Dorian both broke away from their hug. I gained LJ's attention too, the tall man coming forward.

"Good morning, Sloane," he said, taking his wife by the hand. His other went to Dorian's shoulder, and I noticed the dark prince looked at anyone other than me in the moment.

He'd merely pocketed his hands, his eyes to the floor. LJ smiled at me. "I'm LJ. Met you at your brother's birthday party."

I remembered, raising my hand to him. "Thank you for coming."

"We're happy we could be here for our friends," he said, putting an arm around his wife. "You recall my wife Billie too?"

She reached out, taking my hand. "How you doing, honey? You both good?" Her attention traveled back to the dark prince.

"We were good last night," Dorian said, my stomach souring when his gaze completely bypassed me and focused directly on Billie. "Didn't have any problems."

Not with his grandpa, no. So I guess he wasn't lying about that.

LJ rubbed Dorian's shoulder. "Good. Well, we're here to make sure you kids are okay."

"Any updates finding my grandpa?" Dorian asked, his frown heavy. "How are my parents and Ramses and Brielle? Knight, Jax, and everyone else?"

"Everyone's fine." LJ patted the air. "And they'll give us updates when we need them, and I'll give you kids updates when *you* need them. Your parents and the rest of the families are handling this. We haven't found your grandpa yet, but trust us to."

"What's going to happen when you do?" Dorian questioned, and it felt kind of bold to. I hadn't asked this question.

I didn't want to know.

It turned my gut that people were laboring to fix this, and all because of me. No, I didn't want to know, but I wasn't surprised Dorian did.

His hand on Dorian's arm, LJ leveled him a look. "I need you to trust us adults, and I promise you, I will give you updates as you need them. As far as you're concerned, your grandfather is a nonissue and nothing you need to worry about. Either of you."

Except for the fact that we did worry, and definitely if he was missing.

I swallowed, a silent dread in my body. I was well aware of what we were dealing with here. There were like a dozen women and men in here with guns. This security detail was *for us*, and Dorian and I weren't even involved in where the war was supposed to be. I'd overhead Dorian's mom tell him Callum was still in Maywood Heights, so all this was just backup for a man who had power.

Who instilled fear.

"So, with that out of the way, I've also been tasked with 'monitoring' you kids," LJ stated, air quoting. He eyed the dark prince. "As far as all that, I only have to say one thing. I'm not either of your moms and dads, but also don't want to know." He raised a hand. "We'll go with an out-of-sight, out-of-mind approach regarding all that. I remember what it's like to be your age so, yeah. We'll just do that."

LJ scratched the back of his neck, awkward, and Billie laughed. She rubbed her husband's chest. "Oh, honey."

LJ shrugged, and I tried to hide behind my hair. Dorian, on the other hand, stared coolly in my direction. His lips thinned.

"Don't think you'll have to worry about that," he said, basically driving a dagger through my entire chest. He faced his god dad. "I was going to go for a jog. That on the list of approved activities?"

His words had a bite to them, and LJ definitely noticed. LJ's eyebrows narrowed in his direction. "You can go, but someone goes with you. There's about half a dozen guys on the porch right now and more stationing around the perimeter. Pick your poison who goes with you." LJ glanced down. "You need something better for that hand?"

Dorian had a scrap of shirt or something wrapped around

his fist, and I'd noticed his hand last night too. It'd been bleeding, but with all we'd been discussing, I couldn't address it.

He'd also kept our discussion short.

"What happened, love?" Billie asked, raising Dorian's hand, but he waved it off.

"I'm good," he said, barely looking at me before cutting out of the circle. He tugged a hoodie off the couch, and I noticed he'd brought that and other clothes in last night. When I'd asked, he'd said he always kept a bag in his car for the gym.

Of course, this had been before he'd found out I had lied to him and done so with his parents. I folded a hand over my face.

"I'll be back, and I'll tell security," he said, before breezing out of the cabin. The sweatpants and tee he wore he must have gotten from his bag too. It probably wouldn't be enough for most people after the storm we'd had, but I knew he was amped up, simmering. The door closed behind him, and LJ sighed.

LJ rubbed his wife's shoulder. "Well, my godson's in a mood."

"It has nothing to do with you. Either of you." I rubbed my arm. "He's mad at me. That I lied."

I didn't know if they both knew the details there, but when they nodded, I figured they did. Billie came over. "Well, Sloane, it's still early yet. How about some breakfast? We had food brought up so I can make anything you want."

That sounded nice, and I was hungry. We'd made stops on the road, but it'd been a while since I'd eaten.

"I'll help," LJ said, going with us, and I could see what they were trying to do by raising my spirits.

I just didn't know if it'd help.

Dorian

My ax blade split wood, pieces of lumber hitting the snow. Each grip of the ax killed my split knuckles, the impact worse, and I welcomed the pain.

She came from between the trees.

Sloane strode past two security agents, and I pretended not to notice. Instead, I tried to work feeling into my numb hands, my gloves bulky and making it hard to grip the ax. I had tossed them off what felt like forever ago, my hands just as numb as the rest of me. A hoodie and sweatpants wasn't really fucking doing it out here, but I didn't care.

I preferred being numb anyway.

Sloane's smell ghosted on the wind when she approached, reminding me I wasn't numb. Reminding me that I *felt*. I absolute hated that because I felt severed in half, her hands in her pockets when she stopped next to me. "Dorian?"

Chop.

Wood hit the ground again, no words from my lips. Sloane's gaze hit the heavens, a flush across her cheeks. She actually had her coat on, being smart. Her full lips pressed together. "Dorian, you're being immature."

Was I?

Chop.

I kicked the wood off to the side, and she laughed a little, dry. Her throat jumped. "You know what? You can be mad at me, but you can also use your words and tell me about it."

She didn't want me to fucking talk right now, *my laughter* dry.

"Instead, you're out here pouting like a big baby and wearing *no* coat." Her dark eyes peered over me, sounding like a straight-up mom.

Or a concerned girlfriend.

Chop.

I picked up the wood off the snow, stacking it. My parents' cabin ate a lot of wood, more than one fireplace in there that needed it. I'd noticed the woodpile outside was looking thin after my run, and anything I could do outside of that cabin and away from Sloane I needed right fucking now. I didn't want to say anything stupid and make shit worse. I was in my feelings. I was *mad,* and I wasn't good at talking about shit. My therapist knew about that firsthand.

I noticed the agents' eyes on us while I stacked, well aware they were watching over us. A couple had ended up going with me on my run and more had stayed with me after when I'd come back outside. They were just doing their job, and I knew they probably wouldn't tell me to go inside, even though I'd been out here for probably too long.

Sloane studied me, not wearing enough clothes herself out here. She had on a pair of leggings that made me want to drop the ax and bend her over in front of me, shove those things to her ankles while I filled her with my cock. I'd been cold before she came over, but so much blood rushed to my dick now, I could probably split wood without the fucking ax.

Adjusting myself, I ignored it, fighting it. I didn't want to do this shit with her. Hell, I didn't even want to be fucking mad at her. Emotions were a son of a bitch, and I was never good at expressing them. I couldn't tell her how hurt I was, angry. I didn't have the right, and I fucking knew that, which made all this so much worse.

The shove came out of nowhere, and I dropped the wood I'd been stacking. Honest to fuck, I just hadn't seen it coming, which was why she'd been able to do it.

Sloane stood there after she did, looking proud of herself even. She was amped up, pumping her lanky little arms. "Well, I'm not just going to let you, so if you're mad, talk about it. I'm waiting."

I blinked, more shocked than anything. The little fighter had actually pushed me, shoved me. Being the bigger man, I tempered my anger, but then she came at me again. I growled. "Noa…"

"He has words, everyone," she announced to the few watching us. They eyed her like she was insane, and she was acting insane. She raised her arms to them. "Maybe he'll actually talk to me now instead of acting like a big ole baby."

Okay, that shit wasn't fucking cool, and she ignited the rage inside me when she got up on the stump I'd been using to cut wood.

She put hands around her mouth. "Let's see if he'll actually—"

I got her by the hips, my favorite means of transportation for her. She squealed when I tossed her over my shoulder, the tactic always a bit caveman-ish, but I didn't give a fuck.

Sloane kicked, of course, always fucking did. She started hitting me too, and all that did was get her ass hit. I gave her a sharp slap to her ass, those cheeks probably nice and rosy under those sexy-as-fuck leggings.

She was screaming by the time I took her to the shed, not far from the wood stump, and security let me. This argument was clearly just a bunch of bullshit between Sloane and me and the trivial crap of two people who couldn't talk to each other right, but if it was, I wasn't going to have it in front of an audience.

I put Sloane in the shed, but the hits only continued when we got there, and I closed the door behind us.

"See. This is what I'm talking about," she cut, her face exploded in red color. She was a madwoman, her dark hair flinging around when she punched at my biceps and chest with her little fists. "You don't talk. You just act like a complete dick, and you have no right to be mad at me. I did what I did to keep you safe. To keep you out of this."

She was right that I had no right to be mad at her. Not after what she'd been through, and I didn't want to be this way.

I just couldn't stop the *pain* of it.

The hurt in full blast, I got one of her fists and pinned it to the wall. "You didn't trust me. You went behind my back and didn't fucking talk to me!"

The words out there, she froze, her throat working, mouth flushed, pink. I wanted to force her on her knees and fill it with my cock, punish her for not believing I could take care of her.

For not having faith.

"I should have been the first person you came to," I said, pressing my body against hers. Our hearts slammed into each other, and I covered her throat with my hand, making her gasp. "So yeah, I'm fucking mad. Yeah, I'm fucking hurt. The girl I love doesn't trust me to take care of her, and that shit hurts."

The words were amplified around us, and I felt things going too far. Especially when I had both hands around her throat. I guided her mouth up, and soft breaths escaped her lips.

"You can't believe that," she gasped. She wet her lips. "You don't believe that."

But I did, and what else could I fucking believe? I shook my head. "You promised me you wouldn't run, but you did. You left. You…"

She'd left *me*, and I couldn't even with that shit. If she was going to leave, we should have left together.

Something in that moment had her emotional, a tear falling down her cheek. Numbness had obviously left my hands because my knuckles felt the heat of it when I dragged my good set of knuckles down her face. They came away wet, and I wasn't thinking when I bit her mouth.

I just wanted to taste her.

I told myself that was the only thing it was, a taste. Our mouths sealed, though, and the euphoria became better than the numbness.

No more pain.

No more hurt.

Just us.

"Dorian," she breathed out, her hands on my arms, her fists clenching my hoodie. She shoved at me when I went to her neck. "No, Dorian. We need to talk. Talk about what you just said and how you feel."

I didn't want to *fucking talk*. Talking just meant more of this back and forth, and I didn't want to *feel* anymore.

Again, I felt this going too far, her heated breath just as persistent as her protests. She wanted to talk as much as she wanted the flicks of my tongue across her skin. Hell, she might have wanted to talk more. She wanted to help me, help *us*, but I was too busy escaping. I wanted her, and I didn't want it on healthy terms. I wanted it raw, sick, and with me holding power over her.

"I want you on your knees," I ground out, making her gasp. I flicked her tongue. "No talking."

As if to emphasize, I filled her mouth with my own tongue, her pants surprised, heated. I kissed her until I felt no physical resistance, tasting her into submission. Her hands eased their grip on my arms, and I unzipped her coat, filling my hands with her tits through her shirt. We were in a shed that barely fit me, let alone both of us.

A moan touched my mouth, hers. I was hard as fucking steel, and I rocked against her. She held my hips. "Dorian—"

"I said no fucking talking," I cut in, forcing her down to her knees. "Pull me out."

I waited above her, mostly waiting for her to stop me. What I was doing was toxic shit right now, avoiding, but I didn't care. I ignored the disappointment that flashed in her eyes when she undid my pants, like she was disappointed *in me*, and I lost it anyway when her focus shifted to other places. A chill hit when my dick touched the air, but then Sloane put her mouth on me.

I saw fucking *stars*.

My hand slammed to the wall, easing in and out of Sloane's delicate mouth. She took me in deep, gagging a little, and I held her there until her throat opened up.

Fuck.

My eyes pinched tight, my hand working around her hair. I rocked deep, gripping hard, enjoying this too much. This was a temporary high, and I knew that.

I just didn't fucking care.

And I noticed Sloane after a beat. She was going faster, sucking *harder*. I gazed down, and she was looking at me, her eyes heated, aggressive. She played with my balls, taking me to the brink too fast, and I wasn't going to last.

"Sloane. Fuck." I spilled down her throat in minutes, seconds. I didn't even have a chance to pull her off and fuck her the way I wanted to, and Sloane held herself to me. She swallowed it all down and licked me clean after.

She even put my pants back up.

After that, she was on her feet, and I didn't know what to make of her expression.

Mostly because she was avoiding my eyes.

Zipping up her coat, she merely wiped her mouth before looking at me. "Let me know when you actually want to talk."

Fuck.

I closed my eyes. "Sloane."

"No." She raised her hand, her head shaking. I tried to touch her, but she wasn't having that. Instead, she left the shed, passing the agents. I didn't know if they knew what we'd gotten up to, but I didn't care. I was too busy running after Sloane and begging her to talk to me. I was starting to wonder if this was it. If this would be the last time I'd be able to go after her and if she'd even let me. With all my toxicity, this might not be the right thing for her, and I was wondering if I even *should* go after her. She always made me better.

But what did I ever do for her?

CHAPTER
FORTY-SEVEN

Dorian

"Good evening, gentlemen." LJ came up behind me, and when the two security guys watching over me noticed, they nodded at him. They didn't leave, but they did give us space when my god dad came over. LJ tossed the blanket he had at me. "So your parents don't kill me for allowing their kid to get frostbite on my watch."

I frowned at the thing, warm enough in front of the firepit I'd been stationed at for more than two hours. I'd gone after Noa earlier today, but she hadn't wanted to talk, and the irony of that wasn't lost on me. I lifted the blanket. "I'm not cold."

"Like hell." Refusing to take it back, my god dad joined me on the cold lawn furniture. His wool coat kept him warm enough, I supposed, and I wasn't so bad in my coat. I'd actually worn one tonight. His head cocked. "Anyway, it's not from me."

He pointed inside the cabin, Billie waving at us both through the glass door.

Not wanting to make her unhappy, I did put it on, and it did help, along with the fire in the pit. The fire there was probably the only reason I *didn't* have frostbite. I'd been putting to good use all that wood I'd cut.

I put my hands near the flames, and LJ did too.

"I noticed you and Sloane aren't talking much," he said, frowning. "Barely even looked at each other at dinner."

She'd ended up taking hers upstairs in the end, saying she wasn't feeling great, and LJ and Billie were too nice to question that.

I shrugged, and LJ smiled.

"What's going on, kid?"

What was going on was I'd managed to fuck things up worse than I already had. I rubbed my mouth. "We're having issues communicating."

"Well, that's evident." He laughed. He kicked my shoe with his boot. "What's the issue?"

I had no words for him and was annoyed with myself for it. I just wasn't good at this talking shit.

LJ sighed. "I suppose that's good you have nothing to say because you should probably be talking to her anyway?" His question had me looking up. He nodded. "I know you know she needs you right now."

That was the thing. I didn't think she did. I rubbed my hands. "I keep fucking up shit with her. I do, and she runs from me, and..." I forced out a breath. "I make things worse. Always make things worse."

"Well, you're young so that's okay." He smiled. "You only got a few years left of that shit, so if I were you, I'd be taking advantage."

Sounding a lot like my father, I laughed, rubbing my arm.

He bumped me with his shoulder. "Go upstairs and talk to her. Whatever is going on won't just work itself out. You gotta be the one to take the first step."

I rubbed my bad knuckles. "She didn't trust me to take

care of her. She didn't come to me about everything with my grandpa, and it's taking everything in me to just sit here after what he did to her." I rocked back and forth. "I want to kill him, LJ. I want him to bleed out while I watch."

I probably sounded evil saying these things, dark, and I was surprised by the look LJ gave me. It wasn't one of judgment. He put his arm around me. "Sounds to me like Sloane may have saved you from that." He nodded. "The mental burden of that?"

He was right, of course, completely right. "I can protect her."

"I'm sure she knows that." He rubbed my arm. "Which is why you're here with her and not in a fight you shouldn't be. We're handling your grandfather, and the best thing Sloane could have done was keep you out of all that. I think we all know what that summer with your grandfather did to you. He manipulated you, and you did things you wouldn't normally do."

I was cold again, chilly.

"She's here with you now, bud," LJ continued. "She is and she chose that, and if that doesn't mean she feels safe with you, I don't know what does."

My heart lurched, my chest tight. "I always goof shit up with her." I swallowed. "I'm not good enough for her."

"Now, I know you know that's not true." Pulling back, he tapped my arm. "And don't prove yourself right by thinking it. Sloane did choose you, so why not have faith in that choice? She believes in you, so why don't you?"

I didn't know why. Maybe because I'd never known anyone like her, someone so patient, strong. I did do things wrong repeatedly, but she always took me back. I shook my head. "I just want to protect her. Even if it's from me, I want to."

"Mmm. So you're falling on the sword, I see." He smirked. "How's that working for you?"

"Completely shitty," I said, laughing when he did. I shook my head. "You're really good at this talking stuff, by the way." My god dad and I had never really had heart-to-hearts, but that had mostly to do with how busy he was. I didn't see him a lot, but when I did, things were really easy like this. It was nice.

He nudged me. "Thanks, kid. It's nice to have a place to use them with you boys and Bow. Billie and I tried for a while to have kids. Just wasn't in the cards for us, I guess."

He sounded more at peace than sad about that, but I was sure he was disappointed. LJ had a big family, and his sisters all had kids. "I'm sorry."

"Don't be. Billie and I have our hands full enough with you lot." He laughed. "And we've also gotten to travel and just live life. It's been good, nice."

He would have made a good dad, though. A brilliant one.

"And who knows, maybe one day we'll foster or something." He shrugged, smiling a little. "If the timing is right, you never known what could happen."

My own smile lifted right. "You'd be great at it. You and Billie."

"Thanks for saying that, but really, we're good. *Happy.*" And he did seem to be, at peace. He sat back. "Jax, Knight, Ramses, and your dad happened to have terrific kids. Between that along with my own siblings' kids, I can't call myself anything but the luckiest man on earth. I am lucky. I get to live the life of my dreams with the woman I love. What else could I asked for?"

When he said it like that, it sounded like he didn't have to ask for anything else. That he truly had it all.

"You go fix things with yours then, yeah?" he stated, my mouth parting. He smiled. "Come on. It's obvious."

His phone rang just then, and upon checking it, he got up. He gave me a hug before saying he'd take the call inside, and I didn't question it. He'd been getting calls all day, but I hadn't asked him about any of them. Mostly because I knew what they were about. It was obvious he'd been talking to my parents on more than one call.

My dad.

I had to trust that they were taking care of things, and after LJ got up, I did too. Sloane may have taken me out of the fight, but that didn't make my new position any less important. I did need to protect her, and I was going to.

I just hoped she'd still let me.

FORTY-EIGHT

Dorian

I found her on the rooftop, hunkered down in the spot where the boys and I smoked weed. She'd found our stash because the floorboards inside her room had been lifted when I'd entered. The guys and me always kept it in that room because no one used it. It was the smallest.

The window open to that room, that was how I found her after speaking to LJ. Sloane had her legs up, a cloud of smoke around her. Her cheeks hallowed when she took a drag, all bundled up in her coat. She noticed me climbing out the window to her and passed me the joint when I sat beside her.

I tasted her cherry lip balm, heaven, before passing it back to her. Some of the best moments between us were when we were doing shit like this. Just relaxing and being with each other. She knew I wasn't great at talking, and she let me be that way.

She was patient with me.

"I was scared."

Her lashes flashed in my direction, her lips in a full pout.

I'd never seen her so beautiful than with a winter flush on her cheeks. Her eyebrows narrowed. "Scared?"

I nodded, getting closer to her. She didn't move away so that was a good sign. "I thought I'd fucked things up so bad that you didn't trust me. That you didn't believe I could take care of you, which was why you went to the parents first and not me."

I thought the words would cut more coming out of me, but speaking to LJ had helped, my fears before me.

A sadness touched Sloane's eyes I didn't expect. She flicked the joint butt off the roof, then raised her legs. She hugged them. "I didn't want your grandfather to use me against anyone and especially you. I wanted to leave so he couldn't, but I didn't even do that right." Rubbing her arms, she looked at me. "You weren't supposed to find me, but when I saw you…"

Her head lowered, and I stayed silent. I was going to listen to her, truly listen. I hadn't been great at that in the past, but I was going to try today. I'd try for her.

"Dorian, no one makes me feel so safe." She gripped her arms, and my breath touched the air. She cringed. "And I couldn't leave you. I should have, and I know it was selfish, but when I'm with you, I can't help it. It feels so good. It always feels so good."

Her gaze took the sky, her head shaking, and I got closer to her.

"I was stupid," she admitted, her swallow hard. "I just hurt you and made you feel like I didn't trust you, but I do. I trust you with everything."

I trusted her with everything too and made her look at me. I scanned her eyes. "You feel safe with me?"

That almost felt more valuable than her trust, her words like a fucking security blanket. I wasn't a monster or even her dark prince.

I was her safety.

I touched my forehead to hers, waiting for the words like my next breath.

She slid her arms around me, tears blinking down from her eyes when she pressed her face into my neck. She gasped. "You're home, Dorian Prinze. You're my home, and I love you. You make me feel safe. So safe, and I've never felt that way before. I've never felt this…"

She gripped my coat in her hands, and I brought her into my lap. She was shaking so fucking bad, and I guided her to look up at me. I'd never felt like this before either, like I couldn't fucking breathe anytime she was in the room, or the sheer agony it felt to ever be under her disappointed gaze. She made me want to be better, stronger for her. I used to feel like emotions were weak.

But with her, it only turned a dark world into light.

I sealed our lips, the kiss salty with her tears. I didn't know if she was crying because she was happy, or just emotional, but whatever the case I wouldn't make her feel like she was weak because of them. Emotions weren't weak, and those who showed them displayed their power. They allowed for vulnerability and allowed me to see her strength.

I carried her inside, too cold for the both of us out here. I stripped her coat off, then mine, our shoes too, before I hovered above her on the bed.

"Make love to me," she gasped, taking my hand and sliding it over her heat. I gripped her through her leggings, and her head touched the bedding. "Please."

She didn't know what she was asking, my nose touching hers. We'd been together many times, but most had been about taking control for me, expressing power, dominance. I scanned her eyes. "I don't know if I'm good at that."

I wasn't good at being gentle, tender. Even when she'd asked me to make love to her before, it hadn't been like that.

She touched my face. "That *is* what you're good at," she stated, kissing my mouth open, and I growled. I brought her arms up, and her hips rose to meet mine. "Loving me? You're so good at it. Great at."

I kissed her, hard, and my eyes itched, her moans in my mouth, her gasps beneath me. If loving her was what she needed, I would.

I couldn't do anything else.

"I fucking love you," I gritted, pinching her lower lips. She sighed, and I caught her bottom lip between my teeth. "And I'm going to make you feel so fucking good."

I was going to take care of her because she was *my* home, my light in the storm.

My calm in the chaos.

Our tongues dueled, her shirt up, her tit under my palm. I squeezed, and when she growled, I sucked her hard through the lace.

"Dorian, oh my fucking God." She reached for the bed posts, her hips rocking, her sex *hungry*. I could smell her, and I didn't even have her pants off. She looped her legs around me, but I forced them off, then up. I had her hips above me when I worked her leggings down.

I took her panties with them, tossing them off before guiding her pussy up to my mouth.

Fucking *heaven*, my dick kicking against my boxers, Sloane's thighs squeezing my face. She was trying to suffocate me, but I'd die a happy fucking man.

"Please. Please," she begged, touching herself, her breast in her hand. The other hand gripped the shit out of my hair, and there was no sexier sight than watching her wriggle, her shirt above her breasts, her body flush and her mouth open. No one could make her feel this way but me.

I blew heat over her sex, not letting her forget that. I unstrapped her bra while I tasted her, my tongue flicking, greedy. "Touch yourself, baby."

I replaced my tongue with her fingers, licking around both

of them and her clit. Her sticky heat weaved around her fingers and across my tongue.

"Dorian, I'm going to come." She said this, but she didn't pull her pussy away, her body midair and grinding against my face. I pinched her nipple, and the sound that escaped her lips bordered on painful. She shoved at my shoulders. "No."

"Yes." I let her rock, nose deep in her scent, her heat. I let go of her nipple to hold her to my mouth. I had no problem with her coming on my face, and she did, beautifully.

Her body quivered, her juices flooding into my mouth. I sucked them up and was greedy as shit about it.

"Dorian," she gasped out my name, still midair. Her hair was down, and she wriggled like a mermaid in the sheets, a sea of ebony locks around her, perfect, gorgeous.

After she came, I brought her up to me by her hair and didn't stop kissing her until she tasted how good she was, until she *experienced* what it was to be with her. She said I made her feel safe, but she had no idea what she did to me. She wasn't just safety for me, and she wasn't just home. She made me feel *human*.

She made me feel alive.

I kissed her hard into the sheets, pinning her until her hips once again started moving against mine. I tugged my shirt off, skin on skin, flesh on flesh.

"Get naked with me." She forced my pants down, the hottest fucking thing when she said that to me. It didn't just feel like that in the physical sense. At least to me. I felt so exposed with her and let her tug my jeans and boxers down. I sprang to the first section of my abs, and I let her use her hips to take me to my back. She grinned. "That's better."

Squeezing her thighs, I brought her hips down to meet mine, making us both call out, and all I did was rub her against me. "Fuck."

A veil of her hair surrounded us, our kisses heated, our

bodies wet with sweat. I hugged her so close I borderline suffocated us both.

"Dorian…" Soft kisses on my lips, tender, sweet. She was more delicate than I could ever be.

Perhaps that was why we worked.

I wrapped her hair in my fist, making her look at me when I eased myself inside her. Her mouth parted, but when she worked her thick hips, I was the one who couldn't keep my eyes open.

"Little fighter." My hand covered her back, her shoulder between my teeth. My hips hit just as hard as hers. If anything, hers drove harder, faster. If she was trying to prove something, she was winning, but I didn't care about the loss. I'd stop winning in this game between us long ago.

And thank God I had.

I came with her above me, a goddess in the night. I milked her heat, in and out until she came too. She was always so good at that, fucking gorgeous. I barely waited for her to finish before I had her under me, kissing her again. I held her to me and didn't allow an inch of separation.

"Will you be my girlfriend?" The words fell out of my mouth, and I felt childish as shit for saying them. I mean, what the fuck was a girlfriend and boyfriend anyway? Whatever we had was much more than that. We'd *been through* much more than that.

But even still, I saw what the sentiment did to Sloane, her face lit up, her hands in my hair. She drew her fingers through it, and I felt that shit through every fucking follicle.

"I thought I already was," she said, laughing a little, and I grinned. I pinched her lips between mine, and she didn't fight me.

Nor when I did what I did next.

I'd heard of guys on the Court giving their girls their rings and thought that shit was basic. I just didn't know what the fuck that meant, but as soon as I took mine off and put it on

Sloane's thumb it made sense. It was like she had a part of me, a part I gave to her and wanted her to have. I was hers just as much as she was mine.

Our fingers threaded together, the ring perfect on her. I kissed her thumb while she kissed me, all of this so fucking surreal. I was starting to forget what life was before her. At least, the bad parts. She'd replaced them somehow.

She'd healed them.

CHAPTER
FORTY-NINE

I studied Prinze in the driver's seat.

We shared a similar state.

Royal Prinze was just as amped up as I was, restless. I supposed that was a big reason we were both in the car instead of somewhere else. We both had conflicts of interest, me for my daughter.

And him for his dad.

The term was loose for that son of a bitch, and had I had it my way, things would be going very differently tonight. I'd made a promise to *my wife*, and that was the only reason things were different. Me being involved with what we were all doing tonight wasn't possible.

I was too close to things.

Instead, I'd been forced to sit here, watch Prinze. His Tesla hummed while we surveyed a parking lot. It was just after 3 AM, and we hadn't heard anything from Reed or Ambrose.

We should have heard something by now.

Prinze's phone lit on the dashboard.

It was as if a call from God, Knight Reed's name on the front of the screen. Prinze and I barely exchanged a look before Prinze swiped it off the dash.

"Brother?" Prinze said into the line, waiting. I'd known Royal for so long, and he was doing his best to remain calm here. I didn't know his thoughts on the matter, but if my friends were inside of a building trying to take care of my father, I might have some thoughts on it. I wouldn't want to have an opinion about that, but...

It was hard, a history there. I knew Prinze's situation was a little more turbulent than mine was with my dad when he'd been alive, but with either of us, one fact couldn't be denied.

They were our blood.

"Royal, you need to come inside. Now," Reed said, his voice steady, low. "We're sending a guy to your car. He'll take you. Hurry."

"What's going on?" I took the phone from Prinze. My throat flicked. "Is the job done? Is..." I closed my eyes. "Did your people take care of it?"

"The job is done, and you both should probably come upstairs." Reed clicked off about the same time one of our guys came to Prinze's car. We both got out, the air chilly. We made haste behind a guy with legs the size of tree trunks. Reed knew military folks, and many of them had volunteered for this. We'd had to act quickly when we finally found out where Prinze's dad was. It'd been a long search, many hours and no sleep.

The job's done.

Reed's voice played in my head, Prinze ahead of me. We met up with Jaxen Ambrose on the way upstairs. He lingered in a hallway, at a post waiting for us.

"Hey, this way," Ambrose said, our location a stairwell of one of the nicest hotels in the city. It was a perfect setting for a man of arrogance, and we'd all been floored to find out Prinze's dad had been staying here. He'd made his threats against my daughter, caused chaos in my family's lives and stolen so much time…

Yet, here he was, the king of his castle. He'd taken over the entire top floor, but no one seemed to be around now but our men. Prinze and I passed them all, Ambrose with us.

"Jax, what's wrong?" Prinze asked Ambrose, but the question stopped in front of the door of a room. The room wasn't empty, several people inside. The first was Knight Reed, the dude built like a semi and basically shielding the scene behind him.

Though, not enough.

He couldn't cover the woman behind him, nor the man who lay on the floor below her. The man was covered in blood, a hand to his chest, his eyes open as if he'd been trying to get in one last sight of the world.

But I wasn't focused on him, and Prinze wasn't either. He rushed into the room, and he immediately went to the woman. She was his wife.

And for some reason was covered in blood.

December Prinze had her hands cuffing her arms, her eyes haunted and scanning the body at her feet. She just stared at it, unblinking. I didn't know if it was Reed or Ambrose, but someone had her sitting in a hotel chair, the rest of the room filled with military people. The men and women in black holding walkie-talkies were clearing out the scene, wiping things down and bagging things. One of those items was a gun, and I panned away just in time to see Prinze grab his wife.

"Em," he said, her head shooting up. December, my best friend of many years, basically launched herself at her husband.

"Royal, oh my God," she gasped, shaking in his arms. She gripped his shirt, blood all over her hands. "It wasn't me…"

She breathed out the words, soft, light, and I swallowed.

Prinze himself appeared horrified, a trembling woman in his arms.

His father at his feet.

Callum Prinze was dead, a jewel-topped cane beside him. It'd been flung across the floor like he'd answered the door, then been surprised from the front.

I came over too, and my own horror at the scene I was sure was just as evident as Royal Prinze's. What was December doing in here?

"Em?" Prinze questioned, blinking back and forth between his wife and his dead father. He squeezed her. "Em, what?"

He couldn't seem to get out the words in the moment, and I had none.

"We found her," Reed explained, Ambrose entering the room too. Reed scanned the room. "Found him here with her."

"He was already dead, brother," Ambrose said, staring at Prinze. At this point, Prinze had his hand behind his wife's head. He cradled her, holding her tight. Ambrose frowned. "She said he was already shot when she got here."

But why was she here?

"Em?" Prinze pulled December back. "What happened?"

"I don't *know*. I..." She blinked down, her eyes widening at the dead man on the floor. "I came in, and he was already on the floor. He was bleeding out. There was so much blood."

"But why were you here?" he asked her, and her eyes averted.

They fell on me.

I came over, my hand on her shoulder. She took it, squeezing before looking at her husband.

"He had to pay for our children," she said, shocking both Prinze and me. Reed and Ambrose looked away, as if she'd already told them.

Maybe she had.

"He had to pay for all of us," she stated, her head lowered. She wet her lips. "But when I saw him there, I couldn't just leave him. Why couldn't I leave him?"

She seemed to ask herself the question, her cringe evident.

Ambrose stepped forward. "She said she was with him in his final moments." He cuffed his arms, eyes heated on the body. "Though, lord knows the bastard didn't deserve it."

"But why would you come here, Em? *Why?*" Prinze asked her, her face in his hands. "You knew we were going to handle this." He brought her close, his mouth to her head. "We were going to take care of this. *I* was going to take care of this. Why didn't you let me?"

She had no words for him, silent. We all stood around as we watched a man comfort his wife, our own wives waiting for us, and I was sure I wasn't the only one who thought about a significant other at this moment. Instead of Prinze and December, I saw Bri and me here tonight, me holding *her* while she tried to explain to me what she'd come to do here tonight. She definitely would have too.

I knew my wife.

She wanted to protect our family just as much as I did because *that* was who she was, so I wasn't surprised to see December Prinze here this evening. We'd all been about to do the same thing and make the same sacrifice. I'd never been responsible for killing a man, but I'd been going to tonight, with the aid of friends, family. There wasn't a distinction anymore, and there hadn't been for a long time. When someone crossed us, they crossed all of us, and these men and their wives definitely had my family's back tonight. I was sure I wasn't the only one who'd never been responsible for taking a life before.

If that wasn't family, I didn't know what was.

CHAPTER
FIFTY

Royal

"She got lucky tonight, Royal. Real lucky." Knight Reed panned over to my car, my wife sitting inside. She'd gotten in after saying goodbye to Ramses Mallick. He had his own car parked away from the scene, and a couple of our military guys had taken him to get it. Knight's lips turned down. "We weren't even sure if we were going to get in tonight, but she managed to."

It hadn't taken us terribly long to find my father, but that hadn't been the problem. He'd been under the eye of many people and hadn't made it easy to get to him.

"How did she then?" I asked, and Knight braced his arms.

"The place had virtually no security," he said, shocking me. "Floor was basically completely clear, which was how we got in."

That didn't make sense.

"Like I said, she was lucky, and even more lucky because she hadn't been caught on any security footage. Our guys went to turn off the systems themselves, but it'd already been done. Apparently, the power went out in the whole hotel before that, and the feeds hadn't come back on with it."

Crazy.

"So you don't have any footage of what actually happened?" I wondered about the details, but honestly, not that much. My father was gone.

Finally gone.

I thought I'd feel something more about that, but I think my father had been dead to me for quite a long time. There wasn't anything to feel, and after the bullshit he'd been pulling in our lives for over twenty years…

My team was in the process of working on what we were doing as far as the Mallick shares Sloane had signed over, and it only helped that my father wouldn't be in the way to stall the process. There was a loophole in the paperwork Sloane had signed that my father had failed to tell her about, and I wasn't surprised he hadn't shared this detail with her. Knight and his online security team had been able to get a copy of what she'd signed, and she, gratefully, had a few months grace period to reverse her decision. This whole mess would be rectified quickly, and my son wouldn't be basically handed down blood money. My father had left all the shares to Dorian in the event of my dad's death, but a legacy like this I tried to keep away from my son. One of power and greed. My son and I weren't like my father.

We were better.

"No, we don't. I'm going to have our guys keep working on it, though," Knight continued, staring at December in the car again. "We'll figure out who did this."

Again, my concerns lay elsewhere, and after tonight, my father would be a distant memory. He'd be nothing but a missing person starting today, and this was something my friends and I were in the process of finishing. Jax was overseeing the cleanup upstairs as we spoke. Once the room was wiped and floor clear, my father's body would be properly disposed of, and then that would be it. He'd be gone, and hopefully, his dark legacy gone with him.

I left my friends to do that, something they volunteered for. Knight and Jax let me go back to my wife and Ramses to his own. They'd taken our burden for us.

They'd relieved us of more suffering.

————

I tended to my wife later that night, took care of her, listened to her. She'd had no business trying to handle my father herself, and it'd been foolish.

If I lost her…

So many things could have gone wrong today, my son without a mother. I couldn't imagine a life in which I didn't have Em in it, and the only thing that kept me sane was that things hadn't turned out that way. December was *safe*, and I was there to help her wash the blood away. We showered for a long time that night while I held her, the woman so goddamn strong and frustrating.

But I wouldn't have it any other way.

After she was clean, we went to bed and chose not to call Dorian until the morning. It was late, and we didn't want to wake him. He'd be coming home to us not long after that, though, and to a safe home. This family had suffered so much in the last year.

"Why couldn't I do it?" December asked me in the night, my arm around her, her face on my chest. She looked up at me. "Why couldn't I just walk away from him?"

She'd asked me this in the shower, wondering why, when she had found my father, she hadn't been able to just leave him to his own demise. We'd come to find out, my father had been shot in the rib cage three times and the murder weapon had never been found. The gun at the scene had been December's, unused, and our team had taken it with plans to dispose of it.

December buried her face in my neck, so warm, soft. She danced delicate fingers over my chest, each touch always giving me life. She pinched her eyes shut. "I even tried to help him."

Jax had told me about that, how she'd gone in and tried to stop the bleeding. That was why she'd had all my father's blood all over her. She'd been trying to help him, and even after she couldn't, she'd stayed.

"Because you didn't want him to die alone." My wife's lashes fanned in my direction after what I said, and I cupped her face, her eyes closing. I pressed my lips to her hair. "Because you're a good person, and you can't watch people suffer."

I honestly didn't know what would have happened had she found my father first. She told me how she'd threatened him, how she'd met with him and warned him. She'd said if he messed with our family, she'd come for him herself, and that was exactly what she had done. Would she have been able to go through with it? I didn't know, but gratefully, she wouldn't ever have to find out. She'd been kept out of this for a reason, all our wives had been. If someone had to get blood on their hands, it'd be my brothers and me. It was our sacrifice and cross to bear. My father may have helped bring me into this world, but I had no problem taking him out of it. The world and *our families* were better off without him.

"That's why you gave him another chance too," she said, her smile small. She touched my face, her fingers gliding over my stubble. "Because you're a good person."

She used to have to tell me that all the time, nearly every night when she did. She used to have to remind me, and it had taken me a long time before I'd actually started believing her. My father and his abuse had left me with so much rage over the years. He'd blamed me for things and his own suffering my entire life. The loss of my mother and sister had broken my father, and he'd chosen to turn into that monster he ultimately became.

But that didn't have to be my story.

I had a wife I adored and a wonderful son. I had a built-in family of friends, and a new story I'd been at the forefront of creating. I'd chosen a different path. Em and I both had. We could have suffered under the brevity of our pain.

We'd chosen to rise.

CHAPTER
FIFTY-ONE

I woke up when someone touched my cheek.

Ramses.

I shifted, but our son was between us, Ares's head on my shoulder. We must have both fallen asleep on the couch.

I played with his curls, smiling when his father eased over. Ramses kissed me with heat, here with us now, safe.

"What happened?" I whispered, trying not to wake our son. Ares had refused to go to sleep once he'd found out the men were moving in on Dorian's grandpa. He'd overhead the mothers talking, and he wouldn't leave me alone tonight. He was like his dad in that way, always trying to take care of me.

Ramses studied our son, adjusting the blanket over us both. "It's done," he said, my heart leaping. Ramses nodded. "We don't have to worry about him anymore."

He went on to tell me how, as well as the blanks in between. Someone had gone after Callum Prinze under our noses and saved this family from more bloodshed. From how it sounded, this had all started with revenge, and though I hadn't wanted this fight to end in more, I didn't think Dorian's grandfather had given us much of a choice.

"I can only sum up that he had a lot of enemies, and it was probably one of them," Ramses concluded, his expression hard, but it softened when it returned to our son. This family had gone through a lot, but *this* was always there to come back to, our peace. Ramses's eyes warmed, his hand on Ares's head. "Whatever the case, it's safe now."

Safe.

My husband told me more about it in the quiet. His night had been a hard one, a long one. Ares woke up as Ramses finished, but his father somehow convinced him to wait until morning to talk in detail about things. We just told our son everything was safe, and that we'd be able to bring Sloane home when the day came. Ares wanted to call her, but *I* convinced him to wait. It was late, and they both needed to sleep.

It was hard to listen to my own words and not call my daughter in the middle of the night, but I forced myself to. Instead, I made sure Ares got to bed, which relieved my husband to go take a shower before heading there himself. Ramses had put on a tough face that he hadn't let tonight affect him, but he looked tired, and he needed to relax.

I told Ares I loved him before closing the door, and when I found the room I'd been staying in, I heard more than one voice inside.

My heart lifted hearing hers.

"Ares said you just got back," Sloane said. "I told him to text me when you did. I hope you don't mind I called. I know you're probably going to bed."

In the two seconds since I'd left him, my son had managed to text his twin. I shook my head but couldn't fight the smile on my face.

"Of course I don't mind," Ramses said, his voice thick, emotional. I eased a look into the room and saw him sitting on the bed. He must have gotten his shower done, his hair wild and perfect like I liked it. He had his phone up, and our daughter's face was on the screen. "I love hearing from you, and everything's fine. I'm fine, and you didn't have to call."

I started to go inside the room but stopped. My head touching the door frame, I enjoyed watching the two of them together.

"I don't know what Ares told you, but everything's safe now. *You're safe,* and we're going to bring you home," Ramses said, smiling. "We're bringing Dorian home too. As soon as we can. Both of you."

She didn't say anything for a beat.

But then…

"Thanks, Dad," she said, my breath in-taking, and Ramses didn't move, his lips parting. She shook her head. "Whatever you and everyone else did, just… thank you. And thank Mom too."

I swallowed, coming into the room. I'd told Ramses what Sloane had said, how she'd told me she loved me and sent Ramses her love too. It'd been an emotional moment for my husband and me on the phone.

I came over, and Ramses blinked in my direction. Taking my hand, he had me sit on the bed beside him. His mouth warmed my hand before he fit us both into the screen.

"We miss you," he said, his voice tight and fighting emotion. Wrapping his arm around me, he kissed my hair before looking at our daughter. "We're bringing you home, as soon as we can in the morning."

"We love you," I said, before touching the screen, and Sloane did too. It was like the distance between us and her didn't matter in that moment. It was inconsequential. I told her Callum Prinze wouldn't break this family, and he hadn't. Not even with everything he did.

I didn't know how long we talked to Sloane, but I remembered every word of that conversation. I'd never forget the day my daughter first called me her mother, nor would her father forget his own acknowledgment. I saw that in his eyes as we talked about it after, emotion taking its hold over us both. I cried, but there was no pain.

Ramses let me cry my happy tears, his embrace warm as we lay together on the bed. Like so many times, he was there to hold me, but this time, he didn't need to tell me things would be okay. He'd said that so many times to me over the years, talking me off cliffs. Especially when Sloane had initially been taken. He'd said I would be okay and that the pair of us would be fine.

But I doubt even he knew how right he'd ultimately be.

CHAPTER
FIFTY-TWO

Ares

My phone rang just when it felt like I'd fallen asleep for the second time tonight.

Bru Sloane.

Squinting at the screen, I found that weird. Bru was just down the hall from me so if he needed something, he just could have come in.

I answered. "Hello?"

"Wolf." Short breaths followed, like he was moving around or something. "Hey. Can you meet me downstairs? I'm out back behind the safe house."

The fuck?

I sat up. "Uh, why are you out back behind the house?"

"I can't explain. Just… can you hurry? Please?"

The guy was breathing, *hard*, and he clicked off the line before I could ask any more questions. He sounded freaked the hell out.

He sounded scared.

I didn't know what to make of it. I just slipped on some

shoes and grabbed a hoodie. What the fuck was he doing outside and not in bed? He didn't know things were safe now and that the parents had stopped Dorian's grandpa. The mothers hadn't shared the details of how when I'd heard them talking to the dads about moving in on the prick.

But I could have guessed.

My dad had seemed okay tonight when I'd seen him, and I'd asked for specifics, but he hadn't given them. I'd actually only gone to bed because he'd promised to talk to me about it with Mom after Sloane came back. They'd said they wanted to speak to us about it together.

I didn't know what that meant either, but I hadn't cared. I just knew our parents had made things safe again, and that'd been enough for me to be able to go to sleep.

I had been until this shit now with whatever was going on with Bru. It shouldn't be physically possible for him to be outside. We had security everywhere at the safe house.

I saw no one on the way downstairs, but I knew we had agents watching the house. There might be less now with Dorian's grandpa no longer in the wind. I didn't know, but Bru definitely shouldn't just be outside.

The cold shot straight through my fucking body the moment I hit the backyard, and I grabbed my arms. "Bru? Kid?"

I whispered-shouted his name, spotting him not far from the house. He lingered in the shadows, appearing to freeze just as much as me. Even in the dull lights on the property, he was visibly shaking, his head whipping around. Snow up to my ankles, I crunched my way out to him. He spotted me and ran straight toward me.

"Wolf? Wolf!"

"Kid? What the fuck you doing out here?" But then, he showed me.

He didn't have to do much.

He merely had to step into the light flooding off the house, his face splattered in red dots.

His hands.

The same pattern followed along his chest, and my eyes widened.

"Wolf, I..." He held his hands out, staring at them. The kid was two shades of white, eyes red and bloodshot. He looked up. "Ares."

I didn't know what I was looking at. I didn't know what he was *showing* me but that was definitely blood. "Kid, are..." I swallowed. "Are you hurt?"

He shook his head, incessant about it. "It's not mine. It's not mine."

"Whose is it?" I stepped close, and he backed up.

"Don't. Don't touch me. Don't—" His lips pinched together, a fear lacing his eyes I'd never seen. "Ares, I need your help. I fucked up and..." He gazed around. "I'm scared, bro. I need help."

"Okay. How can I help?"

"I don't know what to do. I don't. I..." He had his hands up now, looking like he was about to run. He laced them above his head. "I shot Callum."

What?

"I shot him. He went down. I don't know if he's dead. I don't know if he's sending someone for me. I just ran. I *ran,* Ares. Please help me."

Oh my God.

His hands shook in his hair. "He's probably sending people after me, and I—"

"No. He's..." I raised a hand. "Come inside. Come with me."

I waved him to come, but he was panicked and wasn't moving. I ended up grabbing him, physically pulling him with me inside. His legs weren't moving right, and again, I had to drag him to get him to come with me. I didn't think we were making much noise, but Thatcher's door opened as soon as we passed it. The guy had sleep in his eyes, but they shot open when he saw me with the kid.

"The fuck," Thatch started, but I growled.

"Shut the fuck up," I warned, low, but was loud enough that he did. I told him I was taking the kid back to his room, and Thatch said he'd go get Wells. Bru looked like he wanted to protest about that, but at this point, he wasn't able to do much anyway besides walk.

He wasn't even doing that right. The guy was literally convulsing. I got him into his bathroom, and by then, Thatcher had gotten Wells. We all piled into a bathroom that barely fit one of us, the kid in front of the sink while he rehashed what had happened to Thatcher and Wells.

"How the fuck did you even get outside and around security?" Wells asked him while I helped the kid wash his hands and face. He started to by himself but was having a hard time with it.

"I heard. I heard…" He closed his eyes, taking a second when I told him to slow down. With a breath, he opened them. "I heard your moms talking earlier tonight that your dads were going after Callum. Said they'd found him and I heard something about a hotel. Where he was at, I guess."

"I heard the same thing," I said, news to Thatcher and Wells when they looked at me. "You guys were asleep."

"Well, you should have fucking woken us up," Thatcher grit, and Wells nodded.

"Agreed," Wells said. "But that still doesn't explain why you're covered in blood and managed to get around security."

"There weren't many guys around tonight," Bru stated, looking at us. "The ones who were left mentioned that many of them were going over to that hotel to help. They talked about the room too and where Callum was at. Anyway, with security thin, I found an opening. Took a gun before I left. I lifted one off one of the security guys' yesterday. I wanted to go after Callum myself."

What the hell?

Bru rubbed his hands, rocking. "I know your moms said that your dads were going after him, but…" His expression changed, hardening. "I also heard them say Callum had security, and it'd be hard for any of them to get to him. But if Callum knew it was me, just me… that I came to see him, I *knew* he'd see me. If anything, just to use me. Use me against Sloane, and he wasn't going to fucking use her anymore!"

The bathroom silenced, Bru's face red.

He snarled. "He wasn't going to use her anymore. Me." He glanced up. "I wasn't going to let him, and when I got there, he let me right in. I shot him. Shot him three times." He lifted his hands, clean now, but he analyzed them as if he still saw blood. "He went down, but I didn't see what happened after that. I just left like a little bitch."

"Kid…" I swallowed, and he cringed.

"I came back here after. Took a ride share and the guy's probably wondering about that too. I had blood all over me." His lips moved, quivering. "I'm going to go to prison and—"

I grabbed his arms, making him look at me. "What did you do with the gun?"

"Tossed it."

"Do you remember where?"

He nodded. "In a lake. Why?"

"We just need all the facts," I said, putting off that I was calmer than I actually was. I grabbed Thatch. "Go get my parents. My dad's back. He's with my mom, and, Wells, you go get the rest of the moms."

They both started to go without question, but Bru leaped toward them. "No. No, if you do that, they'll call the cops. I'll get locked up. I don't want to go to prison, Ares."

"Hey. Hey." I got his shoulders, keeping his focus. "Our parents are going to help. *My mom and dad* are going to help, and they're not going to let anything happen to you. None of our parents will."

"But Callum," he started, his eyes coated in a wet sheen. "He's going to send someone after me. He's going to *kill me,* Ares."

I shook my head. "My parents told me tonight things are safe," I said, telling the group. "They're actually bringing Sloane and D home in the morning. They wouldn't be doing that if Callum was still an issue."

More than one person went quiet, silent. My parents had told me the situation had been taken care of, but it seemed only the four of us in the room knew how. Bruno Sloane had taken someone out for my sister…

His sister.

The kid and I were connected, and he'd done something for her I could never thank him enough for. If it was true and he'd done what he had, that was something none of us kids had been able to do. We'd been forced to sit back while our parents took care of things. They'd wanted to protect us.

Meanwhile, Bruno Sloane had protected all of us.

"He's dead?" Bru said the words in a haunted state. I was sure he'd wanted to protect Sloane tonight, but who ever wanted to take a life? The kid had a good heart, a pure heart, so doing what he'd done had to have taken something deep inside him.

It might have even taken something from him.

I think Wells, Thatcher, and I all saw what that same sacrifice had done to Dorian. He'd been different after he'd gotten back, darker.

Bru looked at us. "I'm scared."

He'd said that outside, but he didn't need to be. We had his back. *I* had his back. "Nothing is going to happen to you. I'm going to take care of you. You understand?"

"But why?" He shook his head, cringing. "I've been

nothing but an asshole to you lately. Trusted Callum. Let him hurt her. Hurt you and your family."

He kept getting this wrong. Dorian's grandpa didn't just hurt my family. He hurt *our* family, the kid's and mine. "You've had my sister's back basically her whole life. You were with her when I couldn't be, so as far as I'm concerned, that makes us boys for life."

"Brothers," Wells said, taking one of the kid's shoulders. "We're brothers. All of us."

"We are." Thatcher completed the circle, and if D was here, he'd be doing the same. Our brotherhood wasn't just biological, and we weren't just friends. We were champions for each other and protected in whatever way we had to because *that* was what family did for each other. The kid was one of us.

He was legacy just as much as any of us.

CHAPTER
FIFTY-THREE

Prom Night

Sloane

The seasons changed, and once again, my life changed with it. Things slowed down, and my safety, along with my family's, got *safer*. I had a family, and it went far beyond the reaches of Bruno and me. We didn't just have a family. We had a universe of people and love around us, and with that love, came protection. Bru got to spend the rest of his junior year without living in fear, and I got to do the same with my senior year. We got to go to prom.

And my little brother kind of killed it in a tuxedo.

"Stop *messing* with it. You're going to fuck it up," he growled, hitting my hands off his tie. He'd tried to do it himself, but it was all messed up so I was fixing it. His eyes lifted. "Sloane, it's fine."

"It's not fine because it looked like shit before." And if he hit me again, I'd fuck *his hair* up, which was something else he'd spent like a million years on.

Bru growled again, but he did let me fix his tie to my liking. He was letting me do a lot of things these days, and soon, we wouldn't even be at the same school. I'd be graduating and moving on, so we needed to cherish this time together.

I think he knew that, which was why he let me fawn all over him. He'd moved back in, finally *home* and where he belonged, and it seemed so long ago our lives had been upheaved.

We got reminders, though, sometimes, like last week. We'd both been allowed to skip school to take a day trip. The pair of us had arranged a final resting place for Marilyn and Godfrey Sloane, his parents and mine for a time. They'd been that in every sense of the word when it counted and had paid the ultimate price trying to help me.

I could never forget that, so many sacrifices made for me. I'd finally started to talk about those things in my own therapy sessions, and sometimes Bru came with me. He had his own for his own things, stuff that had happened, and with a trusted family counselor. He got to share what was on his heart, and I'd seen the light return to his eyes in the passing days since. My brother had made a mistake by going over the Legacy families' heads and trying to do things himself. He'd acted impulsively, but with the help of those same families, he gratefully wouldn't have to pay for that mistake for the rest of his life. They'd taken care of it. Taken care of us, and Bru had gotten to *walk away* from that night with Callum like we all had.

I couldn't be more grateful.

Of course, those specifics had stayed with the families, the parents. They'd done things behind the scenes to make sure my brother had a life, and as far as I knew, the world believed Callum Prinze to be a missing person. He'd gone on a trip and never returned, and though I didn't condone what Bru had felt he had to do, I couldn't bring myself to ever chastise him when it came up. He'd wanted to protect me, and if the tables had been turned, I didn't know what I would have done. I know I would have protected him too, though, and done whatever I had to do to make sure that happened.

I suppose, I know what I would have done.

"Not bad, I guess," Bru said in the mirror, admiring my work. He was rocking Armani today, and I'd heard Ares had a similar tux. I hadn't seen him yet. I'd been trying to help Bru make sure his tie didn't look like crap. Bru's gaze hit me in the mirror. "Nothing like you, though."

My eyes lifted, my black dress long and with a shimmer. The slit basically hit my hip and was held together by a single strand of delicate rhinestones across my thigh. The dress itself was backless too, and the dark prince would probably have my ass tonight for being so revealing. I cared less about that and more about pissing him off, though. He'd told me I had to wear black tonight because he was a control freak and said we had to match each other.

Not liking being told what to do, I'd found the most scandalous dress I could find, and Bow had nearly fainted at the shop when I'd picked it out. She'd called me trouble and told me I was looking for it. Apparently, wearing black was just what Legacy did at these things, and Dorian would get me for being defiant.

I'd like to see him try.

"You look truly gorgeous, sis," Bru said. He eyed my necklace, the one Ares had given me. I never took it off, but I never went anywhere without my own personal Court ring either. Yes, Dorian had convinced me to join, and Bru had too.

Bruno and I had the same rings.

The dark prince had rubies in his for the eyes, but Bru and I had had black diamonds put in ours. The diamonds were *our* thing and something we shared, just like I had with Ares and our necklaces. My necklace looked even more fancy these days since that was where I now wore the dark prince's gift. He'd given me that ring with rubies for eyes, and I wanted it close to my heart.

That was the place it should always be.

I touched my ring with black diamonds to Bru's. I did have that bond with Ares and our necklaces, but I also had a bond with Bruno.

"Thanks, dork," I said, referring to his earlier compliment, and he smiled.

"No problem, dorkette." He nudged, and I'd give him a noogie except for the fact that he had spent so much time on his hair. He smiled, and I hugged him, telling him he looked beautiful too. This got me another nudge, but we both looked up when a knock hit Bru's door. He told whoever to come in, and the room filled quickly.

"Are you guys ready? We need pictures." Her camera recording, the mayor of Maywood Heights made it into the room. She was all grins, her husband's hand in hers. Ramses wasn't without his own phone, taking impromptu pictures of Bru and me like paparazzi.

He even made sound effects.

The gesture was as completely nerdy as it was wonderful, and Bru and I made a show of trying to hide our faces.

"Please. Please. No pictures," I stated, joking and being overdramatic about it. Ares brought up the rear behind the parental units, and when he closed the door, his eyes expanded in my direction.

He shot a finger at me. "You're wearing that?"

"Tried to tell her," Bru said, looking at me, and I lifted my eyes.

"Well, I think she's beautiful," came from the smallest paparazzi in the room. Brielle took my hand. "Truly lovely, honey."

"Thanks, Mom," I said, and she pulled me in for a hug. I

squeezed her just as hard, having an out-of-body experience here. I had a mother. I had one and she was taking pictures of me before *prom.*

I had a father too, and though my dad didn't look like he loved my outfit, he was definitely too polite to comment about it. Ramses's eyes warmed. "You do look beautiful, love."

"Thanks, Dad." He hugged me too while Brielle gushed over Bru in his tux. Meanwhile, my twin gave me the stink eye over her shoulder.

"He's going to kill you," I heard Ares growl before our mom shut him up and made us take a picture together. Ares forced a smile with fake teeth, which dropped the moment the photo was taken. In fact, he'd done it so well something told me he'd probably had to do quite a few of these photo ops before everyone came in here. His eyes narrowed coolly at me. "If he doesn't, I will."

"No one's killing anyone. Jeez," Brielle stated, her eyes lifting. She forced all three of us in a picture together before getting one with just Ares and Bru in their tuxedos. They stood like a pair of dudes with their hands clasped in front of their tuxes, no smiles, of course, because again *dudes.* Ares had actually done something with his hair too, his curls up and his undercut freshly buzzed. He also wore his necklace like me, the silver beneath his bow tie. He never took it off, also like me, and I suppose I'd never told him what that meant to me, or what the gift of my own necklace meant. I guess I never had to.

It was unsaid.

I honestly still couldn't believe I had a twin, and if he hadn't come at me all aggressive, I might have told him how handsome he looked. As far as I knew, he didn't have a date tonight, but I'd heard that was by choice. Word through the grapevine was, Legacy didn't take dates to dances, the arrogant fucks. I, of course, was the exception with Dorian, but that didn't really count, considering I was Legacy.

I definitely would be giving them all a hard time about that when I saw them tonight. They were all supposed to meet us at the house in a bit. Apparently, whenever Legacy went to a dance, the parents all met up at one of the Legacy homes to do all the necessary pictures with the kids. I thought that was sweet, but Dorian had rolled his eyes when he'd told me about it.

The three of us here now allowed Ramses and Brielle to get their own pictures in, and Ares only grumbled through, well, all of it. This was old hat for him, but I loved every minute of it.

It was fabulous.

It was so nice to have a family, Bru and I really hamming it up and enjoying it. We all broke Ares down a bit too and got him to smile in a few. A real one, not a fake one. Ramses announced the group would probably all get here soon, and I thought we'd go downstairs right away, but we didn't. Ramses and Brielle actually asked Bru and me to sit because they wanted to talk to us.

Ares chose to stand, his hands in his pockets. He lounged against the wall with what I'd call something of a knowing expression, and when I eyed him, he shrugged.

"We've been wanting to ask you both this for a while actually," Brielle said, taking Ramses's hand. He squeezed it before Brielle's eyes warmed in Bru's and my direction. "And to Bru specifically."

"We know you're seventeen, but we wanted to know if maybe you'd like to be an official part of this family," Ramses said, his smile wide. "On paper and legally."

"Basically, they want to know if you want to be my sibling in the official sense." Ares touched his chest, being cocky about it. He grinned. "Because being a Mallick is great, but being my legal brother is obviously the best part."

"Ares," Brielle chastised, and I would have said something too if I wasn't in shock.

Bru was too. His lips parted. "Like adoption? You want to..." He swallowed, glancing at me before his attention returned to the couple. "Adopt me?"

Ramses lifted a hand. "Like I said, I know you're seventeen, and it probably sounds silly, a technicality, but..." Putting his arm around Brielle, he rubbed her shoulder. "It's not to us. We'd *love* for you to be an official part of this family, and if you'd have us, we'd love for that to be the case and for the world to know your place in this family."

I covered my mouth, no words. We'd really all come a long way since the holidays and everything that had happened. We'd been able to reverse everything with the Mallick shares. Dorian's father had spotted a provision in everything I'd signed, and with Bru coming back here and moving in, things had started to feel, well, amazing and *finally*. The scars were still there, and I didn't think any of us would ever truly move on from what Callum Prinze had done to cast a shadow over our lives, but we were trying. We were *all* trying.

Bru had been trying too and had been a part of this family. Reaching out, Brielle took his hand. "Of course, we aren't trying to replace your own parents," she said, and I think all of us knew that Godfrey and Marilyn Sloane did have a place in all this too. They'd helped Callum steal time, yes, but they had tried to fix things in the end.

And that did mean something.

Ramses put his hand on Bru's shoulder. "But we'd love to be there for you in their absence."

Bru looked at me then, his face flushed, but his attention drifted to my twin when he came over. Ares touched his arm too, squeezing it, and if two people had gotten close recently, it was definitely the two of them. Ares had been there for Bru when he'd come forward with the truth, and Bru had trusted him that night. Bru had gone *to him* instead of against him, and something had happened that night after he had. The two had their own link, a brotherhood, and that went for Bru and the other Legacy boys as well. I always caught them all playing basketball with each other, and in the halls together at school. They all *welcomed* Bru, along with Bow, the little sister of the group and one of my best friends.

I had too many to count these days.

Bru was in this world just as much as me, and it seemed like now, he knew it. He smiled at Ramses, Brielle, and Ares.

"I'd like that," he said, scanning the circle. "I'd really like that actually."

I hugged him, and he laughed when Ares brought the circle in. Ares chuckled. "Another Sloane-Mallick. Definitely like the sound of that."

Recently, I'd gotten my name changed. I was Noa Sloane-Mallick now, but this was a technicality too. It'd never been about the name.

It'd been about this.

My mother, when she put her arms around her three kids, and my father, when he put his arms around her, embracing us all. That first day Ramses had put us in a huddle the world had seemed so dark, and I wasn't sure we'd ever get to this point.

We'd ended up traveling so far beyond it.

CHAPTER
FIFTY-FOUR

Sloane

"Big?"

My voice startled Ares. Jumping, he'd been lingering outside of Ramses's home office, the door cracked. He lifted a hand. "Little… Hey, you should be downstairs. The group will be here any minute. You should go meet them."

And why wasn't he? He'd been ahead of me after we both left Bru's room following the pictures.

Ramses had actually been the first to leave. He'd gotten a call, and after looking at his phone, he'd said he had to go take care of something. He'd mentioned heading to his office and said he'd meet us downstairs after he handled whatever he had to handle. I assumed that meant his call.

That had left the three of us kids and Brielle, but Ares and I both had decided to give Bru and her the room. We wanted to give them some time since well… that was his mom.

It'd all been a really special moment, and I was still on the high of it. I angled close to Ares. "What are you doing?"

I started to look into the room, but he raised his hand

again. He put his finger to his lips, and I was definitely intrigued now. His growl was low. "Seriously, little. Go downstairs—"

"Thanks for seeing me, Dad."

What the…

I shouldered against Ares upon hearing *our dad's* voice, and I think he only let me because he didn't want me to make any more noise. He hovered a head above me while we both peered inside that room and saw our father. Ramses was behind his desk, standing while another man stood in front of it, his hair graying white, curly. He wore a silver suit, dark in tone, with a black dress shirt and matching tie.

And he looked a lot like our dad.

My mouth parted. I gazed up, but Ares wasn't looking at me. He had his eyebrows narrowed, hard, and only in the direction of that room.

The man in the silver suit put his hands together, one flesh and the other… something else. Fingers of dark metal braced the man's hand, a prosthetic. The man nodded and was older than our dad, much older. "I was surprised to hear from you, son."

Son…

"I'm sure you know the surprise lies more with me," Ramses said, his hands in his pockets. "You were presumed dead many years ago, Dad. A bombing in Italy."

This was news to Ares, his head lifting. His jaw shifted a little, and I held onto the door.

"The authorities believed as much. I didn't argue with it." The man… *our grandfather* worked his prosthetic hand. He looked at Ramses. "How did you know I was alive?"

"Actually, our family lawyer," Ramses said, causing our grandfather to blink. "He wanted me to know that the kids' shares in Mallick were being talked about, my kids."

Our grandfather said nothing but did wet his lips.

"Said someone wanted to make sure things turned out okay with all that and, well, Callum. That the kids got what was theirs." Ramses nodded. "But most importantly, that what was *theirs* stuck, even if a certain someone was still alive. Said you gave them everything and wanted it to stay that way."

Ares directed a look down at me, his eyebrows squished together, and I was sure my expression matched.

Our grandfather laughed. "Fredrick never could keep his mouth shut. Could he?"

"Well, he cares about this family, and he's also how I found you. He gave me your contact and said you were recently in town," Ramses continued. He drew fingers down his mouth before asking his father to take a seat. Ramses then explained he didn't have long to speak with him. "It's the kids' prom night. I need to be there for that."

"I understand," the older man said, crossing his legs in front of the desk. "Is that why you asked to see me? About the kids' shares? Well, you don't have to worry about anything. Everything unlocked to the children after I was presumed dead, but I made sure with Fredrick that all stayed, regardless of the fact. They have everything, and it's all legal. I assure you."

I shook my head, and Ares did too. I knew he'd never met our grandfather, and after everything with Dorian's, I guess, well, I'd assumed the man was the same. He was a man obsessed with greed and power, and it was because of our grandfather all this had begun. Callum had gone after me due to an obligation *our granddad* had failed to fulfill.

Ramses's smile was subtle after what his father said. He sat back in his chair, his fingers together. "I guess I have another thing to thank you for, I suppose," he stated before opening his desk. He presented a small object, and even from here what was clearly a flash drive could be made out. He put it on the desk. "A man known as Lucas Gray presented this to me not too long ago, a man who, until recently, my friends and I believed had been in the wind."

Lucas?

My heart hammered in my chest. Lucas had worked for Callum.

And if he was still out there…

He'd held me against my will along with Callum, helped him, and killed Godfrey. He'd been a part of this whole thing.

My grandfather simply stared at the drive as Ramses rolled forward in his chair.

"Told me it was everything I needed to let the world know what Callum Prinze did to my daughter and your grand-daughter." Ramses sat back. "And to my surprise when I listened, it was. There's a detailed confession on there by none other than Callum Prinze himself. It was the night he told my daughter everything and her voice is on there as well. It's authentic."

What?

Ares blinked my way, his look of confusion shared. Why would Lucas give Ramses that confession?

"Said it was mine to do with as I wished, and when I asked him why, he told me this was at the request of his employer." Ramses eyes narrowed. "Said who he *actually* worked for wanted me to have this, and no one was more surprised than me when I looked into that. I did find a name connected, but it wasn't Callum Prinze or even his alias Callum Montgomery."

The older man shifted in his chair. "Son—"

"It was you, Dad," Ramses stated, causing both Ares and me to twitch. "Lucas works for you, or at least, well, he did before *you died.* He was head of your security, and don't deny it. There's sheets of evidence, and my people are still finding more."

"I wasn't going to deny it, Ramses," the man stated, I think shocking the whole room and even Ramses himself.

Our dad's brow lifted after what his father said. Our grandfather shook his head. "It's just unfortunate. Lucas was supposed to provide you what you needed, and that was supposed to be the end of it. There didn't need to be a spectacle or even this meeting. I just wanted you to have the truth and a way to expose Callum."

"Even in death?" Ramses asked, and our grandfather sighed.

"I wanted you to have that option, yes, felt you deserved it, and needless to say, it was the least I could do. I mean, all this was me…" His voice broke off, thick before he pressed a knuckle to his lips. He faced Ramses. "Had I not been thinking more about the future of my company than the implications my decisions could potentially have on my own family, none of this would have happened. You and Brielle wouldn't have lost eighteen goddamn years with your daughter, and my grandson wouldn't have lost his sister."

My lips parted, Ares's too. I squeezed my necklace, and when he noticed, he braced my arm.

"I pleaded so hard with that son of a bitch. I had no evidence he took my granddaughter, but I just knew… *I knew* he had something to do with it when I heard," our grandpa said, glancing away. "It just made sense, and he had threatened me before. Said he'd take everything I loved away from me, but I didn't take that to mean he'd ruin my family's lives."

Ramses said nothing, watching his father.

"I told him I'd give him everything." Our grandfather looked up. "*Anything* he wanted just to give her back, but he laughed at me and claimed, once again, he had nothing to do with it." His hand covered his prosthetic. "The truth was more than evident when he tried to have me killed. Said the meeting in Italy was to reconcile, but the last thing he said to me before he left that cafe was that karma was a son of a bitch. He'd get what he wanted, and he'd watch my world burn even if I wasn't around to." His head shook. "The bastard left, and the bomb went off shortly after that."

Which meant Callum had cared more about revenge than anything else. Our grandfather had been willing to give him what he'd wanted.

I rubbed my chest, and Ares rubbed my arm. He had this look on his face, a rage heating his dark eyes.

Ramses's lips parted. "Why didn't you come to me, Dad?"

"I had no proof, son. Proof he took her or anything else. Not to mention, I knew you wouldn't have seen me anyway."

Ramses glanced away, the action of which was very telling. Ramses had talked to me about his dad, but it hadn't been easy the one time he had. There was pain there, and though he may have gotten past that in his father's death, that didn't mean this was the case when our grandfather had still been alive. There was ill will just like with Callum and his own family.

"Instead, I kept my focus on searching. Trying to find my granddaughter, and the search never stopped despite time and time again coming up with nothing," Grandpa said. "I looked for her for years discreetly, quietly. If Callum knew I was alive, who knew what he'd do to my family."

"He was good at covering his tracks," Ramses said. "Pretty much anyone connected to my daughter's fake adoption he had killed." Ramses cracked his knuckles. "He made it virtually impossible to find her."

The dark prince had said many of the people who'd helped with my adoption had died. Ares had called that justice.

But none of us had known that justice had been murder.

These were obviously things the parents had found out during their own investigation.

My God.

"But one person who's not so good at covering his tracks is my father," Ramses continued, his head tilted. "And before you try to deny this, I have evidence of this too. More than one person saw your Lucas Gray leaving the room housing the hotel's security footage. Footage that was conveniently *shut off* just before our people were about to move on Callum."

Whoa.

"That was you, Dad, but something tells me that security room going dark wasn't just for us. I mean, how could it be? No one knew we were coming. And yet, there were no feeds available to capture what was about to happen in that hotel. There was also little to no security on that floor, which was quite unusual as well. My people weren't even certain they'd be able to get in and get to Callum Prinze since he had so much, but that night they were just gone. The man was unattended, and the only one around was Lucas Gray, a man who worked for you."

The older man looked up. "What are you trying to say, son?"

"I'm sure you see what I'm trying to say," Ramses continued. "Lucas Gray obviously had a job. And one was obviously this." Ramses held up the flash drive. "This confession. It had Callum's truths, but like you said, these were probably just for me. Justice was going to be ultimately served in another way, wasn't it, Dad?"

The man laced his hands, and Ramses eased forward.

"Lucas Gray was there to carry out that justice," Ramses said. "An occurrence that would have happened had no other forces been at hand."

I think we all knew those other forces. Between the Legacy families and Bru, justice had been served that night.

But it sounded like they had only happened to get there first.

Ramses didn't continue, but the older man's silence was everything. He started to speak, but then Ramses held up his hand.

"And if you did have a guy there, one to get that confession and ultimately take out that hit," Ramses started, his throat jumping. "You had someone watching over the situation. You had someone there with Callum Prinze, alongside him and watching his moves. Maybe even guiding them."

I looked up, my twin brother as well. Ares didn't seem to breathe above me.

"You had someone watching over my kid," Ramses stated, his knuckles touching his mouth. He nodded. "You had someone there to protect her and her brother Bruno."

The chain of my necklace dug into my fingers, my throat thickening, and Ares's nostrils flared above me. There was a plead in my twin brother's eyes in the direction of our grandfather, something deep, and I wondered if I had that too. We'd both had so much darkness in our lives, and *just once*, we wanted to have some light. We wanted something to be true and to be able to believe in it.

We wanted to believe in someone.

The older man cradled his prosthetic hand, and though I wondered if he lost it that day at that cafe, I wondered more about him. I wondered about his soul and if there truly was something to believe in within him. If people could change themselves, change their legacy.

"Dad?" There was a plead in Ramses's eyes too, his voice. "Did you have someone on the front lines looking after my daughter?"

Grandpa Mallick looked up, his eyes sad. "I'm the reason someone had to be at the front lines looking after your daughter, my granddaughter." His gaze cut away. "And Lucas did what he could. Callum didn't always reveal his moves right away. Things like that fire. The plan there was to save Sloane, make it look like Godfrey went insane, and for Callum Prinze to be the one to save her and bring her back to this town. He didn't tell Lucas this until the plan was in action and even had Godfrey fire on Lucas, force him to defend himself to make it look good."

Oh, my god.

"Godfrey Sloane had basically been put on a suicide mission, and Lucas informed me Prinze had been able to convince Godfrey to do it with the promise of keeping his son Bru safe in all this."

Another lie. Callum had every intention of killing my brother. He was sick, a madman.

"I suppose Prinze thought Sloane's save would make him look good to the city, to Sloane herself, and to his family." Grandpa's jaw tightened. "And everything that happened to her I'll never be able to forgive myself for. I'm the reason she needed protection. The choices I made." He squeezed his eyes. "I found out too late where she was. There'd been a leak at Fredrick's firm. A guy there had been feeding Callum information for years about our family. That's how Callum knew to get to her in the hospital and about the births in the first place. The traitor even helped with the goddamn adoption."

His voice rattled the air, and I covered my mouth.

Ares glanced my way. "D said someone who worked for our grandfather helped with the coverup, a lawyer," he whispered. He looked into the room. "Sounds like that's how Callum got intel on our family."

I rubbed my chest, and Ramses nodded.

"We know all about Fredrick's associate Dane Masterson and found out recently about his passing. He'd been in hiding before," Ramses said. "I can imagine because pretty much everyone else involved in my daughter's kidnapping was dead. I'm sure Dane connected the dots that Callum was going after people."

Our grandfather said nothing, and Ramses leaned forward.

"But that one was on you this time, right?" Ramses asked,

both my twin and I blinking. "I could go on about the evidence we've gathered there, but I won't. Dane Masterson's car accident was you, his death you. It was because that one was personal."

A short breath left from our grandfather's lips, his eyes narrowed. "He hurt our family, son," he said, his voice struggled, tight. "And I can make no apologies for that."

He seemed to battle something as he stared away, like he had no regrets but wasn't necessarily at peace with what he'd done.

I suppose those answers only resided with him.

Ramses picked up the flash drive. "You want me to expose Callum then? Tell the world the truth about what he did to our family?"

Ramses asked the question almost like a son to a father, like he truly did want his advice, and our grandfather sighed.

"That information is yours, Ramses. Like I said, it's your right, and I…" He worked his prosthetic again. "I needed you to have it. I only wished I'd been able to get it to you sooner. It took Lucas some time to get Callum's confession. Longer than either of us hoped. My guys only found out about the leak in Fredrick's firm and the information Dane had about who your daughter was now shortly before Callum made moves to bring her to the city. We had to act smartly after that, the situation delicate. Her safety was priority, and we didn't know Callum's plans for her. We also couldn't have him deny anything. He was so good at that."

He was. He'd had the whole world believing he'd been helping me, had *me* believing that.

Ramses braced the drive. "Had we not interceded that night at the hotel, it really would have been you, wouldn't it? Taking out Callum Prinze?"

The older man's lips turned down, but he didn't have to say anything. During the entire conversation, the evidence was clear. He'd had Lucas there for a reason. He had been given the job to look after me while he sought for the truth, and once he'd gotten it, he'd been given next steps to take care of Callum. Lucas Gray was supposed to kill Callum Prinze, and those directions had been made by none other than my grandfather, a man who was now giving my twin brother and me all he had. Ares and I had heard crystal clear that our grandfather's shares were now ours, and that was insane. Especially considering how all this had started.

What had started out as a plot for revenge by Callum Prinze had ended in a man trying to make things right. Callum had been doing nothing but trying to take power, power from me and my family to give to his own. Meanwhile, my grandfather had sacrificed his. He'd done everything he could to make things right and protect his family.

He'd protected me.

Ramses started to say something after his dad didn't speak, but then the door cracked.

It was on purpose.

Ares, who'd been watching with me, left the door frame. He strode over to our grandfather, and I wasn't far behind.

Ramses rose from his chair. "Ares…"

I didn't know why Ramses didn't continue with what he said. But I think, like me, he was wondering what his son was doing. I was wondering what *I* was doing, but whatever that consisted of would be standing by my brother. Ares worked his hands, and our grandfather got up from his chair. He was a tall man too, broad-shouldered. He stared at Ares and me in awe as we came over, and by then, Ramses came around his desk.

Our dad stood behind us, a hand on each shoulder. He exchanged a glance between Ares and me. "Ares, Sloane, this is your grandfather," he said, his hands leaving us. "My father."

The older man stood there before us, and from the way his suit fell, that prosthetic went clear up to his shoulder. He started to reach that hand out, but stopped as if he'd just noticed it. He clenched the metal hand, hesitating. He didn't approach any farther.

He didn't have to.

Ares took a step forward, and I think to everyone's surprise. He wet his lips. "You really did all those things?" he said before looking at me. His jaw shifted. "You helped my sister?"

I glanced our grandfather's way, the man's hands coming together. His chin lifted. "I hindered her more, and I'm sorry for that." He looked at me, his smile shaky, small but also sad. "I'm sorry."

My throat thickened, my vision blurry. I didn't know what to say, but like that first step forward, my twin took another. Ares put his hand out directly in front of our grandfather. He reached for the man's hand, but only the one my grandfather was trying to hide.

"Thank you," Ares said, waiting for his grandfather to shake his hand. His cheeks flushed. "Thank you for helping her and helping us."

The air silenced, and slowly, Grandpa Mallick did take his grandson's hand. Something touched the man's expression when he did. He'd had a hard demeanor before, and it was something he'd clearly been trying to uphold.

That faded away as he shook Ares's hand, and then mine when I reached mine out.

"Thank you," I told him, my dad squeezing my shoulder. Ramses squeezed Ares's too, his smile subtle and his eyes warm. He let us shake our grandfather's hand, and I didn't know what would happen after this. I didn't know what the future held for all of us, but in that moment, we all did have peace.

All finally felt well.

CHAPTER
FIFTY-FIVE

Dorian

My mother was basically attacking me with a lint roller. I got her arms. "Mom, there's literally no more lint for you to find."

Ignoring me, she nudged my hands away, then proceeded to roll the thing across my shoulders. "I don't think I need to explain this is your last one of these things," she huffed before her face scrunched up, a happy-sad smile on her face. "This is your last high school dance before you graduate, so yes, you're going to let me do this."

I had a weak heart for my mother, and I wasn't the only one. Wells was getting a similar treatment in his tux, except his mom Cleo had run out of sheets on her lint roller. The woman resourceful, she had masking tape wrapped around her small fist. She gave Wells a quick swipe across his tie.

"You're all letting us do this," Cleo quipped, tapping Wells's nose with the tape. His eyes lifted, but he grinned too, which let me know he didn't mind either.

The only one not getting this treatment was Thatcher who was actually using his mother's roller to get the lint off *her* dress. He'd already finished rolling himself and apparently needed someone else to make pretty.

Smirking, I eyed him, Wells too, and he flipped us both off behind our moms' backs.

Apparently done with me, my mom stepped back. "You look great, baby," she said before taking my face. "Reminds me of Charlie last year when he, well, did this." Her voice thickened, and my throat did as well. She brushed my shoulder with her fingers, flicking at invisible dust. "He would have loved to see you. Be here."

I knew he would have and definitely would have given me shit for not letting Mom fawn all over me. That was one of the things I missed the most, him goading me and being the older brother.

His presence was definitely missed amongst my brothers and me tonight, but he was with us, with all of us. I smiled. "He's here, Mom."

"I know, babe." She cupped my face, and I guess she wasn't done because she continued to move that lint roller over my shoulders. I let her because I did have a weak heart, the guys and me all wearing black tonight. We did rock different styles, though. People expected Legacy to show up to this shit, so we did, cuff links shined and tuxes designer. The next time I wore shit this expensive would probably be at my wedding.

Not that I was thinking that far ahead.

I was antsy waiting for my little fighter, and she and Wolf were making us all wait. Brielle and Bru had come downstairs what felt like forever ago. They'd come down together, greeting all the Legacy families at the door. Brielle had said Ramses was in the middle of something in his office, and shortly after that, she said he'd texted that Wolf and Sloane were up there too. I didn't know if Ramses was talking to them about something or what, but I definitely didn't want to disturb that. It was nice if they were just all talking and spending time together.

But still, I was getting antsy, and the Legacy dads had all basically checked out. My father and all my god dads were on their cell phones sprinkled around the Mallicks' foyer while the mothers fawned all over us and Bow. She was only a sophomore, but she was coming tonight too. Greer, her mother, had a lint roller on her while Thatcher kept his going on their mom's dress.

"It was so nice of you to ask your sister to the dance tonight, Thatcher," his mom said, angling a look back to him. "I'm sure she appreciates being able to go to the dance with you all tonight even though she's a sophomore."

Underclassmen usually didn't get to go, but since Thatch was a junior, he'd obviously gotten her the ticket.

He grinned at his mom like a cocky little shit.

"That's just me. So kind and nice. Right, sis?" Thatcher tapped her with his lint roller, which made Bow's eyes lift to the chandelier. The only reason he'd asked her was because Legacy had caught wind she might be asked by a senior from a rival school to his own prom. That night had happened to fall on the same night as ours, so yes, he'd asked her.

And now he was taking credit for that shit.

I'd forgotten how we'd all found out, but I think it'd been Wells to get the intel. Actually, it was, and I didn't know who he'd heard from, but I wasn't surprised it had been him to sound the alarm. He was quite vocal when it came to Bow, and since I generally tried to stay out of drama and politics when it came to my boys, I'd gone along with intercepting her potential date.

The history of all that drama left my mind when I noticed someone coming down the stairs. It ended up being only Wolf, though, his hair up, and he did look fly as fuck. After speaking to his mom a second, he came to the three of us guys.

He bumped my fist before tapping Wells's and Thatcher's. "You fuckers won't believe who's here right now and what just happened."

He guided all of us away from the chaos of the parents for a bit, but something told me whatever was going on, they were aware. Brielle was talking to the mothers. Bow was with them while the dads listened on, and Wolf himself proceeded to tell us guys the quick version.

All our jaws dropped.

"Fucking serious?" Wells asked, and Wolf nodded. He'd said his grandpa had helped him in more ways than we had ever known, that he was *alive* and upstairs right now.

"He's going to wait until after we leave, though, to head out," Wolf explained. "Doesn't want to make him being here a thing. I honestly don't think he would have told us everything if my dad hadn't figured it out. He gave Sloane and me everything, guys. All his shares… everything."

Sounded like the father my dad had never gotten to have, my grandfather more selfish than anything else.

Wolf started to tell us more, but then Ramses came down the stairs, his arm hooked with a girl much smaller than himself. My attention drifted from my god dad upon seeing her.

And hardened my shit in my fucking boxers.

The slit of Sloane's dress went up to her thigh, a flash of smooth skin exposing every time her black heels hit tile. Her dad helped her down the stairs, something sparkly keeping her dress closed at the hip.

A low *fuck* fell from my lips as I watched her descend, tits high, perfect, golden. The front of her dress cut low between them, her back out and shimmering just as the rest of her. Something she'd put on made her skin glow more than it already had, her lips red, her hair wavy. She tucked some of it behind her ear, and I lost my fucking breath.

I think along with the rest of the room.

Parents were taking pictures, everyone moving in that direction, but I got to her first. "Hey."

"Hi."

I started to say something else, but a throat cleared, and I looked at Wolf. He had a look on his face that was something between a sneer and a grimace. He raised a hand to her. "You see this shit?"

I definitely saw this, peering completely over her but stopped again when a chuckle sounded beside me. It was from Wells, but both Thatcher and Wells were laughing. Thatcher came from behind his hand. "Bro, she's basically naked."

What the fuck?

Blinking out of my stupor, I shot my gaze Sloane's way, then blinked again when I did actually look at her. I pulled her close.

"Uh, what the fuck is this?" I asked, voice low. It had taken me a second, but now that I was seeing this shit, I was *seeing* this shit. "What are you doing? You're basically wearing no clothes."

Her eyes rolled back, hard, and my friends were cracking up behind us. All but Wolf, who looked just as pissed as I felt.

Sloane placed the daintiest of kisses on my cheek before she put her arms around me and got close. "Don't act like you didn't stand there and eye-fuck me from across the room," she quipped, using something I said to her all the time about how she looked at me. Her breath heated my ear. "Like you didn't like it, and you don't want to completely fuck me right now."

I did want to fuck her, and that was the problem. I got her arm, so much blood pumping to my damn dick it was *painful.* "You're going to pay for not letting me do something about that right now." She was cock-teasing me, point blank. "And for showing everyone what's *mine.*"

No one got to see her but me.

She shrugged as if she placed no stake in my threat, and I let her slither away only because our parents were probably wondering what we were talking about.

Immediately, my little fighter went to Bow, the two basically jumping up and down at the sight of each other. Girls.

I was forced to let my girlfriend parade around the goddamn room in what she wore, or I guess lack thereof. At one point, my dad surfaced from somewhere and put his arm around me. He and the other parents couldn't have heard Sloane's and my short exchange, but his subtle look of remorse was quite telling. I definitely had my hands full with Noa Sloane tonight, and she would pay for what she did to me.

I always came to collect.

CHAPTER
FIFTY-SIX

Sloane

I'd never gone to prom before. This time last year, I'd been too poor to attend and hadn't had any friends anyway to experience it with.

Going with Legacy was an experience.

The world just seemed to part for the elite squad of boys I'd believed held nothing but a chip on their shoulders when I'd arrived in this town. I hadn't experienced their aura and the harsh love/bond that was Legacy. It went beyond friendship and even a brother or sisterhood. It was the unshakable bond of a built-in family, and now, Bru and I were a part of that too.

There was nothing like it.

Prom was a celebration of many things that night, triumphs and wins outside of a football field. A state title couldn't touch the shit we'd *all* fought for, this life and our family. We were all dancing to our own beat. The dance floor was ours tonight, though Thatcher Reed and Wells Ambrose may argue something different. This was junior prom, and they both happened to be awarded prom *kings*. Apparently, they weren't even the first to accomplish such a feat as Dorian and Ares had won the year prior. As Rainbow Reed once told me, Legacy isn't popular.

Popularity is Legacy.

And yes, the prom kings threw their weight around. Thatcher and Wells wore those crowns all night, saying they owned this evening, and that continued on to the prom after-parties. It was all Bow, Bru, and the rest of us could do to get away from the fuckers' egos.

God love them.

Honestly, it didn't bother me as much as the coalition the Legacy boys (Bruno included) created to *attempt* to keep me dressed most of the night. They actually all took turns putting their jackets on me, which pissed me the fuck off, and I definitely knew who the culprit was behind the idea.

Not that he tried to hide it.

Dorian's jacket seemed to make it to my shoulders more often than not, and the latest happened to be while Bow and I tried to dance. We'd all hit one last after-party around 2 AM when suddenly, a heavy jacket that smelled of boy and after-shave hit my shoulders. The dark prince had a specific smell, and that *really* pissed me off because I took more than one moment to soak it in before wrestling it off.

Wells had raised his hands after putting it on me, that damn crown still on his head. He grinned. "Don't shoot the messenger, princess. I was only sent to deliver the jacket."

Growling, I left Bow to dance with our group of friends, Bru amongst them. Last I'd seen Ares he'd been on the rooftop bar, chatting up a girl, and though I hadn't seen Thatcher in equally as long, I could guess what he was up to. Odds were, he was off fucking something somewhere, but his prom night hookups (and yes, there'd been more than one) hadn't kept his own jacket from getting to me on more than one occasion this evening. It was like these boys were taking shifts.

I knew they were and by no one other than their beautiful prince. Apparently, Dorian wasn't bluffing about messing with me tonight for wearing this dress, and the only reason he probably wasn't putting his jacket on me himself was because he'd gone outside for a smoke break earlier.

I ended up finding him by the pool, alone, and I hated I hesitated a beat. The pool lights reflected off his impressive physique, his bow tie undone and his sleeves rolled above his forearms. He had a flush to his skin and a messiness about his hair that told he'd danced more than once tonight, danced with me. Basically, he looked hotter than fuck, a joint at his lips while he smoked by some lawn furniture. Seeing me, he allowed the smoke to fall from his lips, his chuckle light. "I see you got my gift."

I basically threw it at him, his chuckle heavy this time, throaty. He tossed the jacket on one of the lawn chairs before fingering through his mess of gold, and I hated how hot that shit was too. I sneered. "You can stop your games now. You made your point."

His laughter was cocky, his lips flushed. He flicked his joint butt in the pool before getting my arms behind me, a stream of smoke curling from the side of his lips. He grinned. "I don't recall saying the jackets were your punishment." He pulled me close. "Too many people saw what was mine tonight."

That'd been the point, to fuck with him. But somehow, he was fucking with me, his hands on my ass, his mouth too close to my ear. I braced his arms. "I don't like being told what to do."

"Clearly." His knuckle followed a line down the chiffon, basically parting my ass cheeks, and when I gasped, his smile pressed into my neck. "But you like this, don't you?" He gathered my dress in his hands, squeezing my ass. "How bad do you want my cock?"

Hot lava buzzed beneath my skin, my body shuddering. I didn't want it *at all*, but my body was betraying me. I wanted to teach him a lesson for telling me what to do.

Dorian swayed us to invisible music, lulling me, and that reminded me so much of the dance earlier tonight. There had been dozens on that dance floor at any given time, but whenever we were together... like this, it just felt like the two of us.

His strong arms covered my back, holding me close. "Tell me you want me."

His teeth pinched my ear, and I quivered, his biceps under my arms. "Dorian..."

"Say it, Sloane," he said, his voice teasing light, and I *loved* him like this. When we'd met, he'd had the weight of the world on his shoulders, but like my world, something had changed in his too. He'd fought for something and was stronger on the other side because of it. He'd called me strong recently, but I begged to differ, compared to him. Dorian Prinze was the strongest person I knew.

And that was incontestable.

I let his hands touch me in ways they probably shouldn't. No one was out here, but still, we were in a public place.

"Tell me, Noa," he rasped, his voice heated, gravelly. "Say you want this. Say you want me."

He knew I did. I could merely nod, and it took me a second to realize what he was doing. He'd swayed me dangerously close to the edge of the pool, his hands on my waist. His arms extended, and I squealed. "Don't you fucking dare!" I slapped at him, but all he did was laugh when he picked me up in his arms. I kicked my heels. "I swear to God, Dorian Prinze, if you throw me in this pool—"

He didn't throw me.

He jumped with me.

Together, he submerged us both, and I flailed, kicking at

him, then the bottom of the pool to push myself to the surface. Dorian was right behind me, and I gasped for air above water.

"Are you fucking kidding me!" I growled, but all Dorian did was bark out a laugh. "Have you lost your mind?"

"Actually, I'd say *this* calls us even." He splashed water at me, and I came for him, manicured claws first. It'd taken me forever to get dressed tonight, and he was fucking laughing about this.

Dorian was all grins and smiles my way, his tongue out. He only let me get a little bit close before he turned the tables and had me pinned against the pool.

"Dorian," I warned, my breath hiking. I gripped his shoulders. "What are you doing?"

He was too close, too… beautiful. His dress shirt clung to his brawny frame, the onyx buttons laboring across his firm chest. Wet skin glistened above, muscular, flushed. His hands covered my back, and we sloshed against each other, that same flush across his chiseled cheekbones and full lips. He looked magnificent in the pool's lights and under the night.

"My eyes are up here, little fighter." His cocky chuckle followed, and before I knew it, he was holding me close and stepping backward. "Do you trust me?"

"Hell fucking no." And to show him that, I messed with his hands at my back, which was pointless. If Dorian was good at anything at all, that was the use of his hands. Besides being good at football, he was just… talented.

I forced those other talented things out of my head as it seemed he planned to drown me in this moment, drown us both. He had the two of us out to the center of the pool, and I stilled.

"Dorian—"

"*Trust* me," he said, then together, he brought us down under the water again. Expecting it this time, I didn't flail, but I most certainly didn't like it.

At least not at first.

Dorian let go of me under the water, but he didn't release my hand. They stayed locked together, but with a tug, I was right back to him. He spun with me, holding me close, and I felt him laugh under the water.

I saw it too, his joy, and I felt mine. We were two kids doing something stupid in someone's pool.

And it was fun as hell.

We wrestled for a bit before surfacing, but the dark prince barely let me take two breaths before he had me under the water again. We went together this time, me floating while he swam around me like a fish, and not once did his hand leave mine. We breached the surface again, but this time when he went under, he hooked his arms under mine. Our lips sealed, and his teasing smile melted over my lips, his kisses hungry, his hands in my hair. It was a good thing my lipstick was smudge-proof.

I looped my legs around him.

I held his face, teeth biting, mouths searching. It didn't feel real sometimes, being with him. It felt otherworldly, magical. There were no sounds down here and no air either. There was just us and this kiss.

And it was glorious.

He held me close, and I felt so safe, invincible, powerful, and I wondered if this was how he always felt. Being in his presence was just that magnetic. We came above the surface, and he pinned me to the side of the pool again, his hands still in my hair and my legs around his waist.

"Dorian, we can't," I gasped, looking over his shoulder. The wall we were on didn't face the house, but anyone could come out here. There were like a million fucking wasted teenagers at this party.

His laughter against my neck heated my blood. My lower lips pulsed, and I was so fucking turned on it was ridiculous. Like he knew, Dorian slipped his fingers under my dress, my panties hooked over, his digits gliding over my sex beneath the water.

"I told you, Noa, no one sees what's mine." A warning touched his voice when he bent his knees and lowered us below the wall. This took us out of view from anyone in the house. He touched his forehead to mine. "Trust me. No one's here but us."

His tone had softened, rough when his fingers parted my pussy lips. His thumb strummed my clit, stroking back and forth, and I rocked against his hand.

"Dorian, this is crazy," I laugh-gasped. My fingers curled into his dress shirt, my body bumping his palm, the pair of us sloshing, colliding. "You're fucking crazy."

"Completely subjective." He bit my mouth, covering a moan. His hand covered my throat, and I couldn't scream if I wanted to.

His hand below the water didn't stop, his grip on my throat tightening. The dark prince had a choking fetish, and apparently, I had one too.

"Don't stop," I breathed out, my eyes shut tight. His hand left my throat, but only to pinch my nipple through my bra.

"So greedy, Noa," he said, his head lowering. He eased part of my top away, my bra going with it, and I was too far gone to stop him before his teeth clamped down over my beaded nipple.

"Shit." My thighs hugged his hips, my sex bumping against his hand. He covered my mouth with his palm the same time he undid his pants, letting me say nothing when he eased his dick past my panties, then guided himself inside me.

He fucked me with a hand over my mouth, water splashing around us, his eyes heated, black. I never saw them so dark than when he was fucking me.

It was a good thing he covered my mouth.

I choked out a scream when he drilled me deep, his teeth

at my ear, his tongue flicking my lobe.

"That's it, baby. Sing for me," he coached, making me scream again when his thrusts slammed my ass against the pool. "Only for me."

Only for him.

I gripped his wet hair, holding on for the ride. He didn't stop until he'd thoroughly fucked me, and my walls closed so hard around him I thought I'd faint.

I felt like I did for a second, seeing stars when he himself flooded inside me. His dick pumped, relentless until he emptied himself. His body sagged over mine, his hands gripping the pool wall. He took a moment to get his bearings before he tucked himself away, then slid my panties back over. But after that, he was right back on my mouth. He kissed me, hard, and I wrapped my arms around him.

I couldn't get enough of him.

There was something about this dark prince, something beautiful and raw but also incredibly flawed. We both were, and I think that was what made us so awesome. We'd get to grow together and become the best versions of ourselves alongside each other. We weren't perfect.

And that was okay.

I brushed fingers along his jaw, kissing him. "I love you," I said between gasps, and he grinned.

"Fucking always," he said, guiding my mouth open. He went for a deeper kiss, but then someone called both our names.

"Holy shit. You're both in the pool," Wells chanted, his jeweled crown twinkling under the pool lights. I'd bet he'd go to sleep tonight with that thing on. He pumped a fist. "I'm going to go get everyone else."

Had he come out like a minute and a half before, he might have seen something, and Dorian and I both chuckled. It seemed we'd both forgotten ourselves, and thank God, he'd had us *below* the wall when he'd been fucking me.

Dorian posted his hands to the wall, laughing, and I smiled too, my arms still around him when Wells returned sans jacket and tie. Actually, the only thing he had on still was pants and his crown. Running at full speed, he cannonballed into the pool, his crown and snowy locks disappearing under the water. He ended up losing the crown, the thing floating on the top of the water while he swam to the surface. He came up with a snap of his hair, but he wasn't the only one to join us out here.

On the pool deck, Bru had his fist to his mouth, completely losing it that we were all in here. He shook his head, but next thing I knew, he was stripping off his jacket. We all called out to him before he jumped in too, the look of disbelief on his face hilarious when he surfaced. This was definitely out of his comfort zone.

A charged, "Sweet!" hit the air before Thatcher Reed ran to the pool deck too, his own crown on his dark locks. He actually tossed it off before he started disrobing, onyx studs in his ears. He'd retired his crosses tonight and was down to his pants too when a smiling Ares and mortified Bow came up behind him. The little rabbit literally had her hands on her cheeks.

"Oh my God. What are you guys doing?" she squeaked, but Ares continued to smile beside her. He chuckled.

"You fuckers," Ares said while Wells yelled at his ass to get in here with us, and Bru was beside him doing the same. I found myself cheering too, pumping my fist.

"Come on, big. What are you, a wuss!" I called out, using his nickname the others had thought was hilarious when they'd heard it. I think my twin brother was regretting letting me name him anything, but he'd get over it. "Come on in. The water's fine."

Ares didn't look like he wanted to, but in the end, he literally let his hair down. He tugged his ebony locks free, those crazy curls of his flying everywhere. He shrugged his jacket off, then side-flipped into the pool with everyone else. He came to the surface, laughing with the rest of us, and on the deck, Thatcher was attempting to get his sister to join the party. He had the little rabbit by the arm, guiding her while she smacked at him.

"No way. You guys are crazy," she said, folding her arms, and Thatcher must have been over it because he left her and jumped into the pool. He went straight for Wells, taking the platinum blond with him underwater. They came up, and Wells was on Thatcher's back, punching at his ass, which had Dorian, Ares, Bru, and me roaring.

"Come on, Bow!" I called out to her. This party wasn't anything without her, and the others joined to help me get her out here. The boys coached her on while I cheered, and when the moment of decision hit her face, she pressed hands to her cheeks.

"I can't believe I'm going to do this," she said, completely cute when she held her little nose. She jumped, black heels, black dress, all of it, and I pumped my fist, Dorian holding me and doing the same. She came up quick, and when she did, she was laughing.

We all did.

In our own Legacy world, we splashed each other, boys dunking girls, girls dunking boys, and boys dunking each other. Eventually, we gathered a crowd when others from the party came out to see what was going on. The spectators watched on, cheering before, ultimately, joining us too. Before we all knew it, the entire pool was filled with splashing and laughter, but no one would forget who started this. This was Legacy, a coalition of family and friends, and it almost felt like a last night for antics for the group of us. It was the last chance to be a kid before everything changed for many of us with graduation and college. We got to just be *us,* wild and free. On this evening, we owned the night.

And what a night it was.

EPILOGUE

Sloane

"Ready. Set." Wells paused, his grin cockier than hell. He loved these races. He winked at me from the start line. "Let's get it."

His fist dropped, and my sneakers shot me off the street, Ares's too. Gone were the days he let me get ahead.

I didn't need the help.

Sheer speed backing me, I pumped my arms, racing past Bru, Thatcher, Bow, and Dorian from the side lines. They all cheered from the side of the street, but the only one who had a knowing smile was my boyfriend. I'd happened to beat him in a race just this morning, my best time ever.

I was about to break that record now.

I didn't know if Ares had let himself go in the days following graduation a few weeks ago or what, but I left him behind me, knowing I'd won this shit before I even passed the finish line. We had the line marked at the end of our parents' street, and we were able to hold our races out here now that summer had hit. Add that to the fact the press were finally leaving us all alone and allowing us to live our lives, my twin brother and I got to finish our grudge match. I was going to beat him in a foot race before we headed off to college in the fall, and today would be the day.

I heard Ares growl right as I accomplished that very feat. I blazed past the finish line, easily a few strides ahead and immediately broke out into a dance.

"Oh, shit!" I chanted, dancing around him when he came to a stop. He had his hands on his knees, winded, but that didn't stop me. I pressed hands to my chest. "Oh, shit. Did she just do that?"

Obviously, I was referring to myself, and I rubbed that win all up in his face as the rest of the group strode up to join us.

Grunting, Ares stood up. He tried to play it off he wasn't completely gassed, but he had to gulp in a few breaths before looking at me. His eyes rolled. "Good job, little."

It was better than *good*. I'd been training for this shit every morning since we'd graduated, a little obsessed, but I didn't care. I wanted bragging rights and something to hold over his head.

I continued to dance around the same time my boyfriend got me around the waist. The dark prince was all grins when he picked me up, my legs looping around him.

"Fuck yeah, my girl did that," he said, kissing me, and Ares's eyes lifted higher.

"She had a good day," he gritted, downplaying my win, and I smirked. Good day or not, I *beat his ass*.

I shot a finger at him. "I guess you were right about those genetics, bro." It was so much easier to call him that now, normal. I smiled, hugging the dark prince. "And I did do that."

"You did, baby." Chuckling, Dorian braced my waist. He

set me down while he proceeded to give me another congratulatory kiss, and I think Ares groaned for a different reason then.

As well as the others.

Dorian got swats at his head, and they were lucky his lips were preoccupied. I'd seen him get in street fights with his friends over less. Especially whenever Thatcher or Wells got flirty. They still liked to poke and tease me because they were horny fucks. I took it in good stride, knowing their personalities now. That was just their way, but whenever they did, they made sure to stop before Dorian came around. They'd gotten more than one punch to the gut for it.

These boys were characters, and though they loved each other, they checked each other too. If one was out of line or being stupid, they definitely called each other out, and I enjoyed their dynamic. I enjoyed seeing that strong bond and how much they did look out for each other.

I think Dorian and I only stopped kissing because *I* thought it was rude, and Bow was jumping to show me my race time.

"A new record," she said, nudging me. She showed me the time on her phone, and my jaw dropped. "You killed this."

"Seems she had more than a good day." Dorian dropped his meaty arm across my shoulders, hugging me close, and Thatcher and Wells punched at Ares's arms.

"Yeah, she kind of blew your shit out of the water, bro," Thatcher stated, which got him a quick knock across the head by Ares, along with a more than heated *shut the fuck up.* Thatcher pouted, his hood up, his dark locks messy and tousled at the front. He messed with them more. "Dude, just speaking facts."

Ares came for him again, but Thatcher chose to hide behind Wells, which was hilarious. One, because Wells lacked the surface area to be able to even do so with his leaner athletic build, and another, because Wells sidestepped every time he tried, Wells's grin high. Giving up on him, Thatcher tried to hide behind Bru, but that was pointless too. At least when he'd been hiding behind Wells, he'd had the boy's height. Wells was shorter than Thatcher, but Wells was still way taller than Bruno.

Bru raised his hands. "Uh-uh. Keep me out of this."

Bruno sidestepped too with a chuckle, and eventually, Dorian shut it all down when he left me and broke his friends up.

"Calm down. Shit," he told Ares, a hand on his chest. It was crazy the three of us were actually graduated now and were supposed to be the *older* ones. Dorian frowned. "Don't be an ass. You lost, so just take it and move on."

My twin brother's expression could be described as nothing but sour when he bunched his arms over his chest. I came over, grinning. "Don't be sour, big. Maybe you'll get a win in next time."

Reaching out, I tapped his face to be an asshole and definitely wasn't stupid enough to stick around to see what he'd do about it.

I heard Bru said, "Here we go," as I shot off, and Ares immediately raced off behind me. Ares spouted heated curses from his lips, but I ignored them when Dorian called after us.

"Use those legs, little fighter." Dorian barked a laugh, the rest of the group yelling after us in the same fashion. I got lots of, "Run!" and I definitely wasn't slowing down.

"You're so fucking dead." Ares charged after me, but he wasn't fooling anyone. Laughter hit his voice as soon as we entered our house, and when I cut into the kitchen, someone immediately separated us.

"Hey. Hey. Hey," Ramses said, getting Ares by the shirt just when he'd been about to grab me. Saved by the dad! Ramses directed a look at my twin. "What's going on? Why are you chasing her?"

"She hit me," Ares accused and was being *so* dramatic. He acted like I'd slapped him. He posted hands on his hips. "Legit slapped me. Right in my face."

His eyes danced deviously behind the bullshit, but as Ramses's attention was on me now, our dad didn't see. I frowned. "He's being overdramatic. I tapped him on the face *lightly*, and that was after he was being a big baby because I beat him in a foot race."

This conversation was hilarious right now, our dad keeping the two of us away from each other while we both pleaded our cases over laughable bull crap. It felt so normal and reminded me of Bru and me growing up.

"A race?" Ramses's brow lifted. He faced me. "You beat him in a race?"

"Uh, yeah. I really didn't hit him. At least, not hard." I shrugged, and Ramses nodded.

But only after he smiled.

He knew I'd been training to one day beat my ridiculously fast brother firsthand.

He'd been training with me in the mornings.

Of course, he couldn't let that be known, my dad's and my secret. I'd told him not to tell anyone about the training because I wanted to surprise Ares when I beat his ass.

Ramses's smile wiped away before he faced my twin. He eyed him. "I'm sorry you lost but killing each other is definitely not the answer."

Ares lifted a hand. "She hit me first, though."

"And you're going to let it go because you're just the bigger person." He put an arm around his son. "And the reason I get to tell my friends I have such a great kid."

Ares's frown was evident, but a smile pulled at it too.

Ramses wrestled his hair. "You'll be okay. There'll be other races."

Ares pointed at me, the promise of that apparently ahead.

I laughed as he did let go what I'd done, leaving the

kitchen. Laughing himself, Ramses watched Ares's exit so he didn't see me until I got him in a hug.

"Thanks, Dad," I said, squeezing. He had definitely just let me get away with hitting Ares. Not to mention helping me in the mornings. I squeezed him harder. "And for the training."

I was still blown away I got to hug my dad and have moments like this. Godfrey had been my father, but it wasn't like these times with Ramses. Godfrey had never been one to express much emotion, even when he had been well.

Ramses was never guarded with his, hugging me back and instantly. He rubbed my arm. "No problem," he returned, and I noticed he held that hug for a second before letting me go. Brielle did too sometimes when I hugged her, but I didn't mind. There'd been a lot of hugs we didn't get to have.

And we were making up for that.

There'd been a lot of hugging too at Ares's and my graduation party, grandparents, friends. Ramses's dad hadn't been there, but Ramses had talked to our whole family after that prom night. If Ares and I wanted to see our grandpa, we could, and Ares and I had had more than one discussion about it. He wasn't quite ready yet, but when he was, I'd be with him.

At least, the potential of that was out there.

I stayed in that hug a little longer too before letting my dad go. I told him I loved him as well before I left the room, and I'd never forget what he mentioned as he said it back.

"Never gets old hearing you say that, kid," he stated, his eyes warm. "Never gets old."

———

Legacy pizza night happened to be at the Mallick household tonight, which was great because that coincided with date night for Ramses and Brielle. They'd been doing that a lot less recently with Bru, Ares, and me being home for the summer. They wanted to spend time with us.

We actually all had a big trip to Greece coming up, a family trip Ramses and Brielle had gifted Ares and me for graduation. I still couldn't believe this was my life sometimes. That I had two parents and a family of not just two brothers but four with Thatcher and Wells. The two were a couple of characters, but they definitely held a place in my heart. I had a little sister too with Bow, and our crew spent as much time together as we could. I ended up getting accepted at Pembroke University, which was an Ivy League not far from town. I'd been floored I'd gotten in with the year I'd had, but I'd managed it. Ramses had gone there so that helped, but I tried to do my part academically.

I had help.

Bru and Ares both were geniuses, and they'd helped me prepare, alongside the dark prince. He was modest about how smart he was too, and he'd also gotten into Pembroke University. Apparently, he was legacy there too, with others in his family having gone there.

I was looking forward to the fall semester, but things would change once again. I'd be headed to a new school, and even though I could come home and see my family (the school was only a couple hours away), things would be different again in my life.

I hoped they'd be good changes, and discussions surrounding college did come up during pizza night. The crew had all been raiding the kitchen for snacks before the pizza delivery when Wells strode into the room with a joint behind his ear. He had a letter in hand, and when Ares noticed it, he grabbed it.

"You in my shit?" Ares asked, slapping his friend's chest with it. Wells lifted his hands.

"Chill, my guy. I was looking for your stash." Wells pulled

the joint from behind his ear as proof, and at this point, the whole room's attention had shifted toward the conversation. Wells braced his arms. "I didn't know you applied to Pembroke."

"Because it was supposed to be a surprise," Ares said, looking a bit sheepish when he noticed us all looking at him. Dorian reached for the letter, and when he read it, he smiled.

"You going to Pembroke?" he asked before returning his arm around me. He never went far. Dorian grinned. "I thought you were going to design school in New York or something."

That'd been the plan, and though Pembroke had excellent options for Ares, they were nothing compared to the schools I knew he'd already gotten offers from. Our senior project had basically gotten him his pick of any school he wanted.

I took the letter, and Ares watched me scan it.

He shrugged. "I just figured with you and little going there…" He scratched his neck. "I don't know. I just thought it'd be cool."

"Aww. Wolf." Thatcher dropped an arm around Ares, jostling him. "Buddy, I didn't know you couldn't stand to be away from all of us," he said, obviously referring to the fact the university was so close to Maywood Heights. Thatcher, Wells, and Bru still had a year before they graduated too, and Bow wouldn't be far behind. Thatcher grinned. "That's so adorable. I didn't know you'd miss me so much."

Ares growled when he shoved Thatcher off him, and Wells threw popcorn at Thatcher, which, *of course*, made everyone else want to throw popcorn at Thatcher. Bru and Bow had their own bowls, and Dorian and I reached into them. We all threw popcorn at the Legacy boy while he flipped the bird at us.

The large man-boy wrestled kernels out of his hair, calling us all assholes, and he was right, but that was just Legacy. There were antics, but there were always good times.

Ares barked at Thatcher to let the college thing go, and I think he only did because he didn't want to get any more snack foods tossed at him. In any sense, the doorbell rang, and the whole kitchen basically evacuated to assault the pizza guy. The only people who lingered back were Ares, Dorian, and me, but I think Dorian noticed I wanted to speak to my twin. I started to approach Ares with the letter, and Dorian nodded at me.

"I'm going to go make sure Thatcher leaves some pizza for the rest of us," Dorian said, kissing my cheek with a full hand on my head. He always loved to manhandle me. He hit my ass before he left (another favorite of his), and Ares laughed.

"Yeah, I'm kind of starting to rethink my decision. Four years of the two of you doing that shit?" he groaned but was mocking about it, teasing when he nudged me. He sat on a barstool. "I was considering D as a roommate, but I might have to think of other arrangements because nah. Seriously, won't be able to take y'all doing all that shit."

Smirking, I leaned back against the counter. "Why didn't you tell me you applied to Pembroke?"

"I applied to a lot of places," he said, tilting his head, and I shook mine. He shrugged. "What? Pembroke's a good school. Ivy League?"

"Yeah, but it's nothing like the places you applied to in New York *and* got in." I nudged him. "Is Thatcher right? You'll just miss us so much you can't bear to be without us?"

His eyes lifted, his smile small. "I don't know about all that, but I know you and I haven't gotten a lot of time togeth-er," he said, surprising me. He nodded. "I guess I just figured these next four years would be a good time to make up for that. Get to know my sister. Really know her."

"Aww. So, you will miss me?"

"Don't make me regret this decision, little," he sighed, and I laughed, definitely putting on a front here. I hadn't said it, but I wouldn't have argued if I'd found out he'd applied to Pembroke.

I wanted to get to know him too.

I hugged him, and just as hard as I had Ramses in this very kitchen. I hugged my mother in the same way, hugs like that I got to share more and more these days. It'd just been Bru and me when we'd got here, and there were so many more people to hug now, so many more to love.

"Love ya, big," I said, and he chuckled, hugging me back.

"Love you too, little." He said it begrudgingly, like it was a chore, but he was bullshitting. He had to have been. I mean, he'd uprooted his plans, and if that didn't say something, I didn't know what did.

Pizza night ended up being an evening of laughter and good times, great times. I got to watch a movie under the dark prince's arm, my friends and family around us sprinkled on various couches/the floor. I'd lost count of all the people in my life I cared about.

Brielle: Love you, honey. Your dad and I will be out late. You might be asleep by the time we come home. We just wanted to let you know. Sending you love from us both.

Dorian's hand brushed my arm when I got the text, the same words said to me every night whether I saw my parents or not. If they worked late, I got a *love you, honey.* If they were home, the same. It was usually the last thing I saw before I fell asleep.

Tonight, it was Dorian's eyes, the glow of the television on his handsome face. The credits were rolling, and everyone else in the room was out, Wells and Bru on the floor, Ares on the couch. Thatcher had actually fallen asleep with a bowl of popcorn on his chair, his head back and earrings dangling. Bow was nestled up against my side, and I was with Dorian. He played with my hair, just looking at me.

"I love you," he mouthed into the night, no teasing, not an ounce. He wet his lips before pressing our mouths together, tasting my tongue. If heaven was this, I'd take more of it. I'd die happy like this. He was my dark prince, but there was no darkness in my happily ever after. There was a boy who had both black and white wings.

But every day, he chose the light.

Get the bonus epilogue to Tiny Dark Deeds! This epilogue is FREE and available to all my newsletter subscribers. Join my newsletter today to get your free epilogue!

https://bit.ly/tddepilogue

Thank you so much for reading *Tiny Dark Deeds*! Get the next book in the Court Legacy saga, *Eat You Alive*, on Amazon today! <u>Amazon</u>

Royal Prinze—yes, that's actually his name—walks around both the school and the town like he owns them. His affiliation to the prestigious Court only gives him more clout. These boys do anything they want. They take anything they want, and they f*ck anything they want... in that order.

Then there's me.

I came to Maywood Heights to live with my virtually indifferent father because my sister went AWOL. She chose to move with him after our father decided to uproot years ago and forget anything related to our late mother. I stayed with our aunt, but my sister and I had always remained close.

She'd never gone off the grid.

The new girl, I arrived at Maywood Heights to find her. The last thing I imagined when enrolling at her school was that she'd be connected to a group like the Court, and boys like Royal. She's nothing like them and so much better than Royal and his elitist attitude...

Check out the other books in the Court universe:

<u>Brutal Heir</u>
Knight's & Greer's story
(Thatcher's and Bow's parents)

<u>Kingpin</u>
LJ's story
(Dorian's god dad)

<u>Beautiful Brute</u>
Jax's & Cleo's story
(Wells's parents)

<u>Lover</u>
Ramses's & Brielle's story
(Ares's and Sloane's parents)